DATE DUE

THE DROWNED CITIES

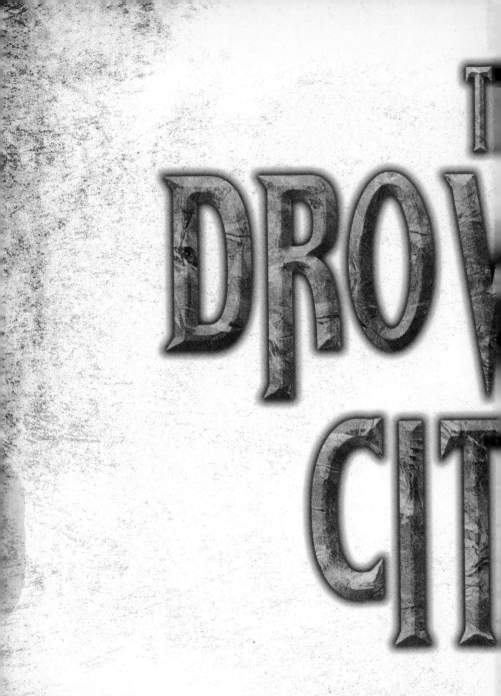

THE DROWNED CITY

Ⓛ Ⓑ LITTLE, BROWN AND COMPANY
New York · Boston

THE DROWNED CITIES

BY PAOLO BACIGALUPI

Copyright © 2012 by Paolo Bacigalupi

Little, Brown and Company

Hachette Book Group
237 Park Avenue, New York, NY 10017
Visit our website at www.lb-teens.com

Little, Brown and Company is a division of Hachette Book Group, Inc.
The Little, Brown name and logo are trademarks of Hachette Book Group, Inc.

The publisher is not responsible for websites (or their content) that are not owned by the publisher.

First Edition: May 2012

Library of Congress Cataloging-in-Publication Data
Bacigalupi, Paolo.
The drowned cities / by Paolo Bacigalupi. —1st ed.   p. cm.
Companion to: Ship breaker.
Summary: In a dark future America that has devolved into unending civil wars, orphans Mahlia and Mouse barely escape the war-torn lands of the Drowned Cities, but their fragile safety is soon threatened and Mahlia will have to risk everything if she is to save Mouse, as he once saved her.
ISBN 978-0-316-05624-3
[1. War—Fiction. 2. Soldiers—Fiction. 3. Survival—Fiction. 4. Orphans—Fiction. 5. Conduct of life—Fiction. 6. Genetic engineering—Fiction. 7. Science fiction.] I. Title.
PZ7.B132185Dro 2012   [Fic]—dc23   2011031762

10 9 8 7 6 5 4 3 2 1

RRD-C

Printed in the United States of America

For my father

THE DROWNED CITIES

– PART ONE –

WAR
MAGGOTS

1

CHAINS CLANKED IN THE darkness of the holding cells.

The reek of urine from the latrines and the miasma of sweat and fear twined with the sweet stench of rotting straw. Water dripped, trickling down ancient marble work, blackening what was once fine with mosses and algae.

Humidity and heat. The whiff of the sea, far off, a cruel, tormenting scent that told the prisoners they would never taste freedom again. Sometimes a prisoner, a Deepwater Christian or a Rust Saint devotee, would call out, praying, but mostly the prisoners waited in silence, saving their energy.

A rattling from the outer gates told them someone was coming. The tramp of many feet.

A few prisoners looked up, surprised. There was no

stamping of the crowd, no soldiers shouting for blood sport coming from above. And yet the prison gate was being opened. A puzzle. They waited, hoping the puzzle wouldn't touch them. Hoping that they might survive another day.

The guards came as a group, using one another for their courage, urging each other forward, jostling their way down the cramped passageway to the last rusty cell. A few had pistols. One carried a stun stick, sparking and cracking, the tool of a trainer, even though he had none of its mastery.

All of them carried the reek of terror.

The keymaster peered through the bars. Just another dim, sweltering lockup, straw strewn and molding, but in the far corner, something else. A huge shadow, puddled.

"Get up, dog-face," the keymaster said. "You're wanted."

No response came from the mountain of shadow.

"Get up!"

Still there was no response. In the neighboring cell, someone coughed wetly, a sound heavy with tuberculosis. One of the guards muttered, "It's dead. Finally. Has to be."

"No. These things never die." The keymaster pulled out his baton and rattled it against the iron bars. "Get up now, or it will be worse for you. We'll use the electricity. See how you like that."

The thing in the corner showed no sign of hearing. No sign of life. They waited. Minutes passed. More minutes.

Finally, another guard said, "It's not breathing. Not a bit."

"It's done for," agreed another. "The panthers did the job."

"Took long enough."

"I lost a hundred Red Chinese on that. When the Colonel said it would go up against six swamp panthers..." The guard shook his head ruefully. "Should have been easy money."

"You never seen these monsters fight up north, on the border."

"If I had, I would've bet on the dog-face."

They all stared at the dead mass. "Well, it's maggot meat now," the first guard said. "The Colonel won't be happy to hear it. Give me the keys."

"No," the keymaster rasped. "Don't believe it. Dog-faces are demon spawn. The beginning of the cleansing. Saint Olmos saw them coming. They won't die until the final flood."

"Just give me the keys, old man."

"Don't go near it."

The guard looked at him with disgust. "It's no demon. Just meat and bone, same as us, even if it is an augment. You tear it up, you shoot it enough, it dies. It's no more immortal than the warboys who fight for the Army of God. Get the Harvesters down here. See if they want its organs. We can sell the blood, at least. Augments have clean blood."

He jammed the key into the lock. Reinforced steel squealed aside, an entire grate specially designed to hold the monster. And then, a second set of locks for the original rusting bars that had been good enough for a man, but not enough to hold this terrifying mix of science and war.

The door scraped back.

The guard started for the corpse. Despite himself, he felt his skin prickling with fear. Even dead, the creature harbored momentous terror. The guard had seen those massive fists crush a man's skull into blood and bone fragments. He'd seen the monster leap twenty feet to sink fangs into a panther's jugular.

In death, it had curled in on itself, but still it was huge. In life, it had been a giant, towering over all, but its size hadn't been what made it deadly. The blood of a dozen predators pumped in its veins, a DNA cocktail of killing— tiger and dog and hyena, and Fates knew what else. A perfect creature, designed from the blood up to hunt and war and kill.

Though it had walked like a man, when it bared its teeth, tiger fangs showed, and when it pricked up its ears, a jackal's ears listened, and when it sniffed the air, a bloodhound's nose scented. The soldier had seen it fight in the ring enough times to know that he would rather face a dozen men with machetes than this hurricane of slaughter.

The guard stood over it for a long time, looking at it. Not a breath. No hint of movement or life. Where the dog-face had once been strong and vital and deadly, it was now nothing but meat for the Harvesters.

Dead at last.

He knelt and ran his hand through the monster's short fur. "Pity. You were a moneymaker. Would have liked to see you fight the coywolv we was lining up. Would have made good ring."

A golden eye flared in the darkness, full of malevolence.

"A pity, indeed," the monster growled.

"Get out!" the keymaster shouted, but it was too late.

A shadow exploded into motion. The guard slammed into the wall and crumpled to the floor like a sack of mud.

"Close the gate!"

The monster roared and the bars clanged shut. The keymaster frantically tried to relock the cell, then leaped back as the monster hurled itself against the cage, snarling, tiger teeth bared.

Iron bars bent. The guards yanked electrical prods from their belts. Blue sparks showered as they beat at the creature and the bars, trying to keep it away while the keymaster fought to close the reinforced second gate. They fumbled for pistols, hardened killers reduced to gibbering terror by the monster's snarl. The creature slammed against the bars again. Rusted iron cracked and bent.

"It won't hold! Run!"

But the keymaster held steady, reworking the locks of the more powerful cage. "I almost got it!"

The monster ripped a rusty bar free of its mooring and lashed through the gap. Iron smashed into the keymaster's skull. The man collapsed. The other guards fled, plunging down the corridor, screaming for help.

The monster tore more bars free, working methodically. The rest of the prisoners were all screaming now, shouting for help and mercy. Their cries echoed in the prison like trapped birds.

The first layer of bars gave way, allowing the monster access to the second cage. It tested the gate. Locked. Growling, the creature crouched and slid one huge fist through the bars, reaching, stretching for the keymaster's foot. It dragged the man close.

In another moment, the monster had the key in its hand and the key in the lock. With a click it opened. The gate screeched aside.

Carrying the iron bar of his prison, the creature called Tool limped down the cellblock to the stairs, and climbed into the light.

2

TOOL COVERED MILES. He was built to do so, and even wounded, he moved with a speed that would have exhausted a human being within minutes. He forded algae-thick canals and limped through bean fields and soaked rice paddies. He passed farmers with wide broad hats who stared up from their sweating work and fled in fear. He circled and doubled back through bomb-shattered buildings, confusing trail and scent. Always, he moved farther from the Drowned Cities, and always the soldiers pursued.

At first, he had hoped his pursuers would give up. Colonel Glenn Stern and his patriotic army had more than enough enemies to keep them occupied; the Drowned Cities were full of fighting factions, perpetually tearing at one another's throats. A single escaped augment might not be worth the Colonel's attention. But then the panthers had caught up with Tool, and he'd known that the Colonel would not let his prized fighting monster slip free so easily.

Pain lanced through Tool's body as he limped onward, but he ignored it. So what if he'd torn his shoulder from its socket in his mad attack on the bars? So what if the hunting panthers had laid long, deep gashes down his back? So what if his one eye was blind? He was moving and free, and he was trained to ignore pain.

Pain held no terror for him. Pain was, if not friend, then family, something he had grown up with in his crèche, learning to respect but never yield to. Pain was simply a message, telling him which limbs he could still use to slaughter his enemies, how far he could still run, and what his chances were in the next battle.

Behind him, the hounds began to bay, picking up his scent.

Tool growled in irritation, unconsciously baring teeth as cousin creatures called for his blood.

The hounds were perfect killers, just as he. They would throw themselves mindlessly into the fight again and again until they were torn to pieces, and they would die content, knowing that they had done their duty for their masters. Tool's dog nature—spliced into his genes by scientific design—knew their mastiff urges. They would never stop until they were dead, or he was.

10

Tool didn't blame them. He, too, had been loyal and obedient once.

Tool reached a new thicket of jungle and plunged into its shadows, tearing through tangling vines. He moved like an elephant through the vegetation, crashing and crackling. He knew he was leaving a trail that even a stupid human being could follow, but it was all he could do to keep moving.

Well-fed, with all his limbs working, he could have run these sad dogs and soldiers for days, doubling back and destroying them one by one in the jungle, whittling dogs and humans down to a huddled fearful tribe around a solitary campfire. Now he doubted he could kill more than a few. Worse, after the last ambush he had set, they had become clever to his ways. They understood—now—how easily their bones snapped.

Tool stopped, panting, his tongue lolling from his mouth, chest heaving. He sniffed the humid air.

Salt breezes.

The sea.

Somewhere north there was an inlet. If he could make the sea, he might escape them still, might dive into the ocean and become one with the marine world. He could swim. It would hurt, but he could do it.

He turned north and east, pushing on by force of will. Behind him, the dogs followed.

Tool almost wanted to laugh. They were such good dogs,

and because of it, many of them would die. Tool, on the other hand, was a very bad dog. His masters had told him so many times as they beat him and trained him and molded his will to match their own. They had forged him into a killer and then fit him into the killing machine that had been his pack. A platoon of slaughter. For a little while, he had been a good dog, and obedient.

Platoon. Pack. Company. Battalion. Tool remembered the Red Standard of General Caroa, waving in the breezes above his encampment in the Kolkata Delta when the Tiger Guard came down on them.

Bad dog.

Tool had been such a bad dog that he still lived. He should have been dead on those muddy tidal flats outside of Kolkata, where the waters of the river Ganges met the warmth of the Indian Ocean, and where blood and bodies floated in salt waves as red as General Caroa's flag. He should have been dead in wars on foreign shores. He should have been dead a thousand times over. And yet always he had survived to fight again.

Tool paused, chest heaving, and scanned the forest tangles. Iridescent butterflies flitted through beams of reddening evening sunlight. The forest canopy was turning dark, emerald leaves becoming muddy as night came on. The black tropics, some people called this place, for its winter darkness. A sweltering humid environment where pythons and panthers and coywolv stalked at will. Killers all. It galled Tool that he was now prey, and weakening.

The guards had been starving him for weeks, and his untreated wounds oozed pus. Only his massive immune system kept him on his feet at all. Any other creature would have succumbed weeks ago to the superbacteria that coursed through his veins and seethed in his wounds, but his time was running out.

When he had been a good dog, an owned dog, a loyal dog, his masters would have stitched and treated wounds like these. General Caroa would have worked hard to protect his battle investment, showering Tool with trauma care so that he could once again become the apotheosis of slaughter. Good dogs had masters, and masters kept good dogs close.

Behind him, the hounds bayed again. Closer.

Tool stumbled forward, counting the steps until he would fall, knowing that flight was hopeless. A final stand, then. One last battle. At least he could say that he had fought. When he met his brothers and sisters on the far side of death, he would tell them that he had not yielded. He might have betrayed everything that they had been bred for, but he had never yielded...

Salt swamps opened abruptly before him. Tool sloshed into the water. Huge snakes slithered away in ripples, pythons and cottonmouths recognizing that they wanted no traffic with a creature like him. He waded farther and suddenly found unexpected beckoning depths. The swamps here were deep, many meters deep. A welcome surprise. This landscape hid sinkholes of water.

With a sigh, Tool sank into the swamp, feeling bubbles forming around him.

Down.

The slits of his nostrils tightened, sealing in his breath. A translucent membrane slid across his remaining eye's iris, protecting his vision as he sank into the depths of the swamp, down amongst crawdads and mangrove roots.

Let them hunt me now.

Above, soldiers came crashing close. The voices of men, and others, younger. Some of them small enough that Tool could easily eat one in a day. But all of them armed and all of them adrenalized by the hunt. They shouted and called, their voices twining with the barking and stampeding of their dogs, all of it filtering down through the waters to Tool's listening ears.

Splashes in the shallows. Dogs swimming about, their legs windmilling above him, baying in confusion, trying to find Tool's direction. He could see them up there, canine shanks cycling madly. He could swim up and yank them down, one by one...

Tool resisted the urge to hunt.

"Where the hell did it go?"

"Shhhhh! Hear anything?"

"Shut your dogs, Clay!"

Silence fell. At least as much silence as pathetic human beings and dogs could summon. Even through the waters, Tool could hear their attempts at stealthy breathing, but they were trying, in their childlike way, to hunt.

"No spoor," one of them muttered as footsteps stalked through the grasses. "Tell the LT, we got no spoor."

Tool could imagine them all on the edge of the swamps, staring out at black waters. Listening to the pulse and scratch of insects and the far cry of a wild panther.

They were hunters. But now, as night closed in on them, and the swamp became black and hot and close, they were becoming prey.

Tool again shook off the urge to hunt. He must still think like prey and take advantage of their failures. He could lie below the surface for as long as twenty minutes, slowing his heart rate, slowing his bulk so that he needed almost nothing at all.

Without exertion, he might even be able to lie there longer, but twenty minutes, he knew for certain—much as he knew that he could run for five miles without rest amongst the high passes of Tibet, or for three days without pause across the blistering sands of North Africa's Sahara.

He counted slowly.

The hounds paddled and circled as the soldiers tried to figure out what to do.

"You think it doubled back again?"

"Could be. It's crafty. Ocho can take a squad—"

"Ocho's all ripped up."

"Van and Soa, then! Go back along the trail. Spread out."

"In the dark?"

"You questioning me, Gutty?"

15

"Where the hell's the LT?"

The ripple and bubble of the swamp flowed into Tool's finely tuned ears. He let them spread wide like fans, cupping the waters. Listening.

The flash of tiny pike. The skitter of crawdads. The distant womblike slosh and surge of salt water as it blended with cousin waters on the shore, where swampland and surf smashed together and sought ever higher tide lines.

"It'll head for the ocean," one of the soldiers said. "We should put another squad up on the north side."

"No, it will hide here, in the swamps. It'll stay right here. Safe enough."

"Maybe the coywolv will get it."

"Not likely. You saw how it did those panthers when it fought in the ring."

"There's a lot more coywolv out here."

Deep in the waters, something dark and hungry stirred.

Tool startled, then froze.

A monster was easing through the waters, vast and silent, a shadow of death. Tool stifled a growl as it passed, fighting to keep the rhythms of his heart slow, fighting to save precious oxygen. Meters and meters of leathery hide slid past him, a great king of a reptile. The creature was bigger than the largest Komodo dragons of the equator. A massive horror of an alligator, tail and legs moving easy, propelling it through darkening waters with a predatory grace.

It circled, attracted by the frenetic hounds and their fool-ish splashing.

The first dog sank before it could yelp. The next went under in a snap. Blood filled the water.

The soldiers yelled and gunshots flashed. Automatic weapons. Shotguns. Sparks of fear as the soldiers peppered the water with their bullets.

"Get it! Get it!"

Heavy impact. A sharp pain blossomed in Tool's shoul-der. He flinched at the bad luck but held still. He'd been shot before; this was not the worst. The bullet had smashed into the meat of his body. He could survive the wound.

"It's not the dog-face! It's a damn gator!" The soldiers unloaded more angry shots into the water. Whistled back their hounds. "Heel!"

Blood smoked from Tool's shoulder. He pressed his fist to the wound, trying to staunch the flow. There was enough blood in the water that Tool's own blood might not be the bait that it would have been, but he smelled of wounded sickness.

The soldiers remained at the edge of the pool, shooting at whatever moved and cursing the alligator. The monster circled in the water, finishing the remains of the hounds, unperturbed by the powerless soldiers above.

Tool watched the alligator, measuring this new variable in the equation of his survival. He felt no brotherhood with this beast. Reptiles, if they were any part of his blood design, were deeply buried in the helixes of his DNA. This creature was nothing other than an enemy.

Above, the soldiers' voices finally faded, seeking their prey in other places.

Trapped in the deepening darkness, Tool continued to study the alligator. If he moved, the monster would sense him, and now his lungs were beginning to heave, demanding air.

Tool clenched his jaws and waited, hoping that the alligator might still move off.

Instead, the lizard sank to the bottom of the pool, sated.

If Tool was fast, he might make it out of the water in time, but he would have to be quick. He knew that he had only two hundred heartbeats of air before he became too weak to fight. The blood thudded in Tool's ears, counting down his death. He could slow the beat of his heart, but he could not stop it.

Tool reached up and took hold of a thick mangrove root, preparing to propel himself upward.

The alligator whipped about. Tool had been about to kick for the surface, but now, if he let himself float free, he would be easy bait. The alligator flashed toward him, jagged mouth hungering. Tool levered himself aside, using the roots to maneuver. Teeth snapped, missing.

The alligator came around. Its tail slammed Tool into the mangrove roots. Tool's vision went bloody. The alligator arrowed in again, and Tool grabbed for a weapon. He tore at the mangrove roots, but the wood ripped free with only a stub.

The alligator's maw gaped wide. Vast oblivion.

Tool lunged for the monster, the chunk of splintered root clenched in his fist. With a silent roar, Tool rammed his fist into the monster's mouth. The alligator's jaws snapped shut. Its teeth crushed Tool's shoulder, piercing flesh. Pain like lightning.

The monster rolled and dove, dragging Tool with it. Instinctively, the alligator knew it needed only to suck the air from its enemy. It was born for this fight, and in its decades of life, none had ever bested it. It would drown Tool, as it had drowned so many other unwary beasts, and then it would feed well.

Tool struggled, trying to pry open the monster's mouth, but even the half-man's strength was no match for the alligator's bite. The teeth were clamped like a vise. The alligator rolled, slamming Tool into the mud, pressing him down.

Panic swept through Tool. He was drowning. He barely fought off the instinct to breathe water. Again he pried at the lizard's jaws, knowing it was pointless, but unable to surrender.

The reptile is not your enemy. It is nothing but a beast. You are its better.

A foolish stray thought, and small comfort—killed by something with a brain the size of a walnut. Tool's teeth showed in a rictus of contempt as the alligator plowed him through more weeds and mud.

This dumb beast is not your enemy.

Tool was not some brute animal, able to think only in terms of attack or flight. He was better than that. He hadn't survived this long by thinking like an animal. Panic and mindlessness were his only enemy, as always. Not bullets or teeth or machetes or claws. Not bombs or whips or razor wire.

And not this dumb beast. Panic only.

He could never break free of the alligator's jaws. They were perfect clamps, evolved to lock down and never release. No one pried free of an alligator's bite. Not even something as strong as Tool. So he would no longer try.

Instead, Tool lashed his free arm around the beast's head, locking it in a bear hug, and squeezed. His grip forced the alligator's jaws tighter around his own arm and shoulder. Its teeth pierced deep. More of Tool's blood clouded the water.

In the dim recesses of its tiny brain, perhaps the alligator was pleased to have its teeth sink deeper into enemy flesh. But Tool's other arm, engulfed in the monster's maw, was free to work. Not from the outside, but from within.

Tool turned the shattered chunk of mangrove root and began methodically ramming it into the roof of the monster's mouth. Ripping through flesh, driving the wood deeper and deeper.

The alligator, sensing something was wrong, feeling the

tearing within itself, tried to open its jaws, but Tool, instead of letting go, now clamped the monster tighter.

Do not run away, he thought. *I have you where I want you.*

Blood misted from Tool's shoulder, but battle fury strengthened him. He had the advantage. He might be running out of air and life, but this ancient reptile was his. The alligator's bite was deadly, but it had its own weakness: It lacked the muscle strength to open its mouth easily.

The mangrove root ground to dust, but Tool continued, using his claws, ripping deeper and deeper.

The alligator thrashed wildly, trying to shake free. Decades of easy killing had never prepared it for a creature like Tool, something more primal and terrifying than even itself. It writhed and rolled, shaking Tool the way a dog shook a rat. Stars swam in Tool's vision, but he held on and tore deeper. His air ran out. His fist found bone.

With one final heave, Tool rammed his claws through the lizard's skull and tore into its brain.

The monster began to shudder and die.

Did it understand that it had always been outmatched? That it was dying because it had never evolved to face a creature such as Tool?

Tool's fist crushed the lizard's brain to pulp.

The great reptile's life drained away, victim to a monster that should never have existed, an unholy perfection of killing, built in laboratories and honed across a thousand battlefields.

Tool's claws carved out the last of the brain meat of the ancient lizard, and the alligator fell limp.

A rush of primal satisfaction flooded Tool as his opponent surrendered to death. Blackness swamped Tool's vision, and he let go.

He had conquered.

Even as he died, he conquered.

3

"THAT'S ENOUGH, MAHLIA." Doctor Mahfouz straightened with a sigh. "We've done all we can. Let her rest."

Mahlia sat back on her heels and wiped her lips of Tani's dying spit, giving up on breathing for the girl who had already stopped breathing for herself. Before her, the young woman lay still, empty blue eyes staring up at the bamboo spars of the squat's ceiling.

Blood covered everything: the doctor and Mahlia, Tani, the floor, old Mr. Salvatore. Ten pints, the doctor had taught Mahlia in her studies; that was what filled a human being. And from the look of it, all of it was out of their patient. Bright and red. Rich with oxygen. Not blue like the placental sac, but red. Red as rubies.

What a mess.

The squat stank. Burned vegetable oil from the lamp, the iron spike of blood, the rank, sweaty smell of desperate people. The smell of pain.

Sunlight speared through cracks in the bamboo walls of the squat, molten blades of day. Doctor Mahfouz had asked if Tani and Mr. Salvatore preferred to do the birth outside, where it would be cooler and they'd have better air and light, but Mr. Salvatore was traditional and wanted privacy for his daughter, even if she'd been anything but private in her love life. Now it felt as though they were swaddled in the smell of death.

In the corner of the squat, tucked under a pile of stained blankets, Tani's killer lay quiet. The infant had nursed for a second, and Mahlia had been surprised at how happy she'd been for Tani that her little wrinkled baby was healthy and that the birth hadn't been as long as she had expected.

And then Tani's eyes had rolled back and the doctor said, "Mahlia, come here, please" in the way that told her something was really bad but he didn't want to scare the patient.

Mahlia had come down to the doctor where he knelt between Tani's legs and she'd seen the blood, more and more of it, his hands covered with it, and the doctor had wanted pressure on her belly, and then he'd wanted to cut.

But they didn't have any drugs to knock Tani out, to make the cutting easy, nothing with them but his last black market needle's worth of heroin, and then he'd had his scalpel out and Tani was gasping and asking what was wrong, and the doctor had said, "I need you to hold still, dear."

Of course, Tani panicked. Doctor Mahfouz called for her father, and Mr. Salvatore climbed up the ladder into the squat, and when he saw the blood he shouted, demanding to know what was wrong, and of course he panicked Tani even more.

The doctor ordered him to her head, to hold her shoulders while he sat on her legs, and then he asked Mahlia to help him even though all Mahlia had was a right hand stump and her lucky left—which didn't seem so lucky when she needed both hands to get the job done.

The doctor set to work by the flicker of the single vegetable-oil lamp and the burn of candles, and Mahlia was forced to lean close, using her eyes to tell the older man where to set the scalpel. With her guiding voice, she helped him make the bikini cuts low across Tani's belly. The cuts that he'd taught her from his medical books, because he couldn't see so well, with Mahlia handing him the implements as quick as she could with her one good hand until they were in Tani's belly and found where the blood was coming from.

By then Tani's struggles had stilled. And after that, she was gone, with her belly cut open like a pig's, and old Salvatore holding his daughter's limp shoulders, and blood all over the squat.

"That's enough, Mahlia," the doctor said, and Mahlia

straightened from trying to rescue-breathe for the poor dead girl.

Salvatore was looking at them, accusation in his eyes. "You killed her."

"No one killed her," Doctor Mahfouz said. "Birth is always uncertain."

"That one. That one killed her." Salvatore pointed at Mahlia. "You should never have let her anywhere near my girl."

At the man's accusation, Mahlia palmed a bloody scalpel into her good hand, but didn't show anything on her face as she turned to face him. If Salvatore made a move, she'd be ready.

"Mahlia..." The doctor's voice held warning. He always knew what she was thinking. But Mahlia didn't put down the scalpel. Better safe than sorry.

"Castoffs like her are bad luck. Got the Fates Eye on them," Salvatore ranted. "We should have run her off when we had the chance."

"Mr. Salvatore, please." Doctor Mahfouz was trying to get the man to calm down. Mahlia didn't think it would work. The man's daughter was dead on the table with her belly cut wide and there Mahlia was, standing right in front of him, the perfect target for blame.

"Bad luck and death," he said. "You were a fool to take that one in, Doctor."

"Please, Salvatore. Even Saint Olmos calls for charity."

"She kills things," Salvatore said. "Everywhere she goes. Nothing but blood and death."

"You're exaggerating."

"She put the Fates Eye on Alejandro's goats," Salvatore pointed out.

"I didn't touch them," Mahlia retorted. "Coywolv got them, and everyone knows it. I didn't touch them."

"Alejandro saw you looking at them."

"I'm looking at you," Mahlia said. "That mean you're dead, too?"

"Mahlia!"

She flinched at the doctor's shocked remonstration. "I didn't do nothing to your girl," Mahlia said. "Or any goats." She looked at the grieving father. "I'm sorry about your girl. Wouldn't wish that on anyone."

She began picking up the stained medical implements while the doctor kept trying to soothe Salvatore. Mahfouz was good at that. He knew how to talk people down. In all her life, Mahlia had never seen someone who was so good at making people stop bickering, sit down, talk, and listen.

Doctor Mahfouz was gentle and calm in an argument, where most people went off and started shouting. He brought out the good. If it hadn't been for him, Banyan Town would have run her off long ago. They might have let Mouse stay, even though he was a war maggot, too. But a castoff like her? No way. Not without the doctor talking words like *charity* and *kindness* and *compassion*.

Doctor Mahfouz liked to say that everyone wanted to be good. They just sometimes needed help finding their way to it. That was when he'd first taken her and Mouse in. He'd said it even as he was sprinkling sulfa powder over Mahlia's bloody stump of a hand, like he couldn't see what was happening right in front of him. The Drowned Cities were busy tearing themselves apart once again, but here the doctor was, still talking about how people wanted to be kind and good.

Mahlia and Mouse had just looked at each other, and didn't say anything. If the doctor was fool enough to let them stay, he could babble whatever crazy talk he wanted.

Doctor Mahfouz gathered up Tani's baby and poured it into the grieving grandfather's arms.

"What am I supposed to do with this?" Salvatore demanded. "I'm no woman. How will I feed it?"

" 'It' is a 'him,' " the doctor said. "Name *him*. Give your grandson a name. We'll help you with the rest. You are not alone. None of us are alone."

"Easy for you to say." Salvatore's gaze went to Mahlia again. "If she had two hands, you could have saved her."

"Nothing could have saved Tani. We might wish otherwise, but the truth is that sometimes we are powerless."

"I thought you knew all the peacekeeper medicine."

"Knowing all and having the necessary tools are two different things. This is hardly a hospital. We make do with what we have, and none of that is Mahlia's fault. Tani is the victim of many evils, but Mahlia is not the beginning of that chain, nor the end. I am responsible, if anyone is."

"If your nurse had two hands, it would've helped," Salvatore insisted.

Mahlia could feel the man's gaze on her back as she dropped the last of the clamps and scalpels into Mahfouz's bag. She'd have to boil everything when she got back to Mahfouz's squat, but at least she could get out of here.

She snapped the bag closed, using the stump of her right hand to stabilize it while she worked the clasps with the fingers of her lucky left.

The bag's leather was stamped with the Chinese characters of the peacekeeper hospital where Doctor Mahfouz had trained before the war started up again. 华盛顿美中友谊医院. 华盛顿 was an Accelerated Age word for *the Drowned Cities*. 中 was for *China*. And she could pick out other characters as well: *friendship* and *surgery*, the character for *courtyard*.

Roughly translated, it meant "friendship hospital." One of those places that the Chinese peacekeepers had created when they'd first shown up to try to stop the war. A place with sterile boiled sheets and good lighting and blood packs and saline for transfusions, and the thousand other things that a real doctor was supposed to have.

These days, their hospital was wherever Doctor Mahfouz set his medical bag, all that was left of the wonderful hospital that the Chinese had donated, except for a few rehydration packets still stamped with the words WITH WISHES FOR PEACE AND WELL-BEING FROM THE PEOPLE OF BEIJING.

Mahlia could imagine all those Chinese people in their far-off country donating to the war victims of the Drowned Cities. All of them rich enough to send things like rice and clothes and rehydration packets all the way over the pole on fast-sailing clipper ships. All of them rich enough to meddle where they didn't belong.

Mahlia avoided looking at Tani as she got the medical bag closed. Sometimes, if there was a blanket, you could pull it over the body to make a shroud, but they'd used all the bedding for the new baby.

Mahlia wondered if she was supposed to feel something at seeing Tani's corpse. She'd seen plenty of dead, but Tani was different. Her death was just bad luck. Not like most of the deaths she'd seen, where someone died because a soldier boy didn't like the way you talked, or wanted something you had, or didn't like the shape of your eyes.

The doctor interrupted her thoughts. "Mahlia, why don't you take the baby over to Amaya's house while I speak with Mr. Salvatore. She'll be able to nurse the child."

Mahlia eyed Salvatore uncertainly. The man looked like he wasn't going to give the baby over. "I don't think he wants me near."

Doctor Mahfouz counseled Salvatore. "You're distraught. Let Mahlia take the infant. At least for a little while. We still must arrange for your daughter. She'll need your rites to send her on. I don't know the Deepwater prayers."

The man continued glaring at Mahlia, but some of the rage was draining away. Maybe later, he'd have some fight, but now, he was just sad.

"Here." Mahlia inched forward and eased the baby from his hands, not looking him in the eye, not challenging him. When the baby was in her arms, she bundled it up. With a last glance back at the dead girl, Mahlia hustled the baby down through the trapdoor in the floor.

There was a whole crowd waiting below.

People backed away as Mahlia came down the bamboo ladder using her left hand to catch the rungs while she cradled the baby in her right arm. Minsok and Auntie Selima, and Reg and Tua and Betty Fan, Delilah and Bobby Cross, and a bunch more, all of them caught in the act of lingering, heads cocked up and listening to the tragedy taking place above.

"Tani's dead," Mahlia said as she reached the bottom of the ladder. "If that's what you're wondering."

Everyone except Auntie Selima looked at her as if it were her fault. A ripple of warding went through the crowd, people touching blue glass Fates Eyes, or kissing green prayer beads, lots of motions to push off bad luck. Mahlia pretended she didn't see. She folded a triangle of blanket over the infant's face to shade it, and pushed through the crowd.

Out from under the squat, the sun glared down on her. Mahlia made her way down a weedy trail, heading for

Amaya's place. Crumbled buildings loomed on either side of her, cracked sentries robed in jungle growth. Trees sprouted from their crowns and kudzu draped over their slumped shoulders. Birds clustered in the heights, making mud nests, flying out of empty window eyes, chattering and fluttering, sending down droppings on the unwary.

From amongst the green and leafy faces, more people peered out, watching Mahlia pass, families who lived on the old buildings' upper floors while they kept the ground for chickens and ducks and goats that ran wild during the day and were penned at night, keeping coywolv and panthers from getting at them.

All along the lower walls of the buildings, the tags and colors of various warlord factions were splashed, painted scrawls competing with one another—Army of God, Tulane Company, Freedom Militia—evidence of the armies that had controlled and taxed and recruited in Banyan Town over the years.

Mahlia didn't like any of them, but then, since most soldier boys would kill her on sight, the feeling was mutual. But the villagers held on to the illusion that they could assuage the soldiers who warred around them, so they still hung the patriotic flags of whatever faction was currently in power, and hoped that it would be enough.

This year, rags of blue dangled in upper windows signaling support for Colonel Glenn Stern's United Patriot Front, but Mahlia knew the townspeople also kept red stars close, in case the Army of God regained the upper hand and took back this territory. A few buildings still showed the stars and bars of Tulane, all chipped and peeled and defaced and mostly covered over, but not many anymore. No one had seen Tulane soldiers for years. Rumor had it that they'd been pushed into the swamps, and had turned to fishing and crawdad hunting and eels because they didn't have enough bullets to keep fighting. Either that, or else they'd made a desperate run north and their bones were now being picked clean by the army of corporate half-men who patrolled the northern borders and let no one pass.

Mahlia's father used to spit whenever he said any of the warlords' army names. It didn't matter if it was Army of God or Freedom Militia or the United Patriot Front. There wasn't a single one of them that was worth anything. A bunch of *zhi laohu*, "paper tigers." They liked to roar, but they blew away like paper in the face of the slightest breath of real combat. Whenever her father's troops showed up, they ran like rats or died like flies.

Mahlia's father had always talked about the ancient Chinese general called Sun Tzu and his strategies, and how all the paper tiger warlords had no strategy at all—he used to joke about what garbage they were as soldiers.

Laji, he'd said. "Garbage." Every one of them.

But in the end, the warlords had won, and her father had left with the rest of China's peacekeeper army while the paper tigers roared their victories from the rooftops of the Drowned Cities.

Sweat dripped down Mahlia's back, soaking her tank as

she walked. Being out in the middle of the day was crazy. The humidity and heat made doing everything more miserable. She should have been hunkered down in the shade, instead of sweating her way across town with blood all over her and a baby in her arms.

Mahlia passed the shop where Auntie Selima sold black market soap and cigarettes hauled from Moss Landing, along with whatever junk she could scavenge from the suburban ruins that surrounded them. Old cups made of glass that hadn't shattered in the fighting. Rubber tubing for moving irrigation water. Rusty wire for binding together bamboo into fences. All kinds of things.

A couple of Chinese-made sheet-metal stoves were stacked in a corner, from when the peacekeepers had been around, trying to make friends. For all Mahlia knew, her own father's battalion might have been the ones who'd delivered the stoves out here, showing people how they burned better and hotter than an open campfire. Trying to do all that peacekeeper outreach that was supposed to make Drowned Cities people who fought one another all the time focus instead on taking care of themselves. Soft power, her father had called it, the winning of hearts and minds that was just as important as the peacekeeper ability to smash the local militias' combat units.

Ahead, Amaya's squat waited. It was small, scabbed into the second story of an old brick building that had tumbled in on itself. On the ground floor, Amaya and her husband had restacked the crumbled bricks to form a strong pen for their goats.

Mahlia ducked into the shade of the open ground floor. Amaya's ladder was painted blue, and little ragged UPF talismans hung like prayer flags to Kali-Mary Mercy, thin offerings meant to keep Glenn Stern's soldier boys at bay.

When Mahlia first saw Banyan Town, she hadn't understood why everyone lived in the upper stories. Mouse had laughed at that, calling her a swank city girl for not knowing about the panthers and coywolv that stalked the night. Mouse's family had grown soybeans on a farm way out in the suburban collapse of the Drowned Cities, so he had known all about living in the middle of nowhere, but Mahlia had had to learn everything from scratch.

"Amaya?" Mahlia called.

The woman appeared from behind her goat pen. One of her licebiters was slung on her back, a tiny snotty-faced creature. Another kid peeked down from the squat above, dark eyes and brown skin almost as dark as Mahlia's, peering down the ladder, serious.

At the sight of Mahlia covered with blood and carrying the baby, Amaya's eyes widened. She made a sign of warding, putting the Fates Eye on Mahlia, who pretended not to notice.

Mahlia held up her bundle. "It's Tani's."

"How is she?" Amaya asked.

"She's dead. The doctor wants you to take care of her

baby. For Mr. Salvatore, since you're nursing anyway. Until he can take care of it on his own."

Amaya didn't extend her arms to take the bundle. "I told her those soldier boys weren't any good for her."

Mahlia still held out the baby. "The doctor says you'll nurse it."

"He does, does he?"

The woman was a brick wall. Mahlia wished the doctor had come instead. He could have convinced her, easy. Amaya didn't want the baby, and if Mahlia was honest, Mahlia didn't blame her. She didn't want it, either.

"We aren't doing it any favors," Amaya said finally. "No one needs another mouth."

Mahlia just waited. She was good at that. When you were a castoff, it didn't do any good trying to talk to people, but sometimes, if you just kind of waited them out, people would get uncomfortable and feel like they had to do something.

Amaya wasn't really complaining about more mouths, exactly. She was talking about orphans. And when she said that, she really meant war maggots. Orphans like Mahlia, who had shown up in Banyan Town with a chopped-off right hand, bleeding, dying for help. No one wanted a war maggot in their midst. It meant they had to decide one way or another about a peacekeeper's castoff, lying in the dirt in the middle of their town. Most people had decided one way; Doctor Mahfouz decided different.

Mahlia said, "You don't need to worry about the extra mouth. Salvatore's going to take it back as soon as it can eat on its own. And Doctor's going to send you more food for your trouble."

"What's that man see in a one-handed nurse?" Amaya asked. "Is that why Tani's dead? Because you got no hand?"

"Wasn't my fault she got herself pregnant."

"No. But she didn't need a useless crippled China girl for a nurse."

Mahlia bristled. "I ain't Chinese."

Amaya just looked at her.

"I ain't," Mahlia repeated.

"You got the blood right there on your face. China cast-off, through and through." She turned away, then stopped. Looked back at Mahlia.

"The thing I keep wondering about is what was wrong with you, girl? How come the peacekeepers didn't want you? If the peacekeepers didn't care enough to take you when they went back to China, why in the name of the Fates would we want you, either?"

Mahlia fought to keep down the anger that was starting to bubble in her. "Well, this one ain't Chinese, and it ain't castoff. It's Banyan Town's. You want it? Or am I telling the doctor you dumped it?"

Amaya looked at Mahlia like she was a sack of goat guts, but she finally took the infant.

As soon as the baby was in Amaya's hands, Mahlia pressed close. Right in Amaya's face, as eye to eye as she could make it with a grown woman. Mahlia was a little surprised to find that she almost had the height. Amaya backed up against the ladder of the squat, clutching the baby as Mahlia pushed closer.

"You call me castoff," Mahlia said, "Chinese throwaway, whatever." Amaya was trying to look away, but Mahlia had her pinned, kept her eye to eye. "My old man might have been peacekeeper, but my mom was pure Drowned Cities. You want to war like that, I'm all in." Mahlia lifted the scarred stump of her right hand, shoved it up in Amaya's face. "Maybe I cut you the way the Army of God cut me. See how you do with just a lucky left. How'd you like that?"

Amaya's eyes filled with horror. For a second, Mahlia had the satisfaction of at least getting respect. *Yeah. You see me now, all right. Before I was just another castoff, but you see me now.*

"Mahlia! What are you doing?"

It was Doctor Mahfouz, hurrying toward them. Mahlia backed off. "Nothing," she said, but Doctor Mahfouz was staring at her with dismay, as if she were some kind of animal gone wild.

"What's going on here, Mahlia?"

Mahlia scowled. "She called me Chinese."

Mahfouz threw up his hands. "You *are* Chinese! There's no shame in that!"

Amaya broke in. "She threatened me!" she said. "That *animal* threatened me." She was furious now that she had backup from Doctor Mahfouz. Angry that she'd been scared by a castoff war maggot. Mahlia braced for the tongue-lashing, but before Amaya could get going, the doctor took Mahlia's shoulder.

"Go home, Mahlia," he said.

To Mahlia's surprise, he wasn't mean when he said it, or mad. Just…tired. "Go see if you can find Mouse," he said. "We'll need to gather extra food to help Amaya with this new child."

Mahlia hesitated, but there was no point sticking around. "Sorry," she said, not sure if she was saying it to the doctor, or Amaya, or herself, or who. "Sorry," she said again, and turned away.

Mahfouz was always telling her to stand down, to let the insults roll off, and here she was, picking fights she didn't have to. She could practically hear his voice in her head as she plodded back toward the doctor's squat and her friend Mouse: "A harmless war orphan is something they may not love, but still, they can empathize. But if you seem violent, they'll see you the same way they see coywolv."

Which meant they'd leave her alone as long as she looked soft. But if she stood up, they'd put her down right quick.

Sun Tzu said that you had to pick your battles and fight only when you knew what victory was supposed to look like. Victory came to people who knew when to attack and when to avoid, and now Mahlia suspected that she'd just done something stupid. She'd let the enemy goad her into exposing herself.

Her father would have laughed at that. A hasty temper was one of the greatest faults a general could have, and people who were provoked by insults were easy to defeat. Mahlia had done what Drowned Cities people always did: She'd fought without thinking.

Her father would have called her an animal for that.

4

DOCTOR MAHFOUZ'S SQUAT was tucked into a five-story war ruin. Missiles and bullets had left holes in its concrete walls, and the upper floors were missing entirely, showing where bombs had dropped down through the roof and blown the top to smithereens. But even with all the wreckage, the building still had good iron bones, and the doctor had chosen to nestle his squat in the second story, amongst those solid iron ribs.

A home.

When the doctor first took Mahlia and Mouse into his care, the squat had barely been sufficient to hold a single person. Not because the squat was tiny—which it was—but because its shadowy interior had been so filled with moldering books that the doctor was forced to sleep in the open air whenever it wasn't raining, all because his books were more important to keep safe than he was.

But with the intrusion of the castoff girl from the heart of the Drowned Cities and the orphan boy from the torched village of Brighton, the doctor at last admitted that his home was inadequate.

With Mouse's help, and later Mahlia's as the stump of her right arm healed, they laid rough planking across the I beams and expanded the doctor's floor space. Using scavenged rusty tin and rough-cut plastic, they made a larger roof to keep off downpours. They'd used plastic for the walls as well, at first. It wasn't like they needed walls for warmth, not even during the dark season. Swamp panthers sometimes leaped up to the second story to prowl, so they'd also cut bamboo for walls and chinked them with mud and straw until they'd made a solid defended space both for people and for even more of the doctor's moldy books.

On the ground floor, the doctor kept his kitchen and a small emergency surgery. The kitchen was stocked with dented pans that hung from bits of bent iron rebar. A large pot that Mahlia used for boiling surgical items sat at the ready atop a cylindrical metal cookstove, one of the many that the peacekeepers had given away in the villages around the Drowned Cities. The humanitarian message on the side of the stove read, BEST WISHES FOR PEACE, FROM THE PEOPLE OF ISLAND SHANGHAI, in English and Chinese.

A little away from their squat, Doctor Mahfouz had

built a livestock house out of carefully masoned rubble, making it so that it stood almost as straight and square as the buildings must have looked during the Accelerated Age, but most important, strong enough to keep out coywolv and panthers. Gabby, their goat, was standing tethered beside the house, placidly chewing kudzu. Mahlia went over to her. Gabby bleated.

"You've already been milked," Mahlia said. "Stop pushing on me."

Mahlia checked the rest of the house. The buckets for washing had already been filled from the pool formed in the basement of the neighboring collapsed building. From that evidence, Mouse was nearby.

Mahlia climbed up the squat's log ladder and levered herself through the trapdoor. The smell of sawdust and rotten paper enveloped her, the smells that she most associated with the doctor. Books lay everywhere, stacked and piled, crowding rough-cut shelves, every wall covered. The man couldn't bear to leave a library alone. Mahlia picked her way around the piles.

"Mouse?"

Nothing.

When Mouse and Mahlia had first arrived, they'd rolled their eyes at the man's obsession with books. There was no point saving books, unless you were going to use them to start a fire. Books didn't save you from a bullet. But Mahfouz had stood tall for Mahlia and Mouse, so if the doctor wanted to keep books stacked to the ceiling until they tumbled over on you, or if he asked you to hike all the way to a place he called Alexandria, then Mahlia and Mouse were going to do it. The doctor had put himself on the line for them. It was the least they could do.

"We're going to Alexandria," the doctor had said.

"Why?" Mahlia had asked.

The doctor looked up from where he'd been studying an old Accelerated Age map, from before the Drowned Cities had drowned. "Because the Army of God burns books, and we are going to save them."

All the way to Alexandria, ahead of the next big push by the Army of God. It was their last chance to save the knowledge of the world, Mahfouz said.

But of course they were too late and by the time they got there, Alexandria was smoking rubble. Corpses littered the town: people who had thrown themselves in the way of an army. People who'd tried to shield books with their bodies, instead of the other way around.

Mahlia remembered looking at all those dead bodies and feeling sad for the crazy adults who thought books were more important than their lives. When the dogs of war came howling down on you, you didn't stand tall; you ran. That was Sun Tzu. If your enemy was strong, you avoided him. Which seemed pretty damn obvious to Mahlia and Mouse. But these people had stood tall anyway.

So they'd been shot and macheted to pieces. They'd been lit on fire and burned by acid.

And their books had burned anyway.

Doctor Mahfouz had fallen to his knees before the torched library and tears ran down his cheeks, and Mahlia had suddenly feared for him, and for herself and Mouse.

The doctor didn't have any sense at all, she'd realized. He was just like the people who'd kept the library. He would die for a few pieces of paper. And she'd been afraid, because if the one man who cared for her and Mouse was that kind of crazy, then she and Mouse didn't stand a chance.

Mahlia shook off the memory and called out again. "Mouse? Where are you?"

"Up here!"

Mahlia lifted a flap of old plastic with a fat Patel Global Transit logo on it and eased out onto one of the I beams that supported the house. Three stories higher up, legs dangling in the open air, Mouse perched on an iron spar.

Of course.

Mahlia took a breath. She kicked off her sandals and balanced her way across a hot rusty I beam. Foot in front of foot, looking down at their kitchen and the makeshift surgery, balancing across the fall until she reached a wall of crumbling concrete and its exposed rebar, where she could scale to Mouse's height with less difficulty.

She started climbing, using her stump for balance, her left hand for gripping, her bare brown toes finding holds as she climbed.

One story, two stories...

Mouse could just shimmy up the vertical I beams, a dexterous monkey climbing with his thin legs and ropy arms and perfect hands. Mahlia had to take the slow way.

Three stories...

The world opened around her.

Five stories up, the jungle spread in all directions, broken only where the war-shattered ruins of the Drowned Cities poked higher than the trees. Old concrete highway overpasses arched above the jungle like the coils of giant sea serpents, their backs fuzzy and covered, dripping long tangled vines of kudzu.

To the west, Banyan Town's shattered buildings and cleared fields lay tidy in the sunshine. Occasional walls poked up from the fields like shark fins. Rectangular green pools pocked the fields in regular lines, marking where ancient neighborhoods had once stood, the outlines of basements, now filled with rainwater and stocked with fish. They glittered like mirrors in the hot sun, dotted with lily pads, the graves of suburbia, laid open and waterlogged.

To the north, trackless jungle stretched. If you hiked far enough, past the warlords and the roaming packs of coywolv and hungry panthers, you'd eventually hit the border. There, an army of half-men stood guard, keeping Drowned Cities war maggots and soldier boys and warlords from carrying the fighting any farther north. Keeping them from infecting places like Manhattan Orleans and Seascape Boston with their sickness.

To the south and east, jungle gave way to salt swamp,

and finally, Drowned Cities proper. Far off in the hazy distance, the sea gleamed.

Mahlia stood tall atop the gutted ruin, squinting in the bright light. Iron burned under her feet and the sun beat on her dark brown skin. It was a good time to be lying low, out of the burn, but here Mouse perched, pale and freckled, staring across the jungles. Skinny little licebiter. Red-haired and skin-roasted, with gray-blue eyes as twitchy as any war maggot she'd ever seen. Not saying anything. Just staring out at the jungle. Maybe looking toward where his family used to have a farm, and where maybe he'd been happy before the soldier boys rolled through and took it all away.

Mouse said his full name was Malati Saint Olmos, like his mother had been trying to make good with the Rust Saint and the Deepwater Christians at the same time. Splitting the difference for luck. But Mahlia had only ever called him Mouse.

Mouse glanced over as she dropped down beside him. "Damn, maggot, you got blood all over you," he said.

"Tani died."

"Yeah?" Mouse looked interested.

"Bled right out," Mahlia said. "Might as well have stuck a knife in her. Baby ripped her inside out."

"Remind me not to get knocked up," Mouse said.

Mahlia snorted. "Too true, maggot. Too true."

Mouse studied her. "So why you look so down?" he asked. "You didn't even like that girl. She was always in your face about being castoff."

Mahlia grimaced. "Amaya and old man Salvatore put the blame on me. Said I was bad luck. Said I put the Fates Eye on her, like on Alejandro's goats."

"Alejandro's goats?" Mouse laughed. "That wasn't no Fates Eye. That was goes-around-comes-around, coywolv-scent-and-Alejandro-deserved-it is what that was."

Goes-around-comes-around. Mahlia almost smiled at that.

The scent had come from a coywolv dissection that she'd helped Doctor Mahfouz perform; he was interested in hybrids and wanted to know more about this creature that no biology book of the Accelerated Age had ever discussed.

Mahfouz claimed the coywolv had evolved to fill niches that had opened up in a damaged and warming world—all the size and cooperation of a wolf, all the intelligence and adaptability of a coyote. Coywolv had come loping down out of Canada's black winter darkness and then just kept spreading.

Now they were everywhere. Like fleas, but with teeth.

When Mahlia and Mahfouz had cut out the female's scent sack, he'd warned her about it, that they should bottle the scent and keep it careful, and wash thoroughly afterward. Which had been all Mahlia needed in order to know that she had something powerful in her hands.

With Mouse, she'd hatched a plan. It hadn't taken much, and suddenly, Alejandro—who'd been all up on her about being a castoff and not worth anything except as a nailshed girl—had his entire herd slaughtered.

"Anyway," Mouse said, "how were we supposed to know the coywolv would figure out how to open the gate?"

Mahlia laughed. "That was purely unnatural."

And it was. Coywolv were scary that way. Smarter than you wanted to believe. When Mahlia had seen the ropes of strewn guts and the last few patches of goat fur in the morning, she'd been as amazed as anyone. She'd been aiming to give the dumb farmer a scare, and she'd gotten a thousand times that.

Goes-around-comes-around to the *nth*.

"Eh." Mouse made a face. "He deserved it. All talking about how you weren't good for nothing but a nailshed girl. All that Chinese castoff stuff. He barely looks at you now. You put the fear of the Fates in him good."

"Yeah. I guess." Mahlia picked at the rust of the I beam. Peeled off a flake as long as her pinky. "But now with Tani, it means all his whispering about me carries weight. It was the first thing Salvatore said right after Tani died."

Mouse snorted. "They'd blame a castoff just for breathing. You could be good as gold and they'd still blame you."

"Yeah. Maybe."

"Maybe?" Mouse looked at her incredulously. "For sure. They're just pissed you actually stood up for yourself. Mahfouz can talk peace and reconciliation all he wants, but if you don't stand tall, no one gives you respect."

Mahlia knew he was right. Alejandro wouldn't have let up on her if she hadn't scared him off. For a little while, she'd been able to walk tall and not feel afraid, thanks to that stunt with the coywolv scent. But at the same time, now she had a cloud of distrust hanging over her, and Doctor Mahfouz didn't let her into his medicines without supervision. Goes-around-comes-around whipping back at her.

She grimaced. "Yeah, you're right. It doesn't matter what I do. End of the day, I'm still a castoff. They either hate me for being weak or hate me for standing tall. Can't win that fight."

"So what's really eating you?"

"Salvatore said something else, too." She held up the stump of her right hand, with its puckered and mottled stub of brown skin folded over. "He said Tani would still be alive if the doctor had more hands to help."

"Yeah? Think he's right?"

"Probably." Mahlia spat over the edge. Watched her saliva do cartwheels to the ground. "Me and the doctor work good together, but a stump ain't no hand."

"If you want to complain about what you got, you can always go back and ask the Army of God to take your lucky left. They'll finish the job."

"You know what I mean. I ain't complaining that you saved me. But I still can't do anything delicate."

"Better than me. And I got all ten fingers."

"Yeah, well, you could do all this doctor work if you tried. You just got to pay attention and read what the doctor tells you to."

"Not hard for you, maybe. I get twitchy just looking at

all those letters." Mouse shrugged. "Maybe if I could read up here, up high, you know? But I don't like being down in the squat, with the lantern and all that. Don't like being closed in, you know?"

"Yeah," Mahlia said.

She had the same feeling herself sometimes. The chest-tight feeling of the Fates setting you up and getting ready to kill you off. It made it hard to focus on a book, or even to sit still. Maggot twitch, some people called it. If you'd seen much of the war, you had it. Some more. Some less. But everybody had it.

The only time Mouse seemed really at peace was when he was out in the jungle, fishing or hunting. The rest of the time he was twitchy and nervous and couldn't sit still and damn sure couldn't pay attention. Mahlia sometimes wondered what he would have turned out like if he'd been able to grow up on his parents' farm, if a warlord's patrol had never had a chance to kill his family. Maybe Mouse would have been real calm and still, then. Maybe he could have read a book all day, or been able to sleep inside a house and not be afraid of soldier boys sneaking up in the dark.

"Hey." Mouse tapped her. "Where'd you go?"

Mahlia startled. She hadn't even realized she'd drifted away. Mouse was looking at her with concern. "Don't go off like that," he said. "Makes me think you'll just tip right off."

"Don't nanny me."

"If I didn't nanny you, you'd be dead by now. Either

51

starved or chopped up. You need Momma Mouse to look after you, castoff."

"If it wasn't for me, you'd have been picked up in a patrol years ago."

Mouse snorted. " 'Cause you're all Sun Tzu stra-tee-gic?"

"If I was strategic, I would have figured out how to get out of this place. Would have seen everything falling apart and got out while there were still ships to sail."

"So why didn't you leave?"

"My mom kept saying there were supposed to be boats for us, too. For dependents. Just kept saying it. Saying that there were supposed to be enough boats for everyone." Mahlia made a face. "Anyway. She was stupid. She didn't think strategic, either. And now there's no way out of here."

"You ever think about just trying to go north? Sneak across the border?"

Mahlia glanced at Mouse. "Coywolv, panthers, warlords, and then all those half-men up there to hold the line? They'd be picking our bones before we even got close to the Jersey Orleans. We're stuck; that's the fact. Like a bunch of crabs boiling in a pot."

"That's Mahfouz talking."

" 'Crabs in a pot, pulling each other down while we all boil alive.' "

Mouse laughed. "You got to say it like he does, though. All disappointed."

"You should have seen how he looked after I pushed up

on Amaya. Talk about disappointed." Mahlia waved the stump of her hand with irritation. "Like if I was nice and polite, they'd think I was some kind of gift from the Scavenge God." She snorted.

Mouse laughed. "You going to sit there feeling sorry for yourself, or you going to tell me something I don't know?"

"Is there something to say? Some fish jump out of a basement and I miss it?" Mahlia poked Mouse. "What's the news, maggot? Why don't *you* tell *me* something I don't know?"

Mouse looked sly; then he nodded toward the Drowned Cities. "They're fighting again."

Mahlia burst out laughing. "That's like saying the cities are drowning."

"I'm serious! They're shooting something different. Something big. I was wondering if you knew it. It's a big old gun."

"I don't hear anything."

"Well, maybe you should listen, right? Show some patience. They been blowing it off all morning. It'll come again."

Mahlia turned her attention to the horizon, studying the wreckage of the Drowned Cities where it poked up above the jungle. Distant iron spires, stabbing the sky. In some of them, beacon fires burned. A haze of smoke hung over the city center, brown and heavy. She listened.

A far-off rat-a-tat of gunfire, but nothing interesting. Couple of AKs. Maybe a heavy hunting rifle. Background noise, that. Skirmishers in the jungle or maybe target practices. Nothing—

The explosion rocked outward. The iron girder of Mahlia and Mouse's perch shivered with its force.

Mahlia gaped. "Damn, maggot! That's a *gun*."

"I told you!" Mouse was grinning. "At first, I thought they were just dynamiting, right? But they keep going. Hammering away. Some kind of big old army shells or something."

As if to underline his words, the explosion came again, and this time there was a flare and a rising cloud in the far distance. Lot of smoke and explosion for such a distance. They were looking out fifteen miles, maybe more, and there it was.

"It's a 999," Mahlia said.

"What's that?"

"Big old gun. Serious artillery. Peacekeepers used to keep them. Dropped shells on all the warlords. Used some kind of spy eye to target it, then they'd drop a big old shell right down on Army of God, UPF, Freedom Militia, whoever. Peacekeepers spiked them all when they rabbited, so the warlords couldn't use them, but that's a 999 for sure."

"You think China's sending in peacekeepers again?" Mouse asked. "Maybe rolling up the warlords for good?"

The idea made Mahlia's chest tighten. It was her own fantasy, the secret one she sometimes curled up to when she went to bed, knowing that it was stupid, but still wanting it, wanting it to somehow all make sense.

Her father would return from China. He'd come back with all his soldiers. He'd pick her up in his strong arms and say that he'd never meant to leave, that he hadn't meant to sail away and leave her and her mother alone in the canals of the Drowned Cities as the Army of God and the UPF and the Freedom Militia came down like a hammer on every single person who'd ever trafficked with the peacekeepers.

A stupid little dream for a stupid little war maggot. Mahlia hated herself for dreaming it. But sometimes she curled in on herself and held the stump of her right hand to her chest and pretended that none of it had happened. That her father was still here, and she still had a hand, and everything was going to get better.

"You think they're coming?" Mouse asked again.

You think?

"Nah." Mahlia forced a laugh. "Warlords must have fixed one of the guns. Or bought one. Or maybe they pirated something off the Atlantic shipping lanes." She shrugged. "The Chinese ain't coming back."

The 999 went off again. A nostalgic sound. The sound of a war that her father had been winning.

999.

It was a lucky number, her old man used to say. He'd sit in their apartment at night, drinking *Kong Fu Jia Jiu* shipped all the way from Beijing, gazing out the window at the orange and yellow flares of the fighting, a fireworks display every night. He listened to the guns.

"*Jiu jiu jiu,*" he'd say. "999."

Mahlia remembered the 999 particularly, because he'd claimed the peacekeepers would knock the warlords back with their lucky 999s and maybe then they'd finally teach these Drowned Cities savages how to be civilized. The paper tiger warlords would learn that shooting and hatred solved nothing. Eventually, the warlords would sit down at the negotiating table and figure out some way to get along with one another, without bullets.

Her father had sat by the window with his clear bright liquor as gunfire echoed through the canals and he had named them all. "*.45, 30-06, AK-47, .22, QBZ-95, M-60, AA-19, AK-74, .50-caliber, 999.*" Mahlia knew the many voices of war from her father's chant.

Later, when those guns were turned on her and she was belly-crawling out of hell, she'd known them, too: the chatter of the AKs and the bellowing of 12-gauges as they ripped the grasses and tore the swamp waters around her.

Mahlia had whispered their names to herself as she'd tried not to be stupid and jump up like a rabbit in the open as bullets zinged all around. Trying to think like Sun Tzu and not make a fatal mistake. Anything at all to keep herself from panicking the way all the other stupid civvies were panicking and getting themselves all shot to hell.

Another explosion rocked the distance—999, for sure. A lucky gun and a lucky number.

For someone, at any rate.

Mahlia looked down at her hand and was surprised to

see blood still on it. Remembered the baby and Tani's death. Remembered why she'd come looking for Mouse in the first place.

"Mahfouz wants us to go find some food and drop it by Amaya's place. Help feed her since she's going to be taking on Tani's baby."

"The doc's too damn nice."

Mahlia jostled him with an elbow. "Well, he takes in lazy-ass war maggots like you, so yeah, you're probably right."

"Hey!" Mouse grabbed for support before he toppled off the beam. "You trying to kill me?"

"Fates, no. You hit the ground, then I got to do all the work myself."

"And we both know you don't got the hands for that!"

Before Mahlia could slug him, Mouse swung down off the girder, dangling nimble as a monkey. He hand-over-handed across open air to a down girder.

Mahlia felt briefly envious of his easy movement. Forced herself not to watch too hungrily. Some things, it was better not to think about. It just made you mad and angry.

Mouse slid down the girder to the next level. "Why we bother working so hard hunting up dinner if we know the doc's just going to give it away?" he asked as Mahlia balance-beamed back to her own route off the building.

"Hell if I know. Because Mahfouz thinks goes-around-comes-around works for the good stuff, too. Balancing the scales and all that."

Mouse laughed. "That's all Scavenge God foo-foo stuff. 'Balancing the scales.'"

"Mahfouz ain't Scavenge God."

"It's still a load. If there was balance, the soldier boys would all be dead, and we'd be sitting pretty in the middle of the Drowned Cities, shipping marble and steel and copper and getting paid Red Chinese for every kilo. We'd be rich and they'd be dead, if there was such a thing as the Scavenge God, or his scales. And that goes double for the Deepwater priests. They're all full of it. Nothing balances out."

"You'd know," Mahlia said. "My family weren't Deepwater."

"Yeah, what do Chinese people worship, anyway? Buddhas?"

Mahlia shrugged. Her father had mostly seemed to worship guns and liquor, though he'd made sure there was a picture of the Kitchen God in their home as well. "My mom was Scavenge God," she said. "On account of all those antiques she sold. Made offerings all the time, so she could find good antiques that the foreigners would buy." She eased down after Mouse, using her lucky left hand for grip, her stump for balance. "Don't worry about the food. We'll hold back our dinner before we give over to the doctor."

"Damn straight we're holding back. I ain't hunting all day and then getting rib-stuck because the doctor's feeling charitable."

"I just said that," Mahlia emphasized. "You don't got to

worry. We ain't starving for Amaya. Now you going to help me hunt, or not?"

"Yeah. Okay." He dropped to the ground and looked up. "Get yourself cleaned up, though. You look like a war maggot with all that blood on you."

Mahlia scrambled down to the ground beside him in a cloud of clattering rubble. "I *am* a war maggot."

"You're dinner for coywolv if you don't get that smell off."

Mahlia reached over and wiped some grime off the boy's own dirty face. "Fussy little licebiter, ain't you?"

Mouse spat. "Only when it matters."

5

Away from Doctor Mahfouz's squat, the jungle lay thick. Trails ran through banyan, kudzu, pine, and palms. The doctor called it a landscape in transition—used to be one way, now it was turning into something else.

To Mahlia and Mouse, the jungle was pretty much the same as it always had been—a whole lot of heat, vines, snakes, and mosquitoes—but the doctor claimed that there didn't used to be swamp panthers or coywolv or even pythons. No gators. None of that. Those animals were all new arrivals, hot-weather animals migrated north, taking advantage of the new warm winters.

Winter didn't seem all that warm to Mahlia. She shivered plenty in the dark season, but the doctor said that not so long ago, standing water used to freeze and ice used to fall right out of the air, which if Mahlia hadn't seen pictures of it in some of his moldy books, she wouldn't have believed at all.

Ice.

Mahlia had eaten ice a couple of times. Her father had taken her to a peacekeepers' officers' club, which had solar generators and power to spare to make luxuries. In exchange for Mahlia's promising to speak Chinese like a civilized person and keeping herself polite, her father had given her ice cream while he'd sipped cold whiskey, diamond cubes of ice floating in alcohol amber.

Ever after, the clink and freeze of ice was something that Mahlia associated with China. A fairy-tale luxury from a fairy-tale land. According to her father, China had ice for drinking and electric bicycles for traveling; they had cities with towers a thousand feet high, all because they were civilized. Chinese people didn't war amongst themselves. They planned and built. When the sea levels rose, they built huge dikes to protect their coastlines, and floated their greatest cities on the waves, like they did with Island Shanghai.

"*You wenhua,*" he'd said. China had culture. It was civilized. Chinese people knew how to *hezuo* — "cooperate." Work together.

Not like the Drowned Cities. Drowned Cities people were like animals. They didn't plan. They fought all the time, and blamed each other for being poor and broken, instead of standing tall. Drowned Cities people were less than animals, really, because they had reason, but didn't use it.

"It's hard to believe this country was ever strong," her father had said, more than once, as he gazed out at the place he had been posted.

The difference was obvious to Mahlia when she sailed through the canals of the Drowned Cities. All the Drowned Cities people were poor and raggedy, while the peacekeepers were tall and healthy. The pictures of Island Shanghai that were printed on the Chinese paper money showed a similar difference: Island Shanghai, tall and gleaming, surrounded by blue ocean, in comparison to the Drowned Cities, where muddy, brackish water swamped every street and ate away at the foundations of buildings.

Mahlia had been glad she was Chinese then, all the way up until her father took a toy wooden horse away from her and she bit him for it. He slapped her then, and said she had too much Drowned Cities in her.

"No respect," he said. "Drowned Cities, through and through. Just like your mother. Animals."

Mahlia's mother fought with him over that, and then he called them both Drowned Cities, and suddenly Mahlia was afraid. Her father hated the Drowned Cities more than anything. And now she discovered she was the same as the people he fought every day.

Mahlia hid under her bed and bit herself for her stupidity. "*Mei wenhua*," she said. "No culture." She bit herself again and again, driving the lesson home. But when she showed her father her bleeding hand, proving that she'd punished herself, he'd only looked at her with more disappointment.

Now, as Mahlia and Mouse padded through the swamps, Mahlia wondered what her father would think of her. A girl with one hand? A muddy war maggot who stole eggs from bird nests to survive? What would he think of her now? She already knew the answer. She might have been half Chinese, but she was pure Drowned Cities. Just another one of the animals he'd found ungovernable.

Mahlia smiled bitterly at that. He could go grind. Her father had run away with his tail between his legs because he'd been too damn civilized for the Drowned Cities. He might have called the warlords paper tigers, but in the end, he'd been the one made of paper. Sure, the Chinese peace-keepers had looked dangerous with their guns and their skin armor, but in the end, they'd blown away like leaves.

If Mahlia had been as civilized as the peacekeepers, she would have been dead ten times over, just getting out of the Drowned Cities. As it was, it had only been luck that had saved her, the Fates putting their touch on her, in the form of a crazy redheaded war maggot who had intruded at the right time and made a distraction.

"Hey, Mouse?"

"Hm?" Mouse was taking his turn with the machete, chopping aside new vines that had filled the trail, not really paying attention.

"How come you saved me?" Mahlia asked. "When the Army of God..." She hesitated, remembering her hand lying on the ground, blood muddy. She swallowed. "When the soldier boys...cut me...how come you made a noise?"

Mouse straightened from his chopping and glanced back, pale brow furrowed. "What do you mean?"

"You didn't have to. It would have been safer for you to just steer clear."

"Just stupid, I guess." He mopped at the sweat coursing down his freckled neck and face and turned back to the vines. "I don't remember this trail having so much tangle on it," he said.

"Here. I got it." Mahlia took the machete and started chopping. Tough weedy vines parted under the sharp blade. When she'd first fled to the jungle from the Drowned Cities, she'd been soft. Now, she swung the machete with expert strength. City girl learning country living.

"So?" she pressed. "How come?"

Mouse grimaced. "Hell, I don't know. Maybe I was crazy. I still get nightmares about that. I'm running through the jungle, but the soldier boys turn out to be better shots, and they light me up." He paused. "I don't think it even was me. Didn't feel like me when I stood up. I just did it."

"But why? I was just a castoff. Peacekeepers were gone. No one was going to give you a reward or nothing. You weren't going to get anything out of it."

"Wasn't about that," Mouse said.

Another nonanswer.

Mahlia slashed through more vines, and the trail opened before her. Instinctively, she paused, examining it for signs of danger.

Sometimes trails went wrong. Auntie Selima's daughter

had blown off her legs that way. She'd followed a little-used trail and ended up in a minefield that dated back to the very beginning of the fighting in the Drowned Cities. The explosion had been loud enough that people heard it in town, but by the time Mahlia and Doctor Mahfouz picked their own way through the mines, the girl had bled out.

Mouse peered over Mahlia's shoulder, examining the trail with her. "Look good?"

The dirt was hard-packed. Lots of people and pigs and coywolv had wandered this way before. "Yeah. Looks safe."

Mahlia handed over the machete and wiped her sweaty face as the redheaded boy took up the blade and the lead.

"So?" Mahlia pressed again.

"So, what?"

He was being deliberately dense. "So, it was stupid," she said. "You just stood up and started throwing rocks at a whole platoon of soldier boys with guns. It didn't make any sense. You could have just snuck away, and you threw *rocks*?"

Mouse laughed. "Yeah. You're right. That was stupid."

"So why?"

Mouse took an idle whack at some kudzu as he passed, but his face was serious. "Hell, I don't know. Why do you care? That was right after our farm burned. They got everyone. Mom and Dad. Simon. Shane got recruited. I saw that. They shot Simon because he was too little, but they took Shane." He knocked aside more kudzu. "Maybe I was hoping they'd just shoot me and get it over with. I was so sick of hiding and scavenging. I think I wanted the bullet."

He shrugged. "And then it turned out that they missed. All those bullets they shot at me, and I didn't take a single one, like the Fates put a hand down between me and them. And then it turned out that you got away, too... Well, you were bleeding out, so there was something to do. And you were hungry, and I knew how to get food. So then I had something to think about, other than... you know." He shrugged again. "Maybe you saved me, right?"

"Yeah," Mahlia joked. "You owe me, big time." She let the subject drop because she could tell Mouse wasn't going to give her any more, but as they continued down the trail, she still wasn't satisfied.

She'd survived the Drowned Cities because she wasn't anything like Mouse. When the bullets started flying and warlords started making examples of peacekeeper collaborators, Mahlia had kept her head down, instead of standing up like Mouse. She'd looked out for herself, first. And because of that, she'd survived.

All the other castoffs like her were dead and gone. The kids who went to the peacekeeper schools, all those almond-eyed kids... Amy Ma and Louis Hsu and Ping Li and all those others... They'd been too civilized to know what to do when the hammer came down. Mahlia had survived because she'd been nothing like Mouse. And then she'd survived again because Mouse was nothing like her.

Mahlia was pretty sure Doctor Mahfouz would have

said that Mouse was right to stand up and she was wrong to duck down, but Mahlia was certain that if she'd been like Mouse, she would have had her head on a stick.

There wasn't any rhyme or reason to it. No balancing of the scales. No reward, unless it was in some afterlife like the Deepwater Christians talked about.

Ahead, Mouse lifted a hand in warning.

Mahlia froze, then crouched. "What we got?" she whispered.

"Dunno."

Ahead, the swamps opened into a clearing, and then into more swamp, waters covered with cattails and lily pads. Mahlia listened, trying to discern what triggered Mouse's concern. The buzz of insects. Nothing seemed wrong. Mouse pointed. Mahlia craned her neck, trying to see—

There.

In the swamp, amongst the cattails, something floated. It didn't move.

After waiting awhile longer, Mouse finally said, "It's clear."

As one, they slipped forward, then separated, scanning the rest of the jungle and swamp, but keeping their eyes on the mass of fur and leathery skin that lay in the water.

The land around the edge of the pool was disturbed, muddy banks torn, grasses trampled. Blood spattered the dirt, blackened with age. Many tracks clawed the ground.

"Coywolv?" Mouse whispered.

Mahlia shook her head. "Too small, right?"

"Yeah." He squatted. "But they're doggy, for sure, not cat. You can see the scrapes where their nails dug in."

He sucked his teeth, thoughtful. Stood up and circled the muddy ground. "Uh-huh." Nodding. "Doggy. Right." He looked up. "War dogs. Hunters, for sure."

"How the hell would you know?"

He waved her over. On the ground before him, another track marked the mud, from another kind of predator. A boot print. A good heavy boot, with a solid waffle tread.

Thick soles might make you noisy, but it also meant you could run over anything. Run over broken glass and rusty wire in the Drowned Cities without slowing down, for instance.

"Soldiers," Mouse said. "Boots like that, it's got to be."

"So we got rich soldiers and their dogs?" She felt a chill of fear. Soldiers. Here in the jungle. Close to town. "UPF, you think?"

"Can't say. But they got boots. If they're that rich, they probably got guns, too. Not just some wannabe warboys with acid and machetes."

"But there's nothing out here. No scavenge. No enemy."

"Maybe they're recruiting."

If that was true, they all needed to run. Everyone in the village. If the soldier boys wanted you, they took you, and Mahlia had never heard of anyone coming back after they got recruited.

"So what's that thing out there?" Mouse asked.

Mahlia followed his gaze to the huge alien mass, floating in the swamp. "Hell if I know. Looks like a gator."

"Not with fur."

Mahlia didn't want to stick around anymore. The jungle was making her skin crawl. "We got to get back to the doc, tell him about the soldiers. Let people know there's military around."

"In a minute."

"Mouse..."

But the licebiter was already wading in, headstrong and crazy.

"Mouse!" Mahlia whispered. "Get back here!"

Mouse ignored her, wading deeper, pushing aside cattails. He prodded the floating mass with the machete. Flies lifted off the dead thing, buzzing and humming. Matted hair and grime, clots of blackened blood, leathery hard skin.

In the light of day, crawdads were in it, and beetles feeding on ragged putrid wounds. Mahlia saw a centipede-like thing come out of a gash and drop into the water, slither-swimming through the water like a cottonmouth.

Mouse leaned against the thing with his blade.

"Damn," he grunted. "It's big."

Huge, more like. Meters and meters of meat, fur, and rough armored skin. It rocked sullenly, so big that it barely moved, even when Mouse leaned hard. Green mossy scum water rippled around it. Rafts of tiny lilies bobbed up and down. Water skippers fled.

"I do believe we've found dinner," Mouse announced.

"Don't be gross."

"It ain't spoiled. And there's enough here for us to smoke. Better than scraping for crawdads and trying to snare lizards and rabbits. Plenty to give to Amaya and her new baby."

"No way the doctor will eat something like that."

"Just because he don't eat pig, don't mean he won't eat this." Mouse spat into the water, irritated. "Anyway, we don't have to tell him what it is."

"*We* don't know what it is."

"So we just feed it to him. We can call it goat, or something. Or make up some of his Latin talk for it. *Deadus pondus*, right? Mahfouz'd eat that right up. He loves those big words."

Mahlia laughed. "You try that, he'll definitely know you're up to something."

"Come on, Mahlia. If we don't carve it up, coywolv will."

Something about the dead thing made her uneasy. She scanned the swampy pools, the jungle all around. Nothing but trees, green leaves, and kudzu draping over everything. Deep mossy pools. And then in the middle of it, this bloody leaking thing.

Mouse was smirking at her.

Grind it. She couldn't be paranoid forever. Mahlia waded in, feeling stupid for her fear. The warm waters of the swamp eased up around her thighs, hot as blood.

"You'll eat anything," she said.

"It's why I'm still alive."

Mosquitoes buzzed around her as she waded through cattails and algae slime. Together, they grabbed the floating mass. Clouds of flies rose up again, a choking tornado.

Mouse caught Mahlia's eye. "On three, right?"

"Yeah. I'm ready."

"One. Two. *Three!*"

They hauled, straining and grunting, dragging with all their strength. The thing moved sluggishly.

"Come *on!*"

Mahlia set her feet and pulled. Her feet scrabbled in the mud, heaving, pulling—

The thing ripped apart.

Unbalanced, Mahlia and Mouse toppled back into the water. Mahlia came up sputtering, expecting to find herself in a sea of guts and blood. Instead, one half of the dead thing had rolled up, revealing a face, scarred and terrible.

"Kali-Mary Mother of God!" Mahlia gave a startled yelp and scrambled back.

"Damn!" Mouse crowed. "I should've seen it before! Should've known!"

It wasn't one creature, but two. Monsters intertwined. A big king of an alligator, and another creature—a thing that Mahlia hadn't seen since the cease-fire died and the last of the peacekeepers cleared out, all of them running for the docks as the Drowned Cities returned to war.

A half-man. A war creature that only the richest

corporations, the Chinese peacekeepers, and the armies in the North could afford to grow and use.

"A dog-face!" Mouse was practically hooting with excitement. "Must've been epic ring!" He splashed over for a closer look. "Must've killed each other! Dog-face killed the gator, gator killed the dog-face."

He shook his head with admiration as he ran a hand down the monster's flank. "Check out those teeth marks. Gator practically tore its shoulder off. Had to be epic ring."

"Mouse..."

"What?" He looked up from his inspection of the battle wounds. "Ain't gonna bite. We'll take the gator. Good eating, for sure. Even old Mahfouz likes gator."

Mouse was right. The monsters were dead. She was being stupid.

After the initial shock of the half-man's face, Mahlia could think through her reaction. It had just seemed too human, that was all. One minute it had been a beast; the next, a person.

"You coming?" Mouse asked. He was looking at her like she was some kind of baby war maggot who'd never rolled a dead body.

"You didn't see its face," she said.

It was submerged again, but it had been terrifying— beast and human welded together in an unholy mix. Her skin crawled at the memory of that visage.

"If you got no spine..."

"Go grind, Mouse. I ain't afraid of the dead."

Still, Mahlia avoided the floating half-man and went straight for the alligator, ignoring the boy's smirk. Together, they grabbed hold of the massive reptile and started hauling it toward shore.

They paused to rest. Mouse leaned his elbows on the floating corpse. Wiped sweat out of his eyes. "Must've been epic fighting," he said. "They got ring fights in the Drowned Cities. Use their deserters and the other warlord soldiers. Panthers. Coywolv. Anything that'll fight. Bet that old monster would've done good in the ring."

"Sure, Mouse. Let's carve up the lizard and get gone."

"Fight like this one, people'd pay Red Chinese cash to see it. Soldier boys would've loved it. Battle to the death. Epic ring."

"Soldier boys do all kinds of dumb stuff."

They started hauling on the gator again, but suddenly the going got slow. Mahlia leaned into the weight, annoyed. Mouse liked to bait her into doing the work and then slack off. Typical.

"Grind it, Mouse! Quit lazing off." She glanced back. "Hey! What you doing?"

Mouse wasn't even helping. He'd pulled out his knife and was wading back toward the floating half-man.

"Got an idea," he said.

"Come on, Mouse! I don't want to be out here in the dark with raw meat. Last time that happened, we ended up sleeping in the trees with a bunch of coywolv down below. Let's get gone."

"We can sell its teeth," Mouse said. "Lucky teeth, off a real dog-face. How many soldier boys got real dog-face teeth? They'd buy 'em for sure. Bet I can find one of these soldier boys who'd pay me all kinds of Red Chinese cash. Good luck, right? Better than a Fates Eye or one of those necklaces the Army of God thinks makes the bullets bounce off. If we take these down to Moss Landing when Mahfouz trades for meds, we can sell 'em quick to the R-and-R boys."

"You're sliding. Soldiers will just take 'em from you. Pay you with a bullet, most likely. Or else just recruit your ass."

"I'll get a nailshed girl to do the deal. They won't even see me. No worries."

He reached the floating monster and leaned on the body until its face came out of the water. He pried open its mouth and hefted his knife.

"Damn, these dog-faces got a lot of teeth."

The monster's eye snapped open.

6

"*MOUSE!*" MAHLIA SHOUTED, but it was too late. The monster exploded from the water. Mahlia watched, stunned, as Mouse flew through the air and hit the bank with a wet thud.

Fates, it's fast.

Mahlia turned to run, but the half-man lunged. He covered distance in a blur, seizing her before she even took a step. Her head snapped and the world spun. She was flying, she realized. The half-man had flung her high in the air, the way a dog tossed a rat.

Swamp waters flashed far below. She glimpsed the half-man, teeth bared, waiting for her to come down. Water rushed up.

"Ugh!"

She slammed flat against the water. Swamp swallowed her. Stunned, Mahlia tried to swim for the surface. The dog-face was coming for her. *No time no time no time.* She surfaced, gasping. The monster was fifteen feet away.

Mahlia thrashed through the weeds, fleeing, but it was like fighting through molasses. The monster leaped and crashed down beside her. A wave of swamp water threw her off her feet. Coughing and retching, she tried to stand. The dog-face loomed. She was surprised to see that it already had Mouse, one huge fist wrapped in the red tangles of his hair.

With an easy swipe, the monster collected her as well. Mahlia tried to scream but the half-man shoved her down into the swamp. Mahlia fought, but it was like a mountain was sitting on her.

I'm going to drown.

With a tooth-rattling jerk, the half-man yanked her up again. Air and sunlight. The flash of tree leaves. She tried to get a breath but the monster sank her again. Slime and hot muddy water jammed down her throat, up her nose. Her face hit mud.

Mahlia flailed at the dog-face's fist, trying to pry free. It was like fighting concrete. The monster didn't care what she did.

Unbidden, Mahlia remembered seeing a squad of soldier boys drown a puppy. They'd taken turns holding it down with one hand as it fought and shook. Then they'd let it up to breathe, so they could laugh at it, before sinking it again. She was a toy, she realized. A kill toy for a monster.

The half-man jerked her out of the water again. Mahlia sucked air, coughing and retching. Mouse was still under-water. His hands poked up from the depths, waving like desperate reeds.

The creature's massive pit-bull skull loomed close. Scars and torn flesh. Animal and human, crushed together in one nightmare beast. Ropy gray scar tissue covered one eye, but the other eye was wide open, rabid and yellow, big as an egg. The monster growled, revealing rows of sharp teeth. A gust of blood and carrion washed over her.

"I am not meat," it snarled. "*You* are meat."

Mahlia pissed herself. Urine streamed down her legs. She didn't feel shame. Didn't feel anything except terror. She wasn't a person anymore. Just prey. It was as if the monster had cut her open and spilled out her guts. She was nothing. Dead already, even if her heart still pounded. Prey for other bigger, stronger animals. Just like all the civvies she'd seen gunned down as she'd fled the Drowned Cities. Mouse was still thrashing underwater, but he was dead, too. He just didn't know it.

Do something.

A joke. They were no match for this monster. Grown soldiers with guns and machetes died like flies before half-men.

The monster stared at her malevolently. The stench of its killing breath overwhelmed her. Mahlia closed her eyes, waiting to be ripped apart.

Go on. Just do it.

But nothing happened. Instead, she heard Mouse come up, gasping. And then she felt herself being lowered into the swamp. Mahlia opened her eyes.

The monster was staring at her with...

Was that *fear*?

The creature dropped to one knee. Sank lower. Swamp waters rose around them. Mahlia tried to pry away, but the monster's fist still held her like a vise. The half-man tried to rise. It took a staggering step toward the bank, dragging them both with it, then toppled. They slammed into the mud. The monster's breath gusted out in a dull huff.

Mouse was coughing and choking, still trying to fight his way free of the monster's grip. The creature bared its teeth and growled, a sound like boulders crushing bones.

"Hold still, boy."

Mouse froze.

The monster's breath came in short gasps. Mahlia realized that they were surrounded by blood. A sea of red, all through the water. The half-man's.

The monster slumped against the muddy bank, half in and half out of the water, its chest working like a bellows, gasping for air. Its yellow dog eye slowly closed, a membrane nictitating over the iris. The lid lowered.

"It's dying," Mouse whispered.

The creature's eye flared wide. Mouse gasped as the monster tightened its grip. "I do not die. You are dying. Not I..." Another pained exhalation, and a gathering of energy.

"I. Do. Not. *Die*."

But Mouse was right. Now that Mahlia could breathe, she could see that the monster's wounds were extensive. Teeth marks. Slashes. Festering torn skin. Blood ran freely from where the king alligator had torn deep into the half-man's shoulder, and those were just the wounds that she could easily see.

The monster's grip was loosening again. Mahlia waited...In one sharp jerk she twisted free. The half-man tried to resnare her, but it was slower now. She danced out of range.

The half-man fell back, but its eye still burned with predatory viciousness.

"So," it growled.

It drew Mouse into a bear hug, keeping him close. Mahlia wondered if she could find their machete, if she could stab the beast somehow. Kill it before it snapped Mouse's neck.

Where was that machete? Lost in the swamp. But she had her own knife.

Maybe if she stabbed it in the eye...

As if sensing her murderous thoughts, the monster said, "Your friend is mine." Its muscles flexed and it began to push Mouse down under the water.

"Mahlia?" Mouse began to struggle, but he was no match. The half-man pushed him lower. Water lapped around Mouse's chin.

Mahlia started forward, barely stopping short of the half-man's reach. "Don't hurt him!"

"Do not test me, then." The monster allowed Mouse to surface, sputtering.

Mahlia paced the shore, still hoping to catch sight of the machete. "Let him go."

The half-man smiled, showing the sharp teeth Mouse had wanted to harvest. "Come a little closer, girl."

Mahlia tried to make her voice reasonable. "Let him go."

"No."

She hesitated. "I can help you."

"No." The monster shook its head. "As your little friend says, I am dying."

"What if we could get you medicine?"

"There is no medicine."

"I know a doctor. In town. He could fix you. Me and Mouse could get him. I know how to doctor, too."

"Ah." The monster regarded her. "You have a doctor, and you will fetch him and he will give the half-man the medicines and care that will save its life, and all will be well."

Mahlia nodded eagerly.

"A pretty fairy tale from the mouth of a pretty child."

Mahlia bridled at the mockery. "I'm telling the truth! Ask Mouse."

A tired snort of amusement. "Your doctor...does he waste his medicines on monsters? When he has humans that already go begging for treatment? When war and pestilence stalk the land, and your kind already pines for help, will he spend his precious medicines on a *dog-face*?"

"He's not like that," Mahlia said. "He listens to me. Me

and Mouse, we can get him to come. He'll help you. If you let us go, we'll bring him back and he can help you."

"No."

"Why not?"

"I do not bargain with liars."

"I'm not lying!" Mahlia felt herself starting to cry with frustration. "I got a doctor. We live with him! He can fix you! I can fix you!"

The monster just looked at her, and then she realized it was observing her missing hand. She could see the contempt in its gaze, seeming to say, *Please tell me more of your silly lies, cripple girl.*

There had to be a way to save Mouse. *Could* she make Mahfouz help? Could she convince him? Mahfouz was kind. He took care of everyone. But this was a half-man.

"I can steal the medicine," Mahlia said, finally. "I can just take it and bring it back to you."

"Oh?"

Mahlia felt a surge of hope at the monster's interest. "Me and Mouse. We can get you medicine. You don't even need the doctor."

"Yeah," Mouse said. "I make a distraction, Mahlia gets the meds, and you get all fixed up." He nodded vigorously.

"The two of you," the half-man murmured. "One to distract and one to steal."

They both nodded eagerly.

The monster snorted amusement and shoved Mouse underwater.

"Mouse!"

Mahlia plunged forward. The half-man lashed for her ankle. She tripped and barely scrabbled out of reach, watching in anguish as the half-man drowned her friend. The muddy water churned.

"Let him go!"

To her surprise, the half-man let Mouse rise again. The boy surged to the surface, retching and coughing, water streaming from his freckled face. The monster shook him once with its huge fist.

"A bargain, girl. Go find your medicines and bring them to me. If they are sufficient, I will let your friend live."

"But—"

The half-man overrode her. "If you bring the wrong medicine, or if you bring soldiers, I will hear you coming and I will snap your friend's neck. And if you fail to return, I will fill his lungs with mud and water. Do you understand?"

"It'll take time," Mahlia protested. "I can't just snap my fingers."

"You cannot bargain with me. My heart is the clock. Find medicine before it ticks dry, and buy your friend's life. Fail and his corpse is all you will find here."

Mahlia started to protest again, but the half-man's glare froze the words in her throat.

"Run, girl. Run and pray to the Fates that you are fast enough."

7

THE JUNGLE TORE at Mahlia, tripping her with vines, clawing her skin with ragged leaves. Already, darkness was falling. Deep amongst the trees, the light faded fast. Shadows leaped at her. Mahlia tripped and sprawled. She scrambled up, ignoring skinned knees and painful scrapes on her palm.

The jungle's paths twisted and crisscrossed, a confusing tangle of deer trails and coywolv hunts and wild pig runs. The darkness made it worse. How long did she have? How long until the half-man's blood ran out?

Mahlia hit a fork in the trail. She crouched, staring at the ground, trying to see a way. Which way had they hacked their way through?

Fates, it was Mouse who liked to track things, not her. She chose the left-bending trail and pelted down it, praying to the Fates, and the Rust Saint, and Kali-Mary Mercy that she wasn't about to run into a minefield.

She hit open water. Tripped and plunged right in.

"Grind it!"

She slogged back out of the water, dripping and angry and scared. Doubled back, looking for the last split. She knew she needed to keep her fear in check, to keep her eyes open, to stay smart in the jungle, but even as she tried to convince herself that she wasn't panicking, she could feel gibbering terror rising in her.

The horrors of the swamps loomed, wild and hungry. Kudzu vines became coiling pythons, dropping from above. Coywolv flitted from tree to tree, pacing her. The jungle had teeth, and suddenly it had become alien and feral.

Mahlia leaped over rotten mossy logs, and nearly tripped again. Had she come this way before? She didn't remember deadfall from their journey out.

Where was she?

There was no way she'd make it to town and back to Mouse before full dark. She'd have to come back by lantern light. Could she even find her way? They'd wandered so aimlessly as they hunted for food, and Mahlia had paid less attention than she should have, never thinking that she'd be coming back in the dark—

Abruptly, jungle gave way to cleared fields.

Mahlia sobbed with relief. She was on the far side of town from where she'd intended, in the fields where every-one tilled crops because the ground was more open, but at least she wasn't lost. Mahlia skirted the dark liquid square of a basement pond and dashed across the fields, weaving around the fins of old crumbled walls that broke the earth.

Ahead of her the town beckoned, oil lamps coming on, familiar yellow glows, soft and comforting. Mahlia slowed, pressing at a stitch in her side. She'd never been so glad to see Banyan Town. Habitation. The sound and smoke of cylinder stoves crackling. The smell of spices. Candles burning beside little metal reflectors, making everything bright as she ran through.

Ahead of her, the doctor's squat loomed in the darkness.

Please be there. You have to be there. Don't be gone on some house call. Be there.

A human shadow stepped out from behind a ruined wall, blocking her path.

"Where you running, girl?"

Mahlia skidded to a stop. More shadows materialized before her, malevolent ghosts rising out of the darkness.

Soldier boys, a whole squad of them.

Mahlia turned and plunged back toward town, but a dog lunged from the shadows, snarling. She leaped back. Hunted for a new path of escape. The dog stalked her, growling, herding Mahlia back toward her captors.

More soldier boys emerged from the darkness. Guns gleamed dully. Bullet bandoliers and scars draped their bare chests. Ugly triple-hash brands scored their faces. UPF for sure. Colonel Glenn Stern's for life. Some of them had blue bandannas tied around their heads, as if the brand wasn't enough. The boys came closer. Eyes bloodshot with red rippers and crystal slide studied her with snakelike hunger. Mahlia scanned the darkness for a way to run, but the soldiers were all around. A perfect ambush.

One of them came up and grabbed her. He twisted her arm behind her back. She felt him scrabbling for her missing hand, and then he laughed.

"Got a stumpy, here!" he said.

His fingers probed at her stump. "Can't even cuff her." The others laughed. Mahlia struggled to get away, but the soldier jerked her around.

"I do that to you?" he asked, gazing at her stump. "How'd I miss your other hand, girl?"

This close, his loyalty brand stood out strong, pale ropy scars against brown skin. Three across, three down. UPF, through and through. Spikes pierced his lower lip. Three in a row, gleaming. Mahlia wasn't sure if they were for decoration, or if they were some other official thing that the Colonel did to his recruits.

"Was that me?" he asked again, but before she could answer, he straightened, surprised.

"Check out her eyes!" he called. "Got us a collaborator, here! Pretty little peacekeeper girl." Mahlia tried to bolt again, but he yanked her back and pulled her into a tight embrace, twisting her arm so hard it almost dislocated.

"Not so fast," he whispered in her ear. His voice had gone cold, dripping with new menace. Before, she'd been a toy to him; now she was something less. "I got plans for you, castoff."

Castoff. His words ran through the rest of the soldier boys like an electric current. *Peacekeeper. Castoff.* Mahlia knew how this would go. First there would be screaming and then there would be blood and then at the end, if she was lucky, she would be dead.

She fumbled for her knife, but with her good hand twisted behind her back, it was pointless. Seeming to sense her intention, the soldier pulled out her knife. Brought it up to her neck.

"What you doing here, collaborator?"

Mahlia felt sick. Already, a part of her mind was preparing for what was about to happen. It was going to be just like when the Army of God got hold of her. Different army, same story. They were all the same, in the end.

"What's a peacekeeper girl doing way out here?" he asked. "This town protecting you?" Mahlia didn't answer. She struggled to twist loose, but the soldier was bigger and stronger. "Why don't you answer? Huh? Someone get your tongue? Or you just stubborn?" A pause then. "Castoff think she's too good to talk to us?" The knife came up to her cheek, touched her lips. "Here. Lemme get that tongue out."

With a wrench of panic, Mahlia almost tore free.

"Hold her, boys!"

Hands seized her, pinning her arms, gripping her head,

forcing her to stare at the soldier who loomed over her. Dirty fingers forced her mouth open. Mahlia tried to bite them.

"Wooo!" the soldier shouted gleefully. "Castoff's got some spirit!" But he didn't let up. He pinched her cheeks until her mouth opened. Slid the blade inside. Mahlia tasted steel against her teeth.

"Didn't know there were collaborators hiding out here," the soldier said. "Thought we cleaned you all out."

"Lay off her, Soa."

At the new voice, the soldier glanced over his shoulder.

"Just getting answers, Lieutenant."

A new shadow rose out of the darkness. Angular, hollow-cheeked. Tall and skeletal. Pale as death. A pink scar split the man's nose, ragged. Gray eyes and wide pupils.

"What answers are you getting?"

"She won't say."

"Then we don't have answers, do we, Private?"

"I ain't started cutting, yet."

"So you're starting with her tongue?"

"Gotta start somewhere."

There was a pause. For a second Mahlia thought there would be violence between them, but then the lieutenant just laughed. He laughed and Soa grinned, and she didn't know if it was all a joke, or if they were going to start cutting, or if it was a game, or if this was just the beginning of the cat and mouse that would still end with her blood in the dirt.

The lieutenant shone a tiny hand-cranked LED light in

her eyes. Bright and painful. She squinted. He lowered the light a little and leaned close to study her with his gray bloodshot eyes. She guessed he might be in his late twenties. Experienced. Twice as old as some of his troops. A real Fates-playing old war dog.

"I'll be damned," he said.

Soa was nodding. "Castoff, right?"

Mahlia summoned her voice. "I ain't Chinese. I'm Drowned Cities."

The lieutenant pinched her cheeks between clawed fingers. Turned her head this way and that while his troops kept her from struggling.

"Half," he said. "For sure, you're half. And you're the right age, all right. Some peacekeeper nailed your old lady, left you behind." He cocked his head. "Don't got much use for collaborators."

His gaze went to the village. "Don't got much use for places that keep collaborators, either. Someone needs a lesson."

"Leave her alone!"

At the voice, Mahlia's knees almost buckled with relief. Doctor Mahfouz was pushing between the soldier boys. Familiar salt-and-pepper beard, broken eyeglasses tied together with bits of kudzu fiber that he had woven himself. Short and slender in comparison to some of the soldier boys. Nut-brown skin and gentle eyes and pure determination as he forced past the soldier boys, ignoring the danger he was in. It was as if he didn't even notice that he was surrounded by boys with guns and scars and a hunger for violence.

But they noticed him, all right. One of them grabbed him. "Slow down, doctor man. Traitors ain't your business. You get back to doctoring."

Doctor Mahfouz didn't even slow. He just turned to the lieutenant, speaking with absolute authority.

"Lieutenant Sayle, that girl is my assistant, she is no traitor, and if you want your soldier to live, I need her help. Now leave her alone. We deal in healing and peace, here. If you want our best efforts, you will do the same. Those are my rules, in my house. We don't deal in bloodshed here."

The lieutenant's gaze went from Doctor Mahfouz to Mahlia.

"That right?" he asked her. "You know doctoring? Got some Chinese medicine up your sleeve? Peacekeeper fix-me-ups?"

Mahlia opened her mouth but didn't know how to answer. Anything she said would encourage him. She closed it, just waiting to see what would happen, knowing she didn't have any influence. It was up to this Lieutenant Sayle and whatever decision he'd already made. She was alive or she was dead. Whatever she said to this UPF lieutenant wasn't going to change a thing.

The lieutenant smirked. He waved her through with a mock bow.

"Doctor-girl, huh? All right. Pull my sergeant back from the Fates, and we'll see how you do."

Mahlia let out a breath she hadn't realized she was holding. She shook off soldiers' hands and made her way to Mahfouz, but as she passed the lieutenant, he jerked her close.

"If my sergeant dies," he said, "I let Soa start cutting. He starts with that leftover hand of yours, then he does your feet, then he just keeps going, till you're nothing but a worm in the dirt. Got it?"

Mahlia stared straight ahead, waiting to be let free. Careful not to say anything at all. He shook her. "You got me, castoff?"

Mahlia kept her gaze forward, nodded once. "I got you."

"Good." He let her go and turned to the rest of his troops. "What are you all staring at?" he bellowed. "Get back on perimeter! Gomez, up above! Pinky, you too! Alil, Paulie, Snipe, Boots...patrol. Van. Santos. Roo. Gutty. Yep. Timmons. Stork. Reggie. Scout the town. See if we got any more castoffs. Maybe we got a whole nest of China rats we don't know about."

The troops saluted and scattered, rattling weapons and ammo, boots stamping across the grasses, acid bottles bouncing, machetes gleaming as they were drawn. Doctor Mahfouz swept an arm around Mahlia's shoulders, drawing her through the activity.

"I'll need your hand and eyes." He waved ahead. "It's not impossible, but there is work."

He led her into his open surgery, and Mahlia gasped. Blood ran all across the cracked concrete of the building's open lower floor.

No wonder the soldier boys were crazy. Four bodies lay before her and blood ran from them in a river. Two looked already dead for sure; another had a leg ripped open, tourniqueted, but he looked so pale she doubted he would last long, even if he wasn't actually dead already.

Only one young man remained. His chest was covered with crimson sopping rags, but he was conscious.

Heavy fighting, for sure. But none of their wounds looked like explosions or gunfire. One of the dead ones looked like he'd been nearly snapped in half. The other had his neck torn and snapped.

The conscious boy's eyes followed her as Mahlia knelt beside him. She peeled away the bloody rags, guessing what she would see, and more afraid because of it.

Four massive, deep parallel gashes cleaved across his chest, tearing his clothes and shearing deep through brown flesh. The white cage of his ribs showed amid the red. Mahlia held her hand over the torn flesh, unwillingly measuring the size of the claw that had dealt the blow.

Mahlia felt sick. It all made sense.

She knew why these soldier boys had come. She knew what they sought, and she knew, too, that if they found it, Mouse would surely die.

8

"OUR FRIENDS TELL US they encountered a wild boar," Doctor Mahfouz said.

It was a stupid lie. No boar could do that. Only a monster. Only a half-man. And Mouse was trapped with that creature, and if Mahlia didn't get him free, he was going to die, and if she didn't get free of these soldiers and find some way to get the meds from Doctor Mahfouz—

"Mahlia!"

She startled from her mesmerized staring at the soldier's wounds. Mahfouz repeated himself. "I have my tools boiling. If you'll wash your hands, I'll need you for the cleaning and stitching."

Mahlia hurried to the boiling water, feeling numb. The

soldiers were everywhere. She snuck glances at them, studying her enemies as she cleaned herself.

They were a raggedy bunch. The kind her father used to scoff at, all beat-up equipment and missing teeth and acid-burned faces, but their guns had bullets and their blades gleamed with razor edges, and they were everywhere. Walking the perimeter, pillaging the doctor's squat, stalking out on patrol. They lit campfires and hauled ancient plastic jugs filled with water from the basement pool next door, and stacked looted piles of everything from rice to dead chickens on the dirty concrete. It looked like they were shaking down the entire village.

A tall black-skinned boy with piercing eyes directed a squad of three in gathering wood and starting a bonfire. Kill scars slashed his bicep, nine enemies ticked off, the way the doctor checked off his medicine inventory.

Mahlia started to count kill scars on the other soldiers but gave up. There were too many; they must have had more than two hundred kills. Even the youngest of them, the little licebiters who were only allowed to carry hydrochlor and machetes, had kills. And the oldest, like the lieutenant and the wounded soldier boy with his ribs opened up, had more than a dozen.

"What we want to do with this?" a soldier called out. Mahlia looked up at the slurred voice. A machete cut had cleaved the soldier's jaw and scarred his face all the way up to the eye. But what drew Mahlia's gaze was his prize, a goat he was leading into their midst.

With a start, Mahlia realized it was Gabby, the doctor's goat. "You can't—" Mahlia started to object, before she shut herself up.

Lieutenant Sayle had been conferring with his sergeants, but now he looked up, a pale cadaverous mantis turning attention to its prey.

"Looks like dinner."

He returned to marking off quadrants on a moldy map, uninterested in what he had ordered, or whom it affected.

The soldier boy looped Gabby's rope around her legs, trussed them, and abruptly shoved her over. It was a casual shove, almost bored. The goat fell with a thud and whuff of surprise, as powerless as a sack of dropped rice.

Lieutenant Sayle was back to talking with his sergeants, his words blending with the rest of the soldiers' activities. "Flush it up against the coast, sweep south." The details of their hunt. "A-6, push along this ridge; it's still above tide line. This river cut might give it protection..."

Mahlia watched, powerless, as the soldier boy knelt beside Gabby, lifted his machete, and hacked into her neck. Gabby bleated once in panic and then the blade sank in and the goat lost her voice. The boy started sawing across. Blood spilled out. Mahlia looked away.

No one else noticed, or cared. It was just something they did. Taking other people's livestock. Other people's lives. She watched the soldiers, hating them. They were different in so many ways, white and black, yellow and brown, skinny, short, tall, small, but they were all the same. Didn't matter if they wore finger-bone necklaces, or baby teeth on bracelets, or tattoos on their chests to ward off bullets. In the end, they were all mangled with battle scars and their eyes were all dead.

Mahlia finished washing her hands in boiled water and rinsed in alcohol, fighting to ignore Gabby's dismemberment.

It's what they do, she reminded herself. *Don't fight things you can't fight.* She needed to think like Sun Tzu. Make her own plans for how to get the meds she needed and escape back to Mouse.

Mahlia focused on Sayle, listening to him plan. "B-6, Hi-Lo Platoon, Potomac..." None of the names meant anything to Mahlia except that soldiers were out there— lots of them—and they wanted that half-man, and Mouse's life wasn't worth rust. If they found the half-man before Mahlia could return, the monster would believe she had betrayed it, and Mouse would die, and she was stuck here, fixing up someone who would just as soon chop off her last hand.

Mahlia finished washing, grabbed boiled forceps and scalpels and needles from their battered cook pot, and shoved through the ring of watching soldiers to the last living victim, wishing there were some way to tell the doctor what was happening to Mouse.

"Ease back," she ordered as she pushed through. The soldiers shifted a little but didn't move away.

The doctor looked up. "Your comrade needs air and he

needs your dirt away from his wounds. Either you listen to the girl, or your friend will not survive."

"He dies, you die," one of them muttered.

Mahlia couldn't tell if it was Soa or one of the others, but the wounded boy reacted to the challenge. "You heard them," he grunted. "Get back. Let the doctors do their thing."

Mahlia knelt down and began swabbing out the wound, plucking bits of fabric from torn brown flesh, inspecting to see if his broken ribs looked as if they had damaged his internal organs.

The boy didn't flinch as she probed. The only evidence of his pain was that sometimes his breath would hold as she dug deep. He stared straight ahead with a fixed expression of contempt. She squeezed blood out of her rag, swabbed the wounds again.

What a fool she had been. Of course the monster had been hunted. There'd been boot and dog prints all over that place. The creature hadn't come from nowhere. It had come out of the Drowned Cities, and the soldiers had followed. In hindsight, it made perfect sense.

"Don't look like a pig did this," she said.

The wounded soldier boy's gaze focused on her for the first time. Gold-flecked green eyes, glinting violence. A face sculpted by war. Hard. "If I say it was pig, it was pig."

Mahlia dropped her eyes. It wasn't worth fighting over. Boys like this had seen too much blood to care one way or the other if they spilled a little more. Antagonizing them was stupid.

"Problem, Sergeant Ocho?"

The voice was soft, but it made Mahlia's skin scrawl. The lieutenant was looking at them. Pale skin, pale hair, gray empty eyes. She'd thought he looked like a corpse at first because he was so pale, and then like an insect, because of his long, thin body and limbs. But suddenly Mahlia knew what he was: coywolv. Pure blood and rust coywolv. A predator. Deadly and smart.

Sayle's gray eyes lingered on her. "Anything I need to be aware of?"

Ocho glanced at Mahlia dismissively. "Nothing here, Lieutenant."

"You let me know."

"Nah. Castoff knows her place."

Lieutenant Sayle went back to his moldy maps and his murmured instructions to the other soldier boys, and Mahlia let out her breath. She went back to work, wishing she dared hurry.

As she plucked out leaves and debris from the wounds, she couldn't help thinking of the meds just overhead, up in the doctor's squat. The soldiers hadn't found them—yet. The doctor kept them hidden in oiled leather wrappings, tucked inside hollowed-out books. Just more books among the many. But they were there. The antibiotics that could buy Mouse's freedom from the dying half-man. If she could just get to the damn things.

The doctor joined her with a needle and catgut. His eyes were bad, even with his jury-rigged eyeglasses. He had to lean close to study the wound.

"The damage isn't as bad as it could be," he said. "His ribs did a good job of protecting him."

Mahlia pointed at one of the wounds. "This is the only one that's bleeding hard."

"Hmm." The doctor squinted. "Laceration to a neuro-vascular bundle. We'll cauterize this first," he said, "then stitch up the wounds."

Their patient suddenly asked, "Can you even see, old man?"

Mahlia looked up at him, trying to remember his name. *Ocho. A sergeant.* "I can," she said. "And I'm the one doing the stitching."

"Blood and rust! Stumpy's going to stitch?"

"Watch your mouth," Mahlia said, "or I'll stitch your guts shut."

The doctor sucked in his breath, but the patient just smirked. "Castoff's got some bark in her."

"No bark. Just a needle."

Mahlia set the point and pushed it in with her good left fingers. The doctor's hand met the needle on the other side and drew the catgut through. He handed it back to her. Between the two of them, they nearly made a whole doctor. They worked the thread through again.

"We don't have any sulfa here," the doctor said. "You will need to keep this wound clean and dry."

Ocho was looking into space again. "Yeah. I know."

From the survey of his body, it looked like he did know. His dark skin was ripped and scarred in dozens of places. He was missing part of an ear, and there was a puckered scar in his cheek, as if he'd been stabbed or burned. A small circular hole, now closed.

The soldier caught the direction of Mahlia's gaze. "Army of God," he said. "Sniper." He opened his mouth, showing her the other side of the wound. His pink tongue was also torn.

"Came right through. Got my tongue, on the side. Came out my mouth. Didn't chip a tooth." He bared them, showing her. "Not a one. Fates got me close."

Mahlia held up her stump. "Me too."

"Don't look lucky to me."

"Still got my left."

"You southpaw?"

"Am now."

She wasn't going to tell him how long it had taken her to train her left to do the work that she'd taken for granted with her right. Even so, sometimes a part of her mind would trip, and suddenly it was like she was in a mirror, looking the wrong way as she tried to use her left to do what her phantom right could not.

"You're pretty good with it," he admitted.

"Good enough for this."

"Can't ask for more," he said.

Mahlia glanced up, startled. Something in his voice was soft, almost apologetic, or pitying.

Can I deal with you? she wondered. *You got something human in there, somewhere?*

Doctor Mahfouz was always yammering on about how everyone had humanity in them. From Mahlia's experience, the doctor was sliding high, but now, as she looked at this sergeant named Ocho, she wondered if there was some bit of softness in this hard scarred boy that she might be able to work.

She went back to the stitching. "How come they call you Ocho?"

He grunted as the needle plunged through his skin. "Took eight of the enemy. Knifed them all. They had guns, but I cut all their throats." He touched the deep burn brand of the UPF in his cheek. Colonel Glenn Stern's mark. "Got my full bars because of it. Legendary."

The soldier boys who were gathered around all nodded. "Legendary eight," they echoed. "Legendary."

"How'd you do that?" Mahlia asked.

"None of your business, castoff."

And just like that, the softness snuffed out. Whatever good had been there was gone, his voice turned hard and brutal as concrete. "Get your stitching done and quit your talk."

"I—"

"I'll fry your tongue in oil, if you don't shut up. Cook it and eat it myself."

Cold as bone, that fast. Just another killer with footprints of blood behind him, and a river of it ahead.

Mahlia ducked her head and focused on the job, suddenly hoping for nothing other than to be forgotten.

At last she and the doctor sat back. "There," the doctor said. "You'll mend." Mahlia's neck and arm were cramped with the work. It was awkward to share the labor this way, but it was the only way.

Ocho studied his closed wound. "That's some tidy stitching." He called out. "Hey, boys, look at me. All sewed up."

Yeah. You're sewed up. Now get the hell out so I can get the meds and get out, too, Mahlia thought.

If she could just get these warboys gone, she could still make her way back through the swamps to Mouse. Even in the dark, she had a pretty good sense of where he was waiting. She'd bring the doctor. They'd make the trade and Mouse wouldn't die.

The lieutenant stalked over. "How you doing, Sergeant?"

"Right as rain." Ocho dragged himself upright. Under his dark skin, he was pale, but he made it to his feet. "Ready to march."

His leader shook his head sharply. "Sit down, soldier. We're not going anywhere. We're going to set up search patterns, base out of here. No reason to live in the swamps when we got this fat little town to feed us." He set his hand on the doctor's shoulder. "Now, where's your antibiotics?"

Mahlia's heart skipped. *No. Those are mine. Mouse's.*

"We don't have any," the doctor said. "Don't worry. It's

a clean wound. Very clean. There shouldn't be complications. Everything was sterilized well. We used sterilized water and alcohol to swab it as we worked."

The lieutenant jerked the doctor close. "You think I'm some dumb war maggot? Animal's got dirty claws. Dirt needs meds."

Mahlia cleared her throat. "I thought you said it was a pig."

Quick as a snake, the lieutenant grabbed Mahlia and spun her about. He looped his arm around her throat, choking off her oxygen. The doctor cried out, but the other soldiers grabbed him and pulled him back.

"Ain't you the hair-splitter?" the lieutenant said. "How 'bout I take you with us? Make you Ocho's nurse? My sergeant lives, I might even send you back with that left hand of yours still attached." His breath was hot on her cheek. "You like that idea? Or maybe I cut it off and string it around your neck. That way you still get to keep it close."

Mahlia couldn't breathe. The man had completely cut off her air. He lifted and her feet came off the floor.

"Or maybe I just stand here and feel you kick. I like it when a pretty girl kicks."

Stars filled Mahlia's vision. From a distance she heard Doctor Mahfouz begging. "Please. We only have a little, for true emergencies. It's so difficult to acquire."

"My soldier ain't an emergency?"

"That's not what I—"

"Get your meds, doc. Your girl's running out of air."

Beaten, Doctor Mahfouz scrambled up the ladder and into the squat. Only when he came down again, with pills in hand, did Lieutenant Sayle drop Mahlia to the floor.

She stumbled away, gasping, her hand on her throat. Air felt like fire as it sawed in and out.

The soldiers caught her and shoved her back toward where Sergeant Ocho lay. Mahlia fell to her knees beside the wounded boy.

Behind her, she heard the lieutenant say, "Dig in, boys. Get that perimeter secure. We'll be here awhile."

No.

9

INFECTION RAGED THROUGH Tool's body like an invading army. Delirium hazed his vision. Darkness had overtaken the swamps. Cricket chirps and the high whine of mosquitoes filled the night.

Tool cracked his one good eye, observing the red-haired boy. Moonlight outlined his skinny form as he pried up a sharp stone the size of an egg.

Tool almost smiled. Human children were always the same. Ribs and hollows sewn together by the barest coverings of flesh. Scarecrows, begging to be torn apart and scattered to the wind, like grass dolls.

It didn't matter what continent he fought on; it was always the same. This one hopped about like a pale, freckled grasshopper, checking every rock in the hopes of finding one that would bash in Tool's head, but he was the same as all the rest.

"I know what you are planning, boy."

The child looked up at Tool, gray-blue eyes glinting like glass shards, then went back to feeling the rocks along the banks, testing each one, reaching as far as Tool's long arm would let him stretch.

"How come you don't stop me, then?" the boy asked.

"Soon enough."

"Mahlia's coming back."

Tool snorted. "Your sister has been gone for hours. And now you are searching for a weapon. I think we are past any illusions about your sister coming back."

"She ain't my sister."

"You are both human. She is your sister."

"That make you a dog, then?"

Tool growled at the taunt. He tried to sit up, but it was too tiring. The mud he had piled against his wounds to staunch the bleeding cracked as he moved. He was surprised to see that it had dried. Time was passing even faster than he had thought.

He lay back, breathing heavily. Best to save his energy.

It was foolish to think that there was anything left to save energy for, but it was his nature. He had been designed too well. Even now, finished and broken, surrounded by hostile humanity, he sought survival. Nature always struggled on, even when hope was gone.

The boy tested Tool's grip again.

"Do not try me, boy."

"You could let me go. I could go get the meds for you."

Tool almost laughed at that. "I think one betrayal is enough."

The boy bristled. "What do you know? You're just a dog-face."

"Also tiger and hyena and man." Tool stared at him. "Which of those do you think is the oath breaker, boy?"

"My name's Mouse. I already told you that."

"Name yourself or not. You are all the same to me."

"You're going to kill me, aren't you?"

Tool made a face, disgusted that the human child could insist that Tool was somehow wrong. "Do not blame me for your sister's betrayal."

"She ain't the one who's gonna kill me."

The conversation was all just a distraction. The boy's hand was out again, worming about in the mud, still seeking a weapon, perhaps hoping he would locate the lost machete. Tool could respect that. He, too, fought to survive.

"I kill because it is my nature," Tool said. "Just as it is yours."

"I kill for food."

Tool bared his teeth. "I, too, eat what I kill."

The boy's eyes went wide at that, and if Tool hadn't been so exhausted and racked with pain, he would have laughed.

10

Moths fluttered and drowned in sticky pools of spilled blood. Mahlia swept a dirty rag through the mess, sopping it up and wringing it out in a rusty iron bucket beside her. As she bent to scrub again, she stole a quick glance at the soldiers, trying to get a bead on them, then ducked her head to her work.

Soa, this time. Watching her from beside the campfire. Thoughtful predatory interest, like being watched by a coywolv.

She didn't like his eyes on her, but when it wasn't him, it was always another. Slim or Gutty or Ocho or one of the other hard-faced boys, as if through some unspoken communication they passed their close attention from one to the next.

No way she could escape with their eyes all over her. She mopped more blood and fought the urge to scream. Mouse was out there in the swamp with that dog-face, and she was stuck here, like a rabbit in a trap.

What would Mouse do in this situation? Would he just be crazy enough to run for it? But she needed to collect meds first. Needed to get away clean. And if she ran, what would happen to the doctor?

There was no way she could just bolt, even if they stopped watching her so closely. It was an impossible trap, with no good solution, Mahlia started scrubbing again, ramming her frustration into the work.

Boot steps, coming close. Mahlia's skin prickled, but she didn't look up. The boots stopped right in front of her, standing in the blood, blocking her work. Soa. She was sure of it.

She steeled herself and looked up.

He stood over her, smiling slightly. "You got a problem cleaning up our blood? Think you're too good or something?"

Mahlia shook her head.

"You sure? 'Cause I saw you making a face." Soa knelt down and ran his fingers through the blood, lifting them up in front of her face. "You think you're too good to clean up the blood of patriots?"

He reached out and slowly ran his fingers down her cheek, smearing her. "Think you're too good for us?" he asked. "Think we're just animals? That's what you peacekeepers always used to say, right? Called us animals? Called us dogs?" He dipped his fingers in the blood again and touched her forehead. Stroking her with wet fingertips.

Mahlia struggled not to flinch at the soldier boy's touch. It was what Soa wanted. He wanted her to act disgusted. Wanted her to act like she was above them. And if she did, she knew he'd kill her. Kill her for spite.

Soa didn't even have a soul. He was just a snake looking for an excuse to bite.

"I don't want to fight," Mahlia said. "You want me to clean, I'll clean. I don't want to fight."

"Don't want to fight." Soa laughed. "More of that peacekeeper talk." He dipped his fingers in blood again, marked her other cheek. Gave her a sharp shove, almost a slap. "Got a surrender slogan for me? One of those peacekeeper sayings? 'An eye for an eye makes the whole world blind?' Some shit like that?"

Behind Mahlia, someone sniggered. Others were watching. All of them waiting to see what Soa would do next.

"Well?" Soa asked. "You got a surrender slogan? I'm waiting."

She knew what he was referring to. When she was little, the slogans were everywhere, painted on the walls of the city. The peacekeepers paid local people to put them up, trying to buy some goodwill and make people think about how they'd gotten themselves into the mess they were in, but the pictures and sayings always ended up getting scrawled with militia and warlord battle flags, and eventually the peacekeepers gave up.

Mahlia cleared her throat, hunting for one that wouldn't set Soa off.

" 'Disarm to farm'?"

"That a question?"

Mahlia shook her head. " 'Disarm to farm,' " she repeated. A statement this time.

Soa grinned, wild eyes. "Oh yeah. I remember that one. That was a good one. All those peacekeeper soldiers giving rice and corn and soybeans if you'd just turn in a gun. I traded them an old .22 for a sack of rice I was supposed to go out and plant. Firing pin was all rusted out, and you suckers still paid."

"I traded a .45, didn't even have bullets," another said.

"What was their whole thing?" Soa asked the group. "Our girl's having a hard time remembering."

" 'Turn the other cheek,' " someone said.

" 'Beat your swords into plowshares!' "

" 'Only animals tear each other apart!' "

More and more slogans poured out, the good intentions of the peacekeepers turned into a grand joke that soon had every soldier boy doubled over laughing as they named slogan after slogan. Every saying the peacekeepers had used as they tried to quell the violence of the Drowned Cities.

When their mirth died, Soa stared into Mahlia's eyes. "You peacekeepers thought we were stupid. Thought we'd just let foreigners take us over. Make us into slaves. But we knew what you were up to all along. We don't roll over; we fight for our country." Soa scooped his hand through the pooled blood and shoved his dripping hand hard into her face, smearing. "When we bleed," Soa said, "you say thank you."

Mahlia fought not to flinch, but it was impossible and Soa didn't stop. Just kept smearing. "You like that, girl? You like that? You too good for our blood, huh, peace-keeper? You too good?"

"That's enough, soldier."

To Mahlia's surprise, Soa broke off. She blinked blood from her eyes.

From his sickbed, Sergeant Ocho was waving Soa away. "Don't let the war maggot rile you, soldier."

"I ain't riled, I'm just teaching her a lesson."

The sergeant's voice was dryly amused, but still it carried authority as he said, "I think she gets it."

Soa looked like he was about to protest, but then he looked at Mahlia and made a face of disgust. "Well, she gets it now."

"That's right, Private. She gets it." Sergeant Ocho waved him on. "Now go ask Gutty when that goat's going to be cooked. Smells good."

And to Mahlia's surprise, Soa actually backed off. With a final jerk to her hair, he set her loose and headed toward the fire.

Ocho watched him go, then nodded at Mahlia. "Get yourself cleaned up, and then get our dead clean, too. They need last rites." He looked at her seriously. "And keep your thoughts off your face. Soa's dying for an excuse to cut you. I ain't going to save your ass twice."

Mahlia stared at the sergeant, trying to figure him out. He wasn't human, but he also wasn't crazy. He wasn't hungry for blood, not like Soa or the lieutenant, but that didn't make him nice, either.

She got a new bucket of water and cleaned herself up as best she could before setting to work on the dead boys, swabbing off their bodies and arranging bloody torn garments. She arranged one of the boys so his broken neck wasn't so twisted. He couldn't have been more than ten years old. One of those cannon-fodder licebiters who got swept up in recruiting drives, and who they shoved out in front to draw fire. Bullet bait. Not even really a recruit yet. Only the first three horizontal bars of Glenn Stern's mark branded on his cheek.

"Half-bar," Ocho said. "They die faster."

Mahlia glanced over at the soldier where he lay. "Not like you."

Gold-flecked eyes studied her, unblinking. "Got to learn quick if you want to stay alive. Drowned Cities eats stupid for breakfast." He straightened, pushing himself up in bed, wincing. "'Spect you know that, though. I ain't seen a cast-off in more than a year. Last time I saw a girl like you, LT had her head on a stick."

"That what you're going to do to me, after I heal you up? Put my head on a stick?"

Ocho shrugged. "Ask the LT."

"You always do what the LT says?"

"That's how it works. I do what LT orders. My boys do what I order." He nodded at the dead boy that Mahlia was cleaning. "Right down the line to half-bars."

"Looks like that worked out real good for him."

"Hell, we're all bullet bait sooner or later. Doubt it makes much difference. You make it to sixteen, you're a goddamn legend." Ocho paused, then said, "If the LT decides to put you down, I'll make sure it's quick." He jerked his head toward the fire where Soa was carving meat off the goat's roasting form. "I won't let Soa near you."

"Is that how you make friends? By promising not to torture them before you kill them?"

Ocho's scarred face suddenly broke into a grin. "Damn. You're pushy for a castoff."

"I ain't castoff. I'm Drowned Cities."

He laughed. "That don't mean you ain't pushy."

It was almost like he was human. Like he didn't have a dozen kill scars hacked into his bicep. He could have been anyone.

A crash resounded from the fire pit. Mahlia jumped at the noise. She spun to see a cooking pot lying on its side, rice spilled across concrete. One of the soldiers, a skinny boy with ears that had been cut off, was sucking on his hand. Soa was shouting at him.

"Grind it, Van! The pot's hot, right?" He slapped the smaller boy upside the head.

Van dodged back and his hand went to his knife. "You touch me again, I gut you."

"Let's see you try, war maggot."

"Shut it, you two!"

It was Ocho, sitting up straighter than Mahlia would have thought he could, his voice full of command. "Van! You pick up that rice. You serve us all off the top, and you eat what touched the ground. Soa, get out and get some fresh water. I won't have you fighting in this unit. We ain't Army of God." He made a dismissing motion with his hand. "Go on. Get to it."

"Trouble, Sergeant?"

Lieutenant Sayle's voice floated down from the squat above, where he had ensconced himself. A voice full of threat. Everyone seemed to freeze. "Anything I need to know about?"

"No, sir," Ocho responded. "Just a little kitchen mess, right, boys?"

They all said, "Yes, sir," and then Van was scooping up rice and putting it onto palm leaves and handing it out to the other soldier boys as they shuffled up and took rice and goat, and then went back to their various posts. Only when everyone else was served did Van squat down and scoop up the last rice for himself.

Mahlia watched as everything got cleaned, trying to figure out what felt odd about it all. It felt wrong. She kept trying to put her finger on it, and then it dawned on her... They were afraid.

They were all staring out at the black rustling jungle

and casting nervous glances toward their dead, and every one of them was afraid. They'd had four of theirs torn to pieces in seconds. Despite all their bravado and threats of violence, these soldier boys were little puppies in comparison to the creature they were hunting in the jungle, and they knew it.

Mahlia wished fervently that there was some way to sic the half-man on them. She went back to her cleaning, imagining the half-man mowing through them. Wishing that the jungle's teeth would just swallow them up.

Teeth. Mahlia paused. She studied the nervous warboys again. The jungle had teeth, and it made them afraid. Mahlia started to smile.

I'll give you teeth.

She straightened and wrung out her rag.

"Where you going?" Ocho asked. "You ain't done here."

"You need better meds. I got something for you."

"Thought you already gave everything."

"Maybe if you act decent toward me instead of treating me like an animal, you get treated better, too."

"That's peacekeeper talk." But the almost-smile flickered again as Ocho said it, and the soldier boy waved her off.

In the squat above, Mahlia found the lieutenant seated at Doctor Mahfouz's rough-cut table, studying an old book of the doctor's, while the doctor sat quietly and answered the man's questions about the jungles in his steady voice.

The lieutenant looked up as she climbed through the hatch. "What you want, girl?"

"I need to fix your sergeant's bandages. And I remember where we had some other meds," she said.

"Other meds?" the lieutenant asked. "You holding out on us, doctor?"

Doctor Mahfouz looked surprised, but he covered well enough. "Mahlia manages our medicines." He touched his glasses. "Because of my sight." He nodded to her. "Go on, then."

Mahlia looked at the lieutenant. "You want me to get the meds or not?"

He waved her on. "Don't let me stop you."

Mahlia went over and crouched in a shadowy corner. Started pulling half-moldy books off a lower shelf. She hated giving away the doctor's hiding place, but she suspected that the soldiers would have found it eventually, or else forced the information from her or the doctor at knifepoint.

Behind the first row of books, more books were tucked away. These, Mahlia pulled out and started opening, revealing the doctor's medicine supply. She extracted blister packs of pills from within the hollowed-out volumes while the lieutenant watched.

"And you said you only had a few," the man said.

The doctor gave a quiet sigh. "It's all we will ever have. They are very difficult to acquire, and we have little to trade. The sort of men who have black market pills aren't the sort who care about what we have to offer."

Mahlia ignored the hungry interest as she went through

the pills. She couldn't read much of the text on the labels, because it was all more complicated than the Chinese she had learned as a child, but the instruction diagrams were made by the peacekeepers for illiterates in the Drowned Cities, so you could mostly tell how many you were supposed to take and what it was for.

She wanted to take them all, but there was no way she could carry everything. She fingered through the blister packs. Black market meds. Old meds that had been hoarded, and new ones the doctor had paid for with great risk and expense by going to the smugglers in Moss Landing.

She took a fistful. It would have to be enough. With that done, she opened another book and found the bottle she wanted. Cloudy liquid corked inside a little green glass bottle, gleaming.

Coywolv scent.

The bottle felt like a grenade in her hand. After Mahlia's first destructive experiment with the scent and Alejandro's goats, Doctor Mahfouz had instructed her explicitly that she was always to ask him before using any of his medicines in the future. He'd never made a direct accusation, but he'd tucked away the scent, and the message had been clear.

Now, Mahlia held up the bottle, showing it to the doctor. "I'm going to use this, right?"

You understand? she wanted to say. *You going to be ready?*

The doctor looked at her, shocked.

For a second, Mahlia was afraid he would stop her, but

really, he was stuck. If he told the lieutenant what was in the bottle, there was no telling what kind of punishment they'd get.

"Are you sure, Mahlia? That's quite strong."

"Lieutenant wants his soldier taken care of."

"That's not a simple medicine."

"It's what we got."

Lieutenant Sayle was looking between her and the doctor, not understanding that there were two conversations happening, right in front of him.

"What is that?" he asked.

"Meds for your boy," Mahlia said. Her eyes went to Doctor Mahfouz, daring him to rat her out.

"Let me see."

Mahlia came over to the lieutenant, her heart pounding. Showed him the green glass bottle. He held it up to the light. "What's in it?"

"Antibacterial. We make it, because other stuff's hard to buy," she said. But the lieutenant wasn't really paying attention. His eyes had gone to the other packages of meds in her hands.

"And those?"

"You want the best, right? Peacekeeper meds. Top grade. Only a year past expiration."

The lieutenant plucked them out of her grasp. He turned the packages over in his hands, studying the foreign script, then handed them back to her with a smile. "Very good."

"Yeah," Mahlia said. "The best."

11

Sergeant Ocho lay still, watching the burn of the fire and trying to keep his mind off the pain in his ribs. When the doctor girl had come back down, she'd given him something that cushioned the pain, and it made him a little hazy. It wasn't as good as the opiates you could find in the Drowned Cities, but it helped a little.

The watches had changed, and his boys were fed. From his sickbed, he studied them, considering them for combat-readiness.

Some of them were still jumpy and on edge from their last run-in with the half-man, but more of them were settling down. Soa was just as crazy as he always was. Van was cracking jokes, which meant he was still afraid. Gutty was sleeping, easy as a baby, always. A few of them started passing a bottle. If they'd been closer to the war lines, Ocho might have shut it down, but soldiers couldn't stand ready all the time, and at least they were out of the heart of the Drowned Cities.

Ocho watched them pass the bottle, listening to their murmured banter and insults. The half-man had hurt them, all right, but Ocho thought their previous encounters had also made them stronger. If it came to another fight, they were ready. They knew what to expect this time.

He lay back, trying to make himself comfortable, knowing the pain in his ribs was too much to let him sleep. He wished there were more of those pink pills the doctor girl had given him, but he was damned if he was going to look like he was begging to get out of a little hurt.

The fire burned lower and the liquor bottle went around again. Or was it a new bottle? Van had rousted more than one off the people in the town. He was good at that—finding the secret stashes.

Soa was complaining again. "What's that stink?" he asked. "Did Slim fart, or what?"

Ocho sniffed. Soa was right. There was a strange nauseous reek of blood and musk in the air. Ocho sniffed again, puzzled. It seemed to be coming off the bodies lying right beside him.

Was the smell something that the half-man had done? He'd never heard of a smell associated with half-men. Just that they were fast and strong and hard to kill. Whatever this was, it was nasty.

Ocho looked away from his dead troops, feeling ill at the losses. Jones and Bugball and Allende. Dead and stinking.

Of all the ways Ocho had expected to die, being torn apart by a dog-face had never been one of them. Bullet in the head, sure. Hands chopped off and him thrown into a canal to bleed out, maybe. Blown to pieces by some leftover land mine from when Tulane Company had occupied all their territory, for sure. He'd come to terms with all those options, long ago.

Instead, he'd taken one impossibly fast and bloody swipe from a half-man and gone flying into a tree. No wonder the swanks who owned the scrap ships always used half-men. The bastards were deadly.

Ocho ran an idle hand over his bandages and stitches. Lucky they'd run across the doctor and his castoff. Those two had done a better job than any of the butchers in the Drowned Cities. The so-called doctors there barely knew how to tie a tourniquet.

He fingered the stitching. Tidy, perfectly even loops pulling torn flesh back together. Ocho's eyes went to the doctor girl, now busily washing pots under Stork's supervision. She'd been the one. The doc knew what to do, but she'd done the doing. Skills like that were good to have in a platoon, even if she was a castoff.

Ocho watched her as she moved around the area, doing her chores. Despite her missing hand, she did pretty good. Not hard to look at, either. Strong cheekbones and dark brown skin and those peacekeeper eyes. As far as Ocho was concerned, she could have had her face burned off with acid and he would still have been interested in her. Not many people stitched skin as good as a machine stitched cloth.

Ocho made a mental note to recommend her to the lieutenant. Maybe burn her in. He'd have to keep Soa off her, though. Soa had some kind of special beef with the peacekeepers. Keeping him off the girl would be full-time hassle.

Even now, Soa was waving at the girl.

"C'mere, castoff. Polish my boots." Soa was grinning and holding them up. "Spit-shine, girl. Get to work. Kiss my boots."

Ocho watched, but didn't interfere, curious to see how far Soa would push his authority. The soldier just didn't let up. Undisciplined that way.

The castoff straightened from her washing. "You want me to scrub your boots?" she asked.

Ocho frowned at her tone, trying to focus through the swaddling blankets of his painkillers. Something about the doctor girl was wrong, and it made his skin prickle. And that weird ripe smell was getting stronger, too. It was all over. Not just coming from his dead soldier boys.

What the hell was it?

The doctor girl had started toward Soa. "You want me to do your boots right now?" she asked. "That what you want?"

Everything about her body language was wrong. She was standing too tall, looking too direct.

Ocho dragged himself upright, fighting the pain in his ribs. She'd lost her fear. The doctor girl had been terrified of Soa before, and now she wasn't. She should have been a frightened little war maggot, quaking and begging, and instead, she was striding toward Soa, and she was smiling.

Blood and rust, Ocho thought. *What you up to, girl?*

Ocho had once seen a nailshed girl go after a trooper with a knife, and she'd looked just like the doctor girl now as she walked toward Soa.

But the castoff was just carrying that bottle of antibiotic stuff she'd had with her all evening. No knife. Nothing dangerous. But she looked like she actually wanted to tangle with Soa.

So where was the weapon?

"Soa..." Ocho started.

At Ocho's words, the castoff glanced over. Something flashed on her face and her step faltered. Hesitation.

Guilt? Fear?

It was weird. It looked almost like she felt bad, like she was apologizing to him for something. And then her expression hardened and she went after Soa, full bore.

Soa never saw it coming. All he saw was an amputated castoff, so he walked right into her trap, even as Ocho started to shout.

The doctor girl swung her arm. An arc of gleaming liquid sprayed Soa, top to bottom. Soa flinched away.

"What the hell?"

For a second, Ocho was sure she'd thrown acid. She'd gotten hold of hydrochlor somehow, and wanted to burn Soa's face off for his hassling. But Soa didn't start scream-

124

ing and clawing his eyes. Instead, the soldier was just standing there. Dripping. Looking nauseated.

"What *is* this stuff?"

A wave of stench rolled over Ocho, emanating from the drenched soldier.

So that was where the smell was coming from.

Soa was staring at the doctor girl incredulously. "This stinks!" He took a step toward her, glaring. "Get over here, maggot! Clean me up!"

But the girl was shaking her head and backing away. Soa took another step after her.

"I said—"

A scream ripped the night, coming from the far side of the perimeter. Gunfire chattered, then opened up full. More screaming, joined by a snarling that made Ocho's blood run cold.

The half-man, he realized. It was coming for them. The gunfire and screaming suddenly cut short. Kilo and Riggs had been out there, and now there was nothing.

Ocho tried to get up and toppled over in his haste. He was more drugged than he'd thought. His head was dizzy with the painkillers. He waved clumsily at his troops. "Get out there!" He waved at his boys. "Dog Squad! Back them up! Don't leave your brothers out there! Help them!"

More screaming and guns were going off, now from the North.

Fates, Ocho thought. *It's back. The dog-face is going to finish us off.*

He cast about for his rifle, feeling suddenly vulnerable and alone. Where the hell was it? Where was his damn weapon?

Soa was unslinging his own rifle, shouting at the doctor girl. He was pissed off, but at least he wasn't hurt.

"Soa!" Ocho ordered. "Get out there!" But Soa wasn't listening. Or maybe Ocho just hadn't said it loud enough. Either way, Soa was all about revenge on the castoff. The girl was backing away from Soa, but the weird thing was, she wasn't panicking. Even as everyone else was shouting and grabbing for their guns and there was screaming and shooting all around the perimeter, the girl didn't look surprised in the least.

She wasn't afraid at all.

Alil's squad dashed toward the sounds of fighting. "Light 'em up!" he shouted. More gunfire ripped the night. Muzzle flashes.

Ocho fought his way to his feet, ribs burning, dizziness washing over him. Where the hell was his rifle? From the corner of his eye, Ocho caught a flicker of movement. A shadow beyond the perimeter, faster than firelight.

"Incom—!"

A whirl of gray fur and fangs exploded from the darkness. Soa stumbled and went down, a beast tearing at his back. Another flashed past, tearing right through the center of the building.

Coywolv?

Blood poured from Soa as more snarling monsters piled

onto him. He was screaming and thrashing, trying to get the beasts off him.

Why the hell were coywolv attacking a whole platoon of soldiers?

The doctor girl dodged past Soa and slipped into the darkness, even as more and more coywolv emerged to tear into Soa.

Why not her?

She was smaller. The coywolv should have been going for her. She was the easy bait. Coywolv always went after easy bait. It didn't make any sense. It was like some kind of strange drug nightmare.

"Get it off!" Soa was screaming. "Get it off!"

Reyes had his shotgun up and was trying to get a clear shot on the coywolv, but they were all whirling motion, and the scatter would tear Soa as well.

"Shoot it!" Soa howled. "Shoot! Shoot!"

He sounded like an animal himself. Reyes sighted again, and then more coywolv piled in and Reyes had his hands full. The soldier boy opened up. One of the beasts' heads whipped back at the blast, blood spraying. Coywolv snarled all around, tearing through the camp, dragging dead soldier bodies out into the darkness, going after the living soldiers as they tried to assemble.

The LT piled down the ladder, shouting for a rally point, the doctor man coming down after. Out beyond the edge of the firelight, the jungle seethed with predatory shadows.

Someone let off a burst of auto.

"Save your shots, you maggots!" the LT shouted.

It was out of control. More and more soldiers were screaming and down under piles of tearing coywolv. Ocho caught a glimpse of the doctor man disappearing into the darkness at the far side of the building, a medical bag in his hands.

"We're losing the doctor!"

But no one was free to go after him. Ocho started hobbling after the man, ribs searing. He fell to his knees. As he struggled to stand, he caught sight of the girl again. Crouched right on the edge of the darkness, watching him.

Why was she still there? Was he hallucinating now?

Ocho again searched for a gun. Finally saw it leaning against a wall, on the other side of Jones's body. He started crawling for it, but a coywolv leaped onto the soldier boy's corpse, blocking Ocho's path. Ocho froze. Another coywolv joined it. They both bared their teeth and snarled at Ocho.

What was he supposed to do? Look them in the eye? Look away? Back off? Don't back off? He couldn't remember.

His questions evaporated as the two coywolv seized Jones's legs in their teeth and dragged the limp body away into the darkness.

Why didn't they go after me? I was right there. And then the answer, as all the pieces of the puzzle fit together. *Because she didn't douse me with that stuff the way she did half the platoon. She set this all up.*

Soa was still screaming. "Get it off! Get it off!" But there were three coywolv on him now, and everyone had their hands full, and then Soa rolled right into the fire and his screaming stopped being words. Coywolv leaped off his back, blazing canine forms, yelping and crazed.

Soa staggered upright, a human torch.

"Get him down!" Ocho shouted. "Roll him!"

But Soa was past hearing. He stumbled about, ran into the ladder, and then it was on fire, too, flames leaping up toward the squat, catching plastics and paper, and then suddenly half the building was on fire.

Ocho gave up on his rifle and started trying to crawl away from the roaring flames. His chest felt like it was being stabbed by knives. His arms and legs felt heavy and clumsy.

Suddenly the castoff was there, grabbing him, hauling him upright. Ocho stared at her, stunned. "What the—?"

She slung his arm over her shoulder. "I didn't spend all that time stitching you up just to watch you get killed. Can you lean on me?"

Ocho felt something tear as she pulled him away from the fire. "You set us up."

She didn't answer, just dragged him into the darkness. Behind them, flames roared higher. Blazing heat. Ocho wished he had his gun, or a knife to stick her, anything at all, but the pain was too much and he was weak and she wasn't stopping to let him catch his breath. "I'm going to kill you," he panted. He tried to grab at her throat.

"Cut it out, I'm saving your maggot ass." She jabbed him in his stitches with the stump of her hand. He gasped and doubled over. He felt like a baby, he was so weak.

"Why are you doing this?"

"Because I'm too stupid to know better." They reached a tree, and she shoved him up against it. "If you climb, you'll make it."

Ocho wanted to turn back, to go to his boys, but she fought off his weak resistance and started lifting him up. "You can't help them," she grunted. She jammed him farther up into the tree. "I'm only doing this because you almost act human. Goes-around-comes-around, soldier boy. Now climb!"

"I can't!"

"You climb or you're coywolv bait." She boosted him higher. "Get up there, you maggot!"

Fire had spread to the rest of the building; it was all going up. Ammo started exploding. *Rat-a-tat*. Probably his rifle on fire. Ocho felt his stitches rip wide as the girl shoved him higher. He almost blacked out from the pain, but he went up.

At last he made it into the crotch of the tree, gasping and sobbing. His side was full of flame, but he was up. Up and safe. Alive.

He looked down for the girl, expecting her to be following him up, thinking maybe he could still pigstick her for doing this to them, but the girl was gone. Swallowed into the jungle. A ghost, just like the coywolv she'd summoned.

Ocho let out a sigh and laid his cheek against the rough bark as the building went up in flames, feeling the knife burn of torn stitches all up and down his ribs. His whole body felt heavy. Maybe that doctor girl's drugs were better than he'd thought.

More gunfire lit the night. Soldier boys doing what they did best. Coywolv were howling, but now the squads had their number and were starting to mop up. Paying back, UPF-style. Ten times over.

Ocho realized that blood was running down his side. He groped at his ribs, fingers clumsy. Too bad about that. It would have made a tidy scar. But then, that was the problem with pretty toy stitches. When real life got hold of them, they always tore out.

The building torched higher, blazing. A bunch more ammo exploded. In his stupor, it was almost pretty. Ocho looked out at the darkness, wondering where the girl had gone.

You better be running for the ends of the earth. If we catch up with you, that last hand of yours isn't the only thing the lieutenant will take.

The warboys opened up, full-auto. More coywolv yelped and died.

Ocho let his cheek rest against the bark, feeling how comfortable it was. He wasn't sure if it was the drugs or the blood loss, but he was fading. He almost smiled as the dark pit of unconsciousness swallowed him up.

The girl had given them a grinding, all right. Gave them a grinding, and they never even saw it coming. He could respect that. Ocho's eyes sagged closed.

You better run, girl. Run hard, and don't you ever come back. Next time, there won't be coywolv to save you.

12

HUMAN BEINGS ALWAYS pretended to a toughness they didn't possess. And perhaps, in their frail human way, they were tough. Places like the Drowned Cities made children strong because the weak ones died early. But whether it was Drowned Cities canals or Kolkata rice paddy, it didn't matter—children were always the same. Lost and running, or feral and fighting. They were always around. Like mice.

Always in the corners of bombed buildings, or splayed facedown in the mud of irrigation ditches. Flies crawling in and out of their noses and mouths and eyes. One mouse here. One mouse there. And stamping them out never filled you with even the smallest sense of victory.

The sun moved across the sky and Tool dreamed of mice running hither and thither.

I am dying.

When Tool was young, his trainers had told him that if he and his pack fought well and honorably, they would ride in the war chariot of the sun. Tool would die and he would go to fields of meat and honey, and he would find his pack and they would hunt tigers with their bare hands.

They would hunt.

Soon.

He remembered the electric prods the trainers used. Showering sparks as they struck his nose. Looming over him, making him cower as they struck him, all of his brothers and sisters pissing and scrambling over one another to get away from them.

Trainers. Hard men and women with their discipline rods. The best of the best, straight from the boot camps of GenSec Military Solutions, Ltd. GenSec knew how to build obedience. Lessons of raw meat and cold electricity. Showering sparks.

BAD dog!

Tool remembered quivering and begging to do as he was told. Begging to fight and kill. To attack when told.

To obey.

And then, their general came. The kind and honorable man who rescued them from GenSec. The general who led their pack out of Hell. They climbed out of Hell together, and stood under the war chariot of the sun and they were born anew. In desperate thanks, they gave their loyalty to General Caroa, forever after.

Rescued from Hell, Tool was meant to serve a lifetime, or however long he lasted. He would fight, but he would also know the pleasure and safety of belonging to something greater than himself. He belonged to army and pack.

Good dog.

The sun was sinking.

Tool noticed a boy squatting beside him like a vulture, observing him with carrion interest.

Tool had seen many of his packmates picked over by vultures. Torn at by lean dogs, ripped at by ravens. They had sailed for far shores, and they had died. When they fought the Tiger Guard in India, the vultures had been circling in the hazy blue skies before the army even waded ashore, anticipating the killing. Knowing that the open swamp waters at the Hooghly River mouth always provided feed. But that hadn't stopped General Caroa.

Tool and his packmates had charged forth at the general's bidding, and they had slaughtered and died.

And now, here, a vulture crouched, waiting.

No, not a vulture...*A boy.*

The mouse boy.

Tool stared at the skinny redheaded creature, wondering why it didn't scamper away. He had this mouse boy by the tail because...Tool searched his memory. It was hazy. The mouse was a prisoner, and prisoners had uses. Sometimes the general had wanted enemy troops taken alive. Wanted them whole instead of gutted...

Tool couldn't remember why he was keeping the boy.

Decided he didn't care. He was dying. Having a companion to watch over one's death was not a bad thing. He himself had watched many of his brothers and sisters as they went from pain into peace. Listened to their recountings. It was good to go into death with someone to remember your passage.

The boy tried to get away, but Tool still had enough strength to stop that, at least.

"No," he growled. "You stay with me."

"Why don't you just let me go?"

"*Let* you go? You're begging?" Tool couldn't help but growl in disgust. "Do you think the First Claw of Lagos offered me mercy when we met in single combat? You think I begged when he placed his blade upon my neck? You think he *let me go*?" Tool snorted. "You think my general offered to let me walk free of his own accord? You think Caroa ever *let* anyone go?" Tool stared at the boy. It was difficult not to despise weakness like this. "Never beg for mercy. Accept that you have failed. Begging is for dogs and humans."

"Is that what you're doing? Accepting that you've failed?"

"You think I've failed?" Tool let his teeth show. "In my years of war, I have never been defeated. I have burned cities and destroyed armies, and the sky has wept flame because of me and mine. If you think I die defeated, you know nothing."

He lay back, exhausted from the exchange. He had never been so weak.

Death is not defeat, Tool told himself. *We all die. Every one of us. Rip and Blade and Fear and all the rest. We all die. So what if you are the last? You were designed to be destroyed.*

And yet still, some part of him rebelled at the thought. He alone had won free. He alone had survived. The bad dog who had turned upon his master. Tool almost smiled, wondering what Caroa would think of him now, lying in the mud, bleeding out. He stifled a snort. Caroa wouldn't have cared at all. Generals never cared. They sent their packs to slaughter, and covered themselves in glory.

Tool stared up at the sun, thinking of cities burned and hearts of enemies he had eaten. Remembering how he and his pack had run streets under fire, blades and machine guns held high. Remembering refugees running before him like a river in flood, tumbling and crashing over one another in their desperation to escape. He and his pack had laughed at their frothing terror, and when Kolkata fell, they roared triumph from the rooftops.

They had done impossible things. They had dropped from great balloon airships, arrowing down from thirty thousand feet to land behind enemy lines and secure the coast of Niger. He had slaughtered the hyena men of Lagos in all their numbers, and had personally eaten the heart of the First Claw.

When the hydrofoil clipper ships of General Caroa arrived to belch forth armies on the beach sands, Tool had been there to greet them, standing knee-deep and laughing

136

in the bloody froth. Wherever he went, he conquered, and the general had rewarded him and his pack.

He had done impossible things, surviving impossible odds. And yet here he lay, just like all his brothers and sisters before him, dying in the mud with flies buzzing around his wounds and not enough interest or energy to swat them away. Apparently it didn't matter what path an augment chose, it always led to this.

"Please."

Tool turned his gaze on the boy. He could barely open his eyes through the blur of fever.

"You're hurting me."

Tool's eye followed the length of his arm, to his fist. Puzzled at what he saw.

The little mouse was pinned by the tail.

"Let me go," the boy whispered. "I can still get you the medicine."

Medicine. Ah yes. That was it. The mouse was nothing. Medicine. That was the thing. But it was too late for medicine. The girl had taken too long. There was only a final bit of payment left. A final promise to keep.

Tool slowly turned his head, his whole body stiff with infection, neck muscles congealed like taffy. Flies rose off his body in a cloud as he dipped his face to muddy water. He lapped, then lay back again, panting, his tongue thick in his mouth. The heat of the jungle felt like a great hand pressed upon him.

"Your sister has left you," he croaked.

"She'll come," the boy insisted. "Just wait a little longer."

Tool almost laughed at that. He wondered how humans could go on trusting one another. Such a fickle species. They always said one thing and did another. It was why his kind had been created. Augments always followed through on their promises.

"It's time," he said. Slowly Tool dragged the boy off the bank and into the swamp. He took the boy's head in his huge hand.

"Just a little longer!"

"No. The girl has forsaken you. Your kind has always been garbage. Willing to run when you should stand. Willing to kill one another for nothing other than scraps. Your kind..." Pain racked him, left him panting. "Worse than hyenas. Lower than rust."

"She's coming!" the boy insisted, but his voice had turned hysterical.

"How long for her to reach this doctor and return?" Tool asked. "Half a day? Two?" He hauled the boy closer.

"Why don't you just let me go?" The boy was starting to struggle, the strength of a gnat against the strength of an ogre. "What difference does it make? You're dead already. It's not my fault. I didn't do nothing to you."

Tool ignored him and started sinking the boy into the swamp's embrace. Strength was pouring out of him, gushing out like water from a shattered dam, but still, he had enough for this. *Pay the girl back. Make her pay for her treachery. Make her know that when the Fifth Regiment is betrayed, nothing is left standing.* The general and the trainers, whispering in Tool's ear, urging him on.

The boy started to thrash and cry. A tiny bundle of bones and scars, freckles and red hair. Just another human who would grow up to become a monster.

"Please," the boy whispered. "Let me go."

Again with the mercy. Humans were always begging for mercy. So willing to do their worst to others, and always begging for mercy at the end.

"Please."

Pathetic.

13

"MOUSE?"

Mahlia eased into the swamp. It had taken her all night and part of the day to find her way back. First to rendezvous with the doctor without getting nailed by the many soldier patrols whom Lieutenant Sayle had sent out in search of them, and then to make her way back to this isolated place of moss-draped trees and stagnant green pools.

Mosquitoes whined in her ears, but nothing else moved. Nothing at all.

"Mouse?"

"Do you see him?" the doctor asked.

Was this the place? Mahlia thought so, but it was hard to —

There. The gator.

"This is it!" She dashed toward the dead reptile.

"Wait!" the doctor called, but Mahlia plunged forward, heedless.

"Mouse!"

She skidded to a halt, scanning the swamps. It had taken too long. Too long to get away, too long to find her way. She fought down tears.

"Mouse?"

Too long to avoid the patrols of the lieutenant as he quartered the wilderness, hunting for her and the doctor, intent on revenge. And now there was nothing.

Where was the half-man? It should have been there, at least.

"Mahlia..."

She turned at the doctor's hesitant voice, and saw what he was looking at.

A small form floated in the water. Arms spread out. Red hair fanned in the water. Floating quiet and still in the emerald pool.

"Fates, please. Kali-Mary Mercy. Oh, Fates. *Noooo!*"

Mahlia splashed to Mouse's body and yanked it up, mindless and desperate. There were ways to breathe life into the drowned and dead. She could still save him. The doctor was good.

But even as her mind told her stories, she knew that they were nothing but silly little licebiter prayers, wishes that would never be answered.

Mouse's head came up out of the water, and suddenly he spit a stream of mud in her face.

Mahlia leaped back with a yelp, trying to understand how the dead spit, all her mother's stories of war dead rising making her skin prickle, but suddenly Mouse was laughing, and now he was standing, and she finally understood that he wasn't dead.

The damn licebiter was laughing.

Mahlia lunged for him and grabbed him and Mouse's skin was warm with life and air, and still he was laughing. Mahlia sobbed with relief and then she slugged him.

"Owww!"

"You maggot! I'll kill you for that!" She shoved him under the water. "You faked me?"

Mouse was laughing and trying to fight her off. Tears blurred Mahlia's sight. She was laughing and sobbing and hating him and loving him, and all her terror that she'd kept bottled up inside came flooding out.

"You maggot!" She hugged him. "Don't ever do that to me! I can't lose you. I can't lose you." And as she said it, she knew it was true. She'd lost too many. She couldn't take any more. Every part of her old life had been ripped away. In its place, there was only Mouse.

Mouse was untouchable. He had the Fates Eye on him. Soldier boys didn't see him. Bullets missed him. Food always found him. Mouse was a survivor. He had to survive. And Mahlia was terrified to realize that she would do anything to make sure of it.

"Damn, Mahlia," Mouse said. "I think you really would miss me if I bit the bullet." He was still laughing. Trying to shake her off, and then he started to hit her, pounding her with all his strength.

"You were late!" he shouted as he beat on her. And then he started to cry. Sobs wracked his small frame.

"You were late."

14

IT TOOK A WHILE to get Mouse calmed down and get the story from him, as well as to tell the story of their own experiences with the UPF soldier boys. The half-man lay in a hollow not far away, huddled amongst banyan roots, like some kind of dead troll from a fairy tale.

Mouse squatted on the swamp bank and stared across at the creature's corpse. He pushed red hair off his freckled face.

"It let me go," he said. "I dunno why."

"Maybe it died too soon," Mahlia suggested.

"No. It let me go. And then it crawled over there and curled up. Could've done me, easy. Had plenty left to sink me and make sure I never came up." He shrugged. "Didn't do it."

The doctor was wading around the beast, staring. Even dead, the monster was imposing. Mahlia had known it before, but seeing the doctor standing next to the creature drove it home. The half-man had been huge. She thought of the three dead soldier boys and the wounded sergeant back at Doctor Mahfouz's squat, and couldn't help wondering what a monster like that could have done if it were healed and healthy.

The doctor waded back to them, moving clumsily through the muck.

"It's not dead," he said grimly.

"*What?*"

Mahlia found herself backing away, even though she was meters distant from the huge body.

"The half-man is still breathing. These creatures are very difficult to kill entirely."

Mouse's eyes had gone wide. "Let's get out of here."

"Yes, I think that's best." The doctor climbed out of the swamp and wrung brackish water from his dripping trousers. "The soldiers will be searching for us. I'd like to be deeper in the swamps before they find this place."

Mouse didn't wait for the doctor to finish. Already he was headed into the jungle, hopping over roots and wading across spongy mosses, moving deeper into the bogs. Soon he would be nothing but a shadow amongst the moss-draped trees and crumbled vine-covered walls of fallen buildings. And then he'd disappear entirely. He was good at that.

The doctor clapped Mahlia on the shoulder. "Come. We should be on our way."

"Where to?"

Doctor Mahfouz shrugged as they walked. "We'll go deeper into the jungle. There are buildings everywhere. We'll find a new place we can use until the soldiers leave. Eventually they'll give up and we should be able to return."

Return? Mahlia stopped short. She looked back toward Banyan Town. *Return?* All she wanted to do was get away. "And then what do we do?" she asked.

"We'll rebuild."

Something on Mahlia's face must have given her away because Doctor Mahfouz smiled. "It's not so awful as that."

"But you know those soldiers will just come back. If it isn't UPF, it'll be Army of God, and if it isn't them, it'll be someone else. And then we'll just have to run again."

"This war won't last forever."

Mahlia couldn't help staring at Mahfouz. "You serious?" But from his expression, she could tell that he was. He really thought things were going to get better, like he was living in some kind of dream. Like he couldn't see what was going on all around.

Mahfouz was like her mother had been, insisting that the soldier boys could be reasoned with, that they could be bribed with the art and antiques that she'd collected, and that they could be safe, even if the peacekeepers had left and the warlords were taking control again.

As troops had swamped the city, she'd clutched Mahlia close and insisted that Mahlia's father was coming back for them. And then when he didn't, she'd insisted that they could always bribe passage on a scavenge ship, even though there wasn't a single one left in the harbor.

Reality was all around her, but she couldn't see it. She just kept pretending.

"Come on, maggot!"

Mouse was perched on a low tree branch, looking back, a small shadow amongst the looming trees and tangling vines.

"We should go, Mahlia."

The doctor stood waiting, expectant in that way adults acted when they thought they were in control. Mouse waved for her to get her ass moving, but Mahlia didn't budge.

Running.

She was always running. Like a rabbit chased by coywolv. Always hunting for some new safe bolt hole, and every time, the soldier boys found her, and forced her to rabbit again. The doctor was wrong. There was no place to hide, and she'd never be safe as long as she remained close to the Drowned Cities.

She looked back at the dying half-man. Amongst the shadows of the banyan roots, the creature was nothing but a black hump blended with thicker shadows. Coywolv bait. Just another skeleton that someone would someday find and wonder what its story was.

Mouse jogged back to them. Gave her arm a tug. "Come

on, Mahlia. Them soldiers ain't going to sleep after how you did them."

She didn't move. "The half-man let you go?"

"Yeah, so? Come on, will you? We don't got much time." He looked back at the inert monster. "I ain't taking its teeth, if that's what you're thinking. No way, no how. Even if it was a hundred percent dead, I wouldn't touch it."

"You couldn't sell them, anyway," she said. "It was a stupid idea."

Doctor Mahfouz also touched her shoulder. "If we move deep enough into the waters, the soldiers won't follow. Their dogs won't track, and we'll be safe. We'll wait them out, just as we always do. But we must go."

Safe?

The word made Mahlia want to laugh. Running didn't make her safe. It never had, and now she was realizing it never would. She'd been as stupid as her father, who had thought the peacekeepers could never be beaten, and her mother, who had thought that a soldier from a foreign country really loved her instead of all her valuable antiques, and Doctor Mahfouz, who thought that there was good in the world.

"I promised I'd give the half-man medicine," she said.

"That's only 'cause it was going to kill my ass," Mouse said. "Now it ain't. Let's go, already."

But Mahlia was working through a new idea in her mind, feeling a different pulse of hope. A scheme that might serve her better than this constant running and hiding. "I said I'd help it. We made a bargain."

148

"That wasn't a real bargain!"

"It didn't drown you, did it?"

"So?"

"Can we fix it?" she asked the doctor. "Is there a way to heal it up?"

"The half-man?" Doctor Mahfouz looked surprised. "Don't be rash, Mahlia. That thing is dangerous. You might as well bring a coywolv into your house."

"I already did," she said. "Whole pack of them." She turned and waded back into the swamp waters, heading for the monster.

The spidery roots of the great banyan tree dangled down all around, brushing her face with feather kisses as she parted them and eased into the sheltered lair the half-man had chosen for its dying place.

"This isn't just stitching up some stray dog!" the doctor called. "You don't know what you're doing!"

Like you do?

If it hadn't been for her, they would have been trapped back in the doctor's squat, waiting for Soa to cut their throats. Mahfouz was smart about doctor stuff, but he was stupid about the Drowned Cities. He couldn't see the truth right in front of him.

Mahlia didn't need someone who talked peace; she needed something that made war.

She scrambled up beside the mountainous creature. Hesitantly, she reached out and pressed her palm to its flesh. Flies rose, buzzing, then settled back. The monster's hide burned under her hand. Sparse coarse hairs, boulder muscles, and blazing blood.

The heat coming from the creature's body was astounding, fevers raging through it, burning it up. Her hand rose and fell with the bellows of the monster's lungs, a shallow rhythm. Faint movement, but it was there, even as the furnace of death raged within.

Mahlia took out the pills that she'd stolen from the doctor's squat and studied them, frowning.

Which ones?

CiroMax? ZhiGan? Eyurithrosan? Chinese characters she didn't know, brand names she hadn't used, for a patient she didn't understand.

She looked over at the doctor, seeking guidance, but he was shaking his head. "Those are the last medicines we have. Now that the house has burned, we don't have anything else. Come away, Mahlia. The soldiers can't miss this place forever. And when they find us, they will make us pay for everything you did to them. We cannot bargain with them now. They won't care anymore that we know something of medicine."

"If you want to go, you can," Mahlia said. "Just show me how to do the meds."

"It isn't just a few pills! It needs surgery," the doctor said. "It has almost no chance of surviving."

"But they're tough, right? These half-men, they build them tough."

"They build them for killing."

Exactly.

Mahfouz seemed to read her mind. "This isn't some fairy tale where beauty tames the beast, Mahlia. Even if you save it, it will not do your bidding. Half-men have one master only. You might as well try to tame a wild panther. It is nothing but a killer."

"It didn't kill Mouse."

Doctor Mahfouz threw up his hands. "And tomorrow perhaps it will rip him limb from limb! You can't know its mind, and you can't control it. This creature is nothing but war incarnate. If you traffic with it, you bring war into your house, and violence down upon yourself."

"Violence?" Mahlia held up the stump of her hand. "Like this, you mean?" She glared at the doctor. "You ever think maybe if we had guns and a monster like this, those soldier boys would think twice about coming after us? You ever think that if we had this thing on our side, we could get away from here for good?"

Mahfouz was shaking his head. "That creature brought the soldiers down on us in the first place. If you seek its company, you will shower all of us in blood. Please, Mahlia, we've already lost our home because of it. Is this how you want to lose your life?"

Was that what she was doing?

Mahfouz pressed on her uncertainty. "Violence begets violence, Mahlia."

Mahlia stared at the wounded monster—the teeth marks, the blood, the stinking rot of its wounds. The carrion scent of its breath. Was she crazy? Maybe the half-man was just like coywolv. Always vicious, even if you raised it from a pup.

But what if it was something else? It hadn't killed Mouse, even when it could have. A soldier boy would have done him in a second, but the half-man had let him go. That had to count for something.

Mahlia set her ear to the creature, listening for the slow thud of its heart. It took almost a minute before she heard it. Huge and thick. Heavy. The heart must have been as big as her head. Crazy big. Crazy dangerous.

She thought of Soa, looming over her: coywolv eyes in the body of a young man. Thought of the lieutenant and his casual way of cutting off her air when Mahfouz didn't jump fast enough. All kinds of deadly there, and she hadn't been able to do anything.

The half-man's heart thudded again under her ear.

Crazy big.

She began inspecting the wounds. *What are you like when you're healthy? How much fight you got in you?*

The doctor seemed to finally understand that she wasn't listening. He waded toward her, pushing through the dangling banyan roots.

"Reconsider, Mahlia. This is not the path you want to follow. You're distraught from everything that's happened." He scrambled up onto the bank. "You need to think clearly."

Something about the doctor's approach warned her. Mahfouz was coming too fast, or maybe there was something of the predator about him. Mahlia couldn't say afterward what warned her, but she yanked her knife out just as the doctor made a lunge for the meds.

She slashed the air between them. He sprang away with a gasp. Mahlia crabbed backward, putting herself up against the dying half-man. She cradled the meds to her chest with the stump of her right hand, keeping her knife raised between her and the doctor.

"Step back, or I swear I'll cut you."

The doctor's eyes widened at the gleaming blade. Horror twisted his expression.

"Mahlia..."

She felt sick in her guts, like dirt, like a worm. She could hear her father sneering at her—*Drowned Cities, through and through*—but she didn't back down. "Don't," she warned.

Mouse was staring. "Damn, Mahlia. And I always thought I was the crazy one."

Mahlia wanted to say she was sorry, to apologize, to make it right, but the knife was already between them, and the doctor was looking at her like she was some kind of soldier boy, a monster without morals.

With a sick feeling, she realized that even if she put the knife down and apologized, there wasn't any going back. She and Doctor Mahfouz stood on two sides now. Pulling the knife had changed everything.

The doctor eased off. "All right," he said soothingly. "All right. Let's not be hasty."

He slowly sat, hands held open and defensive. He looked old suddenly. Old and tired and broken and worn out. Mahlia felt ill. This was how she repaid the man who saved her. No one else had lifted a finger for the peacekeeper cast-off, but Mahfouz had stood tall for her. She wanted to cry, but her voice didn't crack.

"You might as well tell me how to do it right. I'm giving it the meds no matter what."

"Those medicines aren't yours to give, Mahlia. There are people who will need those. Good, innocent people. You can still do right by them," the doctor pleaded. "You don't have to do this."

Mahlia rattled the pills in their fancy blister packs. "How many I got to give?"

Mahfouz's voice hardened. "If you do this, you are no longer my charge. I cared for you as best I could, but this is too much."

Mahlia felt as if she'd stepped out the window of a Drowned Cities tower, and was plummeting toward the canals. Freefall. Nothing to catch her. Just a hard hit, rushing up.

Part of her wanted to take everything back, to apologize for the knife, for the meds, for everything, as the bond of trust that she'd relied on for so long unraveled.

You in or you out?

Mahlia looked from the dying half-man to the doctor.

Was she wrong? Was she stupid? Fates, it was impossible to tell.

But then she looked again at the doctor's disappointed expression and she realized it didn't matter. She'd already chosen, as soon as she'd raised the knife. Old Mahfouz had never hurt anything, and she'd put a knife between them. It was already done. There was no going back. It was like her father said, she was Drowned Cities, through and through. Whatever trust she'd had between her and the doctor was cut now. Cut wide and deep.

"How many pills?"

Doctor Mahfouz looked away. "Four. To start. You'll need four. For that thing's body weight, you'll need four of the blue-and-white ones."

Mahlia fumbled for the meds and started prying pills out. She'd have to grind them, feed them in water to make the thing swallow in its unconscious state. She wondered if she was in time. Wondered if it would all be a waste.

"Four, you say?"

The doctor nodded, disappointment dragging on his expression. "And then more daily, until they are all gone. Every one of them."

You in? she wondered. *You really in?*

Yeah. She was in, all right. All in, whether she liked it or not.

15

Ocho leaned against a sooty wall below the doctor's squat, gingerly probing the wounds that he'd resewn himself. The half-man had ripped his ribs up good, but he was coming back together. The new stitches were messy and brutal, but they'd hold. No way these ones would rip out. They hurt, but they were nothing in comparison to the burn of his back.

Twenty lashes from the cane, for screwing up. Sayle stalking up and down in front of the silent soldier boys, saying, "No one fails, ever! No excuses! I don't care if you're stoned or drunk or you got your legs blown off or you think you're the Colonel himself; you keep on soldiering!" And then he'd laid into Ocho.

Van came over and squatted down. "How's your stitches, Sergeant?"

"Better than my back."

Van smiled slightly at that. He was a skinny little war maggot, missing his ears and his two front teeth. From what Ocho could remember of the firefight with the coy-wolv, Van had been steady. Steady enough that maybe he deserved his full bars. Ocho decided he was going to make the boy a private. Give him a chance to really prove himself.

"You took it good," Van said.

"I been hit worse."

"Everyone knows It wasn't your fault. When we found you, you couldn't even talk."

Ocho snorted. "Don't sweat it, war maggot. LT was right. We got to keep discipline. We don't got discipline, we got nothing. Don't matter who you are. No one gets a free pass."

"Yeah, well, you were so stoned you were drooling." Van hesitated, then said, "LT wants you up top."

"He say why?"

Van avoided his gaze. "No."

Ocho gazed up at the torched building. On its top floor, Sayle had ordered an observation platform built. The concrete and iron was all sooty and scorched and the old doctor's squat was completely burned away, but Sayle still wanted to stand on top of it.

Ocho's instinct had been to pull out of the whole damn building after what the coywolv had done to them, but Sayle had given him a cold look and said if they showed they were afraid, then all these civvies in town would start playing them like that castoff girl had done.

Just because Ocho had coddled himself up with a castoff didn't mean they were going to start sending that kind of message.

So they'd rounded up a bunch of townspeople and put them to work. The maggots had worked damn fast with a gun on their kids.

Now Sayle spent all his time sitting cross-legged on top of the tower, looking out at the jungle, and taking reports from their recon teams as they quartered the jungle, bit by bit, trying to turn up evidence of the dog-face, the doctor, and the castoff who'd done them.

"You need help getting up?" Van asked.

"No." It was a test. LT liked to test. Make sure troops were loyal. Make sure they had semper fi. No way was Ocho going to cry about climbing a ladder, no matter how much it hurt. He pulled himself to his feet with a grunt. "I'll do it myself."

He slowly climbed up the series of ladders to the building's pinnacle, feeling his stitches tugging, feeling the burn of his back. He hoped he wasn't doing some kind of new damage, but it didn't really matter. The only way to survive was to show the LT that he was still loyal, and that he'd do anything for the man. Especially after the caning.

Ocho finally reached the top, gasping and sweating.

Sayle looked up from his maps. Ocho forced himself to

stand at attention. Sayle evaluated him across the short distance. "How are your wounds, Sergeant?"

Ocho stared straight ahead. "Fine, sir."

"And your back?"

"Hurts, sir."

"I went easy on you."

"Yes, sir. Thank you, sir."

"Do you remember how we met, Sergeant?"

Ocho swallowed, forcing down memories. "You saved me."

"That's right. I saw something special in you, and I saved you. I could have chosen anyone, but I saved you. I gave you the gift of life." Sayle's cold eyes narrowed. "And now you give me this..." He trailed off, looking disgusted. "Colonel Stern would never tolerate a failure like that. He'd have your head on a stick. If I were Stern, you would already be a lesson in loyalty."

"Yes, sir."

Far off in the distance, the 999s of the Army of God boomed.

Lieutenant Sayle said, "I made you my second because you have never failed me. You're a good soldier. We all know you were wounded, and drugged by that castoff. It's the only reason you're still standing here. But don't disappoint me again, Sergeant. There won't be any second chances. Not even for you."

"No, sir."

"Good." The LT waved him over. "Now come here. It's time we made plans. We have decisions to make."

Ocho hesitated, trying to tell if he was really off the hook, but Sayle looked up at him, impatient. "I don't have all day, soldier. It's time to work."

Ocho came over and squatted down. "I heard Colonel Stern wants us back at the front."

"That's right. The Colonel is finding himself hard-pressed by our enemy's new artillery."

"When do we march?"

Sayle's cold eyes were like pinpricks. He smiled slightly. "We're not going back."

"Sir?"

"We're not going back. We're staying right here." He looked out at the jungle. "That doctor and his girl haven't come back, and I won't leave until I see them again."

"They rabbited. No way they'll come back while we're around. Might not even come back at all. Jungle's got them now."

"We'll have to give them a reason, then."

"You want them executed?"

Sayle shook his head. "No, I want to know why they left with all their medical supplies. Most of these civvies, they run with food, or a weapon. But these people took their meds."

"Meds are valuable. He's a doctor. The girl's practically a barefoot doctor herself, even with that stump. I'd take meds, too."

The lieutenant nodded slowly, but then he said, "You

noticed that when the girl arrived, she was running? Out of breath. Panicked?"

"Everyone's panicked when they run into us."

"But she was running before she saw us. We surprised her."

Ocho suddenly got it. "You think she was running from something?"

The lieutenant nodded. "It would have to be something big, don't you think? To scare a war maggot like her? Cast-off that's already seen plenty of blood. Plenty of pain." He gazed out at the greenery below. "I think she saw something very frightening out there."

"You think that dog-face got its teeth in her somehow?" Ocho couldn't hide the doubt. "That seems pretty farfetched."

"How long have we been together, Sergeant?"

"Years." Lifetimes.

"Have I ever led you astray? Wasted work on an operation that wasn't worthwhile? That didn't take the fight to the enemy, and come back with trophies for the cause?"

"No, sir."

"I think there are still a few questions worth asking, here in this little town."

"But the Colonel wants us to head back. He won't go easy on us if we don't jump."

Sayle didn't say anything.

Ocho tried again. "You really think that dog-face is still alive?"

"I want to see its body."

"What difference does it make? Colonel doesn't care."

"He does, actually. That dog-face survived in the pits for months."

"Yeah. Epic ring. But we're dead if we don't head back to the front. Stern will execute all of us."

"Stern executes soldiers who fail. It's one thing to loaf out here when the fighting is there, but this is a different case, and demands different thinking." The lieutenant shook his head. "And the Colonel rewards results. The UPF won't be able to hold now that AOG has those 999s. Those cross-kissers will cut more artillery deals, and more scavenge contracts, and the tide will move against us. We'll lose our access to ammunition and weapons, and we will be forced to retreat. The 999s are changing everything. In another year, we could be as lost as Tulane Company."

"What's that got to do with the dog-face?"

"How much do you know about augments...half-men? How much do you know?"

Ocho rubbed his ribs, thinking about how the dog-face had come after him. "All I need to know is that I don't want to fight one again."

Sayle laughed at that. "Have you ever wondered why dog-faces haven't taken over the world? They're better than us. Faster. Stronger. Many of them are smarter. Perfect tacticians. Built for war, from day one."

"Oh, you mean they're war maggots," Ocho joked.

Sayle smiled. "There are similarities. Trial by fire hardens us all. But I'll tell you, that half-man should already be dead."

"I never thought it would beat those panthers."

"No." Sayle shook his head impatiently. "Not like that. Most half-men, when they're trapped, forced to fight for nothing other than survival, they don't last. They pine for their masters, and they die. It's a fail-safe. So they can't be turned. So they can't go rogue against their wealthy masters. So they can't raise a flag for themselves.

"The worst nightmare of any general would be an army of augments gone rogue. They are faster, stronger, and smarter than the average human being. If they were independent as well?" He shook his head. "It would be disastrous. And so when they are cut off from their own, or lose their masters, they die."

Ocho puzzled on that for a little while. "But that one didn't die."

"That's right, soldier. That one didn't die. It bided its time. It survived for months, and then it escaped, and it tore a hole in us and ours. It's all alone, but it's still alive and running."

"So what do you think you can do with it? It'll rip our throats out if we find it. Practically did, already."

The lieutenant shrugged. "Let's just say that it might have a use."

"If it's still alive."

"It's out there." Sayle stared out at the jungle. "It's out there, and that castoff knows where it is. If we find the girl, we find the half-man." He looked over at Ocho. "I have a job for you, Sergeant. It's time for you to redeem yourself."

16

THE PRICK OF a needle. A surprise.

Small pain.

Which meant large pain was receding.

Tool held still as the needle found its way into muscle tissue. Monitored the liquid as it spread warmth into his muscle. A deep injection. 1 cc...3 cc...5 cc...10 cc...20 cc. A great deal of it. An antibiotic, from the way his body drank it in, instead of rejecting it as it rejected toxins.

The needle withdrew.

"That's right. Now check the bandages."

A man's voice. Full-grown. Unusual in the Drowned Cities, where war ate its young long before they reached maturity. And a doctor from the sound of it. Two oddities.

Tool couldn't remember the last time he'd encountered a genuinely trained medic.

"Are these clean enough?"

A girl's voice, and with it, the whiff of blood and fertility. Postadolescent, human, female.

The man's voice responded, irritated. "It's why we boil them."

Delicate hands picked at Tool's chest. Peeled away stinking bandages with a wet tearing. The smell of infection and iron. Blood and stink.

Again the man's voice, flat. Instructive to a fault, but laden with disapproval. Disgust, almost. "That's right. Pluck out the maggots. You don't want them turning to flies."

Tool let them work and listened. No other exhalations nearby, no scuffles or footfalls. Two only, then. And close enough to snap in half. Tool relaxed; he had the tactical advantage. These frail and stupid human beings had no idea that they were being stalked. He was upwind of them.

"If it's healing," the girl asked, "why don't it wake up?"

"It may never wake up, Mahlia. I know you hoped to turn this monster to your purpose, but it's fantasy. Given the wounds it has sustained, you should be amazed that the medicines worked at all. It has taken grievous injuries."

Injuries. Indeed. The catalog of insults he had received was almost infinite. But now he was healing, and soon he would be fully himself. Soon he would hunt as he was meant to.

The hands reset a bandage around his ribs, then moved to the bandages of his torn shoulder. Delicate fingers prodded at the place where the alligator had buried its teeth.

"It's closed up," the girl said, surprised.

The man leaned close, tobacco sweet on his breath. "Don't think of a half-man as human. It is a demon, designed for war. Its blood is full of super-clotting agents and its cells are designed to replicate as quickly as a kudzu grows.

"If you cut a creature like this with a knife, the wound closes itself within minutes. Deep punctures heal in only a few days. Flesh torn down to the bone. Ligaments ripped apart. Bones snapped. None of it matters to a creature like this." The man rocked back. "All the wonders of our medical knowledge, and we use it to create monsters."

Tool could practically hear the man shaking his head.

"Why do you care?" the girl asked.

"Because I'm an old fool who imagines our sciences turned to healing, instead of war. To saving your hand for instance, instead of designing a more resilient killer. Imagine that. Imagine every person in the Drowned Cities with hands and feet, and nothing to fear from soldiers with machetes. Now that would be a true medical advancement."

The girl was quiet. Tool couldn't ascertain from her breathing if it was embarrassment or agreement or thought. Finally she asked, "Will it wake up, or not?"

"It's alive and healing," the man snapped. "It will wake,

166

or it won't. You should be glad it heals more quickly than any human being on the face of this earth."

Quicker than you know, man.

Indeed, even as the man and girl spoke, more of Tool's faculties were returning, the world opening around him like a flower, petals splayed wide: scent, touch, taste, hearing. The world began to illustrate itself in his mind.

Salt scents and rippling water. The ocean whispering, pushing brackish fingers into swamplands. Water skippers skating over glasslike swamp ponds. Sun dappling over his skin. Rustling kudzu. Birch leaves shivering in the wind. Bird calls: crows and magpies, jays and cockatoos. In the far distance, the yip of coywolv and the squeal of a pig.

More and more information poured in. Twenty meters away, a python swished through reeds, a baby practically, no more than two meters long. Overhead, a squirrel's claws scrabbled up a tree trunk—a banyan, judging from the scent and the rustling curtains of foliage and roots that draped all around.

The theater of operation built itself in Tool's mind. From the gaps in rustling leaves, he sensed trails running through the jungle. From the lap of waters, he knew the shapes of stagnant pools. He could guess where gaps in the kudzu led, thanks to the lingering scents of coywolv and deer. Access and egress routes. The most likely paths of enemy attack if he were besieged. The best lines of escape if he was forced to retreat. A battle map, constructed entirely in his head.

He could fight blind, if need be.

A breeze rustled the banyan tree's dangling tendrils, and with it, a whiff of wood smoke carried. Tool's nose twitched. Meat cooking. Snake. Rat. Goat. More than one cookfire, then, and with that information, the knowledge that a village lay not far away, with many families living there.

The man and the girl lifted another bandage. The scent of Tool's own rotting flesh was strong, demanding that he lick the wounds and coat them in the healing enzymes of his saliva. Urging him to seek his packmates. To let their tongues bathe the bloody rents in his frame.

Leaves crushing. Someone coming through the forest.

Tool listened to the approach, accumulating friend/foe data. The dull flip of sandals, stealthy. Another jungle dweller, smaller than the girl. Closer. Closer. Stalking. No scent of metal or gunpowder or gun oil or acid. Not stalking, then—just careful.

"We got soldiers all over," the new arrival said as he came close and squatted. "I covered the trails with all kinds of kudzu and thorns, so it looks like nothing comes this way, but eventually, those soldier boys are going to zero in on this patch, and when they do, we're sitting ducks. You got any idea how much longer we got to stick here?"

A boy. Something familiar about the voice and the scent. Tool tried to recall, but his memories were blotted with fever dreams and nightmare. What was it that he remembered about this boy? About this scent?

"How many soldiers?" the girl's voice asked.

"Forty? Fifty? More?" The boy paused. "They call it a platoon, but there's more soldiers around than Army of God uses for its platoons."

The girl snorted. "Yeah. My old man used to say they didn't know squat about organizing armies around here. You catch sight of that lieutenant?"

"Yeah. And those soldier boys you sicced the coywolv on are pissed. They had Tua up against a wall when I was there, and just kept asking him questions. Even Auntie Selima was up on me, asking about where you'd gone, and what I knew. I thought she was going to turn me over to them."

"Figures."

"Stop it, Mahlia," the doctor said. "Your actions are costing others. Right now, innocent people are paying a price for your rashness. You're the one who stirred that hornet's nest, and now everyone but you is getting stung."

"You mean because I saved you?" the girl answered testily.

The man didn't answer, but Tool could smell the tension between the two. The boy broke the impasse.

"I told people I hadn't seen you, or the doctor. Said you must have bailed, 'cause you're castoff and got no loyalty, but they barely let me off even so. You made a big stir with that coywolv stunt." A pause. "The soldiers are looking for the dog-face, too. They don't say it outright, but they're asking if people have seen any big kills out in the jungle.

169

Pigs. Panthers. Coywolv. Bet they'd be real interested if I said I'd found a huge dead gator out here."

Of course.

It was all coming back now. Tool knew this boy's scent, and the girl's as well. Pieces were clicking together in his mind. The castoff girl, the boy called Mouse, and a doctor with medicines.

The young ones hadn't been liars after all. They really did have medicines and a trained physician. And now, close by, the reek of rotting lizard made sense as well. Another piece fitting into place. Tool's last opponent. That massive reptile, now dead and bloating, six days gone judging by the stench and frenetic buzzing of flies around it. It was dead, and Tool was still alive.

Astonishing.

"So? How much longer we got to stick?" Mouse asked.

An uncertain pause followed.

"Don't look to me, Mahlia," the man said. "You chose this path. Don't look to others to save you from your rashness."

"Maybe a couple more days," Mahlia said finally.

The boy let out a slow hiss of breath. "Dunno if we can keep hidden that long."

"We just need a little longer," Mahlia said. "It should wake up soon."

The doctor broke in, exasperated. "You can't be certain it will ever wake up, Mahlia. At least be decent enough to Mouse to speak honestly to him."

"I thought you weren't going to say what you thought."

"Be realistic. Even monsters like this one die. They are powerful, but not immortal. Even if its flesh heals, perhaps its mind was burned in fever. You don't know all the injuries it has sustained, and it's disingenuous to involve Mouse in your plans. Perhaps it's time for you to pursue another path, one that doesn't involve fantasies of war and killing."

"No," Mahlia insisted. "I already got a plan. If we're going to rabbit, we're getting all the way out. All the way to Seascape Boston."

"You speak with certainty about things you don't understand," the doctor said. "Even if the half-man returns to fighting strength, you will have to cover hundreds of miles infested with warlords and their armies. And after that? You still have to get past the border. No one in Manhattan Orleans or Seascape Boston wants this war flooding north. They protect their borders with more than a single half-man. If you think the UPF or the Army of God is dangerous, then you have no idea what a real army, well-equipped, can do."

"So we're supposed to just keep running around like chickens while the soldier boys try to chop off our heads? Pray to the Fates and God while they pick us off?" The girl's voice was angry. "If anything can get us out, it's a half-man. I don't know about you, but as soon as it heals up, I'm going. I'm done with running and hiding. This monster is my ticket out of here."

Tool stifled a growl as he finally understood the terrain

around him. He knew his physical surroundings by scent and touch and hearing, and now he understood the human landscape as well.

The girl sought to chain him to her. To make him into her loyal fighting dog.

You think to do what General Caroa could not? You think to own me?

17

A LOW GROWL issued from the half-man.

"I am not your dog."

Mahlia turned with a start. The monster was sitting up. It slowly climbed to its feet, a looming shadow in the space under the banyan tree. The doctor was scrambling back, shielding Mouse as he retreated.

The monster snarled. "You do not reward me with raw meat, you do not scratch me behind the ears, and YOU DO NOT OWN ME!"

Carrion and death washed over her. Mahlia gaped up at the half-man, fighting the urge to run. Knowing instinctively that if she fled, the beast would leap on her and devour her.

Fates, what was I thinking?

She'd forgotten what a monster it was. It dominated its surroundings. Its one good eye studied her from the wreckage of a bestial face, the yellow eye of a dog, huge and malevolent. Its lips drew back, showing rows of sharp teeth.

Mahlia swallowed. *Don't run. Don't make it think you're prey. Oh Fates, I was stupid.*

It was one thing to think that you could make a bargain with a monster when it lay dead and still, another to face it, all muscles and teeth and rippling primal hunger.

"Mahlia?" A whisper from behind. Mouse.

Mahlia tried to answer, but her voice was missing. She tried again. "I'm fine," she croaked.

"No," the half-man growled. "You are nothing."

For a second Mahlia thought the monster was about to tear her apart, but then it straightened and turned away, as if it was dismissing her entirely.

Mahlia let out a breath she hadn't realized she'd been holding. The monster was shambling toward the water, stiff at first, then faster, even if it was limping. Mahlia couldn't help but feel a prickle of awe at the sight of the wounded monster, now almost fully healed. Nothing should have been able to survive so much abuse, and yet the half-man stood strong.

It reached the water's edge and crouched. Lowered its face to the brackish slime.

"That's salty," Mahlia called out, but the monster drank anyway.

Mahlia expected it to lap at the water like a dog, but it drank like a human being. When it finished, it glanced at her with a brief flash of a superior smile. "My kind tolerates impurities better than your sort," it said. "We are better than you, in all ways."

The half-man started to straighten, but then it sank to its knees. Its eye widened with surprise as it caught itself. It growled, and then forced its legs under it. Staggered upright once more. It was big, but still, it was weak.

Something about the moment of vulnerability pleased Mahlia. The half-man wasn't unstoppable. It might be strong, but it had its weaknesses, too.

The monster limped around the edge of the swamp pool.

"What the —" Mouse started to ask, but Mahlia already guessed what it was doing. The corpse of the alligator still lay in the water, bloating and torn. The half-man waded slowly into the reeds and seized it. Dragged the body onto the bank, grunting and growling with the effort.

With a low snarl, the half-man tore open the alligator's belly. It dipped into the reptile's entrails and began to feed, unbothered by the miasma of carrion.

The half-man looked up at them and bared its teeth. "My kill," it growled, and then it plunged an arm deep into the alligator. Came up with the heart. "Mine." It bit into the red muscle. Gulping it down.

"Damn, that's nasty," Mouse said.

Mahlia's stomach churned in agreement. Watching

something that looked so nearly like a human being feed like a beast—it wasn't natural, and it filled Mahlia with queasy dread.

What was this thing that she had persuaded them to save?

The half-man continued to feed, tearing and gulping. But there was something else there, too...the way the monster crouched over its kill, victorious, dining on the heart of its enemy...

"Ritual," the doctor murmured.

The monster looked up, gore dripping from its muzzle. The yellow dog eye fixed on him. "We are nourished by victory, Doctor. Life's blood, from the beating hearts of our foes. Our enemy fortifies us. The more enemies we have, the more we feed. And the stronger we become."

"And you never stop fighting," Mahlia whispered.

The monster smiled, all razor teeth and bloody humor. "Conquest feeds itself, girl." It gulped down the last of the alligator's heart. "We welcome our enemies, as we welcome life."

The half-man seemed about to say more, but instead it froze. Its ears pricked up. The monster sniffed the air, broad nostrils flaring. Its ears spread out wider, then snapped back, close to its huge pit-bull skull.

"My name is Tool," it said. "It seems that your enemies have found something to feed upon as well."

18

"WHAT ENEMIES?" MAHLIA ASKED.

"I smell a great deal of smoke. Wood. Plastics." Tool's nostrils flared. "Flesh. A town is dying."

"They're burning Banyan?" the doctor demanded.

Tool was quiet, his ears twitching, listening to things beyond Mahlia's senses. "People are fleeing—"

Gunfire echoed over the jungle, something even she could hear, despite the distance. Startled ravens and magpies filled the air. Flocks of sparrows rose and swirled overhead. More gunfire. Mahlia exchanged worried glances with Mouse and the doctor.

The half-man was still listening and sniffing the wind. "Our mutual enemies seem to have tired of their failures."

"So they're going after the town?"

The doctor was starting to grab his medical tools, throwing them into his hospital bag. "We have to help. Quickly! They'll need us."

As Mahlia gathered the last of the much-reduced supplies and handed them to the doctor, she noticed her hand trembling. She remembered other villages where soldiers had swept through, recruiting and burning. Remembered picking her way through blackened homes, with nothing but skinny dogs and coywolv flickering in the shadows.

"Doc?" she asked. "Shouldn't we be running instead?"

Tool laughed, a low rumbling sound. "The girl shows wisdom. Better to run and live than walk into a tornado."

The doctor glared at Mahlia and she shrank from his gaze. "You caused this," he said. "Violence feeding violence. I've told you again and again and again, but still you never listen. You loose coywolv on soldiers and now the soldiers burn Banyan Town. Tit for tat until the whole world dies."

Smoke was starting to blow over them. Acrid scents of the world on fire that even Mahlia could smell.

"Why are you mad at me? I'm not the one burning the town!"

Doctor Mahfouz snapped his bag closed and looked up at Mahlia. "Are you coming or not?"

"Back to town?" Mahlia stared at the doctor. "Are you sliding? We got no guns. They'll kill us."

"We're not going back to fight. We're going to help as many people as we can."

"I'm not going anywhere."

"You understand how hard I fought for you, Mahlia? How many times I convinced our neighbors not to run you off? I stood for you. I guaranteed you."

Beside them, the half-man growled. "People are coming. You should flee, or else go to your death. Choose now, before the choice overtakes you."

Mahlia turned to the half-man. "Would you come with us?" she asked. "Would you help us help them?"

Tool laughed. "This is not my war."

Mahfouz glared up at the creature. "You brought the soldiers here, and you accept no responsibility?"

Tool's teeth showed in a cold smile. "I neither started this war where your kind tears one another apart, nor did I choose it. I carry no burden of guilt." He sniffed the air, then waved toward the swamps. "If you wish help in escape from your enemies, I offer you aid, willingly, in thanks for medicines." Tool straightened to his full height, looming over them. "But I will not seek out a fight that cannot be won. And I will not suicide on any human being's behalf."

Their conversation was cut short by running feet.

Everyone tensed except for Tool. Mahlia expected soldier boys to come bursting into the swamps, rifles blazing, but it wasn't soldiers at all, it was a woman...

Amaya.

She stopped short, staring. Her eyes widened in shock. "*You,*" she gasped as she saw Mahlia. And then she caught sight of the half-man.

179

"Amaya," Doctor Mahfouz said. "What's happening? What's going on? Where are your children? Where is Salvatore's grandchild?"

"You!" she said again. "They want you!" Her eyes narrowed. "This is your fault, castoff. They're looking for you! We took you in and you brought the soldiers down on us!"

"Amaya—" the doctor tried again.

But Amaya had already turned. She was running back the way she had come.

"She's going to tell them!" Mahlia said. "She's going to give us up to the soldiers."

She leaped after the woman. If she could take Amaya down before she made it back to town, before she could spread word to the other villagers, she might—

A hand grabbed Mahlia's shirt and yanked her around. She spun with the force of it and landed in the mud. Doctor Mahfouz stood over her.

"Mahlia, don't."

Mahlia scrambled to her feet. "She's going back to the soldiers! If she rats us, we're all dead. Once they got our scent and our direction, there's no way we shake free." She made another run for the trails, but the doctor grabbed her.

"That still doesn't justify whatever you were planning for Amaya," he grunted.

Mahlia struggled to break free, but the doctor was surprisingly strong.

"She's going to get us killed!" Mahlia's hand went to her knife. Where was it?

The doctor must have felt her motion, because he caught her hand. "Always that's your solution! Is that what you are?" he demanded. "Just like those soldiers out there? Always killing?"

Mahlia looked around frantically, still trying to fight free. Caught sight of Mouse. "Get her!" she said. "Don't let Amaya get back to town!"

Mouse looked from the doctor to Mahlia, uncertain.

Mahlia glared at him. "She's going to do us, unless you catch her."

"Stay there, Mouse," the doctor grunted. "Make the right choice."

Mouse looked down the path after Amaya, then back to Mahlia. Finally shook his head. "She's bigger than me. I don't think I can catch her before she's back in town."

Mahlia twisted and fought, finally threw herself sideways, taking both of them to the ground. The doctor's grip popped free and she tore loose. She scrambled back to her feet, glaring at Mouse. "You chickenshit farmer."

Mouse hung his head, but he didn't go running after Amaya. The doctor slowly got to his feet, panting. Tool was watching them all, curious, almost amused.

Mahlia looked toward the town. The smoke was thickening. The soldiers had to be burning everything. Not just the town. Probably the crops as well. Scorched earth. More smoke billowed over her. Mahlia swore. She'd hoped to have more time to prepare for a journey north, but with Amaya ratting them out, it was time to run. Ready or not, it was time to run.

Mahlia turned to Tool. "Can you travel?"

Out of the corner of her eye, she saw Doctor Mahfouz shift in disappointment that she wasn't interested in suicide. That was Mahfouz's problem, though.

Tool's yellow dog eye regarded her. "There is no choice. We travel or we fight. And if we fight, we die."

That pretty much summed it up. So why was she even delaying?

They didn't have enough food. Didn't have tools. No machetes, no nothing.

"Okay," she said. "Okay." She wanted to scream in frustration at how quickly her bare plan had fallen apart. Her father had always said that battle plans fell apart. It was to be expected. A general had to adapt—that was what distinguished good soldiers from poor ones. So, she needed to adapt.

"We got to lose the trail," she said. "We're going into the swamp. Water travel." She pointed. "Mouse can show us a way. He knows these swamps. We can still lose them."

The half-man inclined his head in agreement. He limped over to a tree and took a branch in his fist. With a crackling explosion, he tore it free, making a staff to support himself.

"Damn," Mouse muttered. "That's what you do when you're weak?"

The half-man showed his teeth and leaned on the make-shift crutch. "Come, boy. Show us this secret way."

They all started into the water, but a moment later Mahlia realized the doctor wasn't with them.

Mahlia turned. "Doc?"

The doctor was looking at her sadly.

"You can't be serious," Mahlia said. "You think you're going to stay here? Let Amaya bring soldiers down on you?" She motioned for him to follow. "They hate you as much as they hate me, now."

The doctor just looked at her. It made her uncomfortable.

"I thought for a little while that it was possible to save you," he said. "To do some good. To stop..." He shook his head. "To change the sickness of this place." He looked at Mahlia. "I taught you to heal, not to fight."

"You think I was wrong to drop coywolv on them?" Mahlia said. "You wish you were back there with the soldier boys? They were going to kill you, too, you know. They deserved it. They started it."

"And you did nothing to end it."

Mahlia glared. "If I had some guns I would have."

The half-man laughed, a low rumbling. He clapped Mahlia on the back approvingly. "War feeds itself well, don't you think, Doctor?"

Mahfouz looked at the half-man with disgust. "I should never have allowed her to heal you."

"A good thing, then, that I do not rely on a pacifist's

goodwill." The half-man's fangs were showing, sharp knives all gleaming.

The doctor started to retort, but the half-man interrupted him. "Save your shaming for the girl, Doctor. If I cared for human approval, I would have been dead long ago." He turned and started wading into the swamp. "Time is passing. I, for one, have no intention of remaining here for your betrayer to bring back the soldiers and their guns."

"Doctor?" Mouse asked.

Mahfouz shook his head. "I'm not leaving these people to the soldiers. Come with me, or go with the half-man. But these people need our help."

Smoke was blowing more strongly, gray mist thick with the scents of burn.

Mahlia's eyes began to tear. She looked at the doctor, wishing that he wasn't as crazy as he was, and realizing there was nothing she could do to move him.

"Come on, Mouse. Let's get gone." She turned and started walking. Behind her, she heard Mouse say something and then he was catching up, splashing into the water after her.

"You sure about this, Mahlia?"

"There's nothing we can do back there."

"They took us in."

Mahlia looked at Mouse. "We got to look out for ourselves, first. If we don't, we're dead."

"Yeah. Except I saved you."

"And now I'm saving you, right? We ain't going back there."

Mouse subsided. Soon they caught up with the half-man.

"The doctor chose not to accompany you?" Tool asked.

Mahlia shook her head. "He's stupid."

"He has a cause," the half-man said. "It makes him dangerous."

"I got a cause," Mahlia said. "It's keeping my head from getting shot off."

"A worthy one, I'm sure."

Mahlia couldn't tell if the half-man was mocking her or not. They kept walking through the swamp.

Abruptly the half-man said, "It seems your brother Mouse has found his own cause."

"What's that supposed to mean?"

"Look and see."

Mahlia turned to look behind her. Mouse was gone, disappeared into the thickening smoke.

19

MAHLIA AND MOUSE, Mouse and Mahlia.

She'd been the one who'd always been good at keeping them from getting killed; he'd been the one who'd always been good at keeping them alive. She'd kept them out of the bullets, using everything she'd ever gleaned from her old man about Sun Tzu and warlords.

Mouse had been the one who knew how to dig for ant eggs under a rock, or knew how to go hunting for craw-dads. How to catch a frog. They didn't have anything in common, not really, but they'd been a unit. A tight little unit. And because they'd been tight, they'd survived.

While people were running across the fields ahead of Freedom Militia, she'd grabbed Mouse and held him low while the bullets flew overhead and mothers and fathers and kids and grandmas all flopped in the weeds.

You didn't rabbit when they had all the guns; you played dumb and you played dead, and you lay with your face beside some bleeding dead woman and wiped her blood all over you and Mouse, and then you lay like the dead until they'd walked right over you.

You lay like stone, with your blood pounding in your ears and your eyes open and staring straight into the sun like the true dead while soldier boys stepped over you and macheted the ones they'd only wounded.

She'd done that. She'd saved his licebiter ass when he didn't know enough to lie low.

And then, when the Army of God bagged her and she hadn't seen it coming, when they'd chopped one of her hands off already, and were going to do the other, while they were all laughing, Mouse had been the one who'd eeled up to their camp and started throwing rocks—rocks against bullets, of all the crazy things—and while the soldiers all ran and grabbed for their weapons, she'd run the other way, blood pouring from her stump, but still, alive and running, alive when she would have been chopped down to nothing but stumps and hung off a tree the way the Army of God liked to do with all the nonbelievers.

And then they'd found the doctor and he'd fixed up her stump, and it had all settled. Except that Mouse was an idealist.

Mahlia peered back into the thickening smoke. *"Mouse!"*

She couldn't make out a thing beyond a dozen meters. Where was he?

"Grind it." She started back through the bog.

"You'll die if you follow him," the half-man said.

Mahlia realized that the monster had been watching her closely. "You knew he was running?" she demanded.

"I assumed that he had some purpose." Tool's ears twitched. "He only now has turned his path definitively away."

"So can you tell where he is?" Mahlia asked. "You can track him?"

Tool listened for a moment. "A few hundred meters, perhaps. He moves quite quickly."

Mahlia turned and shouted again. *"Mouse!"*

No response. Mahlia grimaced. "He's good in the swamps. We gotta go catch him before he does something stupid."

"He already has," Tool said. "And he will die because of it. And you will die, too, if you follow him. There are patrols moving toward us now. Many ants marching."

"But you're fast," Mahlia said. "Just go after him."

"You remind me of General Caroa, in miniature. Always demanding more of your troops. You think it is easy for me to walk? Let alone run?" He hefted his makeshift staff. "You think I carry this for pleasure?"

188

Mahlia cursed Mouse. They were supposed to stick with this old war monster and it was going to get them away from the Drowned Cities for good. Not just living in the swamps, but all the way out. North. To those places like Seascape Boston and Beijing that weren't swallowed by war. With the half-man, it was possible. He'd be able to sense the patrols, to work them through the battle lines. And now Mouse was turning around and going back to town?

Mahlia looked to the half-man. "You can tell where the soldier boys are, right? You can tell where the patrols are?"

Tool nodded slowly. "I can."

"Then help me go get Mouse."

Tool snorted. "I'm not so eager to die that I will walk into an enemy position with neither weapons nor support."

"I saved you."

"And I am grateful."

"Why won't you help?"

"Why should I throw my life away, when it has just been reclaimed?"

Mahlia wanted to scream at the brute monster. "Because I'm the one who saved you! Without me, you'd be dead already. Mahfouz and Mouse would have let you bleed and die. I gave you every med the doctor had to get you up and walking."

"So you believe I owe you."

"You do! You owe me big-time. And you know it."

Tool slowly squatted, bringing them eye to eye. "Perhaps I do owe you. Perhaps my honor even demands that I pay you back in some way.

"But listen to me, girl. If you come with me now, you have a chance to survive and leave this place. I will take you with me, and I can help you escape." He straightened. "Or you can return and try to save your friend from his own foolishness."

"You can track him, right?"

The half-man's lips drew back, showing teeth. "You still think I'm your dog?"

"No!" Fates, it was impossible to deal with the monster. Even soldier boys made more sense. The half-man seemed like a person, but then it would turn cold and she'd think it was about to tear her apart. "Can you help me? Please?"

"If I do, do you consider our debt settled?"

"Help me get Mouse."

"What is he to you?"

"He's my friend."

"Friends are easy to find."

"Not like him."

"You're willing to die to save him?"

"Fates." Mahlia looked away, feeling lost. "If he dies, I'm dead anyway. I don't got nothing else to lose."

The half-man looked at her, scarred and huge. It didn't move.

"Never mind." Mahlia turned and started back into the

swamps. "Do what you want; I got to get him back. If he's dead, I'm dead. It's how it is."

"Pack," the half-man said. "He's of your pack."

The way the half-man said it made Mahlia think that it was more than just when you talked about dogs or coywolv running together. It was something absolute and total.

"Yeah," she said. "Pack."

20

THE SMOKE THICKENED about them. Mahlia cut a strip of fabric from her tank and soaked it in the swamp, bound it around her nose and mouth, and fought to keep from coughing.

The half-man didn't seem affected at all. Even as Mahlia's eyes teared in the smoke and she fought against sneezing and coughing, the half-man eased through the trees and pools and kudzu like a wraith. Sometimes, he would hold up a hand and she would freeze and he would sniff the air.

Three times, he motioned her off the trail and into the tangled vines of the jungle. Then they lay on the muddy ground, listening as snakes slithered through the undergrowth and then, just as Mahlia was becoming annoyed at the charade of hiding, she would at last hear footsteps and people would be on top of them.

Twice it was people from the village. She was tempted to call out, but then remembered Amaya and knew the villagers were just as much of an enemy as the soldiers.

They lay under smoke and vines and watched the shapes of the refugees rise out of the smoke, sobbing. Clutching themselves. Old man Salvatore, but not his baby. Emmy Song. Alejandro, who had given her so much trouble, hurried past with two young children Mahlia didn't recognize and didn't think were his. People. Old, young, children. So much like other refugees she had seen.

The townspeople had always hated war maggots and now they were just more of the same. Displaced and on the move, hoping they'd find some solace or safety. And despite all the antipathy Mahlia had for them, she found herself wishing them luck, and an easy path under the eye of the Fates.

The people fled with rice and sacks of potatoes and anything that they could carry, and it was heartbreakingly little. She watched them rise from the fog, and disappear again, and she wondered at their future.

Would they ever have a chance of settling again, or would they all end up like her, cast off and wandering, without hope of shelter ever again? Would another village take them in, or would it fight them off?

And then Tool would tap her shoulder and they would climb from their hiding place and glide deeper into the thickening smoke.

The third time Tool motioned Mahlia off the trail, he didn't make her hide, but instead he stopped short, sniffing, and then turned and guided her back the way they'd come. She wanted to ask what he was doing, but she took her cue from his absolute silence.

Ever since they had started toward the village, he had not used his voice, and even now, as he guided her off the trail and into the tangling kudzu, and then onto another path that she hadn't even guessed was there, the half-man didn't say anything.

"Why?" she whispered.

The half-man motioned her sharply to silence. He mimed with his hands, as if he were holding a rifle, then held up fingers, pointing back the way they had come. Pretended as if he were squatting. Held up six fingers again, looking at her significantly.

Six soldier boys. Sitting on the trail, waiting in ambush. Without Tool, she would have walked right into it.

They eased down the new path. Mahlia's anxiety increased. The silence was terrifying.

Suddenly Tool grabbed her and pushed her down, hand over her mouth. She tried to fight him off, but then the guns opened up and she heard people crying and screaming, and soldiers laughing and shouting, and then more shooting, and all the while, Tool lay beside her, hand over her mouth so she wouldn't cry out and give away their position.

They weren't more than fifty feet away. That close. She could hear someone moaning in the smoke, sobbing. She heard footsteps. There was a quick scuffle and someone cried out. The sobbing stopped.

"Dumbass civvies," someone said. Someone else laughed. The soldiers. Right there beside her. Not more than a couple yards away. Slowly their voices moved off. Another person cried out in pain.

Tool motioned and then they were up and sneaking past, moving through the smoke, Mahlia praying that she wouldn't cough and give herself away, and then they were past the ambush and Tool was motioning her onward, urging her faster. She hurried after the hobbling monster.

She was moving so fast she almost stepped on them before she realized what was happening. Bodies lay everywhere. Dozens and dozens of dead. Mahlia jerked up short, on the verge of crying out. She was surrounded by a carpet of bodies. Her breath came out in a low, trembling exhalation. She took another breath, fighting for calm.

It's just the dead. You've seen plenty of them. Just keep going.

She started picking her way over the bodies, trying hard not to tread on them, trying hard not to look at their faces, at the blood, how torn and broken they were. Trying hard not to see Bobby Cross where he lay.

195

But even as she tried to ignore the carpet of death, a part of her was seeing the wounds and trying to fix them in her mind. All her doctor training, plucking at her conscience, telling her how to fix up something that couldn't be fixed. Doctor Mahfouz instructing her in that calm voice of his that first she should stabilize the patient, make sure that breathing and circulation weren't compromised. First fix that. Close the hemorrhaging wounds. Then onto the splints and sewing and...

Had she really brought this down on them? Was this all her fault? Was this an army's revenge for the coywolv?

Mahlia started to retch, and suddenly it came out, all of it. The doctor was right. Everything you did just made it worse. One thing spinning into the next, into the next until a whole village was dead—

Tool clamped his hand over her mouth. "Be silent!" he growled. And though she struggled, he didn't let her go. He buried her face against his body so that even her screams were barely sounds at all, and then her sobs poured out and he stifled those as well with his huge body.

"Lock it away," the half-man whispered. "You feel, after. Not now. Now you are a soldier. Now you do your duty for your pack. If you break, your Mouse will die, and you with him. Feel, after. Not now."

Mahlia wiped at her watery eyes and snotty face, nodding, and they went on.

The smoked lessened. They came to the edge of the blackened fields, with fires guttering all around. Ravens

196

picked at the burned remains of the place. Across the fields, she saw the soldiers. Lieutenant Sayle and his pack, all together, standing around a cluster of people kneeling, and in the center of that knot, under cover of weapons—

"Fates."

21

OCHO WIPED SOOT from his face. All his boys were a mess. The burning had taken longer than the lieutenant had wanted. Some of the crops had been wet, so setting the villagers to work ripping up their food and then lighting it on fire with cooking fuel and wood that his boys made them gather had taken longer than they'd planned, but Sayle wanted scorched earth and Ocho was going to make damn sure he got it.

There'd been a bit of resistance from the villagers, right at the beginning. Some of them had tried to run for the swamps, just as the lieutenant had planned, and Ocho heard gunfire and screaming as a bullet squad tore them apart with heavy weapons. After that, they had fewer defectors. Ocho ordered an acid squad to round up stragglers, while he limped behind.

His rib splints were hurting him, but he wasn't going to show anyone how bad it was. He wasn't showing a bit of weakness, today. The LT had given him a second chance. By the time they finished this operation, he wanted to be back in Sayle's good graces, solid. Ocho wasn't drugged on painkillers now. He was ready for war. And by the end of the day everyone would know it: Sayle, soldiers, civvies. Every one of them.

Ocho gritted his teeth through the pain and soldiered on, ordering half-bar patrols up into abandoned buildings, trying to ferret out the last of the people who were still hiding in the ruins. Getting others organized to put the townspeople to work, burning their own town. He was just assigning a new squad when the doctor came back into town.

At first, Ocho couldn't believe what he was seeing. While half the villagers were scheming to flee, slipping out through the LT's security nets, or dashing off into the jungle when they got half a chance, here the doctor was, coming out of the jungle with his damn doctor bag.

"Well, I'll be damned," Van said as he watched the doctor come on. "LT was right. We got ourselves a doctor. Bo-na-fide human-ee-tarian."

Ocho spat, watching. The doctor was a fool. He'd kind of suspected it, the way he'd stood up to Lieutenant Sayle on their first night in Banyan Town, but here it was again.

The doctor, striding across the blackened field like he was the Rust Saint himself, coming to save everyone.

From the jungle, a bunch of gunfire opened up. *Ch-ch-ch-ch-ch.*

The doctor spun, and fell.

"Dammit!" Ocho waved his hand. "Make Hoopie stop shooting shit, will you?"

One of the licebiters was dispatched, running back across the sooty, uneven ground. Ocho headed across the fields toward the doctor, moving slowly. The man lay in the soot and muddy soil, facedown, but trying to sit up. He groaned as Ocho arrived.

"Whoa there, Doc." Ocho knelt beside the man. Saw the blood. Sayle was going to be pissed.

Another bullet winged overhead.

"Blood and rust! Make that Hoopie stop with the shooting, or I'll ram that rifle up his ass!"

"I got it, Sarge."

Van took off running. A second later, the gunfire stopped and then Hoopie was making his way out of the forest. His skin was all torched and scarred up from the disaster with the castoff girl and the coywolv. He came and stood over the doctor.

Ocho scowled. "LT wanted this one alive."

Hoopie looked down at the doctor. "He don't look too good."

"'Cause you shot his ass!" Ocho waved at Pook and Stork. "Get this one back to the command."

He turned and caught sight of movement in the trees. "Dammit, Hoopie! You got your zone controlled or not?"

It was some little civvy licebiter, watching from the jungle. "Get that civvy. See if he knows anything about the half-man." He grabbed Hoopie as he was about to go. "And if you bring him back like the doc, I'll put a bullet in your head, personal."

Hoopie's bloodshot eyes regarded Ocho with total enmity, but he saluted and headed out. Ocho wondered if the armies up north, all those big corporate war bosses, had so much trouble keeping troops in line. Hoopie would need discipline, for sure, for tagging the doc. Maybe Ocho would bust him down to half-bar again. Give his rifle to someone who at least knew who to shoot.

Ocho stared down at the doctor. The old man was gasping and blood was coming out of his mouth, staining his salt-and-pepper beard. Already his eyes were glazing over.

Pook and Stork grabbed the doctor's shoulders and got ready to drag him, but Ocho motioned them off. "Don't bother. He's already dying." Ocho sighed as he looked down at the old guy.

"What were you thinking, old man?"

Maybe there was someone he wanted to save. But that doctor girl of his hadn't been anywhere in the area. Maybe someone else, then. Ocho scanned the village. It didn't make sense.

The man gasped again, and more blood came out of his mouth. It looked like he'd taken a couple in the chest.

Surprising that he was even breathing, but the blood and bubbles frothing his lips made Ocho think the man wouldn't last long.

Ocho squatted down beside the dying man. "Hey," he said. "You remember me?" The man's hand came up. Ocho took it. "Yeah. You fixed me up." He looked down at the man's blood-bloomed shirt. "Sorry about that, right? None of these warboys got any discipline. Half the time, they don't even know which way to point a gun."

The doctor wasn't looking at him. Ocho couldn't tell if the man was hearing him, or if he was already gone to his dying place. It was a stupid way to die. Hoopie's squad just pinging him for no reason. They were supposed to herd people back into town and put them on work gangs, but this had just been an execution. Hoopie had been pissed about how the girl had gotten him burned, and figured the doc deserved it.

No damn discipline.

The doctor's breathing slowed. Stopped. His hand went limp, and Ocho let it fall. "Sorry, old man." He straightened. "Get that licebiter out of the trees, and make sure Hoopie doesn't smoke him before I get to ask some questions."

He strode back across the muddy fields, leaving the dead doctor behind, still irritated at Hoopie.

Sayle talked a good game about unit discipline, but at the end of the day, they might as well have been coywolv for all the restraint they had.

*   *   *

Mahlia watched from the trees. There was a cluster of soldiers standing in the blackened fields and then one of them straightened, and she recognized him.

Ocho. The sergeant she'd saved. Her hand curled into a fist, and then she saw what he and his boys had been standing over, and she gasped.

Doctor Mahfouz. She recognized the green pants and dirty yellow-and-blue shirt he'd been wearing. Stupid clothes for running and hiding, but the man had liked bright things. And now he lay in the mud. Stupid. Too damn stupid.

Soldiers were jogging in her direction. Tool pulled her back deeper into the jungle. For a second, she thought she'd been seen, but then soldier boys dove into the trees a hundred meters off. Gunshots echoed, followed by shouts. A moment later, they reemerged with some licebiter—

Mouse.

Mahlia lurched forward, but Tool grabbed her. He brought his head close. "You cannot survive this fight."

Mahlia watched, sick, as Mouse was dragged across the fields. Beyond, the town burned, buildings flaming like monumental torches. A roof crashed down, blazing bright, and a cheer went up from the soldier boys.

Somewhere far away, Mahlia could hear a girl screaming, but Mahlia only had eyes for Mouse. The skinny red-headed boy, small between the older soldier boys. Mahlia tried to shake Tool's hand off her shoulder. "They're going to cut his hands off," she whispered. "It's how they do."

Tool's grip tightened. "You cannot save him."

"He saved me! I owe him."

"I'm saving you," Tool said. "I owe you."

"There's got to be a way."

"Why? Because you wish it? Because you made offerings to the Fates or the Scavenge God? Because you repented to the Christians and drank their deep waters?" Tool shook his head. "As soon as you start crossing those fields, you will be spotted. There are fire teams to our left and right, still combing the trees, and they, too, watch the fields. That"—he pointed to the open land—"is nothing but a killing field."

Mahlia gave him a withering look. "Don't you care about anyone?"

Tool growled. To Mahlia's surprise, he suddenly released her. "You wish to prove your love for the boy? Go, then. Prove it." He gave her a rough shove. "Charge. Attack. Take your little knife and attack. Show your love and bravery, girl."

Mahlia glared up at the half-man, hating him. "I'm not a half-man," she said.

"And I am not your dog."

Mahlia looked back at the village. The soldiers had dragged Mouse close to the torched buildings and forced him to his knees. A figure emerged from the sooty wreckage...

Sayle.

He had a pistol in his hands. Mahlia watched the man stalk around the boy, then step close. She squinted, trying to see, not wanting to, afraid, but unable to look away. Sayle put his pistol in Mouse's mouth.

Tool's ears pricked up, cupping the wind.

"He wants to know where we are," the half-man said. "They're threatening him. It won't be long until they know, and then they will pursue."

The half-man's hand fell on Mahlia's shoulder, heavy and solid, even as the monster's deep voice became soft. "Come," he said. "It is best not to watch these things."

Mahlia shook off his hand, still watching. Unable to pull away. She heard the half-man give a low growl of frustration. She was surprised he didn't just grab her and drag her. Instead, he waited.

"They're going to kill him," she said, feeling sick.

When she had needed help, Mouse had stepped up for her. He'd thrown rocks, of all things. He'd done the brave and stupid thing, and saved her. And here she crouched amongst kudzu vines, unable to make her limbs move, terrified and a coward.

"They're going to kill him," she whispered again.

"It is their nature," Tool said. "Come away. This will only make your nightmares worse."

22

SAYLE JAMMED HIS PISTOL into the prisoner's mouth. "You're dead, licebiter." The kid tried to speak, but he couldn't get words out around Sayle's 9mm. Little pale runt, all crying and begging.

Ocho stood by, watching the jungle, waiting for the bullet.

The kid kept on with his whimpering and begging, and Ocho tried not to listen. He'd learned long ago that if you treated maggots like people, it just ripped you up. Gutted you and made you weak when you needed to be strong.

The kid went on whining, though, pissing his pants.

Just get it over with, Ocho thought.

But Sayle liked the maggots squirming.

It was another thing Ocho didn't like about the LT. The

man was crazy. One of those bastards who'd grown up and found out that war was where he lived best. Sayle enjoyed suffering.

Sayle kept on, questioning the prisoner, making him think he had a chance. Like baiting a dog with meat and then pulling it out of reach again and again. Making the pathetic little licebiter stand up and bounce around on his hind legs, tongue hanging out.

Sayle offered freedom. He coaxed people to rat their relatives, to rat their food stores. He was good at it, the dangling. But it made Ocho ill, and he tried to be away from it when he could. Couldn't pull it off every time, though. If the LT thought you were a weak link, bad things happened. So sometimes you just had to stand by while some war maggot begged.

"She ran! She went away. Her and the half-man. They headed out. She was going to leave. Go north."

It made sense to Ocho. The doctor girl had seemed like the kind who had a plan. For sure, she'd ripped the hell out of the platoon.

"You're covering for her," Sayle said.

"No! I swear it! She told me not to come back here. Told me not to do it. She said the doctor was stupid. Said I was." He spat blood and the despair in his voice made Ocho look over. Little war maggot looked like he'd lost her, all right. No hope there.

Sayle caught Ocho's gaze. "What do you think?"

Ocho leaned against a flame-blackened wall, trying not

to show how much his ribs hurt. Wishing that Hoopie hadn't shot the doctor. It would have been good to recruit a real pill pusher into the company. Now Ocho's survival was pretty much up to the Fates; if he picked up an infection, he was done.

"I think he's telling the truth," Ocho said. "Doctor was crazy, for sure. I can see him coming back alone. Humanitarian, right? All kinds of do-gooder."

"This one, too? And ditch the girl?" Sayle looked down at their prisoner.

Ocho shrugged. "Doctor was surprised when the coywolv came in. The girl's pure Drowned Cities. Don't matter if she's a castoff or not. She's got the war instinct."

"Maggot was smart, all right."

"Yeah. But the doctor?" Ocho shrugged.

The body in the field said it all. The old man had no survival instinct. Marching into a combat zone like he had a big old red cross on his back and a company of Chinese peacekeepers behind him. Stupid. They weren't fighting that kind of war. Ocho wondered if maybe the doctor had just gone crazy. Sometimes it happened. Civvies went out of their head and did stupid stuff. Got themselves killed, even when they could've gotten away clean.

But not the castoff. That girl knew what was what. He'd seen it in her eyes, right when she brought the coywolv down on them. Killer instinct.

Ocho scanned the torched village again. A dog was picking

through the smoke, circling in on a body. Ocho wondered if it was coming back to its owner, or if it was looking for dinner.

"Got to figure the castoff headed north with the half-man." He spat. "I would've."

"Yeah." The lieutenant stared down at their prisoner. "That how it went? She just left you to die, huh? Headed north and ditched your maggot ass?"

The kid looked like he was about to cry again. Ocho wished the LT would just hurry up and do the job. He stared out at the jungle.

"It's going to be hell trying to pick up their trail," Ocho said. "All those civvies out there, running around, trampling things down?" He shook his head. "Lot of jungle to search."

"Missed our chance, you think?"

Ocho glanced over at Sayle, trying to tell if he wanted an honest answer or if he was trying to trick Ocho into showing weakness. Showing he wasn't all in for the cause. But the lieutenant was just staring out at the jungle, too.

Finally Ocho said, "I don't see how we're going to pick up its trail. If that girl did a doctor job on the dog-face, that means it's mobile now. It was just dumb luck that we even got close to it before, and it ripped us up." Ocho touched his ribs. "Did four of us, and that was when it was down and out."

"It's still wounded," the LT said. "It isn't made of magic."

"Yeah, but it sounds like it's doing a hell of a lot better than the last time we tangled with it."

Lieutenant Sayle snorted. "You may be right, Sergeant." He turned and headed into the village, waved back at Ocho. "Get rid of the maggot."

Ocho looked down at the kid. He had snot all over his face from crying and his eyes were red.

"Sorry, maggot." He waved for his boys. Tweek and Gutty grabbed the maggot and scooped up a machete. Good soldiers. They knew better than to waste a bullet.

"Put his neck over some wood," Tweek was saying. "I don't wanna dent the blade."

Gutty got the kid laid over a log, and then the maggot seemed to snap to awareness. Like he finally realized what was up. He started struggling and screaming, while Tweek and Gutty tried to control him. For a skinny bastard, he sure fought.

And then, all of sudden, the boy stopped fighting. His chest heaved and he was covered with sweat, but his fight was gone. He looked up at Ocho, as Gutty and Tweek knelt on his back. Ocho had the unnerving feeling the licebiter was putting some kind of Deepwater hex on him, but the kid didn't say anything.

Ocho turned away and headed into the burning town.

Sorry, maggot. Wrong place, right time.

It was the same problem all the time. Sometimes you got lucky, ended up recruited instead of dead. Got a machete and a bottle of acid, and you ran around trying to show everyone

210

how you were worth keeping. Putting as much blood on you as you could, so that Sayle wouldn't dump your body in a ditch. Sometimes you just got your head chopped off.

Behind him, he could hear the kid start struggling again.

"Dammit! Would you hold him, Gutty?"

"I am! Licebiter's strong."

Ocho turned back. He limped over to the licebiter and squatted down in front of him. Waved his boys to leave off trying to chop him.

"You want to live?" he asked.

The kid didn't know how to answer. The way he'd been pushed over the log, his face was all red and puffy with tears and fear. Ocho waited, then prodded him.

"Speak up, maggot. You want to live?"

The kid nodded hesitantly.

"You think you got some soldier in you? Wanna fight for the UPF? Sign on? Fight the patriotic fight?"

The kid sort of grunted, still held down by Tweek and Gutty.

Ocho grinned and slapped the kid on the back of the head. "Sure you do." He glanced over at Tweek. "Go get me some hot metal."

"You gonna brand him?"

"Sure. Born out of fire, right?" He stared into the war maggot's eyes. "It's how we all are."

A minute later, Tweek came back with a hunk of rebar, glowing and smoking from a burned building. He held it in one hand, by smoking cloth.

Ocho took the metal bar. Even with a cloth wrapping, it was hot in his hand. He squatted down by the small shivering boy. It was hot. Good and hot.

"What's your name?"

"Mouse."

Ocho shook his head. "Not anymore. We got to give you a new name. You ain't Mouse, anymore." He studied the village and destruction, hunting for a soldier name.

The place reminded him of his own town, a long time ago. He was surprised this place had lasted as long as it had. You couldn't live close to war and not have it grab you eventually. His own family had always been sure that war was going to stay down in the Drowned Cities, where all the fools were, but war was like the sea. It just kept rising, until one day the tide rolled in and you were up to your neck in it.

The wind shifted and smoke poured over them. Was that this boy's name? Smoke?

Ocho scanned the blackened place, considering. The trees guttered with flame, some of them half-burned, twisted into spooky shapes by the fires. Stones sizzled with heat. Ocho thought he smelled meat burning. Pig or human. One or the other.

He considered names as he studied the kid. *You were dead*, Ocho thought. *And now you're not.*

Raised up from the dead. Got a mission, still. Yeah. That was all right.

Ocho smacked the kid on the back of the head again. "Your name's Ghost."

He crouched down with the brand. "This is gonna hurt, little buddy. You better not cry. You cry, Tweek here will chop your head off. UPF's tough, right? We don't flinch, we never surrender. You're Ghost. And you're UPF, forever, warboy. Forever."

He stared into the face of the sniveling war maggot, all pale and sooty with his wide scared eyes. "You ain't going to thank me, maggot. But it's better than dead." And then he pressed the brand into the little war maggot's face, three horizontal lines.

The cooking smell of pig curled up from the brand. The boy shook and fought, but he held on and rode through the pain, just like they all had.

When Ocho straightened, the warboy was gasping, but he hadn't cried and he hadn't begged.

He slapped the kid on the back. "Good job, soldier." He waved at Tweek and Gutty. "Go get our brother drunk."

"You going soft on me, Sergeant?"

Ocho stiffened. The lieutenant's voice was soft, but there was a warning there. Like the movement of a cottonmouth in the swamp, coming at you, and then you were bit and poisoned and dying.

Ocho turned. The boys had found a bunch of antique furniture that they'd hacked up and piled into a bonfire, and everyone who wasn't standing patrol against civvies coming back and looking for revenge was drunk off their asses. One of the soldiers had put the head of an old civvy lady on a stick and was running around saying, "But I don't even like castoffs!" while everybody laughed.

And now Sayle was standing beside him. "You going soft?"

Ocho drank from his bottle. It was some bottle that had used to hold...what? He studied the label. Some kind of cleaning fluid, if the bleached-out picture on the plastic was right. Showed a Chinese lady with a floor that was sparkling bright as the sun. Ocho drank again.

Van had found the liquor store in the back of the old lady's sundries shop, hidden. She'd tucked all the booze away as soon as UPF showed up, but Van had that nose for liquor. Ocho drank while he considered his answer.

"Soft?" he asked, and handed the bottle up to the man who controlled his world.

Sayle snorted. "*Soft?*" he mimicked. "You know what I'm talking about." He waved the bottle over at the company. "You recruited that war maggot?"

Ocho followed the man's gesture to the bonfire, where the new recruit stood surrounded by soldier boys. At their command, Ghost was taking drinks from a bottle that they were passing around the fire. He was scared. Eyes like a rabbit, looking for a way out. The half-bars Ocho had laid on his cheek stood out, red and blistered.

"He's tough," Ocho said. "And he's loyal."

"How you figure?"

"Followed the doctor into hell."

"That's not loyal. That's just stupid."

"There's a difference?" Ocho deadpanned, making Sayle snort his alcohol. "I figure if he's fool enough to follow that crazy doctor, he might be smart enough to follow someone who saves his maggot ass."

He took another swig of burning liquor. It was trash. Nowhere near as good as the stuff that got smuggled in on Lawson & Carlson ships when the recycling went out, but that was what you got with the homegrown stuff. Probably make him blind if he drank enough of it. His old man used to say you could drink homemade hooch and go blind.

"What you going to do when that little pup turns and tries to bite you?" Sayle asked. "Maybe puts a bullet in the back of your head?"

Ocho shook his head. "He won't."

"Big bet, Sergeant."

"Nah. I'd put a million Red Chinese on that boy." Ocho studied the recruit. "We're all he's got."

When you were alone in the rising ocean, you grabbed whatever raft passed by.

23

COWARD.

Coward. Coward coward cowardcowardcoward...

The word kept running through Mahlia's head, and with every step away from the village, the accusation echoed louder.

I tried to tell them. I tried to save their dumb asses. They would have been fine, if they'd just listened to me.

Doctor Mahfouz was always talking about places where kids grew up without worrying about bolt holes and what to do if soldier boys came. Places where you lived past twenty. Mouse should have been born there. He just didn't have the Drowned Cities instinct. He was too nice for his own damn good. Just a sad-sack farm kid who didn't know how to stay alive.

Yeah. He was so dumb, he saved you, *right?*

Mahlia hated the thought, but couldn't keep it from surfacing. Mouse had charged, when he should have run in the opposite direction. He threw rocks and drew gunfire, even though it was the dumbest thing in the world.

Why didn't you do the same for him? You owe him. If it had been you in that village, he would have done something.

And that was why he'd gone back for the doctor, and all the townspeople, and how he'd gotten himself killed.

Coward.

The word kept running through her head as she stumbled through the jungle, accompanied by the silent, shambling half-man.

Coward.

The thought burrowed into her heart as darkness fell. It coiled in her guts as she wedged herself amongst the boughs of a tree to sleep. And in the morning, it woke with her and clung to her back, riding on her shoulders as she climbed down, hungry and exhausted from nightmares.

She was a coward.

Yellow dawn light filtered through the jungle, highlighting misty humidity. Mahlia looked around at the greenery, feeling sick, knowing she would feel this way until she died. She would never escape it. She'd run away instead of helping the only family she had left.

She was just like her father.

When the peacekeepers finally gave up on their fifteen-year attempt to civilize the Drowned Cities, the man hadn't

217

even looked back. He'd just run for his troop transport with the rest of his soldiers as the warlords flooded back into the city.

Mahlia remembered the gunfire and explosions. Remembered how she and her mother had run frantically for the docks, sure that the peacekeepers had saved berths for them. She remembered people leaping into Potomac Harbor as the last peacekeeping troop transports and corporate trading ships set sail without them. Remembered those huge white sails unfurling, clipper ships rising on hydrofoils as winds caught canvas.

Mahlia and her mother had stood on the docks and waved and waved, begging for the ships to come back, begging for her father to care, and then they'd been shoved forward into the ocean by the desperate press of others behind, all of them begging for the same thing.

Her father had abandoned her, and now she'd done the same. Mouse and the doctor had risked everything for her, and she'd just walked away. Saving her own skin, because it was easier than risking everything in return.

That's how people get killed. If you did like them, you would've been dead a hundred times over.

She'd seen it often enough as she tried to escape the Drowned Cities, after the collapse of the peacekeepers. She'd seen people stand up, determined to hold on to principles. People who thought there was right and wrong. People who tried to save others. People like her mother who had died so horribly that even now Mahlia's mind shied from the jagged memory. Only Mahlia had survived. While all the other castoffs were getting cut down by Army of God and UPF and Freedom Militia, Mahlia had taken Sun Tzu's principles to heart, and survived.

The problem with surviving was that you ended up with the ghosts of everyone you'd ever left behind riding on your shoulders. As she stood in the cool jungle dawn, it felt like they were all there with her. School friends. Teachers. Shop owners. Old ladies. Families. Her mother. And now, Doctor Mahfouz and Mouse.

No one else could see all the bodies she'd left behind, but they were there, looking at her. Or maybe that was just her, looking at herself, and not liking what she saw. Knowing she could never escape her own judging gaze.

"I'm going back," Mahlia said suddenly.

The half-man turned at her voice. In the dawn, he showed as something stranger and more alien than she had understood before. He was eating something that looked like it might have been snake, but he gulped it down before she got a good look. For a brief instant, it was like she was seeing the entire unnatural melding of his DNA: the tiger, the hyena, the dog, the man, all smashed together.

"It is too late," the half-man said. "If there are any survivors, they will not thank you for your return. The ones you care about are dead."

"Then I'm going to bury them."

Tool regarded her. "You increase your danger if you circle back."

"Why're you always afraid of things? Don't you want to fight? They hurt you, too, right? Why don't you got any fight in you? I thought you were all blood and rust and killer instinct."

Tool growled. For a second Mahlia thought he was about to attack. Then he said, "I do not fight battles that cannot be won. Do not confuse that with cowardice."

"What happens if you don't get to choose the fight? What if it just comes for you?"

Tool regarded her. "Is this such a case? Do I have no choices? Is this battle preordained by the Fates?" He pointed northward. "There are more than enough battles ahead of us, and those ones at least have the merit of being to some purpose. Going back to your village is pointless."

Mahlia glared at his mocking words. "Fine. Do whatever you do. I'm going back."

She turned and started down the jungle trail. Tool was right, she knew. They were already dead. It was stupid to even bother. The doctor was gone. Mouse was gone. Going back wasn't going to fix any of it. But she couldn't stop herself.

Going back didn't make her any less of a coward, but it was the only thing she could do to get rid of the disgust for herself that weighed in her guts. Maybe if she went back, the ghosts wouldn't hang on her so hard. Maybe she'd be able to sleep, and not feel shame.

Tool called after her, but she ignored him.

*   *   *

The sky overhead was bright and blue, but Banyan Town was black.

Mahlia crouched on the jungle verge, studying the place, trying to see the hidden dangers. Sweat dripped from her chin. Mosquitoes whined in her ears, but she kept watching.

Nothing moved.

Silent fields stretched to charred, smoking rubble. Black ash coated the ground, drifts filling furrows where crops had burned. Even after a day, smoke still rose in coils, gray snakes writhing up from the ground, marking where tree roots smoldered beneath the dirt. A couple of fruit trees guttered with flames deep in their bowels, black and tortured ribbons of glowing coals clawing the sky like charred fingers, all that was left of Banyan's orchards.

Every part of Mahlia's survivor's instinct told her to lie low.

Walk away. Just walk away.

But still she crouched, staring at the open expanse.

She hated how exposed the fields looked. As soon as she started to cross, she'd stand out like a flare. She kept looking for better cover, some way to sneak into the town without giving herself away, but there wasn't anything left standing.

You a coward, or not?

After half an hour of watching swirls of ravens and vultures rise and fall over town with no sign of other life, she gave up on being smart. Whatever had happened to Mouse, she needed to know, and the only way she was going to find out was if she went in.

She started across the fields, watching for signs of ambush. Ash rustled under her feet like leaves. Insects creaked and sawed in the humidity, but nothing rose to challenge her.

Halfway across the field, she found Doctor Mahfouz.

He was facedown in a black slurry of mud and ash and half-burned wheat. The mud stuck to Mahlia's feet and legs, staining them black. She crouched and rolled him over. His glasses were shattered. She realized that the mud was from his own blood, mixing with the dirt and ash. Fates. What a mess. She wiped at the muddy shattered lenses.

He'd walked right into it. Like he was one of the soldiers who fought for the Army of God. One of those soldier boys who wore an amulet that was supposed to protect them from bullets.

"How could you be so stupid?" she asked, and then she felt bad for saying it aloud. He might have been stupid, but he'd been kind. It seemed like he deserved some respect, or something. Not this, at least. Not to end up with his face shoved into bloody char.

Mahlia started to try to put his glasses back on, but it was too hard to get them to fit, and it was pointless, anyway. She crouched there, holding the glasses, feeling stuck.

He'd been kind and compassionate, and he'd stood tall

for her when no one else would, and now he was just as dead as all the people who'd spit on her and called her castoff.

So what was she supposed to do now? Was she supposed to pray or something?

Everyone had different rites for their bodies, offerings they were supposed to make, but the doctor hadn't been Deepwater Christian, or Scavenge God. He'd had a little prayer rug that he sometimes got out to pray on at different times of day, and he'd sometimes read out of a book with script that Mahlia couldn't piece together and that he'd called Arabic, but she wasn't sure what Arabics did for their dead.

Fire, maybe. Her father said that the Chinese burned their bodies. Maybe that would do. She grabbed the doctor under the shoulders and started pulling, grunting with the effort. Dead, he was surprisingly heavy. A leaden sack, passively resisting every tug.

Mahlia kept at it, dragging him through mud and ash. She grunted and sweated and hauled. His shirt tore away under her fists. She lost her balance and thudded back in the ash, exhausted and defeated.

This was crazy. There wasn't even anything left to burn in the town. The UPF had already burned everything. There was no way she could build a funeral pyre.

Mahlia sat in the middle of the field, dripping sweat, staring at the dead man.

They don't even let us die right.

She wanted to cry. She couldn't even get Doctor Mahfouz passed on to whatever afterlife he was supposed to have. She didn't know how long she sat, staring at the man's body. Minutes. Hours.

A shadow loomed.

Mahlia gave a startled gasp. The half-man stood over her.

"The dead are always heavy."

The half-man scooped up the doctor, and even though the man's body was stiff with rigor mortis, Tool lifted him easily and slung him over his shoulder.

24

TOOL LISTENED TO the girl as she searched the village, while he dug into the earth, preparing a grave with a shovel he'd found abandoned. He heard her calling Mouse's name, over and over, and had to stifle the urge to silence her, to remonstrate with her for breaking sound discipline. She was foolish with her grief.

Let the girl mourn, he told himself. *The soldiers are gone.*

Still, it irritated him. She had no discipline. If they were to march north together, she would be a liability.

Leave her, then.

But he didn't, and Tool wondered at it. It was time to move. Past time. He could sense more and more eyes returning. He wanted to be well clear of the village by nightfall.

And yet still Mahlia searched, calling Mouse's name, turning dead charred bodies and digging through burn-hollowed buildings, and still Tool lingered with her.

Eventually, Mahlia stumbled back to where Tool was lowering the doctor into his grave.

"Maybe they buried Mouse," she said.

Tool shook his head. "No. These ones do not waste effort on such niceties."

The girl looked for a moment as if she was going to cry, but then she mastered herself, and helped him move the earth back over the doctor's body, filling the grave. Tool went and found large chunks of concrete lying in the blackened rubble and piled them over the grave, moving slowly, testing his strength against his memories of what he should have been able to carry.

He moved the last of the rubble into place.

"Will that keep the coywolv out?" Mahlia asked, looking at the pile of concrete and stones.

"It's more than anyone has given me or mine," Tool said sharply. He almost smiled when she flinched at his words.

Humans were so precious about their dead. When his own people died on distant battlefields, no one cared to gather them or bury them. If you were lucky, you were present to hear their stories, and if not, you told their stories after the battle. But you did not linger like this.

Human beings lingered. It made them vulnerable.

The girl stood, staring at the pile of rubble. Her face was smeared with mud and blood and ash. Just another bit of debris in the wreckage of war. Just like all the other children of all the other wars that Tool had ever fought.

If she had been born in another place, during another time, he supposed she might have been the sort of girl who concerned herself with boyfriends and parties and fashionable clothes. If she had lived in a Boston arcology or a Beijing super tower, perhaps. Instead, she carried scars, and her hand was a stump, and her eyes were hard like obsidian, and her smile was hesitant, as if anticipating the suffering that she knew awaited her, just around the corner.

A little ways off, a dog was picking through the ashes, hunting for prizes. It started to nip and tear into a dead goat. Finally succeeded in ripping out the goat's intestines. Another mongrel approached, teeth bared. It snarled, and the first sped off with its prize of guts.

The girl watched.

"That was Reg's dog," she said. And then she said, "That was his goat, too."

Tool wondered if the girl was going mad. It happened to people. Sometimes they saw too much and their minds went away. They lost the will to survive. They curled up and surrendered to madness.

Tool decided there was nothing he could do for the girl, but he wouldn't leave good meat to feral dogs. He left the girl standing by the grave and headed for the goat.

The new dog lowered its head and bared its teeth. Growled as Tool approached.

Tool's own lips peeled back.

Oh? You think to challenge me, brother?

He snarled, and the dog fled, cowering. Tool almost laughed at the pathetic mongrel. He gathered up the goat, feeling increasing satisfaction. He was healing, and he would eat well. Soon, he would be himself again.

It had been a mistake to drift close to the Drowned Cities, to think that there would be a place for him in its chaos.

But now he was healing, and soon he would be gone.

Mahlia watched Tool stalk the dog. The half-man's snarl echoed in the ruins, full of blood and challenge.

The dog fled, its tail between its legs, looking back in fear to see if it was being followed. Beyond the half-man, Mahlia caught sight of something else: a person scuttling through the ruins. Hiding.

For a second Mahlia hoped it was Mouse, and then she was afraid it was soldiers returning, and then she realized it was neither.

A woman emerged into the open and stopped short, staring at them. Amaya. Her clothes were torn. She was nearly naked. Bloody streaks marked her body. Beatings or forest scratches, Mahlia couldn't tell. She froze at the sight of Mahlia and Tool.

"Amaya?" Mahlia whispered.

Horror filled Amaya's expression. To Mahlia, she looked like a dog that had been beaten. Amaya's frightened eyes flicked to Tool, then back to Mahlia.

"You," she whispered. "You did this."

Mahlia took a step toward the woman, wanting to help, or apologize, to do anything at all. "What happened?"

"You did this," Amaya said again. And then, with hatred. "You did this!"

Mahlia took another step toward her, but at her approach the woman's face filled with fear, and she fled.

Mahlia stared after the ragged woman stumbling away. Was she supposed to go after her? Amaya wouldn't stand a chance on her own. Did she owe Amaya something for everything she'd lost?

"You cannot help her," Tool said as the woman disappeared into the jungle greenery.

"She won't make it on her own," Mahlia said.

"No. But there are a few other villagers who escaped. More like her. They are returning."

"If I hadn't riled the soldiers, none of this would have happened."

Tool snorted. "Do not overestimate your own importance."

"But it's true. If I hadn't set the coywolv on them, the soldiers wouldn't have done this!"

Tool growled. "Soldiers have been looting and burning for generations. Perhaps they burned the town because of you, or perhaps they did it because they disliked the whiskey. Soldiers kill and rape and loot for a thousand reasons. The one thing I am certain of is that neither you nor I did this burning." Tool reached down and turned Mahlia's gaze to meet his own. "Do not seek to own what others have done."

Mahlia knew that Doctor Mahfouz would have disagreed with everything Tool said. She could practically see the doctor shaking his head at the creature's words.

Tool seemed to wall himself off from any responsibility at all. Like nothing he did mattered. Doctor Mahfouz would have said that every action connected to every other action, and that was why the Drowned Cities was the way it was.

The Drowned Cities hadn't always been broken. People broke it. First they called people traitors and said they didn't belong. Said these people were good and those people were evil, and it kept going, because people always responded, and pretty soon the place was a roaring hell because no one took responsibility for what they did, and how it would drive others to respond. Mahlia wanted to argue with the half-man, but he suddenly stiffened. His ears pricked up and he sniffed the air.

"It's time we were on our way," he said. "I smell more villagers returning."

"I still can't find Mouse," Mahlia objected.

"No. And you will not." The half-man paused, regarding her. Seeming to consider his words. "There are tracks on the far side of the village. Not just the boots of soldiers. Bare feet, too. Sandals. All sizes. They took prisoners."

Mahlia felt a sudden rush of hope. "So you think they took Mouse? You know where they went?"

"He is an ideal age. Big enough to carry a gun and use it well, young enough to train and fanaticize."

Understanding dawned on Mahlia. "You think he's recruited? You think he's gone soldier boy?"

"With the proper stimuli, anyone can be turned into killer."

"A killer like you?" Mahlia asked, but Tool didn't seem offended; he just nodded. "Very much like me. I was bred to kill, but I was *trained* to do it well."

"But Mouse isn't a soldier boy," she said. "He's not like that. He's good. He's kind. He..."

He likes dumb jokes, and he likes to catch snakes and eggs, and he's always up for a trip into the jungle, and he can't read books for the life of him, and he's scared of sleeping inside at night, and when you're feeling like hell because you're a castoff, he comes around and sits with you. And when the Army of God's got you by the hair, and you got one hand already lying on the ground, he steps up and saves you.

"He's not that kind of person."

"Soon, though. These armies are experienced in recruiting the young. They will bind him to his comrades, and they will mold him to their needs."

"He's not like that!"

Tool shrugged. "Then they will kill him and find someone who is."

The half-man spoke with infuriating detachment. Mahlia wanted to punch him in his giant doglike face. "We've got to save him."

Tool just looked at her. She could almost see the smile

there, the joke of her saying it, but she pressed. "We can't just let them have him. We got to go after him."

"You will fail."

"Not if you help me."

The half-man's lips curled back, revealing teeth. "You presume too much, girl. My debt to you is more than paid."

"So why are you still here?" she asked. "Why come back here? Why help me at all?"

Tool growled. "I balance my debts. If you wish my help in escaping from this place, that is fair. You saved my life when those others would have let me die. But those soldiers take their prisoners into the heart of the Drowned Cities. It was difficult enough for me to escape Colonel Stern last time. To do it again would be impossible. Suicide is not something I owe you or yours."

"What if we saved Mouse before they get there?"

"You overestimate my health and abilities."

"When you jumped me and Mouse, you were scary fast."

"Even I cannot destroy a company of trained soldiers, not without weapons or support."

"We could stalk them."

"We?" Tool raised his eyebrows, looking down on her. "You think you are some fine predator? A swamp panther or coywolv?" He pretended to inspect her. "Where are your teeth and claws, girl?" He bared his teeth. "Where is your bite?"

Mahlia glared up at him, hating him. Hating how he

dismissed her. She turned and stormed into the ruins, hunting. She found a burned machete, sooty and blackened, but with metal still sound. Tool watched her with a bemused expression as she returned. She held it up.

"I got teeth."

"Do you?" Tool's features turned predatory. "They have guns and acid and training." He leaned close, his monstrous gaze blazing with promise of hell. "They will break you bit by bit, and then, when they have turned you into a cowering, begging animal, they will kill you. Don't tell me you have teeth. You are a rabbit attacking coywolv."

Part of her knew he was right. If a half-man wouldn't face all those soldiers, what made her think she could? It was stupid. The kind of war maggot fantasy that got you killed.

"I go north now. If you are wise, you will accompany me."

Mahlia wanted to listen to him. Hadn't she already lost enough here? She had a way out. With the half-man to help, she could make it past all the armies and war lines. She could get away from the Drowned Cities for good.

Mahlia tried the idea out in her mind, trying to imagine a safe life in a place like Seascape Boston. Maybe she could doctor there. Maybe she could just not wake up in the middle of the night, having a nightmare that the Army of God was coming for her.

But even as she tried to imagine some better life, all she could really think of was Mouse, jumping up and hollering and throwing rocks at soldiers, like the Rust Saint rising up, blessing her with a second chance at life.

"You do what you do," she said finally. "Mouse would come for me, and I'm not leaving him. Not again. I'm done with that. I'm done with running."

"You will die."

"I guess. I don't know." She shook her head, trying to pick through her feelings. "I used to think I was alive just because I kept getting away. If someone didn't put a bullet in my head, I was winning. I was still breathing, right?" She looked at the blackened land around her, feeling tired and sad and alone.

"But now I'm thinking it ain't like that. Now I'm thinking that once you got enough dead looking over your shoulder, you're dead anyway. Don't matter if you're still walking and talking, they weigh you down." She looked up at Tool, hoping against hope. "You sure you don't want to help me?"

The half-man didn't say anything at all.

Tool watched as the girl departed from the far side of the village. She crisscrossed the ground, trying to pick up the trail, and then headed into the jungle. One small and determined girl, stalking into the teeth of war.

Tool could respect the stubbornness, but it was difficult to respect the stupidity. A lone girl with a broken blade against an army. Tool had faced terrible odds in his life, but the girl faced worse.

What honor was there in suicide?

The boy is her pack.

Not mine, though.

With a growl, he turned in the opposite direction and started walking north to safety. He would need to be clever, but it was more than possible to penetrate the borders that Manhattan Orleans and Seascape Boston had thrown up to contain the chaos of the Drowned Cities. Though they might patrol their borders with armies full of his brethren, there were always weak points, and Tool was very good at exploiting others' weaknesses.

Tool glanced over his shoulder, looking to see if the girl might have changed her mind, but she was gone. Swallowed up by the land.

The Drowned Cities ate its children.

You fight for yourself now. Do not mind that girl.

But still it rankled that a one-handed girl had the temerity to demand his loyalty, just as Caroa always had. People were all the same. Always demanding that others do their killing for them. Tool had slaughtered tiger guards and hyena men, but it was the humans who were most frightening. Humans had created generals and colonels and majors, people who kept their hands clean while they ordered others to cover themselves in blood.

Tool wondered if it was his loyal nature, bred and trained into him, that made him feel guilty for leaving her to her fate. Some vestige of the training that had made him so obedient to his original masters. Was that why he kept following her, trying to persuade her to leave this doomed land? Had he simply been reverting to his original conditioning? The loyal dog who would not leave its master?

Is she your master, then?

Tool bared his teeth at the thought.

But still he heard the girl's taunting voice: *How come if you're so strong, you're so afraid of everything?*

He didn't fear death. But he would never throw himself into pointless battle again. That was what the generals and their war machines demanded. He was not that sort of dog. Not anymore. He had fought too long, at too much cost, to allow anyone such power over him.

Are you afraid? a sly voice insinuated.

Tool snarled at the thought. *I have never lost a battle.*

But have you ever won?

25

PURSUING THE SOLDIERS was easy. Between them and their captives, they left a wide trail.

Mahlia slipped through the jungle, following.

The trail wound along one of the old roads, made of concrete and now carpeted with soil and leaves and vines. New trees punctured the way, poking up through cracks in its tortured surface, but still, the way was wider and more open, and the vegetation wasn't as thick as the true forest. At times, the trail leaped into the air, arching high on concrete pylons, following the ancient expressways and byways from the time when everyone had had gasoline to burn and cars to drive.

Up high, Mahlia would pause and look ahead, seeking signs of the soldiers, but for all her speed, they seemed to move faster. And she had to slow and forage as she went.

Her feet became sore. She became thirsty. She drank from brackish water, pushing aside slime and water skippers, and always she kept alert. At times, she could hear the boom of the 999 off in the distance, the far roaring of the Drowned Cities, and it frightened her to think of what she was walking into.

But she kept going, knowing she couldn't live with herself if she didn't. Knowing that she was doing exactly what her father had always scorned about Drowned Cities people. They were stupid and never thought strategically. They rushed pell-mell into revenge and bloodshed and war and death, even if it made no sense.

Mahlia remembered her father kicking off combat boots and cursing the Drowned Cities and its thirst for conflict. Stripping off body armor as her mother had clucked around him, cleansing wounds.

"They're animals. Nothing but dogs, tearing at each other."

"Not all of us," her mother said soothingly as she helped him into a steaming bath. "Just because you've been here a few years doesn't mean you know everything about us."

"Animals," he repeated. "You only defend this place because you don't know how good life can be. If you'd seen Beijing, or Island Shanghai, you'd know. In China we aren't like this. We aren't dogs tearing at one another's throats. We plan. We think ahead. We cooperate. But you people?"

He snorted. "If you had any sense, you'd spend less time shooting at one another and calling each other traitors, and more time building seawalls." He closed his eyes in the steaming bath. "*Sha.* Stupid. All of you. Too stupid to drink water even when it's given."

On the second day, the coywolv caught her.

She'd found a new ruin of a town, and amongst its rubble had found some sun-cracked sandals lying in the junk of the place. She remembered the wire and glass and rubble of the city. Her feet were tough, but she doubted she could walk over raw glass.

She sat on the ground and slipped the sandals onto her feet, but their plastic cracked as she walked on them, so she tossed them aside. They were too old, and too sun-broken to be any good. But she spied a plastic jug that looked good for carrying water, and there was some rope as well, and then she'd straightened.

The coywolv was staring at her, eyes like lamps. Yellow eyes as predatory as the half-man's.

Mahlia's skin prickled. She slowly retreated, looking left and right. Sure enough, she saw other shadows flitting through the ruins.

Fates. Who knew how long they'd been stalking her? If they were revealing themselves, it meant that they'd already set up their kill.

Coywolv were smart like that. Liked to follow and circle and evaluate, and then they came in on you and you were dead. Sun Tzu would have approved, but all Mahlia felt was a sick fear as she realized the beasts had chosen to attack her in an area of ruins that had nothing but weedy little trees no more than the width of her wrist, and few rubble-pile walls. Nothing to climb up on. No place easy to flee.

She hefted her rusty machete. The coywolv before her seemed to understand the challenge. Its lips drew back, showing fangs, and it started to growl. But it wasn't the one she needed to worry about. Behind her, the wind rushed.

Mahlia spun and swung. The second coywolv twisted aside, easy and nimble. Her blade whistled harmlessly through empty air. The coywolv lunged again, snapping, baring teeth and growling, circling as its partner nipped at her heels.

Mahlia spun again, swinging, warding off the pair. She needed to get to a tree. If she could get up high, they'd trap her for a while, but they weren't hunting dogs. They'd eventually move on to easier prey after a few hours or a day. But the closest tree that looked climbable was more than a hundred yards away.

Don't panic. Don't run. Just get moving.

If she panicked and ran, they'd bring her down just like a small forest deer. They'd rip her legs out and pile on top of her, and she'd never stand up again.

Claws scrabbled on rubble behind her.

Mahlia turned and swung. She hit fur with the flat of her machete. The coywolv snarled, leaped back, then lunged again. Mahlia screamed and charged it, swinging again and this time the blade cut across the coywolv's mouth.

Turn! TURN!

There would be a third attacking now. They always coordinated. They worked together. She spun, swinging the machete, and slashed it away. It snarled. The first one circled her, nipping in, faking an attack. She feinted at it, trying to run it off, but it bared its teeth and hardly backed off at all.

She spun, swinging, expecting another attack from behind, but the other coywolv were out of reach. She was starting to panic, jumping and turning at imagined sounds.

The coywolv all circled, darting in on her, growling and snapping and then twisting away.

Fates, she needed her back against something. But the weedy trees offered no cover, and now a fourth coywolv joined its brethren. Ears flat back, head low, stalking.

She'd been so busy worrying about soldier boys and villagers she'd forgotten the jungle had hunters of its own, and now she was going to die for it.

Behind her, a whisper of motion. She whipped her machete about and caught the coywolv in midleap. The blade bit deep but the coywolv crashed into her and she went tumbling. The other coywolv leaped for her. Teeth slashed at her face. Another went for her legs, teeth tearing.

Mahlia threw up the stump of her arm. A coywolv bit deep. She screamed. Suddenly, a roaring filled the air. The coywolv was jerked off her and blood rained down. Howling and yelping. A hurricane of movement. The coywolv that had been attacking her legs evaporated into a whirl of fur and showering blood. Mahlia curled into a ball as the roaring increased, shaking the world, louder then war.

Suddenly everything went silent. Mahlia scrambled to her feet. All around, torn and twisted coywolv bodies lay scattered.

Amid the carnage, Tool stood tall. Battered but vital, covered in blood. His machete dripped with gore. Mahlia clutched at her wounded arm, staring at the transformed battleground. All the coywolv were torn apart. One of them lay against a tree, broken and whimpering. One was ripped in half. Another had its head cleaved open.

Tool knelt down over the carcass of the last.

With his machete, he pried into its body, then set the blade aside and punched his fist through the coywolv's ribcage. A second later, his hand emerged gripping the heart of the beast, and Tool bent his head to feed.

Mahlia felt a chill. As quickly as the place had become a battlefield, now it was nothing but a slaughterhouse. They were all dead. Every single one of them. In seconds, Tool had torn them all apart. The carnage was astounding. Worse than what soldier boys did, and a thousand times as fast. She'd never seen anything like it.

She must have made a sound, for Tool looked up at her, blood dripping from his muzzle. He eyed her wounds. She could see him evaluating her.

Doctor Mahfouz would have rushed to her and clucked

and worried after every scratch and bit of blood. Tool simply glanced at her shredded arm, scraped face, and clawed body, and dismissed it all.

"You truly believe you can reenter the city?" he asked.

It took a second for the half-man's words to sink in, and then Mahlia got it. She wasn't alone. This warrior monster was with her. Her heart leaped. She wasn't alone. She wasn't powerless. She had a chance.

"Can you do it?" the half-man asked again.

Mahlia hesitated, remembering the terrors of her previous escape, the panic, the huddled hiding places, the nights spent in murky drowned buildings, then nodded. "I got out, didn't I?"

"It will have changed."

"I can get us back in. My mother, she had places where she hid her antiques, before she sold them. There's places we can hide. And there's ways through the buildings, if you can swim."

Tool nodded. "So."

He straightened and went over to the coywolv Mahlia had chopped with her machete. It still writhed on the ground, whimpering and baring its teeth. With a swift motion, Tool snapped its neck, then set his grip on the animal's body. His muscles bulged.

The coywolv's ribcage shattered like matchsticks.

"If we are pack, then conquest is our sustenance, sister."

He plunged his hand into the coywolv's frame. With a wet tearing, the heart came out, glistening and full of

243

blood, veins and arteries torn. The muscle of life. Tool held it out to her. "Our enemies give us strength."

Blood ran from his fist. Mahlia saw the challenge in the half-man's eye.

She limped over to the battle-scarred monster and held out her hand. The heart was surprisingly heavy as Tool poured it into her palm. She lifted the muscle to her lips and bit deep.

Blood ran down her chin.

Tool nodded his approval.

-PART TWO-

THE
DROWNED
CITIES

26

MOUSE'S FACE BURNED, a constant reminder of his new associates: Slim and Gutty, Stork and Van. TamTam and Boots and Alil, and dozens more.

They stood around and laughed and pointed their guns at the prisoners where they lay flat on the ground with their hands on the backs of their heads, and every one of the soldiers carried the same burned brand on his cheek that Mouse carried on his own.

"You're Glenn Stern's now, warboy," Gutty said, holding a pistol up to Mouse's head. "Elite! Best of the best."

Mouse held still, not sure what he was supposed to do. The barrel of the gun pressed behind his ear.

"Half-bar like you, there's only one question..." Gutty went on. "Do you got what it takes?"

Mouse hesitated.

Gutty jammed the gun hard into his head, and Mouse finally understood.

"Yes," he said.

"Yes, what?" Again the pistol jab.

"Yes, I got what it takes?"

"Then say it!" Gutty shouted. "I want to hear my warboy say it proud!"

"I got it!"

"GOT WHAT?"

"I got what it takes!"

"WHAT?"

"I GOT WHAT IT TAKES!" Mouse shouted as loud as he could, sure Gutty was going to blow his brains out.

"I CAN'T HEAR YOU, SOLDIER!"

"I GOT WHAT IT TAKES!"

"YOU A SOLDIER?"

"YES!"

"YOU CALL ME SIR, HALF-BAR! YOU CALL ME SIR!"

"YES, SIR!"

"THAT'S RIGHT, HALF-BAR! SING IT OUT!"

"I GOT WHAT IT TAKES, SIR!"

Mouse was shouting so loud his voice cracked. Gutty started laughing, doubled over with hilarity. Some of the other warboys were laughing with him.

"Damn," Gutty said. "You got what it takes, huh?"

Mouse wasn't sure what he was supposed to do, so he shouted again, "YES, SIR!"

Gutty slapped him upside the head, hard. "Shut up, maggot. You keep shouting like that, you'll bring Army of God down on us, get us all killed." He slapped Mouse again. "Now go get us some water. Fill our canteens."

He tossed a bunch of plastic bottles over to Mouse, a big pile of them, all covered with pictures of Accelerated Age cars. One of them said MOTOR OIL on the side. A big yellow one read ANTIFREEZE.

"Move, soldier!"

Smoldering with fear and humiliation and adrenaline, Mouse gathered up all the bottles.

Every minute with the UPF soldiers felt like he was balancing on a slime-slick swamp log, always about to slip and drown. He clutched all the bottles to his chest, and then, with a surge of hope, he realized that he was being sent away from the camp.

Just himself.

He was a dog sent to fetch, and they didn't take him seriously. But if he was quick about it, he could simply slip away. Disappear into the swamp, make like a lizard and disappear into the greenery.

Mouse glanced around, gauging the soldiers. They were all busy guarding prisoners. Talking with one another. Kicking back after their march. He gathered up the bottles and started off, forcing himself not to glance back, not to give away his intentions.

Don't look sneaky, he told himself. *Pretend like you're a good soldier boy.*

He walked quietly, listening to the jungle. No one was following. He was sure of it. He moved on through the jungle to where swamp water turned the ground squashy. Just a little farther. He reached the water.

Now, he thought. *Run.*

It was his chance. He needed to do it while they were distracted setting up camp. But something stilled him. Instead, Mouse crouched down and started filling bottles, listening to the jungle around him. Something didn't sound right. He listened to water gurgling into the jugs, and to the jungle, trying to figure it out. It was too quiet.

With a chill, he realized that he wasn't alone. Someone was watching him. He filled another canteen and casually let his eyes wander the greenery, as if he were simply bored and watching butterflies.

Nothing. But he was almost sure that he was being watched.

He finished filling the bottles. Straightened. Still nothing. But he couldn't get rid of the fear that he was being watched. Mouse knew the jungle. He'd lived in it and hunted it, and foraged it, and there was someone out there.

He hefted the water bottles. *Last chance to run. It won't get any better.* But he didn't move.

Why was he so scared?

The boys back there weren't supernatural. They were just thugs with guns. That was all. They couldn't watch him all the time. They weren't watching him now.

So why did he feel so afraid?

With a sick feeling, Mouse turned and started back toward the voices of the soldiers' camp. Knowing that he was chickenshit. Knowing that he should run for it, but too afraid to risk it.

He came into the clearing and dropped the water bottles in a pile. The camp was just as he'd left it. Soldiers joking. One of them, a blond kid with an acid-burned face who he thought was called Slick, was kicking the villagers every time they looked like they were lifting their heads or looking around. Other soldiers were squatting down, eating smoked jerky. Sergeant Ocho sat against a tree, looking sleepy, holding his side where he'd been ripped up by the half-man. Nothing out of place —

Mouse froze. Lieutenant Sayle stood on the far side of the clearing, smoking a hand-rolled cigarette. And he *was* watching him. Cold gray eyes, watching. They didn't show a thought or a feeling, his gaunt face was expressionless, but the man's eyes lingered.

Mouse made a hesitant salute as his skin prickled, aping what he'd seen the other warboys do. The lieutenant's lips quirked into something like a smile, mocking, but he gave a lazy return to Mouse's gesture of respect.

"Ghost!" someone shouted. "Hey, half-bar!" Mouse finally realized that he was being called and turned away from the lieutenant.

Gutty, the slack kid with the flappy skin on his arms and legs and belly.

"Go get us some firewood!" he ordered. "On the double,

251

boy! We don't keep no lazy maggots! You're elite! Let's see the sweat! UPF ain't afraid to sweat! Get on it, warboy!"

Mouse tried another salute. He was as exhausted as everyone else, but he stumbled for the forest again.

Maybe this time, he'd get free.

As he headed into the jungle, he saw a pair of soldier boys emerge from the trees, liquid shadows, from the direction of the swamps where he'd just been, gathering water.

For the barest instant, they glanced at Mouse, and his gut tightened into a knot of fear as they crossed the camp, headed for Lieutenant Sayle.

They were all around, Mouse realized.

It was all a test. Every bit of it. He wasn't crazy. There really were eyes on him.

"Make sure it's dry!" Gutty shouted. "I don't want no damn green wood smoking and going out!"

The jungle travel continued, warboys joking and talking themselves up, kicking the prisoners when they didn't move fast enough. They put Mouse on guard duty, standing over people who had been kind to him.

Sometimes one of the soldiers would come over to him and tell him that one of the prisoners had disobeyed.

Mouse was supposed to kick them in the ribs, or else pour acid on their backs, to make their skin smoke. He called them maggots and worse.

He kicked them to stand up when they lay on the ground.

Made them put their faces in the dirt, when they were standing tall.

Mouse kept expecting someone to give him a gun and order him to kill one of them. He'd heard stories about how the warlords recruited. He knew what was coming, and he dreaded it.

He kicked and beat and burned the townspeople, waiting for the next horror, and the people of Banyan Town looked at him with all the hatred that they used to reserve for soldier boys.

The warboys laughed and encouraged him.

Mouse wanted to cry, to make it all stop, to just refuse, but the one time he flinched, they made him do more. They made him hit harder. He hesitated to thrash Auntie Selima with a bamboo cane the way they wanted, and so they made him do it again and again, until her back was bloody ribbons. And then they made him salt the wounds.

Mouse wanted to vomit, but he learned the lesson.

Once, he apologized to Mr. Donato after he'd kicked the man in the ribs, for being too slow getting up, but he couldn't tell if the man was even listening.

"I'm sorry. I don't want to. I'm sorry."

But he was too much of a coward to stop doing what Lieutenant Sayle and the others ordered him to do.

One night, in the darkness by a campfire, Mouse finally just gave up and asked when it would happen. When would they make him kill these people who had taken him in?

Sergeant Ocho had plopped down beside him and asked, "How you doing, soldier?"

Mouse stared at the prisoners, but didn't answer.

Keep silent. Ride through. Don't let them know what you're thinking.

He thought of Mahlia, who tried so hard to never let her feelings show on her face. To never let anyone know what was going on inside her head. No weakness. The only way to survive amongst these coywolv was to hide all your fear and weakness. Never show anything.

But Ocho saw right through. He followed Mouse's gaze to the prisoners.

"It's hard to get broke in, no doubt. This is the hardest part."

Mouse kept his mouth shut, not daring to say anything. It was another test. If he said what he was thinking, they'd come up with some new way to hurt the townspeople and him. If he showed where he was vulnerable, they'd put a knife right there and twist and twist, and then after he'd cried and hurt enough and given away another weakness, they might just decide to blow his head off.

"After we get rid of these maggots, it'll be better," Ocho said. Then he gave a sort of laugh and said, "Well, it'll be clearer, anyway. When you're shooting at Freedom Militia or Army of God, you don't got to feel sorry for them, 'cause you know they'll do you the same."

Mouse looked at the sergeant. "How come you don't make me kill one of them? You make me do everything else."

Ocho looked at him like he was crazy. "We ain't animals! Not like the Army of God. Godboys, they shoot you for no reason at all. They shoot you if you ain't wearing a patriotic shirt, or if they think you don't sing loud enough for their general, or they think you got the wrong religion. We ain't like that. These maggots are our prisoners, now. They try to run, or they hurt one of us, then they get themselves a bullet."

He shrugged. "But we don't just go around wasting people." He nodded out at the prisoners, all lying flat on the ground, shadow lumps that might as well have been corpses for all that they moved. They'd learned that movement got them kicked, so they lay still like stones.

Ocho continued, "Dead maggots ain't any good to us. They might not look like much, but all those maggots, they're walking resupply. Every one of 'em. We start knocking them off, we hurt ourselves, too. We gotta keep them alive, get them earning. Maggots like that work scavenge for us, we sell the scrap to the blood buyers, we get bullets to fight the war. Without these maggots here, no way we can take this place back from all the traitors and collaborators and maggots who tore this country up..." He trailed off.

"You don't get all this, cause you ain't with us, yet. You don't think you're a soldier. Don't got the feel of it."

He patted his rifle, then nodded out at the troops. "You got to know that these boys here, they'll back you up. Maybe they give you all kinds of hell right now, but when

255

the bullets start flying and you got one in the leg, they'll come get you. They'll get you back to camp and doctor your ass, even if all they got is a bottle of Black Ling whiskey and a shoelace to do it. As long as you're still yelling and flopping, they'll put it all on the line to make sure AOG don't get their knives on you. We're brothers. You're our brother."

"Doesn't feel like it."

Ocho laughed. "You only got half-bars, and you want them to treat you like a soldier?" He shook his head. "Nah. You got to earn that, little war maggot.

"We make the Drowned Cities, you see the real war— that's when you show your boys that you're worth calling a brother. You do that, and they'll never let you down. The Colonel says it don't matter where we come from before. Don't matter what we did before. Here, we're UPF. We back you up right."

He clapped Mouse on the shoulder. "Don't think you ain't doing good, half-bar. Soon as we get a little blood on your prick, you'll be golden."

He flicked the brand that still throbbed on Mouse's cheek. "We'll give you some verticals to go with those horizontals. Burn you right. Let you stand tall."

I don't want this, Mouse thought. *I don't want to be golden with the boys. I don't want blood on my prick. I don't want them to burn me again.*

It felt like some part of him was dying inside, but there were soldier boys all around, and wherever he turned, they were looking at him, making sure he followed the path they'd laid out.

Either he followed it, or he was dead.

Doctor Mahfouz used to talk about how everyone had choices, and when he said things like that, he made it seem so possible. And maybe for him, it had been. Mouse didn't think the doctor would have whipped Auntie Selima or poured acid down Mr. Salvatore's chest. He would have stood tall.

And the soldier boys would have shot his head right off and gone on to someone else without a second thought.

I don't want to be a warboy.

But there was no escape. There was no other path that didn't lead to death.

I'm a coward, he thought. *I should stand up and fight them or run away, or something.* But he was still afraid, and the soldier boys were always watching.

Three days later, they hit the Drowned Cities.

27

MAHLIA AND TOOL lived in the jungle, feeding off the dead coywolv for a week, while her torn-up arm healed and while the half-man gained back his strength.

Gradually their diet expanded. They caught fish and frogs. Mahlia ate ant eggs and grasshoppers and snared crawdads, and every day she improved.

She knew it was time to go when Tool came back with a wild pig slung over his shoulder, moving at a stride that would have made her jog to keep up. They were ready, as healthy as either of them could hope to be. That night, they roasted slabs of the pig over a fire of old cardboard boxes and timber chunks that she'd rooted out of one of the ruins.

She knew she needed to be on her way—Mouse was out there, trapped with those soldiers—but still she let days pass. It was like she was frozen in place. Here, she was safe. As long as she just lingered with the half-man, she was as safe as she had ever been since the peacekeepers left. Once she started pursuing Mouse, it would all be lost.

Memories of her escape from the Drowned Cities were flooding back. The mobs and the soldiers, the torches and dripping machetes. The cleansing of everything the peacekeepers had wrought during their years of trying to civilize the city and make the different warlords stop fighting, once and for all.

She remembered hiding in the flooded lower floors of towers and apartment blocks, after her mother had been caught. Living in shadows. Praying that no one would notice her as she moved by darkness from one swamped building to the next. Praying that she wouldn't run across someone in those rooms as she swam and waded and crawled to the city outskirts. Night after night, she lay in darkness, watching troops set up perimeters, waiting to slip past. She'd had two hands then.

And now she was going back.

On the tenth day of her recuperation, Mahlia clambered up onto one of the great vine-covered overpasses and looked toward the Drowned Cities.

From a distance, if you didn't listen for the warfare, the place could have been abandoned. But as you got closer, you could make out details. Trees sprouting from windows, like hair from an old man's ears. Robes of vines draping off slumped shoulders. Birds flying in and out of upper stories.

Mahlia tried to imagine what the place must have been like without all of that. She'd seen pictures of the old Drowned Cities, the version from long before, in one of the museums the peacekeepers had been trying to protect.

Her mother had taken her to the museum, wanting to examine what other old things might be of value to foreign collectors, and Mahlia had seen the photographs. But it had all been surreal. Open roads with cars on them. No boats at all. A river that cut through the place, instead of swamping it. A different place. She'd looked at the pictures and wondered where everyone had driven their cars away to. Or maybe they were just at the bottoms of all the canals. Sleeping.

The whole museum felt a little like a cemetery. A place where you came to look at the dead. And really, the artifacts weren't anywhere near as good as the ones that her mother kept in her warehouse.

"People value history, Mahlia," her mother said. "Here, look at this one." She lifted a piece of parchment, holding it gingerly. "You see these names? This meant war. When they signed this, it changed the course of the world." She laid the parchment down again, exquisitely careful. "People will spend fortunes to touch the paper that these men touched."

She smiled then. "No one here knows the stories behind these things, so they don't know the value. To them, this all looks like junk," she said, and she waved at the warehouse around them, filled to bursting with her mother's selections.

Old flags. Paintings. The marble heads from statues of old men that had had their heads knocked off and found their way into her shop at the mouth of the river, where collectors came to buy history and scavenge.

Her mother had a tiny shop on the storefront, where she studied potential buyers. But it was the warehouse that was truly astonishing. She'd installed it in the belly of a huge building near the city center, several apartments that she'd bought and then carefully bricked up, hiding them away from prying eyes. It was there that she brought her best buyers.

When Mahlia was small, she was sometimes allowed to watch as men and women surveyed the paintings leaning against walls, the statuary of presidents, the murals chipped from government buildings and transported whole to the warehouse.

Her mother said that was how she met Mahlia's father.

He'd had a passion for history, just like her. He'd bought little silver snuffboxes from revolutionary times, and quill pens that had signed famous documents. Handwritten letters. All sorts of things. He'd kept coming back, again and again, until her mother finally understood that it wasn't just antiquities that her father loved. And that was where Mahlia had come from.

"You think you have a path?" Tool asked, breaking her thoughts.

Mahlia startled. For all his bulk, the half-man was silent. It was spooky to have him suddenly appear. "Yeah," she said. "There's a way."

"Undetected?" the half-man pressed.

Mahlia bristled. "Well, if it ain't, we're both dead pretty fast, right?"

Tool smirked. "Escape is simpler than infiltration, girl. Just because you managed to flee that place doesn't mean that you can reenter it. The direction of your passage is not the only variable. Where will you lair once you have passed within? How will you survive until you find your brother?"

"He's not my brother."

Tool growled at that. "Then leave him to the Fates."

Mahlia knew what Tool was getting at, but she didn't like his bringing it up again.

"I owe him," she said.

"Debts are a heavy burden. Throw them off, and you walk free."

It was tempting, for sure. Just run away. Pretend that the licebiter who had cracked the jokes and played the pranks and who had rooted up an entire nest of pigeon eggs when they were starving had never existed. That he'd never saved her from all the pain the soldier boys had wanted to slash into her.

"Can't." She grimaced. "Anyway, why are you helping me? Why don't you just run off? No one's keeping you here."

"I have my own reasons."

"It's not because I saved you?" Mahlia taunted.

Tool's bestial face swung back to regard her. "No."

The tone of his voice frightened her, because she realized that she had no idea what drove the half-man. When they'd been foraging for food together, she could sometimes forget that he was something other than human. And then suddenly the creature would be looking at her with his huge yellow eye, and scarred face, and doglike muzzle and tiger teeth, and she felt as if she was staring into the face of something that occasionally saw her as food.

Mahlia steeled herself. "So why?"

"I have decided I have unfinished business there."

"Since when?"

Tool regarded her for a long time. Mahlia forced herself not to look away. Finally Tool said, "When Colonel Stern held me captive, he used me to fight. I fought panthers, and Army of God captives. I fought his own soldiers, the ones who ran from battle, or who failed him in some way. Stern enjoyed that. He used to sit just outside the fighting cage and watch me kill his enemies. He cheered a great deal when I tore off a man's arms. I think that I would like to meet him again, without a cage between us."

"That's impossible."

Tool smiled at that. "And saving your friend isn't?"

Before Mahlia could answer, he turned and swung off the overpass, dropping down to a tree. It swayed and bent with his weight, leaves rustling wildly. Mahlia listened, expecting a thud as the half-man hit the ground, but she heard nothing. It was as if the jungle had swallowed him into its belly. Disappeared without a sound.

"Tool?"

"It will take two days for us to reach the river," the half-man called up. "If you wish to have a chance of saving your friend, it's past time we were on our way."

28

WHEN MOUSE HAD been younger, his family had all talked with hushed tones of the Drowned Cities' lawlessness and decay.

His father had sometimes gone there with a skiff full of chickens in bamboo cages, to sell to the city people and to the army soldiers, but his father's face had always been grimly set when he poled off through the swamplands, and grimly set when he returned.

He'd always gotten the money they'd needed, along with the new hoe or the new barbed wire for fencing their pigs better, but he'd never been happy about it—the going out, or the coming back.

Mouse's brother said it was because the soldiers shook

you down as you crossed their territories. If you looked at them wrong, they'd call you a traitor or a turncoat or a spy or Chinese collaborationist, and just shoot you outright.

They made up things to call you. Anything would do. They'd call you a left-hand dog. Put a bullet in your face and laugh at your body while it floated in a canal.

Mouse had felt bad that his father needed to kiss soldier boots just to get the few things that they couldn't make themselves or get from a merchant on his sales circuit. He'd also been secretly glad he never had to go himself.

Mahlia had her own stories of the Drowned Cities, from when she'd grown up there. Her stories and Mouse's father's were as different as night and day.

Mahlia talked about the city's great rectangular reflecting pool that stretched more than a mile, and the vast marble palace that overlooked it with its great high dome where the peacekeepers ran their administration. She talked of *shaobing* sellers who sold their sweet roasted breads to the peacekeepers. She told of company offices and clipper ships in the harbors and biodiesel rafts running the canals, jostling through floating markets that sprang up every day as farmers like his father poled their way into the city to sell. She told of green bok choy, bitter melon, red pomegranates, long pork bodies hung above the water, fresh and clean from slaughter.

But that had all been peacekeeper territory. The rules had run different in her part of the city, where the Chinese intervention had pushed the warlords out. Her life sounded like heaven to Mouse, at least until China got sick of trying to make everyone get along, and took its peacekeepers home, and let the Drowned Cities get back to its business of killing.

Regardless, Mouse's impressions of the Drowned Cities were all secondhand. His life had been made up of his family's flooded fields and their little home that his father had built in the second story of an old redbrick ruin. His life had been defined by planting times, and getting a mule to till the mud when the rains stopped, and thinking that if they made enough money, they might get a big old water buffalo like the Sims had, and then life would be good and easy.

A farm boy, Mahlia had called him. Just a silly little lice-biter farm boy who didn't know squat about the city.

Mouse thought about that as he stood atop a crumbling ten-story building, with a machete and a couple bottles of acid dangling from his belt, surveying his territory for Army of God infiltrators.

Now, he was more Drowned Cities than the girl who had come out of them, but he had to admit that the place looked like nothing he'd imagined.

He'd expected the city to look more...dead.

Instead, he surveyed miles of ancient buildings and swamped streets turned into canals. Networks of algae-clogged emerald waterways were dotted with lily pads and the stalks of white lotus flowers. Block after block of buildings and apartments were swallowed up to their second stories and sometimes higher, like the whole city had suddenly wandered off and decided to go wading in the ocean.

Creeping vines and kudzu covered tower faces. Trees sprouted from window ledges and rooftops, green parasols that leaned out over the waters while their roots clung tight to masonry and concrete. The shortest buildings were entirely submerged, and made for nasty snags, but many of the buildings still stood above the sea, waist deep in saltwater swamps that rose and fell with the tides, green leafy giants squatting in warm ocean waters.

UPF warboys poled through the canals on skiffs or ran along bamboo boardwalks that they'd constructed to float on the waters. Troops were everywhere, traveling over fixed bridges from block to block, moving through the city's orleans, sometimes wading, sometimes swimming. Sometimes catching rides on biodiesel zodiacs if they could manage to snag one from the reclamation companies that paid them for access to the scavenge in their territory.

Above all, Mouse was aware of how alive the city was, and not just with gunfire and soldiers and fighting. That was all there, for sure. The slathered colors of territory and control, the troops, the echo of gunfire and artillery along the contested borders. Sector numbers were painted slapdash on buildings along with painted names for canals: Stern's River. Easy Canal. Gold Street. K Canal. Green

268

Canal. Peacekeeper Alley. He'd expected all that. The bullets and the buildings.

But he hadn't expected to see flocks of birds roosting in broken windows. Or eagles wheeling overhead, diving for fish in the canals. He hadn't expected to see a deer swimming across open water, or to listen to coywolv yipping and yowling at night, calling to one another across the rooftops.

There was war and ruin, and heat and sweat and mosquitoes and brackish water, and there was also a strange life in the Drowned Cities, as the jungle busily took back its own territory, reaching deeper and deeper into what had once been a place solely for human beings.

And then there was the scavenge.

Mouse had always thought of the Drowned Cities as a war zone, but what it really was, was a scavenge mine.

On his first day in the place, he watched a city block being torn down to raw parts. Clouds of concrete and rock dust, piles of pipes and ducts, steel and copper and iron being dragged out. Tangled heaps of wiring separated by weight and metal and color.

Some of the buildings were old, made of pink and white marble, and the marble was being mined and placed on barges, while the rest of the stone and concrete was heaved into the canals, filling up the waters and making new streets, raising the level of the city above where the tides could reach.

He'd stared at all the people swarming through the rubble. Hundreds and hundreds. They made long lines of wheelbarrows, filled with stone, and they gathered in clots around massive iron I beams that they lifted with kudzu ropes and hauled to the barges.

Dog Squad, the one Mouse had been assigned to, had guided the captives of Banyan Town into the mix of laborers.

"Get in there!" Gutty yelled. "Make yourselves useful!"

The other soldiers jeered at the captives and switched at them with bamboo canes as they were led away into the scavenge operation. Mouse knew those people. Knew Lilah and Tua and Joe Sands and Auntie Selima, who had been so kind to him. Mr. Salvatore, who had lost daughter and grandson both, looked at Mouse like he was dirt as he was chivied past.

Sergeant Ocho slapped Mouse on the back of the head.

"Ow!"

"Better not look too long, half-bar. LT will think you don't want to be a soldier boy. Maybe think you want to join the rest of the war maggots."

Sure enough, the lieutenant was watching Mouse again, cold gray eyes evaluating. It was like he was always watching. More often than not, Mouse could feel Sayle's eyes, dragging on him, even when he wasn't doing anything wrong. Even when he wasn't fantasizing about making a run for it.

Had he given himself away?

Maybe the lieutenant had seen him as they marched toward the Drowned Cities. Seen Mouse as he sat by the campfire, looking again and again to the shadows of the jungle for some way to run off. But always there'd been some other soldier with a gun nearby.

"Look away, Ghost," Ocho said. "Those prisoners ain't even people now. They're just maggots. They ain't your business."

The soldier boys herded the prisoners down into the mess of rubble. Clouds of concrete dust roiled around them, and then they were swallowed in the work.

When Mouse finally dared to glance after them again, they were lost amongst the many ants, just a bunch of dusty dots mingled with the many. But Ocho still caught the backward look and he jammed Mouse in the ribs with the butt of his rifle.

"Last warning, Ghost. You got a ways to go before you get your full bars. Don't give anyone a reason to think you got no semper fi."

And to Mouse's everlasting shame, he turned away from the scavenge workers and the prisoners and did as he was told.

Even now, it still sat badly with him. Standing at his watch post atop a building, he could see the concrete dust and hear the clatter of the recycling work half a mile away.

His cheek still ached where they'd seared Glenn Stern's mark into his face, but the pain was fading. And even though everyone still called him half-bar, and still made

271

him do their chores, whether it was fetching water or scraping pots, or cooking a deer they'd gunned down, they had also armed him with a machete and acid, and he stood watches with the rest.

He might have been their dog to whip around, but it was better than what the people who worked the scavenge operation were getting. He was fed and armed, and standing watch was easy work.

It frightened him to think about it. That the captives had been swallowed in that sea of labor, and that he walked free, for no good reason at all.

None of it made any sense. He hadn't done anything one way or the other to end up where he was. The tide of war had rolled in and swallowed him up, and Banyan Town with him, and they'd all tumbled in the surf. And for reasons he couldn't understand, he'd broken the surface and managed to breathe, while everyone else was drowning alive.

His parents had been Deepwater Christians, and they'd always told him the world might move in mysterious ways but God had a plan for them.

As Mouse stared across the clatter and roar of the recycling operations with its seething hordes of dust-covered slave labor, Mouse thought that if there was a plan, then it was a cruel and vicious one.

In the distance, gunfire chattered.

He couldn't tell who was fighting for the territory. Could have been United Patriot Front or Army of God, or Tulane

Company, or Taylor's Wolves, or the Freedom Militia. Impossible to guess. Just more gunfire.

Gutty came up behind him and clapped him on the shoulder. "C'mon, Ghost," he said. "We're doing patrol. Guess who walks point?" and then he laughed, because to him, it was funny.

29

MAHLIA AND TOOL reached Moss Landing in the afternoon of the second day. Twice they had to double back and work their way around patrols that Tool sensed, and so their route was circuitous, but eventually the broad muddy swathe of the Potomac River opened before them.

Mahlia had been to Moss Landing twice before with the doctor, but each time she had remained on its fringes while the doctor went into its heart to bargain for medicines from the troops who smuggled black market goods in from the coast.

As long as there was a river, there was transport, the doctor had said. Medicines were smuggled upriver from where the big scavenge companies and their corrupt workers would sell to the troops, and guns moved downriver, magically penetrating the war lines, even though armies and refugees could not.

More guns and bullets for the struggle.

"Why do they keep fighting?" Mouse had asked once. "Wouldn't it be easier to just stop? Everyone would make more money."

Mahlia had almost laughed at that. He was basically repeating what her own father had said every night for years.

"They're stupid and crazy," she'd said.

But Doctor Mahfouz had shaken his head. "Not crazy. More like...rationally insane. When people fight for ideals, no price is too high, and no fight can be surrendered. They aren't fighting for money, or power, or control. Not really. They're fighting to destroy their enemies. So even if they destroy everything around them, it's worth it, because they know that they'll have destroyed the traitors."

"But they all call each other traitors," Mouse had said.

"Indeed. It's a long tradition here. I'm sure whoever first started questioning their political opponents' patriotism thought they were being quite clever."

Now, Mahlia and Tool crouched in the jungle on the outskirts of town. It looked much as she remembered it. Troops on R & R. Nailshed girls. Guns and booze and drugs and laughter and screaming. Guns firing randomly, like Spring Festival fireworks going off, but all the time. The place seethed with ring fights and red rippers and white dust and bloodshot eyes watching from the shadows. Mahfouz had never wanted her to go into it, and she'd been glad to stay out.

Beyond, on the river, she could make out a few sails. Smugglers, probably, with their little skiffs. No rich ones, though. The last time she'd been here, there had also been the buzz of biodiesel zodiacs, running upriver on behalf of Glenn Stern and his UPF soldiers.

She watched the soldiers and the nailshed girls. Suddenly gasped as she caught a better glimpse of a soldier. He had a green cross tattooed on his bare chest, and now that she looked, she caught sight of a glinting amulet of aluminum strung around his neck. They were all like that. All of them with their crosses and their amulets.

"Army of God," she whispered. She started worming backward, trying to escape. "It's Army of God."

Tool gripped her arm, stopping her flight. "This is a change?" he asked.

"Used to be United Patriot Front."

"War is fluid." Tool studied the town. "There are still soldiers on the river, and crates being unloaded on the dock. Black market goods still move on the waterway. The players have changed, but the business of smuggling remains the same."

"Yeah, except if we have to cross back into UPF territory downriver, we're dead." She looked out again at Moss Landing. Rough-cut buildings scabbed inside older fallen-down and overgrown concrete and brick. The troops were singing some patriotic song about how their general would never die until the last God-haters were swept away.

"That is not why you try to flee now," Tool observed.

Mahlia's heart was pounding. She swallowed. "They're the ones that caught me. Last time. The ones that took my hand."

Tool nodded slowly. "Still, you must go down. See if the route remains open."

"Not me." Mahlia shook her head violently, fighting down memories of trying to break free. The soldier boys laughing as they laid her hand across the log. "They got no love for castoffs."

A shout went up. Mahlia flinched. A couple of soldier boys stumbled out into the middle of the street, leaning on nailshed girls. They were all drunk or high. Crazy and mindless because they weren't on the front.

UPF had been the same way, when they owned the town. Moss Landing was safe territory. R & R ground. Safe upriver from the Drowned Cities. Easy duty.

Unconsciously, Mahlia found herself reaching for a rock, prying it up, preparing to defend herself if they came her way.

She looked down and almost yelped. Her hand gripped a skull, lying buried, meat still on the face. It was past stinking, but she could make out the triple hash of Glenn Stern on the warboy's cheek. With a chill, she realized that she and Tool were lying on a graveyard of bodies, UPF soldiers shallow-buried all around.

"Fates," she whispered.

Tool's bestial face showed amusement. "I thought you knew."

Mahlia dropped the skull, wiping her hand on her hip, trying to make it feel clean, knowing it wouldn't work.

"It's why I chose this vantage," Tool said. "The soldiers down there will avoid their killing ground. They will detour around the history they have made in this place."

"You smelled it?"

"Of course."

It made sense, but still, Mahlia felt nauseated, knowing she was lying atop piles of bodies. Her skin crawled with a superstitious need to get away, but she forced it down. She'd seen plenty of bodies. This was just a few more. And a good reminder of what the Army of God was capable of.

As if she didn't know already.

"We got to find another way," she said.

Tool looked at her. "Afraid?"

"Damn straight. Army of God..." She shook her head. "You can't argue with fanatics. They'll just cut us down."

"How is this different from the UPF?" Tool asked. "Your plan was sound. Go to the banks. Seek a guide."

But now Mahlia saw how risky her plan had been. Even with UPF around, it had always been Mahfouz who had gone down into Moss Landing and come back alive.

She watched the people standing around bonfires. Girls laughing in that way that made you know they were trying to keep soldiers happy but that they were scared.

A man wandered to the edge of the jungle and pulled down his shorts. Urinated. A grown-up. How many actual adults had she seen since the war started up again? The ones in Banyan Town, sure, but out of the Drowned Cities? Just the big names. The ones who ran things. Lieutenant Sayle. The face of Colonel Glenn Stern, head of the UPF. And yet here was a man. Full-grown.

Behind him, a couple of his troops stood waiting. War maggots. Didn't even have hair on their upper lips. Mean-ass licebiters with guns, probably high on red rippers, probably crazy. One had a shotgun, the other a hunting rifle, not just machetes or acid, which meant they were probably bloodthirsty, especially if they were standing bodyguard on the grown-up. Boys with guns scared her. Guns gave them swagger, and swagger made them vicious.

Somewhere inside the town, someone was sobbing, begging and in pain. She couldn't tell if it was a boy or a girl. It didn't even sound like person, hardly. Mahlia realized she was shaking. She knew that sound. She'd made exactly that sound once, when they got hold of her hand.

"I ain't going down there. We got to find a different way."

Tool's huge head turned to regard her. "There is no other way, and you are the one who must go." He nodded toward the town. "Augments like me are blood enemies to soldiers like that. They will shoot me on sight. I am their greatest nightmare. They fight my kind in the North, where the war lines bottle them up. If they see me here, they will assume I am a scout or an attacker, and they will shoot."

"What if you were just passing through?"

"Half-men do not simply 'pass through.' I learned that to my cost the last time I tried," Tool said. "Those soldiers believe that we always have masters, and we always work to our master's purpose. My kind would have no business here, other than war with them."

He nodded at the town. "You must go down to the waterfront, and you must find us a smuggler."

"What do I do if someone comes at me?"

"We need a skiff and we need a person who knows how to move into the Drowned Cities. Without an alliance, we have nothing."

"We don't got anything to pay them."

"Bring them to me." Tool bared his teeth. "I will arrange the payment."

Mahlia shook her head. "I don't think this is going to work."

"Be strong, wargirl. It will only get worse."

Mahlia stared out at the town, hating what she had to do. "In the morning," she decided. "I'll go when they're all hungover and sleepy and stupid. Not while they're all sliding and crazy and looking for someone to hurt."

Tool smiled. "A decision worthy of Sun Tzu."

30

THE PROBLEM DIDN'T develop right away.

Mouse's squad was deep inside UPF territory, so they should have been safe. The only things to keep an eye on were chain gangs and farmers. Mouse and all the other soldiers were standing around joking and watching as big old barges eased through K Canal, and they had no idea what was coming.

The barges were massive things, ironclad and rusty. A whole long line of them clogged the canal, with a webwork of ropes leading to the boardwalks on the sides, where people were harnessed to the ropes in long lines, leaning forward, dragging.

A few people had mules that they urged forward, but

mostly, it was stringy people with dirty matted hair and torn skin, white and brown and black and tan and all of it whipped and torn by labor.

The braying and complaining of the mules and the groaning of the prisoners filled the canal and echoed off the buildings. The stink of them as they passed was almost overwhelming. Mouse stepped back as the haulers leaned against the weight of the filled barges.

The first barge just had a bunch of green logos and a Lawson & Carlson stamp. The second one, though…

"Is that Chinese?" Mouse asked.

The side of the barge had a big old logo with writing on the side, just like on the packs of medicines that Doctor Mahfouz used to dole out.

Gutty looked over. "Sure."

The warboy went back to shaking a bottle of his acid. He squirted a little out and it smoked and hissed as it hit the boardwalk. "Bunch of the blood buyers come from over there. We got 'em all."

He pointed at the succession of barges and logos. "Lawson & Carlson, they're out of the Seascape. GE…dunno where. Stone-Ailixin, I think that's from over in Europe. Patel Global, they're Seascape Boston, too."

"I thought the warlords—" Mouse paused, adjusting his words. "I mean, I thought we kicked the Chinese out."

"Just the peacekeepers. If buyers got cash for bullets, we let 'em have scrap, just like everyone else. Long as they don't try no more invading or telling us how to run a democracy or whatever, they can have as much marble and steel and copper as they want."

Mouse frowned, thinking. Remembering Mahlia, and how everyone treated her as a castoff. And here everyone was happy to take bullets from the same kinds of people as who'd left her behind. All that patriotic talk about kicking China out of the country, and taking the country back, but they were happy to trade with Chinese companies. They'd kill castoff peacekeeper kids, but were willing to take China's bullets?

The air whistled.

Mouse looked about, trying to figure out where the sound was coming from.

Beside him, a barge exploded. Debris screamed past.

The blast threw Mouse and Gutty into a wall. A chunk of granite rained off the building above them and shattered on the barge iron. More stone showered Mouse, cutting flesh. A granite slab slammed down beside him, shattering the boardwalk and leaving a hole down to the canal waters. He stared dumbly at the hole.

Where was Gutty?

Another whistling sound. Another barge exploded. The thing started to keel over, dragging mules and workers into the water. Screams echoed as the sinking barge dragged people under.

Chaos was erupting all around. People running, diving

into the water, or crawling out of it. Everyone trying to escape the kill zone. Workers thrashed in water, tangled in their harnesses. Mouse's ears rang with the explosions. The screams seemed distant. He'd lost his hearing, he realized. Another explosion dropped into the canal, sending up a spray of water.

The 999, he realized. It had to be. The Army of God had a 999, and they were dropping shells right onto him. He stared around himself, shell-shocked. Watching all the people thrashing and frothing and drowning.

A bunch of his squad were waving him at him from a window alcove.

Cover.

He dove for them as another shell hit. Somewhere behind, rifle fire opened up. Bright red blood stained the boardwalk before him. He started to panic, checking his body, but he had all his arms and legs. Where was the blood coming from?

Another shell whistled overhead. Everyone curled into balls as it hit the half-sunk barge. It was like the sky was raining fire and there was nothing they could do.

Mouse started to panic, but Van grabbed him. "Don't you run, Ghost! You stick with your squad, boy!"

Mouse nodded dumbly as another shell hit the building beside them. Rubble poured down.

Ocho was staring up at the buildings around them. "How'd they get our position?"

Bullets ripped down the canal. Ocho ducked behind a

fallen chunk of granite. Screams of animals and prisoners filled the air. Mouse's ears were ringing. The bullets kept coming, bouncing off the walls like the Army of God had enough ammo to last them all the way to eternity.

All he had was a machete and an acid bottle. Mouse curled lower as more weapons fire ripped around them, showering them with shrapnel. Something slashed past his ear. He felt blood running down his face.

And he was one of the lucky ones. Gutty was gone. When the granite slab came crashing down, one second Gutty had been there, and then he'd been disappeared. Smashed and drowned, Mouse guessed. Gone. Just gone.

The 999 boomed again. Mouse tried to ball himself up even tighter.

They couldn't run or swim back the way they'd come, because the godboys had gotten a pin on them from behind as well, and so now they were sitting ducks amongst the towers, waiting for the 999 to drop a whole building down on their heads.

Ocho stood and sprayed bullets down the length of the canal with his rifle. The boy must have been protected by his Fates Eye, because he didn't take a bullet in reply, and then he was down beside Mouse again, back pressed against the granite.

"They got a spotter," he gasped. "We find him and shut him down, we can get some breathing room."

He nodded toward a building across the way. "They ain't shelling that one."

Pook scanned the building Ocho indicated. "You think that's where they are?"

"It's the only building they ain't blowing up."

The 999 went off again, and they all flattened themselves, but the round went somewhere else. Didn't even explode. They all laughed.

A dud.

"How we doing, warboy?" Ocho slapped Mouse's knee. "Ready to hurt these bastards?"

Mouse couldn't form the words. He was shaking. His face was bleeding from some bit of shrapnel that had hit him and he didn't know where it had come from.

He realized Ocho was looking at him. He tried to speak but couldn't say anything at all. He was surprised to see that Ocho was smiling.

The sergeant leaned close. "I got news for you, half-bar. None of us is getting out of here alive. You get it? We're just walking dead. So don't worry so much about surviving, right?" He slapped Mouse's leg, grinning. "Don't take it so serious. We're just meat in the mill."

Mouse closed his eyes and wanted to cry, but Pook grabbed him. "Come on, half-bar. Time to earn your verticals."

Ocho pointed at the building across the canal. "You get your ass in there and find that spotter. Get the 999 off us, and maybe we get out of here alive. Fight another day, right? Only way out is if we shut down that 999. Otherwise we're kill food." He slapped Mouse on the back.

"Go on, half-bar! Hunt!"

And then he shoved Mouse into the canal, right into a hail of bullets. Mouse went down, came up sputtering. Wondering what he was going to do.

He thought about trying to swim away, to flee, but then Pook splashed into the drink with him.

"Come on, half-bar. Let's get your prick red." And then he was swimming for the far side.

All of Mouse's senses were alive. It felt like he was looking in twenty directions at once. Army of God boys down the canal, shooting at them. Rubble raining down from above. Mules in the water, swimming around, braying and thrashing and climbing up on one another, and being dragged down and tangled by their harnesses.

They hadn't seen it coming. None of them had. One second they'd been patrolling, working muscle while a bunch of civvy slave labor moved scavenge down the canal—just making sure the scavenged wire and marble and pipes and I beams all went out and bought them more bullets—and the next they were in a firefight for their lives.

Mouse made it to the far side of the canal.

Pook had an AK that he held above his head as he swam, and it slowed him, but then he made it, too. They climbed into the building through a shattered window, swimming through the interior of a swamped floor plan, hunting for a stairwell that would lead them up out of the water. Slime and heat hung heavy and the roof was only a few feet above their heads, but it was enough.

"Here!" Pook whispered. They squelched up a stairway, dripping and trying to be silent as they stepped around garbage and dead animals from who knew how long ago.

Raccoons dashed away from them, running up the stairs. Pook pulled Mouse close as they reached the first dry story of the building.

"They got to be on the south side of the building," he said. "Looking down on us. Thought I saw some reflections, up five more stories. Stay stealthy, right?"

Mouse nodded, gripping his bottle of acid in his left hand and his machete in his right.

They stole up the stairs. Outside, another shell whistled down. Mouse was briefly glad that he was inside and not out in that nightmare, but then they hit the floor they'd been looking for and all hell broke loose.

They would have surprised the godboys completely, except that he and Pook had scared up that pack of raccoons. The animals dashed out of the stairwell, scattering like cockroaches, and the Army of God were right there in front of them—three of the bastards, leaning out the window and laying down artillery.

Another shell came booming down and the godboys all whooped when it hit, and then the raccoons came piling through.

The boys turned and grabbed their rifles. Pook dashed forward, screaming and firing. He hit one of the boys. Mouse glimpsed surprised brown eyes wide, long hair spraying, as the boy's head whipped back, and then he went right out the window.

Another godboy took a bullet in the leg but was swinging his rifle around. Mouse ran toward him with his bottle and sprayed him like he'd been trained, right in the face, follow the stream up and down and all over, and suddenly steam was rising and burning and bubbling, the kid's face burning off. But the boy was still shooting.

Mouse dropped to the ground as bullets flew wild. Pook slammed down beside him, blood and shattered face and surprised eyes.

Mouse tried to get his bearings. The godboy with the acid face was on the floor, flopping around and screaming, the other one was dead and gone, out the window like he'd learned to fly. Pook lay beside him with his jawbone blown off.

And then there was the radio boy. Just standing there. Staring.

Mouse and the radio boy both looked at each other, and then the godboy was scrambling for his gun, and Mouse grabbed for Pook's rifle. He couldn't get it off Pook's shoulder. Bullets rained down, chipping concrete as the other boy opened fire. Mouse got Pook's rifle up and took aim as the other gun blazed away. He pulled the trigger once.

A red stain opened on the boy's chest. Blood spattered the wall behind him. The kid just sat down, looking surprised, and suddenly everything was quiet, except for the squawk of the radio asking for bearings.

For a long time, Mouse stared at the boy he'd shot. Blood ran from him. His eyes were staring at Mouse, but Mouse couldn't tell if he was dead or not. He was breathing, Mouse thought, and then he wasn't sure what he was supposed to do. He didn't think he could shoot the boy again.

Mouse started to shake. He was alive. Pook was dead. The other three were dead. And he was alive. Fates. He was alive. He stood up, trembling. Amped with adrenaline. He ran his hands over himself, amazed, trying to find a bullet anywhere on him.

It was just like the Army of God boys said. They were immune to bullets. Blessed. Bullets were supposed to just bounce off them, because their general blessed them. They had amulets to keep them safe. Mouse could see the ones these boys wore, little aluminum disks marked by their priests to ward off bullets. But they were all dead and he was alive.

Mouse went over to the window. From high up, the fighting down below looked like little ants, dancing around without any purpose.

The radio squawked. "Where you want the next one?"

Mouse looked down on the fighting in the streets. He should run. This was his chance. He could run.

But he was deep inside the Drowned Cities—war lines on top of war lines, in every direction. And he was already branded UPF. If he tried to run, UPF would grab him; if he went into Army of God territory, or ran up against Freedom Militia, they'd shoot him on sight. He wasn't just another war maggot, now. He was a soldier boy. Branded, named, and reborn.

"Where you want the next one?" the radio asked again.

He stared down at the fighting. Ocho was down there.

You want to know a secret? You're already dead. Stop worrying about it.

Ghost picked up the radio and clicked it on. "Move it back a hundred yards."

"*What?*"

"Go back a hundred yards. You're way off."

The 999 boomed.

Army of God soldiers started running like ants as a shell dropped behind their lines.

Ghost watched the war maggots run and scatter, and felt a rush of excitement as he walked the 999 down the street, chasing them.

It didn't last long, but it was enough. Pretty soon, Ghost saw the godboys coming back and he knew it was time to go. It was like pranking his brother, back when he was still around. You could poke at him for a little while, but then he'd get pissed and it was time to get out of the way. When a squad of AOG started swimming the canal, it was time to go.

Ghost scanned the room. They'd been set up for a while. Must have been planning the ambush for days and days. He grabbed his dead opponent's gun. Ammo...

He couldn't carry it all. He fumbled through the ammo, trying to match the guns to the ammo. Whole hodgepodge.

He pulled a belt of bullets off one boy, and a couple of cartridges off another, scooped them into his shirt. Time to go.

The temptation to stay there, to try to get the rest...In a sudden inspiration, Ghost grabbed the rest of the rifles and flung them out the window, then the ammo he couldn't carry, and the radio, too, all of it sailing out the window and down, tumbling, into the canal below.

Only then did he run. He went down two flights and this time the raccoons saved him, because they came up ahead with the godboys behind, and Ghost had enough time to slide out of sight. He stealthed down refuse-strewn hallways with mice and rats and raccoons, slipping through the building, keeping the map of the place in his mind, moving and dropping down another stairwell, and then down and down and down again, until he was in the water and swimming back to Dog Squad.

The old boy, Mouse, he would have just swum right out, but Ghost stopped short of the canal, peered out at the water and the canal and the shattered boardwalks.

Boys with guns were all around, but he had a gun, too, now, and the hunt was different. He'd hunted frogs and snakes and crawdads, and if the godboys weren't snakes, he didn't know what was, and so he scanned the canal and the buildings up above, peeking out, looking for glints of snipers, for signs of movement, and then he saw Dog Squad running, leapfrogging as they backed themselves out of the skirmish zone, and Van caught sight of him and then Ghost was out in the water, swimming, knowing his warboys had his back and that he had covering fire.

He came out of the water, dripping, trophy rifle held high, his pockets full of bullets and who the hell knew whether they'd shoot, but one thing for sure was that Army of God didn't have those bullets.

The 999 opened up again, but Dog Squad was out of the kill zone.

Ocho looked at him. "Where's Pook?"

Ghost pointed up at the building.

"Dead?"

"Yeah. Got it in the face."

"You're with TamTam and Stork, then." Ocho waved to the other warboys. "Hey, Stork! Pook's gone. You got Ghost."

Two boys he hadn't worked with. One of them a little licebiter with castoff eyes and a smashed-up nose: TamTam. The other, black-skinned, tall, and gawky, and older. Ghost liked that. If Stork was older, he might not be stupid. Might not get him killed.

Stork eyed him. "Nice job with the 999." He paused, looking at the rifle Ghost had brought back with predatory interest. "Nice gun."

Ghost gripped it warily, knowing what was coming.

"TamTam don't have a gun," Stork said.

"So?"

"He outranks you."

Ghost just stared him down. He didn't let himself blink or show fear. He just looked back at Stork. "If he wants one, I guess he better find one," he said.

Stork almost looked like he was going to be pissed, but then he just smiled and shook his head.

"Yeah. Guess he better."

31

DAWN BROKE STILL and hot and wet on Moss Landing. Rain came down and soaked everything, turning everything to mud.

The place looked almost as bad as Banyan Town had looked after the UPF burned it. If the people hadn't been puking and lying facedown but breathing, they could have been dead. Some of them were so exhausted from debauchery that they weren't even conscious.

Mahlia stepped over the bodies. In the gray flat light of the rainy morning, Moss Landing seemed less threatening. No one wanted to be outside making trouble. No one wanted to be awake. She heard someone shouting, but they were far away. Someone else was singing an old licebiter nursery rhyme about being a soldier boy and winding up dead.

The docks were quiet. Rain pattered down on the Potomac, making rings. Rivulets of muddy water trickled around a couple of raggedy piers thrust into the brown river flow.

This close to the sea, the surge of salt water pushed its way up into the mouth with the tide, then flowed back. What seemed like years ago, Doctor Mahfouz had told her that it was a unique environment. In other places, where a river was less poisoned with war and rotting city, it would have been rich with life, teeming with fish and turtles.

Some of those animals were probably there, but Mahlia had heard that the best fishing was always for bodies. People floating down from other parts of the war, headed for the ocean. Some of them dumped, some of them floated there on little rafts. People were always snagging those.

Mahlia hesitated at the docks. One of the people on the water was a woman. She looked up at Mahlia from under a dripping rain hat. Mahlia started toward the lady, but then hesitated. Just because she was a woman didn't mean she was safe. And Mahlia didn't like the way the woman looked.

She had a pair of pistols strapped to her hips, and her lip was split wide, raggedly sewed back into place. And her eyes were so cold that Mahlia took a step back. The woman might as well have been coywolv.

Mahlia turned and started away and caught sight of the man she'd seen before. The one she'd taken for an officer when he took a leak at the edge of the woods.

He and his two bodyguards were tying gear down on their skiff, covering it with ripped plastic stamped with old Chinese company symbols. Mahlia even recognized an old banner that the peacekeepers had hung when she'd been young.

DISARM TO FARM, it said, in English.

She remembered the campaign. They'd been trying to resettle ex-soldiers back into the countryside, to give them seeds and land and expertise to become farmers again, and all they had to do was turn in their guns.

One of the boys stood atop the torn plastic advertisement, a shotgun held low. For a second, Mahlia thought she was going to be shot, but then the boy's eyes passed on.

The woman was still looking at her. She climbed out of her skiff, striding toward her.

"You," she said. "Come here, girl. Let me get a look at you."

Mahlia started to back away, and then to run, but behind her she heard new movement.

She lifted her machete to defend herself, but the two boys moved past her, ignoring her entirely. Their faces dripped with rain, but they barely squinted as they brought up their rifles.

"Move off, lady," one of them said. He had a head like a bullet and dark black skin. His arms and legs might as well have been sticks, but he had his hunting rifle up and aimed. The other boy was moving sideways, getting clear room. He could have been Chinese, but not like her. Not castoff. Some full-blooded patriot, born and raised in the Drowned Cities, instead of a half-breed like her. He had a shotgun.

"You leave the girl alone," he said.

The woman's hand eased toward her pistol, but the man called out. "They are expert shots, Clarissa. Move on."

She looked at them all, and then she turned and went back to her skiff and untied the lines. A moment later, she was in the river, and drifting away. Looking back at them. And then disappearing into gray and rain and mist.

Mahlia looked at them all, surprised. "Thanks."

The man shrugged it off. "You should go. She is a collector. Even without your hand, she'd be able to get a price for you, and if you had walked right up to her, she would have taken you."

The two boys were looking at her.

"You castoff?" the darker one asked.

Mahlia wondered how to answer, but before she could form a response, the boy answered the question for her. "They don't like castoffs here. You better get yourself clear or tag AOG, real quick, girl."

AOG. Army of God. Of course. Tag herself. She'd been stupid. She needed an amulet, or something. And then, when she got down to UPF territory, she'd need to mark herself again. She'd have to brand her cheek, probably. Put the triple hash on herself, if she wanted to slide past without getting challenged.

"Thanks," she said again.

But they were already securing the last of their bundles in their skiff and unwrapping their ropes.

"Hey!" she called. "You going downriver?"

"Why?"

"I want to come on, if you are."

"You got money?"

"My friend does."

"Yeah?"

"He's hurt. I need help getting him down. We can buy on, if you can take us. We just want to get out of here."

"And you want to go downriver?" Their disbelief showed.

"We got friends," Mahlia said. "They say they got us room on a scrap ship, going out. Going north. To the Seascape."

"First time I heard of something like that. No one gets out of here."

"We got a friend. We just got to get there." She hesitated. "Please. We got to get downriver. My friend's just in the trees. We can pay. We got rice. We got machetes. We got coywolv skin."

In a burst of inspiration, she thought of Mouse and his profiteering schemes. "I got some half-man teeth. Dog-face teeth. You can sell those, right? Lucky charms. Soldier boys love those, right?"

She almost laughed when they perked right up.

Tool took the boys so fast that Mahlia actually felt bad.

The boys came up with their shotgun and rifle, full of swagger and acid, thinking they knew how to fight, maybe still a little high from whatever they'd gotten up to the night before, and Tool...

The boys stood there under the trees, looking around expectantly, kind of pissed that they'd come this far, and it was like the jungle just breathed.

The leaves rustled. The two boys flew. They crashed to the ground and Tool landed atop them. He ripped their guns away and wrapped a boy under each arm.

They kicked and thrashed and flopped around, and one of them started to piss his shorts, and Mahlia almost laughed, except she remembered what it had been like to be on the other end of Tool's attack, and she didn't.

She got down with the boys and said, "I don't got no money, but now I got you." She looked at them. "I'm going to talk to your boss. See if we can work out a trade."

They both stared at her with hatred.

Mahlia sighed. "Don't feel so bad. Half-man teeth are what got my friend Mouse into trouble, too. It ain't your fault." She grabbed the one boy's shotgun. Fiddled with it until she had it open. Checked the load.

"Take the rifle," Tool advised. "The kick will be worse with the shotgun. You won't be able to control it."

Mahlia looked from one weapon to the other. "That little licebiter carries it. Why can't I?"

"He has practice, and two hands."

Mahlia looked from the rifle to the shotgun she held in her hand. "But I can't miss with this."

"If you're close enough. Your stump will make it difficult to control."

"I'll brace."

Tool shrugged.

Mahlia took the shotgun anyway. Stood up, hefting it and smiling. Damn, it felt good to hold a weapon. Not just some machete that you could never get close enough to show what for. She couldn't ring-fight a soldier boy, but she could blow his head off just fine.

The gun felt solid in her hand, reassuring. Powerful. She could stand tall with a weapon like this.

No wonder soldier boys had so much damn swagger. With a gun under your arm, you walked tall. If she'd had a gun when the soldier boys caught her the first time, everything would have been different.

All her life she'd been ducking and running, always rabbiting, while the coywolv did all the hunting. But with this big old gun, she could stand tall.

The weapon was heavy, but she suddenly felt light, as if the weight of all of her past had suddenly fallen off, like a concrete block, tumbling away.

She grinned at the weapon in her hand. Yeah. She liked this gun, all right.

"Brace it against your shoulder when you fire," Tool said. "The kick will bruise you."

"It'll kill, though," she said. "It'll kill good."

"Resist the urge to think that weapon makes you strong."

"It sure don't make me weak."

"Weaker than you think," Tool said. "Resist its swagger."

"I don't swagger."

"Everyone swaggers with a gun. Look at it."

"What about it?"

Mahlia looked down. It seemed fine. Looked clean. In good condition. Ready.

"It gives you confidence." Tool shook the boys under his arms. "It gave these two confidence as well. And look at them now. From a position of strength to an asset of their enemy, and all it took was confidence. The swagger a gun gives when you're following some harmless crippled girl into the jungle."

Tool suddenly snarled. "Now look at it, again!"

Mahlia startled at the force of Tool's words. She looked down at the shotgun. "I am! I am!"

Scrapes and scratches. Heavy black barrel. A wooden stock that had been carved by hand and hammered back on to the main mechanism.

It was painted. Lots of guns were painted, though, and this one wasn't any different. Lots of things on it. Mostly green crosses, for Deepwater faith. The red stars of the Army of God.

"Yeah? What of it?"

It was just like every other gun she'd ever seen. Beat-up, but ready for action.

"Look," Tool said again.

Mahlia stared at it, trying to see what Tool saw.

"The paint is chipped," Tool said.

Mahlia glared up at him. "So?"

"So. Look."

Sure, some of the paint had chipped off. But there was just more paint underneath. Might have been a couple of Fates Eyes, from the shape of them, under the green crosses. Sure. It could be. Something red, too. Maybe a bit of a white star on a blue background. Maybe a UPF tag...

A cold crawling moved up her spine. Mahlia's breath snagged.

The gun gave her swagger, all right. And it had given their prisoners swagger.

And whoever owned it before that.

And whoever before that.

And before that.

And on and on and on...

She could look at the gun and see the history of hands that had held it. Soldier after soldier, making it his own. Covering it with luck symbols and charms, Fates Eyes and crosses and whatever they thought would give them the edge.

And every one of them was dead.

The shotgun didn't care who owned it. It went hand to hand. She was just the latest in a chain that might as well have gone all the way back to the Accelerated Age when people had cities that worked and they didn't shoot at one another all the time.

A lot of hands had held this weapon, and if it had done any of them any good, they probably still would have been holding it, instead of passing it down the line to her.

She shivered, suddenly wondering if she was a dead girl. If just holding the gun made her a ghost.

Tool growled. "You understand, now."

Mahlia swallowed. Nodded.

"Good. Now go and negotiate with our captain. We should go before day breaks on us fully. The town will awaken soon."

Mahlia turned and started to go, then turned back and looked at the boys.

"I don't want it." She held up the shotgun. "It's yours. Soon as we're gone, it's yours. I don't want it."

She couldn't tell what they thought of her. Their eyes looked wide and frightened over Tool's fist and she felt bad, but she didn't trust them enough to tell him to be nicer. Instead, she slipped out of the jungle, stealthing through the misty streets.

The heat of the day was already starting to increase, but the soldiers were still drunk and barely moving. A nailshed girl hurried through the mud of the street, barefoot, clutching torn clothing around her. She took one look at Mahlia and her gun, and steered clear.

Mahlia wondered what she herself looked like, that a girl like that would be afraid of her. She reached the water.

The man straightened at her approach, and his hand went for a gun when he saw Mahlia carrying the shotgun.

"Don't!" She held out her hand, holding the shotgun wide. "Don't."

"What's your business, castoff?"

"Me and my friend got to get downriver. We don't got no money. But we give your boys back if you get us down."

"Maybe I'll just shoot you."

"We need you. Need you to get us past the checkpoints. Tell us where they are."

"Who are you?"

"Just a war maggot, looking to get out."

"There's no way out. No one gets onto the scrap ships. They won't take your kind, or any other. Not unless you've got a king's ransom stuffed down your shorts. No one goes anywhere. The armies up north, all the battle lines. There's nowhere to go. And not for your kind, for sure. Now where's my boys?"

"You want them to live, you go downriver, past town. Tie up just out of sight. We'll meet you." Mahlia turned away.

"Wait!"

"What?" Mahlia glared at him, summoning all her threat. "What? You got something to say, old man?" She tossed the shotgun to him. "Take it. We don't want it. You either come downriver and get your boys back, or you don't—and you don't."

"Maybe I gun you down right here."

"Fates," Mahlia said. "I'm dead already, old man. Don't you get it? You kill me, it don't matter. I'm just another castoff. People won't even blink about it, will they? They'd mourn a nailshed girl more than they'd mourn me."

She held up her arms, stretching them wide. "I got no armor. Got nothing. You want to blow me away, you do it. No one cares." She looked at him. "But if you care about your boys, then you come downriver, and you meet us, and you get them back, all in one piece.

"Otherwise, you got my head, and you get theirs, too."

She turned and headed back into the jungle, not looking back. Her spine prickled and sweat gushed down her ribs. Waiting for the bullet.

A gamble. Everything was a damn gamble. Betting against luck and the Fates, again and again, and again.

She kept walking, waiting for the bullet.

32

"YOU WANT ME to carry *that* downriver?"

The boatman stared at Tool as he emerged from the jungle. They had rendezvoused below Moss Landing, but as Tool materialized from the shadows of the jungle, the boatman was so startled that he almost let the current carry him away.

Tool bared his teeth. "I am not here to war with you. We will pass through your life and be gone and you need never remember that we existed."

The man just stared. He looked at Mahlia. "What are you?"

"Just some castoff," she answered as Tool swung the two captives aboard the skiff and climbed aboard himself, making the sailboat tilt alarmingly.

"It's impossible," the man said. "I can't hide a dog-face on my boat."

Tool growled and bared his tiger teeth. "You may call me Tool, or half-man or augment, but if you think to call me dog-face again, I will tear open your chest, and eat your heart, and sail your skiff myself."

The man recoiled. "It's impossible. There's no way they'll let us pass with…with…" Mahlia could tell he wanted to say dog-face again, but didn't dare. "You," the man finished, finally.

Tool dismissed him. "That is not your concern. Tell us where our enemies lie. I will conceal myself at the necessary moments."

The boatman still looked doubtful. "And you let us go, when you're done?"

Mahlia and Tool both nodded. Mahlia said, "We're just trying to help a friend."

"Helping a friend?" The man looked at Mahlia, askance. "And this is how you repay our kindness? What if we hadn't helped you with Clarissa? Where would you be, then?"

Mahlia flushed and looked away. "It ain't personal," she said.

"It never is with your kind. You pick up guns and you hurt and you kill and none of it is personal." The man looked at her. "Children with guns. We aren't even people to you."

"Hey! I ain't part of this war," Mahlia said. "I didn't ask to be in it. I didn't ask soldier boys to come hunting after me! I ain't part of this."

But even as she said it, she felt stupid. Before her, two boys lay on their backs in the bottom of the skiff, bound in kudzu vines that Tool had twisted into ropes. Her captives. Her victims.

With Tool, she could just as easily cut off their hands and dump them in the water and laugh while they tried to swim. She had power over them, and she'd used it to make sure they did exactly what she wanted.

She was in, all right. All in, and going deeper.

"Just get us downstream and we'll leave you alone," she mumbled. "We ain't here to hurt no one."

The man snorted at that and seemed to be about to say more, but he caught sight of Tool's expression and fell silent. Mahlia felt bad again. Scared boys, all tied up. A man who hadn't done anything wrong to her, and she'd taken advantage of it.

Am I just like the soldier boys?

It wasn't like she'd killed anyone. If these licebiters had been picked up by soldier boys, they would have been dead already, or else recruited like Mouse. No way they'd just catch and release.

The wind filled the skiff's sails and they eased away from shore. The water reflected the light of the rising sun, turning the river into a glittering dragon that twined all the way to the Drowned Cities, and the sea.

"I can take you as far as UPF territory," the man said bitterly. "After that, I have no influence. I don't do trade with the river mouth. I can't take you all the way to the sea."

Mahlia nodded. "That's enough. Just get us through UPF lines."

"With the...half-man?"

"Do not concern yourself with me," Tool said. "The soldiers will not notice me."

"What if I give you up to them?"

Tool looked at him. "I will kill you and yours."

Was this what she wanted? Did she want to play the same game as the soldier boys?

"Untie them, Tool," she said. "Let the boys go. They won't do anything. They've got to be free for the checkpoints, anyway."

Tool shrugged. He unbound their captives. The boys sat up, glaring and rubbing their wrists and ankles. "Knew we shouldn't have helped a castoff," one of them said.

Mahlia glared at him. "Would you have let us sail, if you knew I was with him?" She jerked her thumb toward Tool. "Would you?"

The boy just glared at her.

"Yeah," she said. "That's what I thought."

Ahead of them, the river opened, showing the Drowned Cities poking up above the jungle. The buildings rose up, like bodies staggering up out of the grave. Towers and warehouses and glass and rubble. Piles of concrete and brick where whole buildings had collapsed. Swamp waters all around, mosquitoes buzzing, a miasma.

Mahlia saw it with a strange double vision. When she'd lived in the city it had been a place of play. Her school, her life with her mother and father, the collectors who came to buy antiques from her mother. Now it was burns and ruins and rubble and chattering gunfire, a map of safe territories, mining operations, and contested blocks.

When the peacekeepers had been there, they'd been all about setting up wind turbines for energy, wave generators, had even managed to create a few projects. Mahlia's mother had taken her out to a wind turbine project right in the river mouth, huge white turbines going up like giant pale flowers. Her father had had something to do with it, but whether it had been guarding the turbines themselves, or the Chinese construction teams, or someone else, she had been too young to understand it. But now, as she looked at the open waters, Mahlia saw them again, but the turbines were all torn down.

She pointed to them. "My dad worked on those."

"Castoff," one of the boys muttered.

Mahlia wanted to kick him, but she held off. The man said, "They took them down."

"The peacekeepers?"

"Warlords. As soon as China pulled its peacekeepers out, the warlords started shooting at them, trying to bring down the electric grid. It was a power-sharing arrangement that couldn't last. UPF in charge of the towers, and Freedom Militia in charge of the conversion station, so they'd have shared responsibility." He shrugged. "They shot each other up. UPF bombed the station. The Militia mined the turbines. And then the Army of God pushed them both out and sold the steel and composites, and the turbines all went out to Lawson & Carlson for new weapons."

He nodded at Tool. "Bet that's something his kind would know all about."

Tool didn't respond to the dig. "War breaks things," was all he said.

His ears were pricking to the winds, and his eye seemed to gleam with interest as they cut across the waters. Mahlia watched him.

Sometimes, his strange bestial face seemed completely human, when he laughed at some bit of half-man humor or when he'd tried to show her the folly of swaggering with a gun. But now, as they approached the Drowned Cities, she was aware again of how many layers affected the creature. Part human, part dog, part tiger, part hyena…pure predator.

As they approached the Drowned Cities, Tool seemed more and more alive. His huge frame seemed to pulse with the vitality of war. The hunger to hunt.

The boatman said, "As soon as we make this bend, we'll be in the city itself. Army of God territory. They'll want their bribes."

"You've done this before?" Tool asked.

The man nodded. "I have agreements to let me through. I bring supplies in for the captain who covers the river."

Tool nodded. "How long before they can see us?"

"I'll be sailing into the canals now."

Without another word, Tool flipped over the side of the

boat and into the water. The boys looked at her, suddenly speculative, started to reach for their rifles. Tool surfaced beside the boat.

"Do not think I am gone. I am here, and I am listening, and I can drown you all. Best not to be hasty in your decisions."

He disappeared underwater again. The boat rocked oddly and the boatman grimaced. "The damn dog-face must be right under the boat."

Like some kind of massive barnacle attached to the skiff.

The boatman hauled on his sails and his boys scrambled to pull out oars as they closed on the shore. The boatman looked around the boat, stared at Mahlia. Threw her a blue-and-gold cap with an old Patel Global logo on it.

"Pull that down. You look too much like a castoff."

"Other people got eyes like mine. Your boy, even."

"Other people aren't you. Everything about you screams castoff. You're the right age, and you look too mixed." He glanced to where canals of the Drowned Cities were opening before them. "You have no idea how much danger you put us all in."

They sailed into the canals. From under her cap, Mahlia eyed the city. It was different than when she'd been here last. It all had a dreamlike quality, one city on top of another city. Memory and reality, superimposed.

"The water's higher," she realized.

The boatman glanced over. "When were you here last?"

"When the peacekeepers left."

"Yes. The water here is higher, then. The dike and levee system the peacekeepers tried to install was destroyed as soon as they left. The warlords wanted to flood each another, so they blew them up, and all the drainage projects and hurricane protection barriers with them. So the ocean came flooding back in. All that work to push the water out, and they just let it right back in."

The place was worse than Mahlia had expected. Old neighborhoods were collapsed on themselves. Waterways made a maze through twisting broken buildings and rubble. Kudzu-tangled jungle and swamped buildings intertwined with brackish pools and clouds of biting flies and mosquitoes.

There were bars full of nailshed girls and drunk soldiers, rifles slung over their shoulders, shouting at one another, smashing liquor bottles. Squatters and addicts watched the river traffic with drool stringing from their lips and red eyes. Thick pythons undulated in the canals, and ravens and magpies circled overhead. Mahlia spied a den of coywolv peering from a window, three stories up.

City and jungle bled into one.

River traffic moved sluggishly. The red-starred flag of the Army of God hung bedraggled from building windows, and the face of the AOG's general, a man named Sachs, was slathered everywhere. Pictures of him holding up the green cross to his true believers, or wielding a shining sword and an assault rifle while the AOG flag billowed behind him.

His face stared out at the populace, challenging. Even the

crudest paintings of the warlord drew Mahlia's eye. General Sachs had close-cropped hair and a scar that ran the length of his jaw. But it was his eyes, black and intense, that held her. The man seemed to inhabit his paintings, seemed alive within those eyes, and seemed to promise things.

Other people seemed to think so, too. As the populace of the Drowned Cities walked past the warlord's various images, they made motions of supplication to him. Small gifts of food and flowers and snuffed-out candles were scattered beneath each painting, as if he were the Scavenge God or one of the Fates, but bigger.

His influence seemed to touch every neighborhood. Water sellers and nailshed girls and three-year-old children wore his political colors, and his soldiers were everywhere. In the streets and waterways. Clogging boardwalks as they smoked hand-rolled cigarettes and watched the river traffic. Army of God. Owners of the city. At least for now.

Much like the shotgun Mahlia had inspected, the walls of the city were decorated with the images of previous owners, emphasizing how quickly the tides of war shifted in the Drowned Cities.

AOG colors were slathered over other warlord faces, blotting them out. Other army flags were blacked out or painted over, but some images still peeked out. Mahlia could even make out a few peacekeeper slogans from when the cease-fire had been in effect. IMMUNIZE FOR LIFE. BEAT YOUR SWORDS INTO PLOWSHARES.

Mahlia saw soldiers on a boardwalk, waving them over.

They were just boys, some of them as young as Mouse, all of them armed with assault rifles and shotguns. Bony bodies and knotted muscles and scars that ripped across their bare backs and ribs and chests. All sorts of races and mixes, black and brown and pale freckled pink, and all of them as hard-eyed as their warlord. All of them full of the same hungry swagger as the UPF soldiers who had taken Mouse.

"Who're you, girl?" one of them asked.

Mahlia didn't answer. The boatman answered for her.

"She's with me."

He pulled out papers and handed them over to the soldiers. They looked at her, looked at the papers. Mahlia wondered if they could even read.

The boatman said, "I have an arrangement with Captain Eamons." He lifted a sack, offering it to them. "He will be expecting this."

The boys looked at the sack, looked at the papers. Looked at Mahlia.

Their eyes were bloodshot. Red rippers or crystal slide. All the troops were hopped up on the stuff to give them a combat edge, but it made them crazy and wild, and suddenly she had a bad feeling about the plan.

These soldier boys, they just wanted to kill another castoff. It didn't matter if she had the protection of this trading man or not. Didn't matter if there was some agreement.

A castoff had no chance going into the Drowned Cities. She didn't belong here. The warlords had demonstrated that when she and her mother fled the first time. People who had collaborated with China's peacekeeping mission were public enemy number one. The warlords and their soldier boys had long memories for traitors.

One of the boys was looking her over. He only had one eye, which kind of reminded her of Tool, but this boy's eye was brown and bloodshot and angry and crazy in a way that Tool, even when he seemed ready to kill, never was.

"You castoff?"

She tried to speak, but fear overtook her. Shook her head.

"Sure you are." He looked at the boatman. "What you want a castoff for, old man?"

The boatman hesitated. "She's helpful."

"Yeah? How 'bout I buy her?"

Mahlia's guts tightened. What a fool she'd been.

"She's not for sale."

The boy laughed. "You think you decide what's for sale, old man?"

The boatman shook his head. Even though he looked calm, Mahlia could see sweat dripping from his temples, running down his neck. "Your captain and I have an agreement."

"I don't see him around."

Mahlia thought she felt a thump through the base of the boat. Tool, either drowning, or readying himself to emerge and slaughter.

Stay down, she prayed. *Stay down.*

All the soldier boys were looking at her, hungry and

317

predatory. Their little aluminum amulets of protection glinted on their bare chests. Some of them had a green cross painted on them; others had their general's face painted there, the same one that slathered the walls, with his black skin like her mother's and his hollow cheeks and his wild, intense eyes.

The amulets were different, though. General Sachs was still smiling, but whoever had painted him had made him look almost crazy. Mahlia couldn't tell if it was because he wanted to look that crazy and dangerous, or because the painter just couldn't paint worth a damn, but when she looked up at the boys, she knew she wasn't going to ask. It didn't matter if she thought the general they worshipped looked silly or not.

No one with a gun looked silly, in the end.

The boy looked at the boatman, then looked at Mahlia, weighing his cruelty. His troops all watched, interested. Ready for anything. Happy for everyone to end up dead.

Don't shame him, Mahlia thought. *Give him a way out. Give him some way to not lose face with his boys.*

The boatman seemed to be reading her mind. "Your captain is expecting us." He opened a sack and withdrew a dirty stack of Red Chinese paper money, with pictures of some woman on the front and a tall angular tower on the back. BEIJING BANKING CORPORATION written in Chinese and English.

Red hundreds.

"Once he pays us," the boatman said, "there will be more on the way out."

The soldier boys didn't change their expressions. But the lead boy took the cash and waved them deeper into the Drowned Cities.

33

GLENN STERN'S FACE stared at Ghost from the side of a building.

The man was three stories tall, and ten stories up, and he was eye to eye with Ghost, because Ghost was sitting on top of a barracks building by a bonfire with all his warboys, and Ghost was the man of the hour.

They'd gone into an old building and found a whole bunch of old paintings and furniture, broken them up, and started a bonfire on top of the building, choosing one where they could see out across the Drowned Cities and enjoy the view.

It had been a hell of a time hauling the stuff up, but now it was all burning, and the fire was crackling and hissing, and all kinds of strange colored paints were bubbling on the canvas and going up in smoke.

Sergeant Ocho hadn't wanted to go up so high, but seeing as they were behind the war lines, and seeing as Stork and Van and TamTam and everyone else were begging, he said it was okay.

Stork said the sergeant didn't like getting pinned up in the towers; he'd been caught with an old squad and ended up doing an emergency jump into a canal from four stories up. Broke his leg doing it, but in the end, he'd come out okay.

Still didn't like to get pinned, though.

So now they were up high, looking out over the city, with Glenn Stern staring at them, and they owned the place.

Far in the distance, other fires burned, beacons. Some of them UPF; others, farther away, the campfires of the enemy. Sometimes, some asshole would launch a mortar and they'd watch it arc across, but there seemed to be some kind of agreement between the troops of the different factions that you didn't mess with each other when you did a rooftop camp at night. Skirmishing was a day job. When you cycled back for R & R, they left you alone, and you did the same. Mostly.

Tracer fire launched across a darkened street along with the chatter of a .50-caliber. Ghost was surprised to realize that he didn't need Mahlia to tell him what the guns were. He knew them all.

Van grabbed another big painting and dropped it on the fire. It hissed as the fumes from its paints went up.

The flames cooked through the picture. Some lady, sort of lying on a wheat field, looking across the hills to a house, all the colors kind of washed-out and grayed. The colors were boring, not like the kinds of paint they decorated their guns with. Those colors really stood out.

Ghost was looking at his own gun. It had color after color on it. Bright. A green cross on a red background, a sign that the Army of God had been the last owner.

Ocho squatted beside Ghost, nodded at the gun. "You should paint it," he said. "Make it your own."

"With what?"

"Romey's got some colors; he does the pictures of the Colonel sometimes."

"Like that one?" Ghost jerked his head at the huge image across the canal.

Ocho grinned. "Not quite. But he can get some supply. You can put your mark on it. Put a Fates Eye on it, or something. Get yourself some protection. Make it yours, right? All that AOG crap's got to go, though. No cross-kisser stuff. Fates Eye, or else UPF blue and white, you want to get all patriotic."

"How'd they even get him up there?" Ghost wondered.

Slim looked over at the image. "Patriotic fury, right? They scaled that sucker."

"Ropes," Ocho said. "They dropped ropes over the side,

and lowered themselves off the top. Worked for weeks on it. For Colonel Stern's birthday. Bunch of Alpha Company put the civvies on it."

"I still say they climbed."

"You weren't there," Ocho said. "It was before you even got your half-bars."

"Why you want to run down a good legend? Where's your patriotic fire?"

"I'm all for patriotic fire," Ocho said. "Especially if it's a bonfire." He tossed a cracked chair leg into the blaze, sending up sparks.

Ghost stared across the gap between the buildings. The people who had painted Glenn Stern had done a good job. The man looked like some kind of god. Hard and angular and his green eyes that did the same thing that Ocho's did. Sort of green with gold flecks.

A god, or at least a patron saint. They all toasted the Colonel with their bottles, and then they all toasted Ghost, the hero of the day.

Reggie had bought three bottles of Triple Cross off the boys over in Charlie Company. They had a still that they worked, smuggling food downriver off their territory grant, and then distilling it. No one knew what went into the brew. For all they knew, Charlie Company was distilling fingernails and dogs, but they said it was all real grain. Things like ShenMi HiYield Rice, TopGro Wheat, whatever they could burn out of the fields and get away with before Army of God or Freedom Militia figured out that they'd gone raiding.

Ghost's squad boys kept giving him shots, getting him drunker. He stared up at the image of Glenn Stern.

"You should hear him speak," Ocho said. "He's got fire in him. Make you believe you can walk through a wall of bullets for the cause."

"You got the same eyes," Ghost said.

Ocho glanced at the painting. "Nah. I don't. You look into the Colonel's eyes and you see it in a second. We got the same color, but our eyes ain't nothing the same." He shrugged. "Saved me, though."

"Oh yeah?"

"I wasn't Drowned Cities, originally. Not like most of these dumbass war maggots."

A couple of the other soldiers hooted at the insult, but Ocho waved them silent, smiling. "My family were fishers. We all got blown in on a hurricane, couldn't paddle out. UPF scooped us up."

He shrugged. "Most of us—" He broke off. "Anyway, they thought my eyes looked like the Colonel's, so they recruited me." He held out his hand, waist high. "I was a maggot about this big. They liked me. Like a mascot, right? Little bit of Glenn Stern, to keep them lucky when the bullets started flying."

"Those soldiers still around?"

"Nah. They're dead, mostly. But the LT, he was the one that saved my ass. He likes it when he's got a sign. There are days when all I can do is wake up and thank the Fates that I got the same colored eyes as the Colonel. If I didn't—" He broke off, his expression turning dark.

Ghost hurried to change the subject. "How come he calls himself Colonel?"

"You think he should call himself something else?" Stork asked, an edge in his voice.

"Army of God has a general. General Sachs," Ghost pointed out. "How come they got a general?"

"General Sachs." Stork made a face of derision. "Hell. That man ain't even a soldier. Never even went to war college. He's just some crazy dude who talks fine and got a bunch of sorry-ass warboys to believe they'll go to Heaven if they kill everyone who doesn't bow down to him. He calls himself Supreme Eagle, too."

Ocho broke in. "The Colonel says you can't just give yourself a rank. That ain't military." He nodded across at the huge painting. "He says he won't take a higher rank, because it's not his place to take a rank. That ain't patriotic. He's fighting for the Drowned Cities, not for some kind of rank. He loves this place, for real. He's not just here to scrape some scavenge out and run away like these other dogs.

"Someday, when we get rid of Army of God and Freedom Militia and Taylor's Wolves and all the rest, he's going to build it all back. Make it great again. Maybe then, he'll be like in the Accelerated Age. A president or something, right?"

"President," Stork laughed. "Don't they got one of those in China? Peacekeepers were always going on about stuff like that."

The conversation broke off abruptly as Lieutenant Sayle came up onto the roof. Everyone jumped to their feet.

"Soldiers!" The lieutenant smiled. "I've got good news. We've got a new hero in the platoon. Got to treat our boy Ghost right." He waved to Ocho.

"Burn him in. Give him his verticals, and treat him good. We have twenty-four R-and-R before we go back out and teach the cross-kissers another lesson."

"Burn me in?" Ghost asked.

Ocho and Stork had already grabbed Ghost's arms.

"C'mon, Ghost. Be a man. Get your three." Ghost started shaking at the thought of the iron again, but Tam-Tam handed him a bottle of booze.

"Drink up, warboy. You don't got to do this one clean."

Lieutenant Sayle set a piece of iron in the fire. Ghost stared at it, and then he took a big swig of the booze.

The iron got hotter and hotter.

Ghost took another swig. Ocho tapped him on the shoulder. "All right, warboy, one last drink. Let's get this done."

The boys all grabbed him. Some of them were laughing. Ghost fought to keep himself from struggling.

"Sarge?"

"You know the drill, soldier." Ocho took the brand from Sayle, and carried the red glowing bar over to Ghost. Knelt

326

down in front of him, his own face fierce with its scars. "You're one of us now, Ghost. UPF, until the sea rolls out."

He pressed the metal against Ghost's flesh and Ghost flailed and struggled. But they had his head and he didn't scream even though he wanted to pass out from the pain, and then the bar was on him again. And again.

Three across, and now three up and down. His horizontals and his verticals. Full bars. A real soldier now. The triple hash of Glenn Stern's United Patriot Front on his cheek.

The brand came away. Ghost lay on the rooftop, gasping. Someone pulled him up and then all the boys were slapping him on the back and cheering for him, every one of them with the same deep burn on their right cheek.

Ocho pulled him close. "We're brothers now."

The LT stood to one side, his hollow face smiling. "You did well out there, soldier. Real bravery. Even Colonel Stern has heard about how you turned the 999 back on the cross-kissers."

He took out a glittering golden pin and placed it in Ghost's hand. "The Star of the True Patriot. Your bravery under fire makes the UPF what it is. Keep it close."

Ghost stared down at the gleaming pin. It was a blue star on UPF white, surrounded by gold. The other warboys crowded around, peering at it.

Got himself a star, they murmured. *UPF Star.*

The lieutenant clapped Ghost on the back. "Congratulations, soldier. Welcome to the brotherhood."

And then Ocho shouted, "Who are we?"

"UPF."

"Who we fight?"

"TRAITORS!"

"Where do we fight?"

"WHERE THEY HIDE!"

"What do we do with them?"

"KILL!"

"Who are we?"

"UPF! UPF! UPF!"

Everyone was shouting and high, and Ocho and the lieutenant were smiling. "What are you waiting for?" Ocho shouted. "Show our brother Ghost a good time!"

With a whoop, the boys all grabbed him, and lifted him to their shoulders and carried him off the roof, chanting, showing their new warboy off to the other units. Ghost was theirs.

Ghost rode with his brothers, his cheek blazing with fire that all his brothers had felt before him. One of them gave him some kind of powder to snort, and it was mixed with gunpowder and his head went wild with pleasure and insanity.

The night became a whirl of drinking and powders and celebratory gunfire, and then they were all leading him into another part of the building and there were girls there.

Ghost tried to focus, surprised. He hadn't seen any girls since the village and he was confused by the reek of fear and sex and then his boys were pushing him forward. Someone shoved a bottle of Triple Cross into his hand, and

Slim and TamTam grabbed a girl and shoved her at him, and they all were laughing and drinking while they made the girl do whatever they could think up, and Mouse felt sick but Ghost was high and burning and alive and crazed and Mouse was dead, anyway.

Mouse was just some war maggot. Ghost was a soldier, and he was alive. Even if he was dead tomorrow, he was alive tonight.

34

OCHO WATCHED HIS new warboy go into the nailshed. It was always shaky after you burned them. Sometimes they broke, right after, and you had to put them down. Sometimes they settled in.

He remembered when it had been his turn. He'd never felt anything like it in his life. Being burned in. The smell made him sick. He wasn't like the LT or TamTam, who seemed to like the burning, but he was damned if he was going to show it.

He watched the curtain fall behind Ghost.

Sorry, warboy.

A nailshed girl came up to him, but he shook her off. "Not now." She looked nice, but he didn't want to be distracted. The booze and the red rippers were too much already, and they made it hard to concentrate on what was what.

He'd learned from Sayle that you needed a clear head. Sayle didn't booze at all, straightedge warboy, but Ocho suspected that what got him high wasn't any booze or drug or girl. It was the hurting. Sayle liked people hurt.

Sayle was the one who came up with the new way to deal with war prisoners. Chop off their hands and feet and dump them where their army could find them. Let them decide if they wanted the burden of taking care of someone who couldn't walk or eat or crap without someone helping them.

That was Sayle.

Ocho had watched Sayle do it the first time and then Sayle had straightened and looked at the platoon and said, "That's how we do, from now on." And Ocho had looked at the dying boy with his bloody stumps and he'd seen the future, right there.

That was him.

Not that day, and maybe not the next, but eventually, it would all come boomeranging back at him. Fates coming howling in like a banshee. And sure enough, now everyone did it. Now you always made sure your new recruits killed their own when they got tossed back.

It taught you a lesson, Sayle said: Don't let them catch your maggot ass.

Ocho pushed past the other troops and the girls, past the smell of coywolv roasting and headed down to the canals.

He didn't have any place to go. Wasn't even sure what he wanted, but he needed to think and with the R & R, he was going to take the time.

There was something that he'd been thinking about a lot, ever since the run-in with the 999.

The gun was banging away on them all the time, now.

They'd tightened security to keep spotters from getting deep in again like that. But it meant they needed to worry about more than a company of soldiers actually pushing the territory. Now a couple cross-kissers could sneak in and find a barracks tower and start raining death in on them. And that made Ocho start thinking about the endgame.

A pair of patrol soldiers called out to him. He held up his hands, careful not to make any moves while they came over. For a second he was afraid that he'd forgotten the call signs—but then they came to mind.

"Charlie Sweet Bogey."

Tomorrow it would be something else. The call signs were coming down from above, changing fast and furious. They needed to keep switching up to keep out any more infiltrators. The order came straight from the Colonel.

Ocho doubted it would last. The Colonel would need something better to identify his own. Ocho couldn't even get out to his own boys without almost getting his ass shot off.

It made it almost impossible, really. How were they sup-posed to let farmers in if they were looking for someone with a tiny little radio? They were used to looking for guns, but if it was just spotters now...

He made it to the company HQ, and checked in on the soldiers. He had downtime, but still, he couldn't help checking in.

"About time," someone said.

Ocho looked over at the boys. "Why?"

"Got something."

"Another spotter?"

"You mean forward observer."

"Right." FO was the new term. Forward observers. Handed down from the Colonel, also. Stern had gone to war college. He knew about forward observers. Just no one expected to have to actually fight them.

"You got to see this." One of the boys handed Ocho the squad's binoculars.

"What am I looking at?" Ocho asked as he peered one-eyed through the single good lens.

"You'll see. Just watch the water down there."

And so they sat, taking turns.

Nothing moved for a long time, and then suddenly the water moved and a girl surfaced...

What the...?

Ocho squinted, looking at her.

At first, he thought she was just taking a bath, getting the sweat off, but he'd been watching that spot, and she hadn't gone in. There was something about her...

Were the cross-kissers sneaking girls in as spotters?

Something was off. It wasn't that she was a girl in a war zone. They were around. Here and there. If she had the kill instinct, she was in, just like any boy.

He'd commanded a killer of a girl with curly brown hair that she kept cropped real short. Pale skin and freckles, and crazy as any warboy he'd ever known. She'd gotten blown up working point for a patrol when the Army of God mined a building they'd taken and were trying to clear. Walked right into a wall of nails. But she'd been good. Smart...

Ocho froze. This girl didn't have a hand. That was it. She was missing a hand.

You're sliding, he thought. *That's all. Just a bad slide on the crystal ride. There's no way. She couldn't be here. She can't. There's no way.*

The girl came out again, checking both ways.

Fates. It was the girl. He was sure of it. The one-handed castoff who'd stitched him up. Dark skin and Chinese eyes, and that look of a survivor. On her cheek, he could just make out the triple hash of Glenn Stern's chosen. He had to give her credit. She was almost as sneaky as Army of God.

The girl made a motion toward the water. Ocho stopped breathing.

"Oh shit."

"What is it?" his boys asked. "What you see?"

A huge shape was emerging from the still waters of the canal. Graceful despite its mass. The monster came out of the water and climbed onto the floating walkway. Whole and healthy. Not a sign of a war wound on it.

The half-man paused, crouched there on the edge, head swiveling left and right. Ocho couldn't breathe. Suddenly he was right back in the jungle, the creature exploding from the leaves, slamming him with a clawed fist and sending him flying. It was huge. It was too close.

Ocho yanked the binoculars away from his face. Realized he was being stupid. They were far away. They had no idea he was here. He lifted the binoculars again.

The monster was gone.

"Dammit!"

"What?"

Ocho pointed at the distant building. "I want spotters on that tower. Every side. We know what's in it?"

"Nothing. Old junk. Apartments."

"Get spotters on it. And kick this up to the LT."

"For some girl? You don't want us to just go grab her?"

"No!" Ocho whirled. "Don't go near her. Just watch. If you see her or the half-man come out, stay off them. Put two layers of spotters out, in case they slip by. And watch the water. They're using the canals. Swimming under our lines or something."

He turned and bolted for the stairs, galloping down flight after flight. The half-man was here. In the Drowned Cities. Inside their damn territory. The castoff and the dog-face.

Faster and faster. His trot turned into a flat-out run. The half-man was here. He slammed into a patrol.

"Hold!"

Their guns whipped up. Ocho skidded to a halt. "Don't shoot!" He tried to remember the passwords. Finally remembered, dragging them from his panicked memory.

"You need help, Sergeant?" they asked.

Ocho shook his head. "No. I'm fine. Bad rippers, that's all. Just a little shaky."

"Don't run like that." They waved him past. "We got warnings to be on the lookout for infiltrators, right?"

"I look like I wave a green crucifix?" He gave them a dark look. "Get out there and patrol."

He turned and kept going, but he was gripped with a sense of creeping horror. It was just dumb luck that his boys had picked a new pair of binoculars off the Army of God and were trying them out. Surveillance was at the edges, not this deep in.

What was that girl doing here? Every time Ocho had run into either of them, it had been bad news. And now they were here together, inside the perimeter, stealthy and deadly.

They had no reason to be here unless...

Unless they were hunting.

And if they were hunting, they either wanted revenge, or they wanted Ghost, and either way, it meant he needed to shut them down before they got any deeper.

35

CROSSING INTO UPF TERRITORY was harder than Mahlia had expected, but with Tool, it was at least possible. The half-man could sniff out the patrols, and sense them far away. After abandoning the boatman, they made slow progress across the city, moving at night.

When they reached the boundaries of the war between UPF and Army of God, where gunfire was traded every few minutes and buildings echoed with screams of soldiers trying to break through against one another, Mahlia nearly gave up. There was no way they could cross an active war line.

"We're dead," she said. "This ain't going to work."

Tool just smiled. "Do not be so easily discouraged." He took her hand and led her into the bowels of a swamped building. "We will swim."

"Swim where? They'll see us."

Tool's teeth showed. "Come." He drew her down into the water. "Trust me."

He dragged her deeper into the water. Mahlia started to struggle. Tool said, "Breathe deep," and she did, just as he pulled her down below the waterline. Warm seawater swallowed her. Distant waves and gunfire. Tool drew her onto his back, and then he was swimming.

He swam out through a broken window and into a canal, and still he swam. Water dragged at Mahlia as he accelerated, swimming hard. Mahlia clung to him and tried not to be torn loose by the pressure of the water streaming around her.

Her lungs began to heave with a need for air, but still Tool swam. She needed to breathe. Had to surface. Tool didn't stop. The half-man didn't seem to care. Still he swam. Mahlia started to panic. She tried to let go, to try to surface, but Tool seized her.

I'm going to drown.

She fought to surface, but the half-man pinned her arms, and kept her down. He pulled her close. His great face loomed before her. Blew a stream of bubbles in her face.

For a second, Mahlia was so surprised that she almost drowned herself. And then she understood. Tool had more than enough air for both of them. She steeled herself, and let herself exhale. Nodded to him, knowing the half-man's plan.

Tool's maw gaped wide, showing teeth. He pressed his mouth over hers. Breathed. Mahlia inhaled. Oxygen and carrion. Life and death, all at once. Mahlia's lungs filled to bursting with the half-man's breath.

Tool drew away, and motioned for her to hold on once again.

They swam.

Above them a firefight raged, but down deep in the water, they passed unnoticed. Canal after canal. Block after drowned block. They slipped through the city like fish, unremarked by the warfare that raged above.

At last, they had crossed the final battle lines, and Tool found shelter. He swam into a new building, and they surfaced to the sound of sloshing, salty waves and distant remote gunfire. Mahlia sucked clean air, desperately grateful to be breathing something that hadn't come out of the lungs of the killer. Clean oxygen. She gulped at it, coughed, and gulped air again.

"Do you know where we are?" Tool asked.

Mahlia swam to a window. It was half above the water level, so she could see a bit of the world outside. She peered out, then jerked back with a hiss. A floating boardwalk was right outside, at eye level. People outside, straining to drag a barge, slave laborers, under the eye of UPF soldiers. The barge was full of scrap. Rolls and rolls of wire and cable. Even through the glass, she could hear the groan of the scavenge laborers.

She waited until they were past and scanned the canal again, getting her bearings. "Yeah. I know where to go. We still got a ways."

Tool didn't complain. He just took her on his back once again, and they swam on. Hours later, they reached the place Mahlia had been seeking.

She surfaced first, climbing out of the water and slipping inside the building. She paused, listening. Praying that it was empty. No sounds echoed other than the flutter of pigeons. No voices. No smell of human habitation. Nothing. No one. Just another abandoned building.

Mahlia returned to the canal and motioned for Tool. The half-man surfaced and followed her into the tower of Mahlia's memories.

When Mahlia was young, her father and his peacekeepers had dominated the building. They'd lived in profusion. Here, Mahlia had spoken Chinese, like a civilized person. When she was out on the street, she spoke Drowned Cities, but here, she spoke Mandarin.

She had moved and blended between two worlds, and she'd done it easily. She was like her mother that way. Her mother had had the knack for crossing back and forth between cultures and worlds. She could make foreign buyers look at her and take her seriously. Trust that the antiques she sold were genuine. Get them to give her money. And she'd known how to float the Drowned Cities as well, ferreting out the things that foreigners wanted to buy. She could scavenge with the best, and then she could take her prizes to the foreign buyers and they'd seen her not as just another Drowned Cities con artist, but as a respected handler of antiquities.

"What is this place?" Tool asked.

"I grew up here," Mahlia said. "Lots of peacekeepers used to rent apartments here. The owners had ancestors from China, a long time ago, so they knew how to rent to peacekeepers, make them happy. Make food they liked, stuff like that."

The door to the apartment had been knocked down, furniture had been chopped up and burned. Soldiers had camped in it, and then some other animals had nested after. Pack rats maybe, from the piles of torn fluff and glittering objects in the corner.

Mahlia stood in the middle of the apartment, remembering. It seemed small in comparison to her memories. This place had been so large, and now the halls seemed short and the ceilings seemed lower. She pushed open another door and found her bed. The mattress was missing. She found it pushed up against a window in her mother's room, burned and shot through, as if someone had used it to shield themselves from weapons fire.

Home, now torn apart completely. Bullet holes in the walls, shell casings on the floor. The stink of a latrine long dead. A few pieces of art were still on the walls, but someone had painted a green crucifix over half of them.

Tool stalked the rooms like a tiger, probably building one of those tactical maps that he liked to have in his mind.

Noting every window and every door, every shared wall, every drop to the canals below.

Mahlia peered out a broken window. There was some kind of nest just outside, maybe hawk or pigeon, but it looked like it hadn't been used for a while.

Tool had counseled her to watch not just for people but for animals as well. Running animals, flights of birds, all were indicators of soldiers approaching, and all of them would be savvy for the same dangers from her. If Mahlia scared a group of roosting pigeons up here, she was marking herself as surely as if she stood up and shouted.

Down in the emerald green of the canal, someone was poling a skiff. Some kind of noodle seller. She was still surprised to see that anyone lived in the Drowned Cities other than soldiers, but Tool said that armies always acquired hangers-on — merchants, children, nailshed girls, farmers, smugglers, black marketeers, drug dealers.

Armies had needs, and they found ways to make sure those needs were supplied. They'd shoot every castoff they found, but plenty of other civvies were allowed to survive. It was Glenn Stern's patriotic duty to scrape the Army of God and Taylor's Wolves and the Freedom Militia from the face of the earth, but he needed the support of the people within his territory to carry it off.

And people did support him. After all, they had nowhere to go, either. Just like the soldiers. They were all pinned in by border armies and impassable jungle wilderness and the sea. A bunch of crabs stuffed in a pot, all ripping away at each other.

Mahlia felt a wave of bitterness at the sight of civvies down in the canals, selling their vegetables, meat, hot noodles. They could talk to those soldier boys. Probably, they'd ratted to the soldier boys, too. Probably told the returning armies exactly where to find every single peacekeeper family in the city, currying favor in order to keep the bullets pointed away from themselves.

Mahlia stared down at them, and imagined shooting them. Paying them all back for ratting her out and running her off, for helping to kill everything she'd grown up with and depended on.

"Vengeance," Tool rumbled behind her.

Mahlia startled. "You read minds now?"

Tool shook his head. "Your body is full of rage. Every sinew. It is easy to read. You speak volumes with a clenched fist."

Mahlia laughed shortly. "All those people down there, they didn't have to run."

"And you would like to make them run the way you had to."

Mahlia shrugged. "Sure. Teach them a lesson."

"You believe that seeing your enemies running and afraid would accomplish something?"

"What? You Doctor Mahfouz now?" Mahlia didn't like the tone of judgment coming from Tool. "Don't give me that 'eye for an eye makes us all blind' talk."

Tool's teeth showed briefly, a cynical smile. "Not I. Vengeance is sweet." He was squatting in the shadows, a massive statue of muscle and death. "But this place has gone beyond that. The people here don't even remember why they revenge upon one another."

"Doctor Mahfouz used to say living in the Drowned Cities made people crazy. Like it came in with the tide. When the water came up, so did the killing."

Tool laughed at that.

"Nothing so mystical. Human beings hunger for killing, that is all. It only takes a few politicians to stoke division, or a few demagogues encouraging hatred to set your kind upon one another. And then before you know it, you have a whole nation biting on its own tail, going round and round until there is nothing left but the snapping of teeth. Destroying a place like the Drowned Cities is easy when you have human beings to work with. Your kind loves to follow. My kind at least has an excuse, but yours?" Tool smiled again. "I have never seen a creature more willing to rip out its neighbor's throat."

Mahlia was about to retort, but a 999 boomed, interrupting her. Its artillery shell buried itself somewhere to the east of them. Another followed. And then another. Tool's ears pricked to the sounds. He began nodding slowly.

"What do you hear?" Mahlia asked.

Tool glanced over. "The tides of war. They are flowing strongly against Glenn Stern. The Army of God suddenly finds itself well armed."

"And?"

"The UPF will not last long. If your friend Mouse is still

alive, he will be in greater and greater danger. The 999 means that the Army of God has negotiated a way to bring in weapons past the sea blockades. Presumably they have made promises to share the UPF's corpse with their suppliers, people on the outside who are rich enough and hungry enough for raw materials." Tool shrugged. "It could be any of dozens of countries or companies. Perhaps Cycan Mining? Perhaps Lawson & Carlson. Or Patel Global or Xinhua Industrial. It hardly matters. The Army of God has sold the last scraps of their city so that they can dance on the skulls of their enemies."

"You don't know that's what's happening."

Tool smiled. "I am ignorant of many human things, but war I know. War requires a steady diet of bullets and rifles and explosives shoveled into its open maw. None of that comes cheaply. The only thing the warlords have to offer is the scrap of this city. I very much doubt they even remember what started their fighting with one another. Now they just want the territory so that they can sell a little more scrap and buy another handful of bullets."

Mahlia considered. "So they buy things from the outside?"

"They don't have the intelligence or the wherewithal to make their own equipment. All of them are funded by other groups who hope to profit."

"Those other people," she said. "Lawson & Carlson, or whoever. Would they buy stuff from other people? Not just soldiers?"

"What are you suggesting?"

Buyers. Mahlia tried to control her excitement. There were buyers, still. Just like when she'd been young and her mother had found the rich people who wanted antiques from the past. There were buyers.

She motioned Tool to follow, then guided him down a dusty stairwell.

"You can't tell anyone," she said, her words a whisper. Echoing her mother's own words the first time Mahlia had seen her coming out of her secret place.

Mahlia reached the level above the canals. Scanned the hall. It was abandoned. No one was moving about. She ran her fingers along a wall, pushing on it, feeling for the latch buttons. Pushed hard. They were stuck.

Tool reached past her. He leaned and she heard the click. A portion of wall opened. Tool cocked his head. "A secret door?"

"My mom had it built, my old man's idea. He bribed people. You'll see."

Mahlia waved for Tool to follow. Past the secret door, the warehouse was large. Bigger than two apartments put together. It was dim. The only light filtered in from the outside through high-up slits with bars. Barely noticeable. Barely worthwhile to investigate. With no way into this corner of the building, it had lain undiscovered, even as all the living spaces and apartments were ransacked.

Mahlia squinted in the gloom. Treasures surrounded her. They still existed. It wasn't just her child's dreaming mind that remembered this place.

It was truly here.

Oil paintings in gold-leaf frames. Marble busts of old men and women. Ancient muskets. A tattered banner with a circle of white stars on blue, and bars of red and white. A head, almost as tall as her, marble and craggy, knocked from some forgotten monument and moved by barge to this secret hiding place, until a buyer could be found. Old books, moth-eaten. Bits of paper curled and torn. Manuscripts. Bits and pieces of the Accelerated Age.

Mahlia's mother had known history, and she had had an instinct for what foreign buyers might desire. And it was all here. Still undisturbed. The valuables that she'd been sure the man who had fathered her daughter would never abandon.

Tool picked up a gray uniform of some long-forgotten soldier, and held it up to the light. Set it down carefully. Dust rose. He lifted an ancient musket, peered down its sights.

"Well?" Mahlia asked.

Tool looked over at her, inquiringly.

"Do you think we could sell it?" Mahlia asked. "Do you think this could buy us out of here? Find a buyer and smuggle out? If they smuggle in guns, maybe they'd smuggle out us. For enough money, they'd do it, right?"

Tool set the musket down, thoughtful. "Where did this come from?"

"My mom. She sold this kind of stuff. She did scavenge. But only the old stuff. And then she did a lot more of it when the peacekeepers rolled in and made the war stop for a while."

Tool shook his head, smiling slightly. "It must have been profitable for her."

Mahlia shook her head. "I don't know. That was all bank stuff."

"A bank...in China?"

Again, Mahlia shook her head. "I don't know."

"Your father. The peacekeeper. Did he know of this trade?"

"It's how they met," Mahlia said. "He collected things, too."

Tool snorted. "I'm sure he did."

Mahlia didn't like the tone of the half-man's voice, like he saw things she didn't.

"You think someone would buy this stuff?" she asked again.

Tool looked thoughtful. "Any number of people would buy it. It seems your mother was very good at what she did."

"Yeah?"

"I see things here that were thought lost long ago. These are the sorts of objects that should live in the greatest museums of the world." He gingerly lifted up a piece of parchment and studied it. "Some of them once did."

"So we can sell them?" she pressed.

"Oh yes. You can sell these pieces. The problem is that for every buyer, you will find a thousand others who would cut your throat for the chance to sell it themselves. We are surrounded by the treasure of the ages, and just outside those walls, tens of thousands of soldiers all kill one another over pieces of scrap that aren't worth a tenth of what's in this room."

"You think maybe there's a way to cut a deal?" she asked. "Some way to bargain with the soldiers?"

"A delicate negotiation, when they would just as soon put a bullet between your eyes. Neither of us is the sort the warlords like to speak with. A castoff and a half-man." Tool smiled.

"Mouse," Mahlia said suddenly. "If we can get Mouse back. He could be a go-between."

"You build cloud castles from dream smoke."

"But we could do it, right? If the Fates look right on us, then maybe we could do it, right?"

Tool looked at her. Scars and thought. "Do you believe the Fates smile on you?"

Mahlia swallowed. "They got to sometime, right? Got to."

36

GHOST WAS THROWING UP, head hung over a canal, when Ocho and the LT found him. They dragged him upright and splashed water on his face, and then waited again while he threw up some more, then led him down the boardwalk.

"I thought we had R-and-R?" he said.

Ocho almost looked guilty. "Yeah. Change of plan. We need you to go on patrol."

"Why me?"

"'Cause I said so!" Ocho's expression hardened. "Don't think because you got a fancy pin from the Colonel means I don't still own your maggot ass. I say jump, you jump, got it?"

"Yes, sir."

"Good. Alil's waiting for you."

When they got to Alil, he tossed Ghost his gun. Ghost hefted it, still feeling nauseated, trying to focus on his boys.

"We searching civvies today," Alil said. "Checking all the farmers and the girls, making sure they don't got anything like a radio." He paused. "And check our soldiers, too. If they got a radio, they ain't ours, even if they got a brand."

"Army of God keeps poking us," Ocho said. He wasn't looking right at Ghost, more looking away. Looking toward AOG territory, maybe. "We think there might be some infiltrators, so we want you to go over some of our inside sectors, check them real close. See what crops up."

Sayle was more direct.

"I want you boys to go out and make sure none of those cross-kissers makes it through on my watch. You catch one, you send him back without his hands and feet, right? Teach them a lesson."

"Yes, sir," they all chorused, but Ghost still felt nauseated from the night before and the new brand on his cheek ached like crazy. No way he was going to complain about it, but still.

Ocho gave them their sector. It was odd, because it was way inside their territory, but when Alil asked, Ocho just looked at him and said, "Maybe we got some intelligence, right?"

"Seems like a small area."

"Yeah. Keep close on it. When you finish with it, loop on it again. We got other people patrolling the rest."

A few minutes later, Alil was leading them out over a rubble trail between two buildings, through another, and then out to the floating boardwalks.

"You doing okay, soldier?" He clapped Ghost on the shoulder. "You look like hell."

Ghost just looked at him blearily.

Alil grinned. "Don't worry. This is crazy-easy duty. We're two cordons back from where we're seeing contact. Keep your eyes peeled, though. Maybe the LT really does got a lead on something. We don't want any more of these FOs slipping through. And don't get overconfident. Civvies sometimes get feisty when you search them. Got stuff they want to hide."

Ghost nodded and tried to pay attention. After their ambush with the FOs and the 999, he couldn't afford to lose track of what was going on around him. He wouldn't be overconfident ever again. Hell no. That's what got you dead like... *Pook?*... Was that his name?

Ghost was disturbed that he'd already forgotten the name of the boy who had trained him. Tubby? No... Gutty. Right. 'Cause of his gut. 'Cause he'd been fat, once. Back when the peacekeepers were around.

"Mouse?"

Ghost turned, surprised. The voice was familiar.

Something blasted past him, piling into his friends. They went into the water with a huge splash. Ghost stood frozen, staring at what stood before him. Mahlia. Real as day. Not

352

a hallucination. Not some hangover memory. Mahlia. For real.

"Mahlia?"

She grabbed him and dragged him into a building's shelter, pulling him close. She was talking to him, saying things, but Ghost couldn't stop staring at her face. She had the triple hash, right on her cheek, burned in good.

"When did you get recruited?" he asked, and then all hell broke loose.

Mahlia hadn't expected it to be so easy.

She'd been looking out the windows of her family's old apartment, just killing time, waiting for dark so they could start moving again. She knew she'd eventually have to expose herself and leave her lair, but not yet. She'd wait, and then she'd find Mouse's platoon. She'd look for that Lieutenant Sayle and his soldiers. The boys all had call signs, and she could make her way to them. Lieutenant Sayle, Hi-Lo Platoon, Dog Squad. She'd be a runner. A messenger. And if that didn't seem workable, she'd come up with something else. They were inside UPF lines now. In the dark, with a hat over her eyes, and most of the castoffs long dead, she thought she could pass.

One step at a time.

And then she saw Mouse coming down the floating boardwalk, jumping around splintered bamboo spans — him and a couple of other soldier boys, but practically alone.

She stared.

Was it him? Was it really him?

He had scars on his face, the full triple hash of Glenn Stern, just like she'd burned into her own cheek, and his ear had some kind of brownish bandage on it, but it was him. He had an AK slung over his shoulder, and she had to look at him twice more before she was absolutely sure that he wasn't just another soldier boy, but no, it was Mouse.

He was there. Right there.

"Tool," she whispered. "I see him."

Quick as a knife, Tool was there, looking down. "Only three."

"Two," Mahlia corrected. "Mouse doesn't count."

Tool didn't say anything to that. He saw the world differently. But Mouse wasn't going to shoot them. "I'll talk to him," she said.

"Not with those two."

"If he sees me, he'll break off."

"No. They are together. None of them will separate. They are patrolling. Even these boys know that much about their duties. They are nothing in comparison to a real army, but they have that much training at least." He studied them. "Were either of the others at the village?"

Mahlia stared down at them, trying to remember. There'd been a lot of them. "I don't know."

"If they were, they will recognize you, and they will kill you."

She couldn't be certain. She'd seen a lot of soldiers, but she had no way of knowing how many had been there, and if they had seen her, and she'd been distracted. It definitely wasn't the sergeant she'd worked on. Or Sayle. Or that one who had wanted to hurt her.

"I don't think so."

"Not good enough," Tool said. "I will neutralize them. You get Mouse."

And just like that they set up the ambush. It was easy. The soldier boys walked right into it.

Mahlia and Tool waited in a broken bay window of the building, a nice wide one that would let Tool move easily and that they could step right through and onto the boardwalk...waiting, waiting...and then as the soldiers came close, Mahlia called out to Mouse.

She felt a blur of wind as Tool shot past her and piled into the soldier boys. They went into the canal with a splash. Mouse turned. His gun came up.

Mahlia backed off. "Mouse?" Fates. Was he going to kill her? "It's me. Mahlia! We're here to get you out!"

The gun came down. Mouse looked from her to the water. A few bubbles rose.

"Mouse?"

The redheaded boy looked puzzled. He stared at the water, then back at her. In a minute Tool would have both of them drowned. Mahlia almost felt bad for them, knowing what that felt like. Being held down by a half-man while you drowned. Those two didn't stand a chance. She pulled him into the building.

"When did you get recruited?" Mouse asked.

He was still confused, and then Mahlia remembered her own mark. "No! Fates, no!" She shook her head. "I'm just here to get you out."

She tried to pull him with her, but Mouse wasn't coming along as quickly as she wanted. She saw that his face was nicked and bruised, and the bandage over his ear was bloody. He'd been in battle. He was in shock, she decided. He was still staring at Mahlia, looking surprised and confused, like he was looking at a stranger.

Tool surfaced from the canal. Suddenly the buildings around them opened up. Gunfire chattered all around. Bullets peppered the concrete and stone, whizzing and ricocheting. Debris showered them.

Mouse ducked under cover. Tool leaped from the water, running for the building's entryway, but his back was a carpet of red. For a second Mahlia thought that he was bleeding, but the blood was waving about, bristlelike.

Needles, she realized. Dozens, maybe hundreds of needles, all peppering his back. Tool shoved them both in through the window and stumbled. Kept shoving them forward, and then he toppled. Boots echoed down the boardwalks. It was an ambush, Mahlia realized. She'd thought they were hunters, but they were prey.

Mahlia grabbed Mouse. "Come on!"

She dragged him down a corridor. They weren't far from her mother's secret vault. If they could just get inside, the soldiers might not find it. But Mouse wasn't running, he was dragging.

"Come on!" Mahlia shouted. "Come on!"

Boots echoed behind them. More and more. They were pouring in from all sides. Mahlia slammed up against the warehouse's secret door, feeling for its catches, scrabbling at them, jamming them, pounding them in frustration.

The door swung open. She dove through, pulling Mouse. She heard shouts behind her. She tried to slam the door closed but a rifle jammed its way through, blocking her. Outside, the soldiers were all yelling. They slammed against the door and knocked her back. Soldier boys swarmed through, surrounding her. They grabbed her and dragged her out.

Mahlia caught a glimpse of Mouse, standing still, astonished, and then she was out in the hall, dragged kicking and screaming back the way she'd come. Before her, Tool lay on the floor, animal eye wide with tranquilizers as troops swarmed over him.

Lieutenant Sayle stepped in through the building's huge bay window, and a fresh wave of his troops boiled in with him. He smiled coldly as his boys slapped her and shoved her forward.

Mahlia caught another glimpse of Mouse being pulled away, a look of shame and confusion on his face. Soldiers were slapping him on the back, cheering and calling him Ghost, and more warboys were coming around to point at her and laugh, and spit in her face.

Sayle stepped close, smiling.

"The girl who summons coywolv," he said. "I have been dreaming about you."

37

MAHLIA STARED AT MOUSE, shocked. "You set me up?"

Mouse's eyes went from her to the soldiers, confused. "I didn't know." He finally seemed to be getting what was happening. He tried to push through the soldiers. "I didn't know!"

"Get him out of here!" Sayle ordered.

A couple of soldiers grabbed Mouse and pulled him away while he struggled and tried to get back to her. Mahlia looked to Tool, hoping for help, but he was down and gone. She was on her own.

The lieutenant raised his fist and swung hard. Pain exploded in her face. She tried not to flinch and not to cry. He hit her again. She felt her nose break.

The lieutenant stood before her, gray eyes coldly alight.

Mahlia tried to tear away, but the soldiers tripped her and she landed on the floor. She scrabbled to get up, but they jumped on her and held her down. Someone slammed her face into the cracked tile floor.

Lieutenant Sayle knelt down beside her. He grabbed her by the hair, twisting her head up so he could look into her face.

"You got some payback coming to you, castoff."

Mahlia knew what was coming. It was going to be like it had been for her mother. They'd rape her and break her, make her scream until they got sick of her. Then they'd kill her. Mahlia started to pray. Knowing it was stupid, but praying anyway. Kali-Mary Mercy, Rust Saint, Fates. All the martyrs of the Deepwater Church. Anyone.

Sayle put a knee on her back, pressing her down, and then Mahlia felt something else, too, metal pricking cold against the skin of her spine. A knife.

"Maybe we'll take your kidneys out, before we're done with you," Sayle said. "Harvesters give a good price for pieces and parts. Take your eyes, take your heart, take your kidneys, drain you out." He paused.

"But they don't need fingers, do they?"

Mahlia started to shake. Her fingers. Her hand.

She started bucking and twisting, trying to break free. Knowing it was pointless to fight, but doing it anyway.

The lieutenant put his knife against her pinky knuckle. She felt it slice through.

Mahlia screamed. She screamed and screamed and they didn't try to muffle her. They just laughed as she bucked and writhed under their hands.

"That's one!" Sayle crowed.

He dangled her pinky in front of her while she sobbed and tried to squirm away.

Sayle leaned close, his breath hot on her cheek. "How 'bout we go for two?"

"LT!" The shout came from across the room, interrupting.

Sayle turned, annoyed. "What do you want, soldier?"

"Need your help, sir."

With a curse, Sayle climbed off. Mahlia lay gasping, panting. One of the other soldier boys gave her a shove with his foot.

"Only four more..."

It didn't matter, she tried to tell herself as she lay shivering and whimpering. It didn't matter whether she had one or two, or no hands. She was going to die anyway. But she couldn't help crying.

"Call HQ," Sayle was saying. "Get us some more soldiers. Get us a damn barge. Show some initiative, soldier."

"We got no authority," the soldier was saying. They were all standing around the unconscious mass of the half-man. Some of the other troops were trying to get Tool lifted up. It was almost a joke. He was clearly too heavy for them.

The soldier talking to Lieutenant Sayle said, "We got to hurry. We got the sucker roped, but there's no telling how long till it wakes up. Until we got it chained or something, there's no guarantee it won't just bust loose. It's strong now. Stronger than when we chased it before. We don't want it waking up."

The soldier looked familiar to Mahlia.

The one she'd saved from the coywolv, she realized. The one she and Doctor Mahfouz had stitched up. She regretted it now. Should have let him die. Should have cut him wider open, and saved everyone the trouble. She could have finished it right there in the doctor's squat, a month ago.

Ocho. That's right. For knifing a bunch of other soldiers who all had guns.

Lieutenant Sayle was pissed. He kept looking from Mahlia to Ocho.

"Sir?" the sergeant pressed. "We got to make this happen now."

Sayle nodded impatiently, then stalked over to Mahlia. "We aren't finished, girl. We're just getting started."

He waved at some of his other soldiers and they all headed out, leaving Ocho and another squad behind. Mahlia closed her eyes. The pain in her hand was going away. She couldn't tell if that was because she was bleeding out…No, she couldn't bleed out. Not just from a finger. That would have been too damn easy. Sayle wouldn't let her go easy.

She lay still, trying not to sob. Some of the soldier boys

roped her legs and her arms behind her. The stump gave them a little trouble, so they did her arms above the elbows, almost dislocating her shoulders in the process, using some kind of sticky tape that wouldn't slide off.

Footsteps. Mahlia opened her eyes. It was the sergeant, standing over her.

"What the hell were you thinking?" he asked.

Mahlia summoned all her will, looking up at him, hating him. "You remember me, right?"

"Oh yeah. Crazy girl who brought the coywolv down on us. Ripped up Soa and Ace and Quickdraw."

"Saved you, though." She stared up at him. "You remember that? I saved you."

"Yeah, I remember."

The soldier boy almost looked sad.

Mahlia stared up at him, willing a connection. Willing him to see her as a person. "Let me go," she said. "Just let me and Mouse go."

"You crazy? I let you go, I'm dead. That boy you call Mouse?" He shook his head. "He's already dead. Never even existed. We got a soldier name of Ghost, who might look something like someone you knew a long time ago, but he ain't that boy anymore."

"We could run."

"There's nowhere to go," Ocho said.

"What if we could get away? The half-man could do it. He could get us out."

Ocho smiled slightly. "Now you're just sliding."

It was the same as when the peacekeepers left. Just like when she'd stood on the dock with her mother, waving her arms and jumping up and down, begging for the clipper ships to sail back. It didn't have to be this way. He could choose different.

"Please."

The sergeant fumbled in his pocket, pulled out some pills. "Here."

Mahlia turned her face away, but the boy grabbed her and twisted her head around. "Don't be dumber than you already are. They're painkillers."

"You think that's enough?"

"No. But it's what I got. And it's what I can do."

Mahlia stared up at him, feeling stupid for hoping the warboy would have compassion for her. "Just kill me," she said. "Just kill me and get it over with. At least do that. Don't let Sayle get hold of me again. You owe me that much. Don't let him do any more to me."

The sergeant looked apologetic. "LT would cut my own fingers off if that happened."

"I saved you," Mahlia pressed. "You owe me."

Ocho grimaced. "Yeah, well, no one ever said things balance out. That's for Fates and Rust Saint worshippers."

He forced the pills between her lips with dirty fingers and clamped her mouth shut so that she couldn't fight them off. Pinched her nose. "Just swallow. You'll be glad."

She finally obeyed, staring up at him with hatred. He

nodded, satisfied, and straightened. "They got opium in them. Warboys smoke it, but you can eat it. Takes the edge off, whatever ails you."

Mahlia wanted to keep hating him, but her eyes were getting heavy, and dreaminess overtook her.

38

THE GIRL'S VOICE slowed and went blurry as the meds hit her. Opiates. Good stuff that put them all into a dream state, let them ride out the pain. Ocho looked down on her. Waved at Van. "Bandage that hand."

"But—"

"LT wants to torture her, not bleed her out. Not yet, at least."

He turned away. It was better not to look at her. Better not to put himself in her shoes. That was for sad-sack half-bars who hadn't burned in. You didn't want to overthink. It just got you confused, and it got you killed.

Ocho turned his attention to the half-man. "Get me some more ropes. I want that dog-face looking like a damn mummy. Wrists. Elbows. Ankles. Knees. Upper body. And then double it up."

A couple of the soldiers groaned, but Ocho snapped his fingers and they made salutes and got to work. They were lazy, but they were good boys, when it came down to it. They showed respect when it mattered.

Ocho looked at the unconscious half-man. The monster was stuffed to the eyeballs with tranquilizers. Huge amounts, and Ocho still wasn't sure it would be enough.

Even now, it almost looked as if the creature's one open eye was following him, even if it didn't move, it looked like it was still there, caged by tranquilizers but entirely aware of them. Watching.

Ocho shivered, remembering how deadly it had been when it came after him in the swamps. Then, it had been underfed and wounded. Now, though? Fighting it would be like fighting a hurricane. When they'd first sprayed it with the tranqs, he hadn't even been sure they were going to hit, it had been moving so fast.

"You serious about all this rope?" Stork asked.

"If I had my way, I'd kill it right now," Ocho said. "If it starts to move, stick it with some more of that tranquilizer."

"Don't got any left."

Ocho's skin crawled. "We used it *all*?"

It was like they were tying up some kind of demon. No way this could turn out well. LT wanted it alive, but he was crazy. Always trying to climb too high and impress too many people.

Kill it now.

Ocho knew that was the best way to take care of his boys. Get rid of the thing. Chop its head off. Burn it until there wasn't anything but ash. He felt an almost superstitious dread.

"Wrap it good, then. If it wakes up, we're all dead."

He turned and walked down the hall, wanting to get away. Ahead, he saw the open door, the hidden place in the wall that the castoff had been trying to get into. He peered inside. Whistled.

"Nice bolt hole."

Paintings, statues, all kinds of stuff. Ocho eased inside, awed at the amount of loot that he was looking at, overwhelmed by the feeling that he was looking at something rare.

There were things here that Glenn Stern revered. The faces of true patriots. Images that the Colonel handed out to his boys as luck charms. Old soldiers. Fighters who'd fought the good fight over centuries for the sake of the country.

A scrape of movement behind him. Ocho whirled, his hand going to his fighting knife, and then he relaxed. Ghost.

"What're you doing here?"

"Is it true?" the boy asked.

"Is what true?"

"There's treasure, I heard."

"Yeah, there's treasure." Ocho pushed him out and pulled the door shut. Was surprised that it disappeared so completely. He marked the place in his mind.

Another thing to deal with.

He took Ghost and guided him away from the hidden vault. As they passed the castoff girl, Ghost stared. She lay still, eyes glazing with the drugs Ocho had fed her, trussed and bleeding.

Ocho felt him falter and gripped his arm harder, dragging him past. "Don't look at her. She's not your business."

"But—"

Ocho spun Ghost to face him. Looked him in the eye. "I'm trying to keep you alive, soldier. If people think you're unreliable, they'll kill your ass. Won't even think twice. That castoff ain't anything. Just a piece of meat. Like a cow or a pig or a goat. We all got past lives. Things you might want to think about. Things you might pretend you can get back to."

He gripped Ghost's shoulders tighter. Got his face in close. "Don't you think about any of that! You focus on your job, soldier. You think about your brothers. You think about us. About keeping all of us alive to fight. You think about Army of God and how they'll do us all if we lose focus.

"Now get out there and stand patrol. We got a war on." He shoved Ghost out the door. Nodded at Stork.

"Keep an eye on your warboy. Make sure he don't forget who he is."

Mouse stood outside, shaking. Mahlia was there. *Right there*. If he was brave, he could just walk in and—

And what? Shoot everyone? Kill Stork and Ocho and TamTam and everyone?

Stork came outside. He took Mouse's elbow and tugged him down the floating boardwalk. "Let's walk, soldier."

"I—"

"You can't go back, you know."

"I wasn't..."

"Sure you were." The tall black boy smiled slightly. "Everyone thinks about it sometimes. I even tried." He glanced at Mouse. "After I went full-bar, I tried. You can't go back, because they know. They know what you are now. They know what you done."

He spat into the canal. "They don't want you. It's like you're bad meat. Civvies smell you a mile away, and the only thing they want to do is bury you. You might not like it, but without your squad, you're nothing."

He fished a hand roll out of his pocket and lit it. Took a deep drag and handed it over to Mouse. "After a while, you figure out the only people who got your back is your squad. We got you safe. We're your brothers. We're your family now."

He took the hand roll back and puffed again, before nodding down the canal. "Looks like the LT found us a barge. Time to get to work." He jerked his head toward the building. "That girl, she's just some civvy. If she knew what you done...how much you killed...the girls you done, the bad shit you been up to..." He shrugged. "She'd rather puke than look at you."

"But she was coming for me," Mouse said. "She said she was coming for me."

"Nah. She was coming for some civvy she called Mouse." He flicked the last bit of cigarette into the green waters of the canal.

"She don't give a damn about Ghost."

Loading the half-man into the barge took ten of them working in concert. The bastard was dense. Like its muscles were made of concrete. As soon as they started dragging it, Ocho realized they probably should have improvised some kind of stretcher, but it was too late then, with the LT standing over them and swearing that they needed to hurry up.

So they dragged and grunted and hauled and sweated and cursed and finally got the monster dumped into the barge.

The barge was half-full of iron I beams and sharp chunks of copper tubing from some building's plumbing, which meant the LT must have just grabbed the first barge he'd found. The sullen looks on the faces of all the bond labor seemed to confirm that. They'd probably get hell from their overseers for coming back light, but that was the way of it.

Ocho made a mental note to at least send some kind of report along with them that it wasn't their fault. Sometimes the overseers could smuggle meds and booze and cigarettes and drugs in from the docks, and if you stayed on their good side, it was better than if you didn't. Kept them a little content, at least.

The barge rode slowly through the water. The half-man didn't move. It might as well have been dead, they'd loaded it with so many drugs.

The barge was slow. Ocho hated how slow it was. He split his time between keeping an eye on Ghost, the half-man, and the castoff, who looked like she was starting to wake up.

He looked from her to Ghost, not liking what he saw there. She'd been insane to follow her boy. But she'd come anyway. And it pissed Ocho off.

For a little while, he couldn't decide why it made him so mad, but he kept wanting to hit her. To punch her and shake her.

Stupid-ass doctor girl. Dumb castoff. Didn't she know this was no place for war maggots like her? Nobody wanted a castoff reminding them how China had taken everything over for more than a decade, telling everyone what to do and how to live. Swaggering around with their guns and their half-men and their biodiesel attack boats.

She was stupid. Too stupid to breathe. And now she lay like a dead fish atop a pile of copper. Her eyes were open, watching him. Her hand looked like it had started bleeding again.

You're just parts, he told her in his mind. *Just a bunch of blood and kidneys. Maybe they pop your eyes out and give them to someone else. Harvesters are always buying. You're just parts.*

She deserved it.

So why did it bother him so much?

Ocho was smart enough to know that when you got crazy about something, you needed to think it through. Being crazy meant you did things by reflex, and it meant you made mistakes.

Sayle had been that way with the girl. Going after her, being all over her like that, threatening her. Sayle liked to hurt people, but this was more. This was all about his getting ambushed by a civvy. Pissed off about being embarrassed by a one-handed castoff.

She'd jammed them all good with her coywolv trick, and none of them had seen it coming. But then, Army of God had ambushed them last week with that 999, and that wasn't personal. Sure, they'd chop up the next bunch of cross-kissers and dump them in a canal if they found them, but it wasn't personal.

But the lieutenant was really stewed about the girl. This was crazy stuff coming from the LT, and it made Ocho nervous. He didn't like being on this slow barge, with a drugged-out dog-face and an angry LT, because it meant the LT wasn't thinking straight. Wasn't looking at the big picture. All because of that girl.

Ocho stared at her. He couldn't decide if he was pissed off at her because she'd tried to act like he owed her for saving him from the coywolv—which was a load of crap no matter how you sliced it. She'd sicced the coywolv on them, so saving him wasn't anything other than bringing the scales back to even.

No...It was because she'd come all the way into the Drowned Cities, to get her boy back.

Mouse, she'd called him. She'd come all the way in. And it made Ocho want to shoot her right then and there.

No one ever tried to come for you.

Ocho sucked in his breath at the thought. He coughed, and it almost came out as a sob.

Reggie and Van looked over. Ocho stared them down, face like stone, but inside, it felt like someone had a handsaw and was cutting up his guts, ripping away.

No one had ever come for him. They'd blown into trouble, him and his uncle. And not his mom, not his dad, not his brother, not a dozen people who he'd called his friends back in his town on the coast, not a one of them had ever come looking for him, trying to get him back. They'd just let him go. That was the difference. But this castoff cripplehand civvy girl had come all the way in.

Ocho scowled down at her limp body. *See what loyalty gets you? See?*

Stupid bitch. She didn't have any survival instinct at all. She deserved what she got.

39

MAHLIA STARED DULLY at the world around her. The opiates made the pain...not exactly go away, but made it less important. Irritating, still, but distant. She only had four fingers left.

Four out of ten ain't bad.

It was just like the last time she'd been caught, when the Army of God had taken her good right hand. So much of it felt the same. She wasn't even a person to them. It was all the same.

Except, that time Mouse had come to her rescue. She didn't think that was likely this time.

Mahlia turned her head, trying to see where Mouse was. Someone kicked her. Lieutenant Sayle looked over at the noise and Mahlia froze. She didn't want to show the man how scared she was, but she couldn't help it. She was terrified. Just having him look at her filled Mahlia with a sick animal terror, as if she were a mouse being watched by a panther. All she wanted was for Sayle not to look at her. The man's gray eyes held hers for a long time, promising more evil. At last he looked away. Mahlia lay still, heart pounding. Trying to make herself relax. Feeling the muddy pain of her newly missing finger.

From where she lay atop a pile of copper, she could see big buildings going by, and then the sky seemed to open up. They were out in the open, a huge rectangular lake stretched into the distance. The slaves wading around the edge of it, using floating boardwalks and rubble for purchase as they dragged the barge along. She could hear them splashing. She caught a glimpse of a white monument spiking up into the searing blue sky, right out of the center of the lake, a monolith of marble, its face yellowing in places, and cracked, but still vertical.

The scrap barge creaked as the men and women pulled on their ropes. They chanted and hauled. They were civvies. Or slaves. Or maybe just legs and arms and sweating backs.

Mahlia would have given the rest of her fingers just to be one of them.

Some of the soldier boys were standing up now, looking forward.

"There it is," one of them said. Others stood, talking, craning their necks.

"The palace."

"Damn, it's big."

"Can you see the Colonel?"

"Don't be stupid. He doesn't stand around waiting for a maggot like you to catch sight of him. He's running a war."

The palace, the palace…

Mahlia craned her neck. A huge marble building loomed into view. The palace. Marble from top to bottom. Steps marching up from the lake to its grand presence. A soaring dome stood central, seeming to touch the sky, and it was flanked on either side by broad marbled wings that encompassed more space than Banyan Town. Grand columns and intricate carvings decorated the structure, what must have taken decades of work to create.

From what Mahlia could see, the place looked even worse than when she'd been here before, when her father had taken her to see the eagles and ancient sigils of a long-dead nation.

One wing of the vast structure looked as if it had been hit by artillery, and its facade had turned to crumbling rubble. Scavenge gangs were ripping into it, men and mules dragging material out of the shattered building, skins gleaming sweat under the burning sun. They heaved at huge marble blocks, then slid them onto skids, so that they could ease them down the crumbling marble steps to the waterline, where they were being loaded onto barges.

Not far from the marble mining operation, a line of ancient marble and bronze statues stood, along with other sundry artifacts. It reminded Mahlia of her mother's warehouse, but out in the sunshine, with a half-dozen men in tidy clothing winding amongst the wares, studying paintings and statuary, squatting to inspect tile inlays, running their hands over mahogany desks and antique chairs with curving legs, all while they adjusted their thin ties and fanned themselves with hats that matched their pale tropical suits.

Antiques traders. The sort she'd seen her mother trade with. The war continued, and the buying did as well. Mahlia stared at them dully, wondering if she could have offered them her mother's warehouse, if one of them would have consented to smuggling her and Mouse away from the Drowned Cities and into a better life.

It had seemed like such a good plan when she'd first started to consider it with Tool. Now, it just seemed silly. She lay still, feeling the sear of the sun, and watching buyers and sellers. Fancy corporate logos were splashed on the sides of the zodiacs and skiffs that floated at the waterline, waiting to take away the buyers' purchases. Lawson & Carlson. T.A.M. Worldwide. Reclam Industrial. One of the rafts even carried Chinese characters that she recognized from her time in peacekeeper schools. China might have given up on trying to stop the endless civil war, but some of its companies were still here, picking over history's bones.

Mahlia watched as one of the buyers supervised a statue being loaded into a motorized skiff. Bored UPF soldiers stood around, keeping an eye on the proceedings. They finally got the statue secured, and the man and his bodyguards all climbed in. They fired up a biodiesel engine and buzzed away.

The palace loomed larger. The white dome soared overhead. It had a hole in it, from some missile, or mortar. Another new wound. It hadn't been there when the peacekeepers had owned it; she was sure of that. She remembered standing in front of it, her and her mother, while her father snapped a picture, and at that time, it had still been whole.

Her father had said that it had been the capitol building for political bosses during the Accelerated Age. Nothing like what they had in Beijing, but still, important for its time, and when the peacekeepers intervened in the civil war, they had set up administration there, as they tried to drag the Drowned Cities out of barbarity.

Mahlia had thought the palace looked grand.

Now, though, with one entire wing being torn down and a hole in its crown, it didn't look like much. Just easier scavenge than some of the other buildings that lined the huge rectangular lake, because at least it was up on a hill. Now, it just looked like something that would sell well when the soldier boys traded its marble for more bullets.

A whistling filled the air.

"Down!" Ocho shouted. "Down! Get down!"

Everyone flattened themselves. Another part of the marble palace exploded, right before Mahlia's eyes.

40

INSTINCTIVELY, OCHO FLATTENED himself as the 999 round came screaming in. The palace rocked with the explosion. Debris showered the steps. People screamed and scattered.

A second later, another round came in. It missed the palace and geysered into the lake, sending up foam and froth.

Ocho straightened, trying to get his bearings. They were sitting ducks. He could see people all around the lake, flattening themselves, staring up at the sky as though they'd be able to see the next round coming and somehow dodge it.

Another shell pounded the palace's scavenge side, spraying smoke and debris. A mule was blown down the steps toward the water, smearing red over marble as it tumbled. Ocho's soldiers were all staring, shocked.

"Get your heads down!" Ocho said, even as the lieutenant stood up and cocked his officer's pistol.

"Keep pulling!" the LT shouted at the barge workers. "You keep pulling or I'll put you down myself!"

Another shell dropped out of the clear blue sky.

"They're going after the Colonel," Van whispered. His voice was awed.

Another said, "They can't hit the palace, can they?"

Ocho could hear worry in the boy's voice.

"They just did, maggot."

He couldn't catch sight of which soldier had asked the question, but he knew the feeling. The Army of God was going after Colonel Glenn Stern, and the heart of the city. How was UPF supposed to survive if they lost their leader? What would happen to them if the Colonel died from the shelling? What would be left of the Drowned Cities if AOG was willing to destroy its last monuments?

If Ocho thought about it rationally, of course the Army of God would try to bomb the Colonel, but still, it was unnerving. No one was safe. Not even the Colonel. Suddenly, they were all just scared little rabbits, looking for cover. But the Colonel wasn't supposed to be like that; he was supposed to be above all that.

"Can they kill the Colonel?" Stork asked.

"Anyone can die," the LT said. "High or low, doesn't matter. That's not your problem, soldier."

Stork shut up. Ocho watched the lieutenant. Sayle didn't look worried. He looked completely calm. As if the 999 wasn't a threat at all. The blond man stood tall as another round came down and hit the north wing of the building. He didn't take cover. Didn't even flinch as the explosion rocked outward. Just watched the hit with his cold gray eyes.

"Don't worry, boys," the LT said, smiling. "The Colonel has a plan." He smiled again and looked down into the barge. "Army of God won't know what hit them."

Ocho followed Sayle's gaze to the unconscious half-man. What could *it* do? But he didn't have a chance to question, as their barge bumped up against the steps of the palace.

TamTam and Stork and Ocho rolled out and ran to grab one of the abandoned sledges that the workers had been using to move marble. The LT pointed his pistol at the barge pullers, and put them to work rolling the half-man onto the sledge, urging them to hurry up as everyone watched the sky for more shells. Ocho sweated and swore with everyone else. It felt like they were working in molasses. Waiting for the next shell to drop right on their heads at any moment.

Finally they had the half-man secured and the workers were hauling the monster up the steps. They passed inside, dragging the half-man. Colonel Stern's elite squads watched, interested.

Inside, it was almost cool: out of the sun, surrounded by marble halls. Ocho had never been in the palace. He tried not to stare at the gleaming marble or the vaulted ceilings with their paintings, the intricate carvings marching around their edges.

It was a strange, echoing place. He didn't like being in it at all, not with the 999 trying to bracket them. He kept waiting for another shell to come crashing through one of the beautiful domed ceilings, but the artillery seemed to have stopped for the moment.

Was the Army of God just trying to show they could put rounds wherever they wanted, or were they trying to actually hurt them?

Either way, Ocho didn't savor being blown to pieces. He didn't think he was going anywhere but straight to hell when he died, so he wasn't eager for the afterlife the way the Army of God boys were.

They followed the sledge, and finally got to a spot where Stern's elite all wore black uniforms. Eagle Guard. The best of the UPF. Every one of them was older and more experienced than anyone except maybe the LT. Survivors. They'd grown taller than all the warboys except Stork and the LT, and they looked down on the rest of the platoon.

Ocho was surprised at how small he felt standing in front of them. Of course, he'd seen them in the past from a distance. They traveled with the Colonel when he toured the war lines, but here they were, and they were huge in front of him. Muscled and well-fed, with their black uniforms and their hard eyes.

At the sight of the half-man, though, their demeanors

changed. One of them whistled in surprise. Another, the oldest of the group, a man with small crow's-feet at the corners of his eyes, ran his hand over the inert monster.

"Haven't seen one of these since we fought up north," he said. "Nice work."

Ocho and the rest of the boys straightened at the compliment. The older man motioned to his Eagles.

"We'll take it from here."

They gathered up the ropes to haul the drugged half-man away. Lieutenant Sayle waved to Ocho. "Get the girl. We're done here for now."

But the Eagle held up a hand. "The girl came with the half-man?" he asked. "They slipped in together?"

Sayle nodded unwillingly.

"We'll take her, too. The Colonel will want her."

Ocho could tell that the lieutenant wanted to argue, but he bit it down, and then Ocho caught sight of something more worrying. Ghost was staring at the girl. Ocho could practically see the gears turning in the soldier boy's head.

He went over and grabbed the boy. "Outside, soldier," he said. "We're all going outside."

Ghost resisted. Ocho gave him a shove. One of the Eagles grabbed the castoff girl and hefted her over his shoulder. She flopped limply, drugged and stupid with the opium that Ocho had given her. He couldn't even tell if she was really there anymore.

Ocho wondered what would happen to her. Maybe she'd

be better off in the Colonel's hands. At least she was out of the LT's control. That had to be something, he told himself. As she was carried away, limp like a sack of potatoes, Ocho tried hard to believe it, and then he tried to figure out why he cared.

41

A NEEDLE SLID into Tool's shoulder, flooding him with endorphins and amphetamines. He came alive. Awake and alive. Ready for war.

Men all around. Many of them. Deep voices, echoing dully against hard marble walls and tile floors. *Men.* Adults. Not just child soldiers from the swamps. Steel and iron and gunpowder. Tobacco smoke. The smells and sounds of a war machine's beating heart.

Tool remembered the darts hitting, thinking for a moment that they were bullets and that it would be difficult to survive so much lead, and then he'd been surprised at how little each bullet hurt... Just before the tranquilizers washed over him like a tidal wave.

Captured then. But still alive. He listened to their words:

"*K Canal...Angel Company...Lost fifteen at Constitution.*"

The sounds of an army besieged. It had been a long time since Tool stood in the heart of a command center, but all of it was so familiar that it might as well have been yesterday. Their words and movements told him everything he needed to know about their present circumstance.

"*Artillery support...sorties into North Potomac 6.*"

Tension in the adviser's voices. Worried mutters as they relayed reports from various fronts. Fear. It was rank in the room. They were all going to die, and they knew it. The United Patriot Front found itself hard-pressed. Its Colonel was outmatched, and his soldier boys were inadequate.

Tool waited until he sensed one of military men coming close, smelled his sweat and fear, and then he opened his eyes and lunged.

He slammed up against iron shackles.

The man scuttled back, swearing. "It's awake!"

Metal bit into Tool's arms and ankles. He was still groggy from whatever tranquilizer they'd used on him. He hadn't even realized he was bound.

Tool roared and lunged again, testing the chains, tearing at them. Military men flattened themselves against marbled columns and frescoed walls, eyes wide with fear. Tool strained to reach them and they shrank away, but the bonds held.

Tool lifted his hands to study the inch-thick iron that bound his wrists. More shackles clamped his ankles. All the chains were sunk deep into the floor.

The floor around him was covered with intricate colored tiles as ancient as the building that housed them, but here at his feet, there was new gray concrete. And his iron shackles were embedded in it.

Tool could sit or squat, but he could not rise to stand fully erect. He tested the chains again.

"You cannot escape."

Tool recognized the speaker instantly. The man's face looked down on the canals all across the UPF's territory. Tool had been forced to salute that face each time he entered the ring fights. How long ago was that? It seemed as if it had been years, and yet it was only weeks since he had fought against men and coywolv and panthers at the behest of the Colonel. Only weeks since he had fought free. And now, he found himself the Colonel's prisoner once again.

Tool growled. "You think these small chains will hold me, Colonel?" He set his feet and leaned against his bonds. His muscles bulged.

The concrete began to crack around his feet. Everyone stepped back, horrified. A few of the soldiers pulled out pistols and pointed them, but Glenn Stern just smiled and waved them off.

Tool bared his teeth and pulled harder, every tendon straining, muscles tearing. Concrete popped and cracked and turned to dust around the chains. Tool's skin began to shred, but the manacles neither broke nor slipped.

"You'll rip your hands off if you keep doing that," Stern said.

Tool let himself relax and studied his bonds again. The chains weren't only embedded in concrete; they seemed to be connected to something larger below, something stronger than stone.

"They're looped around the steel beams of the basement supports," the Colonel explained. "It took quite a lot of work to dig up all that stone and marble, but it seems that I anticipated you adequately."

"You planned to capture me?"

"If you recall, I already did capture you. I'd hoped to speak with you weeks and weeks ago, but then you escaped."

"How inconvenient for you."

The Colonel shrugged. "I suppose. But I have you now, and apparently I judged your capacity correctly."

As they spoke, the rest of the Colonel's staff began daring to move. The bustle of the command center slowly resumed, hushed conversations as they leaned over desks and discussed their maps and troops. But Tool noticed how they all looked to the Colonel with increased respect. He hadn't flinched in the face of Tool's threat, while everyone around him ducked for safety.

Colonel Glenn Stern might not have been the finest tactician, but he was a leader. It was no surprise that people followed. He had a faith in himself that appeared unshakeable. People would follow him, even when he was wrong or foolish.

Tool had met similar leaders in his time. Men and women who commanded through the force of their personality and whose words drove their followers forward in frenzied waves. In Tool's experience, they created armies with a great deal of passion, and very little competence.

Tool settled back, accepting that he could not escape by brute force. He surveyed the command bunker, parsing it for clues that would help him survive this new challenge, seeking the cracks in Glenn Stern's army.

The room was ancient. A chamber filled with marble columns and fading frescoes on the vaulted ceilings. Statues lined the walls, men and women cast in marble and bronze, but they had been pushed aside to accommodate the war room and its functionaries.

"Pardon the accommodations," the Colonel said. "We've found it expedient to decamp from the upper chambers." An explosion echoed above. The entire building seemed to shake, and the bare electric bulbs strung across the ceiling flickered. "The crypt is stable," the Colonel explained. "Now that they've dropped so much rubble down on top, it will be difficult for them to reach us, but it's not an ideal location."

Tool assessed the group's assets. A few computer screens flickered and glowed, most likely charged by the same solar systems that kept the lightbulbs glowing, and that hadn't yet been bombed out of existence. The computers would likely be gathering information from the Colonel's battlefields and providing connection to the outside world where he traded his scavenge for the bullets and explosives that kept him in the war.

When Tool had still warred on behalf of his patron, tablets and computers had connected them to ancient satellites hurtling overhead, to gliders and drones that described the tactical realm, and allowed them to rain fire down from above. Here, there were only a few electronic devices. The rest of the place was dominated by dozens of chalkboards hanging on the walls or set up on stands, scratched with numbers. Other parts of the room were papered with maps of the Drowned Cities, its coastline and jungles, hand-inked by soldier surveyors, and tacked with small nails, each painted red or green or blue, to describe the larger battlefield and the UPF's many enemies.

A quick glance at the boards reinforced what Tool already suspected about the Colonel's position and chances for survival. The number of inexperienced child soldiers that the UPF was using only served to confirm it. Some of the children even stood in the command center itself, gawky and thin in comparison to their larger and better-fed leaders.

Tool's eyes fell on a lump of a person, lying chained to one of the columns in the room.

Mahlia.

The Colonel followed his gaze. "You seem to have fared better than your compatriot."

"What do you want, Colonel?"

"You're quite a puzzle. It took a long time for us to discover what you were, and how you survived so long. Questions we had to ask." The Colonel nodded at Tool's neck, where a code was stamped. "We had to go all the way back to your country of origin, and then trace forward. Quite a lot of effort."

"You know nothing about me."

Stern wasn't deterred. "I've only seen an augment throw off its conditioning once. It was one of those beasts that the peacekeepers used. A common breed, not like you. It lost its entire platoon, then turned coward and ran from battle. It harried us for a little while, but even that one only survived another year. Suicidal, it seemed. It lost all its tactical sense. It couldn't die on its own, but it wanted to die, I think.

"It could have escaped us entirely, if it chose, but instead it lingered here, returning again and again to the site of its last battle. We gunned it down in the end. When your kind becomes masterless, you have a difficult time surviving. And yet here you are, years past your expiration date."

"What do you want?" Tool asked.

"I want to win a war."

Tool said nothing, waiting. The man wanted to talk. Powerful men enjoyed their power. Tool had known generals who liked to talk for hours. Colonel Glenn Stern didn't disappoint.

"I want the 999s shut down."

Tool bared his fangs. "Send a strike team."

"Ah. Yes," Stern said. "Actually, I've sent three. The Army of God has been good enough to return my soldiers to me, but without their hands or feet. We know where the guns are, generally. We think there are two. But they're determined to protect them."

"You want me to go," Tool said. It wasn't a question. It was obvious.

"For starters, yes. Lead a strike team."

"What makes you think I can succeed where your soldiers have failed?"

"Come, now. We're both professionals."

The Colonel came closer to Tool, squatting so they could speak closely. Tool measured the distance between them, but Stern remained just out of reach.

"I do what I can with the clay I have," the Colonel said. "But this is very rough clay. Children? Farmers from the jungles? We can mold them, but they are weak material. Fired by war, to be sure, and clever enough, but they are small and they have fought on only one battlefield in their entire lives. We both know that nothing in the Drowned Cities compares to you. I am at war, and you are one of the finest war machines that mankind has ever devised." He leaned forward. "I propose an alliance between us; I want your expertise to bolster my patriotic effort."

"And for myself?"

"Let's be honest, half-man. You need a patron. Alone and independent as you are, it's only a matter of time before a cleanup squad catches wind of you and puts you down for good. You need protection as much as I need a war leader."

"I've had enough of patrons."

"Don't misunderstand me. I propose to hire you, proper. You will forge my war effort into something more than this wasteful detente. Something that can cleanse the Drowned Cities. With your help, I smash the Army of God, and Taylor's Wolves and all the rest of the traitors. I can cleanse this place, and rebuild."

"And then?"

Glenn Stern smiled. "And then, we march. We reunite this country. Make it stand tall once again. We march from sea to shining sea."

"The savior and his war beast," Tool said. "The obedient pet."

"My strong right fist," Stern replied. "My brother in arms."

"Let the girl go."

The Colonel glanced over at Mahlia. "Why would you want her to leave? This friend of yours? This girl who you feel some loyalty to? I think it better if we keep her as an honored guest."

"A hostage."

"I am not a fool, augment. As soon as you are released,

you are dangerous. I do not pretend to know why you work on this girl's behalf, but I am more than happy to have leverage in our bargaining. Her life is, without question, the cost of your good behavior."

The building shook with another explosion. Dust rained down.

The Colonel looked up at the ceiling with a grimace. "General Sachs seems to have decided that he'd rather see me dead than preserve the capitol building."

He looked at Tool. "You see the sorts of barbarians I fight? They care nothing for this place or what it once was. They care nothing for its history. I seek to rebuild, and all they seek to do is to tear down and scavenge."

"I've spent time in your arenas," Tool said dryly. "Your patriotic talk rings hollow."

Stern grinned, unapologetic. "I didn't know you had value then. By the time I discovered what you truly were, you were effecting a rather daring escape. Now I know. And now I offer you a bargain."

Tool looked over at Mahlia. She lay bloodied and bruised, almost lifeless. Stern waited. Tool could feel his eagerness. All Tool's life, men like Stern had found a use for him. The half-man was, as his name implied, useful. Something men sought to wield, again and again.

Another explosion echoed down from above. Stern didn't move, waiting.

"Don't bother," Mahlia croaked suddenly, breaking Tool's thoughts. "He'll just kill us later."

Stern frowned. "Be quiet, castoff. This is a discussion for adults."

"He'll just kill me when you're dead," she said. "He'll use us up, just like they use everyone up."

"Not so different from any other leader," Tool said. "Generals are in the habit of using up all the people around them. It's their job. It's what they do best."

Stern nodded seriously. "We've both walked those paths."

"I never turned children to war," Tool said.

"Only because you fought on the side of wealth," Stern retorted. "You think I *want* to fight with children? This was not my preference. The Army of God started the practice. Or else it was the Revolution Riders, or perhaps it was the Blackwater Alliance. It's hard to remember where these things began, but I assure you, it was not my choice. But I'll be damned if I'll let our effort die because I failed to use every tool at my disposal. And any general worth his rank would do the same. If all you are given is a rock, you still must strike with it."

"I thought you were a colonel."

"Don't split hairs with me. If you don't like the ugly cast of this war, then help me end it. With your help, the war ends, and the children go back to innocence and toys. What say you? I offer you an honorable fight, and a rank that befits your considerable skill, and your friend lives in safety. With me, you are no longer a fugitive, but the commander of an army. What say you to that?"

Tool studied the man, considering his options, but again Mahlia's voice interrupted his thoughts.

"Ask him if he wants to give me back my fingers, too," she slurred. "As long as he's making promises, ask him if he's got my fingers."

42

MAHLIA HAD BEEN watching the conversation for some time. Through the haze of opiates and her own pain, she watched them, faced off against each other. Two monsters. Two killing creatures, bargaining and testing each other.

As the two of them bargained, Mahlia felt an increasing anger. They weren't talking about saving Tool and Mahlia—not really. They were talking about more war and more killing. Changing the tide of blood so that it would swamp the Army of God, instead of the UPF. And if she and Tool wanted to survive, they had to help. Tool would slaughter and leave bodies in his wake, just as he was designed to do.

She remembered how Tool moved through jungles and

tore apart coywolv. A monster. A killing creature. A slaughter demon. She remembered Doctor Mahfouz, what seemed like a million years before, urging her to let Tool die.

If you heal this thing, you bring war into your house.

At the time, she'd thought Mahfouz only meant that the soldiers would come looking for her, that she was putting herself in danger.

But now, as she watched the half-man and the leader of the UPF barter, she thought she saw what Mahfouz had been trying to tell her. She wasn't just bringing war into her house—her house was becoming a house of war. Mouse was recruited, full-bar-branded, a soldier boy now, no different from any other UPF killer, and if she and Tool wanted to survive, they would join as well.

If men like Glenn Stern and the rest of the grown-ups in this room had a use for you, you could live a little while. But you were just a pawn. Her. Mouse. All those soldier boys who'd been hand-raised to shoot and knife and bleed out there in the Drowned Cities.

Mahlia leaned against the pillar, watching the Colonel and his advisers, and finally, she thought she understood Doctor Mahfouz and his blind rush into the village.

He wasn't trying to change them. He wasn't trying to save anyone. He was just trying to not be part of the sickness. Mahlia had thought he was stupid for walking straight into death, but now, as she lay against the pillar, she saw it differently.

She thought that she'd been surviving. She thought that

400

she'd been fighting for herself. But all she'd done was create more killing, and in the end it had all led to this moment, where they bargained with a demon of the Drowned Cities, not for their lives, but for their souls.

"Fight the patriotic fight," Stern said. "Smash the Army of God."

But what he meant was keep on killing. If you wanted to stay alive, you had to keep on killing.

Mahlia was done with it. Done with being shoved around and threatened. Done with the bargaining that always said that if she wanted to live, someone else had to die. Done with armies like UPF and Army of God and Freedom Militia, who all claimed that they'd do right, just as soon as they were done doing wrong.

"Ask him if he'll give me my fingers back," Mahlia croaked. Her throat felt dry from the drugs and it was almost too much effort to speak, but she managed.

"Long as he's making pretty promises, ask him if he's got my pinky somewhere. He gonna sew me back together? He gonna get my hand back from the Army of God? Gonna make it all right?"

One of the Eagle Guards strode toward Mahlia, but Stern waved him back.

"Did you say something, young one?"

Through the muffled distance of opium, Mahlia watched the man crouch over her. He wasn't as big as his pictures. Not that imposing at all. But then he leaned close, and Mahlia imagined that she could smell death rising from him.

"Did you say something to me?" he whispered.

Mahlia wondered if she would have been frightened of him if she weren't so drugged, but as she looked up at him, she felt very little at all. He was a monster. A man made powerful because he strung words together in pretty ways. A man who could get his face painted three stories tall, and get a bunch of war maggots to worship it.

Mahlia cleared her throat. "If you got my hand somewhere, then we can do business."

The Colonel laughed. "You think you dictate for your friend?"

"Nah." Mahlia let her head lean back against the column. "He'll do what he does. I can't control him." She looked dully up at the Colonel. "But that don't mean I got to agree, and it don't mean I got to go along."

"Even if it meant you could go free? Run on to some distant place? Run to Seascape Boston? Manhattan Orleans? Maybe Beijing and your father's people there?"

"You ain't going to let us go."

"After your friend wins the war for us, I will."

Mahlia thought about that for a little while, finding her way around the edges of the man's words.

Finally she said, "No one ever wins, here. Bunch of dogs fighting over scraps of something...you don't even know what it is."

For the first time, Stern looked irritated. "I fight to cleanse this place, and revive a country. You have no right to question the sacrifices we make."

"I bet the guys who started this war said stuff like that, too. Bet they sounded real nice." She let her voice fall to a whisper. "You know something, though?" She let her voice fall lower. "You know what I realized?"

Glenn Stern leaned close, intent. Mahlia gathered her strength, and spat full in the man's face.

"I still want my fingers back!" she shouted.

The Colonel reared back, yelling and wiping spittle from his eyes. He glared at her. "You—"

Quick as a cobra he slapped her. Once, twice, thrice. Mahlia's head rocked back, her face flaming. Stern struck again. Pain exploded between Mahlia's eyes as he pounded her already broken nose. A spike of obliterating pain. Blood gushed down her face.

Mahlia cried out, despite the painkillers. She was almost blind with hurt, but still she forced herself to meet the man's gaze. "That what you got?" Her voice cracked. "That all?"

"You'd like more?" Glenn Stern raised his hand again.

A low growl filled the marbled room, heavy with threat. They both turned at the sound. The half-man was watching them both.

"I do not accept your offer," Tool said. "I will not war on your behalf."

Glenn Stern looked from Mahlia to Tool, and back again. Mahlia smiled.

Stern said, "You're playing a dangerous game, girl."

" 'Cause you'll hurt me some more?" Mahlia let her head

roll back against the column. "That was always the way it was going to be. You got your war and I'm just meat in the gears. So hurry up, old man. Grind me up."

Suddenly, Lieutenant Sayle appeared. "I have a solution, I think."

Mahlia didn't like the way he smiled as he murmured into the Colonel's ear. Glenn Stern's expression hardened as he listened. He turned to Mahlia.

"You want fingers, girl? I can get you fingers."

43

OCHO AND THE REST of the platoon were huddled in a corner of the palace, a huge round room surrounded by more columns and statuary. Ammunition and weapons were stockpiled all around, watched over by more Eagle Guards.

Every once in a while, another round from the 999s whistled in, and Ocho kept expecting a shell to just come smashing through and hit the ordnance and blow them all up, but so far the rubble overhead seemed to be protecting them.

He crouched beside Ghost. The boy was staring at the marble and tile floor. All sorts of intricate patterns covered it, decorative knots and geometric tangles running along the floor to where they were hidden under crates of weaponry.

"You okay, warboy?"

Ghost just shrugged. Ocho didn't like the look on Ghost's face. Too doubtful, too withdrawn, too haunted.

He'd thought that the boy was fully recruited, but now he was wondering. Using him for bait to get the half-man had been a risk. But now that it was over, the boy should have been pulling back together. It wasn't like every soldier in the platoon hadn't had to prove loyalty at one point or another.

"I saved her," Ghost said. "Long time ago, I saved her from the Army of God. When they cut off her hand."

"Best not to think about that. She ain't with us. She ain't a brother," Ocho said. "Don't spend your nevermind worrying about civvies. They ain't us."

"We were all civvies."

Ocho tapped his cheek. "We ain't now. We're above them. Don't put yourself down on their level, soldier. We're UPF. You stand tall."

"Sure."

"I mean it, soldier," Ocho said. "You're something now. We brought you up, 'cause we could tell you were special. Now you got a place and you got brothers who will throw down for you. Don't go throwing that off for some castoff war maggot."

He was about to say more, but he was interrupted by the arrival of Lieutenant Sayle.

"Sergeant," Sayle motioned for Ocho. "You're needed. Bring the recruit." He waved at Ghost.

Ocho slapped Ghost on the back. "Come on, soldier. Time to get back to work."

They followed the lieutenant down a marbled hall and were stopped by a pair of Eagle Guards. "Drop your weapons," one of them said.

"Say again?" Ocho asked.

"Leave your guns here."

Ocho tightened his grip on his rifle. "I don't disarm for no one."

"Disarm, Sergeant," Sayle said, his voice hard. "It's for a purpose." He surrendered his own sidearm as well.

Reluctantly, Ocho stripped off his rifle and bandoliers and motioned for Ghost to do the same.

As soon as they were disarmed, they were led down another hall, past more Eagle Guards, and then into a huge room, full of columns and soldiers and chalkboards. The murmur of strategy surrounded them.

Ocho realized that they were in the heart of the UPF's war room. From here, all orders issued. The lieutenant led them between the carved columns that held up the vaulted roof. They came around a column and Ocho gasped.

Colonel Glenn Stern stood before him, smiling. Ocho jumped to attention and saluted, jabbing Ghost to do the same. The Colonel returned the salute with a quick nod.

"Sergeant," he said, "I've heard good things about you from the lieutenant." Ocho stammered thanks but the Colonel's gaze had fallen on Ghost.

"This is the one?"

"Yes, sir," the LT said.

"Good." The Colonel motioned for them to follow. They

navigated amongst more columns, threading between them to the far side of the room. Ghost sucked in his breath. "Hold him, Sergeant," Sayle ordered.

Ocho looked from Stern to the girl before them, uncertain.

"Hold him!" the lieutenant shouted, and Ocho did as he was told. He grabbed Ghost's shoulder as the LT did the same on the other side.

Ghost started to struggle.

"Don't," Ocho warned. "LT's got a plan."

They muscled Ghost forward. The half-man was chained, ankles and wrists locked down, lengths of chain as thick as Ocho's arms disappearing into poured concrete.

Even captured, the monster was a frightening sight. Not far away, the doctor girl lay roped to her own pillar. Blood smeared her face and her skin was blotched with bruises.

"Mahlia?" Ghost asked.

"LT?" Ocho asked, uncertainly. "Are you sure—"

"Steady, soldier," Sayle said.

Glenn Stern was standing over the girl, smiling. "It's time you learned your choices have consequences, girl."

The doctor girl was looking from Stern to Ghost. "Mouse?"

"What are you doing?" Ghost asked them, looking from Stern to Sayle to Ocho. "What's going on?"

"One last time," the Colonel said to Mahlia. "Your friend wars on our behalf, or you suffer the consequences."

The girl shook her head.

"Mahlia?" Ghost asked. "What's going on?"

Ocho was wondering the same thing. There was a terrible tension in the room. The smell of blood was strong. The girl huddled against the pillar. The half-man was growling, low and warning. Ocho had seen similar scenes, but this one filled him with unease.

Glenn Stern turned to Sayle and Ocho. "Put him on his knees."

"LT?" Ocho asked.

The lieutenant barked at him, "Do it, soldier!"

Reflexively, Ocho responded to the order. Glenn Stern produced a knife. "You want this for the boy?" he asked Mahlia.

The girl was staring in agony. At first, she'd looked like she wasn't even there, so drugged and out of it, she'd seemed, but now she was straining forward. "Don't touch him!"

"Mahlia?" Ghost asked again, his voice cracking. He was starting to fight now, but Ocho and the lieutenant held him. The half-man was growling, louder, deep in his throat.

Ocho knew what was coming, and yet his mind refused to believe it. It felt as if someone else was holding Ghost. Someone else was forcing the soldier boy to hold still as he finally realized the boy was about to be a blood sacrifice.

Is this me? Am I doing this?

Ocho's mind felt like it was molasses. Ghost struggled, but Ocho was stronger. He thrust out his warboy's hand, sickened, as Stern seized the boy's fingers.

"You want this?" the Colonel shouted.

The knife flashed and Ghost howled. Blood poured onto the tiles. And there was a finger, too. Right there on the floor. Ghost shrieked and bucked. Ocho held him, but he couldn't take his eyes off the finger.

Am I doing this?

"What're we doing?" Ocho shouted. "He's our boy!" No one seemed to hear him, though. Ocho wondered if he'd said anything at all.

Had he just turned coward and shut up? Did he imagine that he'd protested?

Ghost was still thrashing against Ocho's restraining hands, and Stern was scooping up Ghost's finger. He waved it in Mahlia's face as she and Ghost sobbed.

"Is this what you want? You want more fingers? *You want them all?*"

"Let him go!" Mahlia screamed. She fought against her ropes. Ghost bucked against Ocho's grip. Glenn Stern stalked back to him. The blade flashed again. Red on the floor. Blood and bright as rubies. Brighter than the sun.

It didn't make sense. Ghost was their boy. Ocho had recruited him. He was theirs. UPF forever. Full bars. The Colonel might have been vicious to the Army of God, or Taylor's Wolves, or civvies, but not—

Sayle's voice whipped Ocho with command. "Hold his hand, Sergeant! Stand strong!"

The Colonel didn't see it coming. Ocho himself was surprised.

One moment Ocho was holding Ghost, fighting to keep the boy from twisting away as the Colonel went after another trophy—and they were all jostling and wrestling now that the boy knew what was coming—and the next moment, Ocho had his own knife in his hand.

He sunk it deep into the Colonel's kidney. In and out, just like he'd been trained. Warm blood poured over Ocho's hand.

The Colonel gave a gasp. The man's own knife fell to the floor with a clatter.

Without Ocho to restrain him, Ghost popped free of Sayle, screaming, and dove for the Colonel's blade where it lay on the tile.

A couple of Eagle Guards were running forward, shouting, trying to figure out what was going on, calling for backup as they ran. Ghost scooped up the Colonel's blade in his good hand and lunged for Stern. The man didn't even dodge as the boy sank his blade.

Glenn Stern's eyes were wide, surprised, his hands trying to reach around to the hole in his back and then reaching around to the front where Ghost had just stuck him. Ocho wasn't even sure if the man was there anymore, or if it was just some lizard part of his brain, still making his hands move, while he bled out...

More Eagle Guards were charging into the room, but they were all zeroing in on Ghost. They fired and bullets ricocheted, missing. The LT was pulling his own knife, staring at Ghost and the Colonel. Ghost jammed the knife into the man's belly again. Mahlia was screaming and struggling to get out of her ropes, and the half-man was roaring, and the LT...He was staring right at Ocho.

Pale gray eyes blazed with understanding as he took in Ocho's bloody hands, realizing that he had a traitor in his midst, even as everyone else was distracted by the captive boy who still drove the knife into Glenn Stern.

Ocho didn't give the lieutenant a chance. He took a quick step up to the man and drove his blade into Sayle's gut. Did it again, to make sure.

The lieutenant gasped. *"Why?"* But Ocho didn't have time for him. He slapped the man's blade away and shouted for a medic, and then he turned as weapons chattered on full auto.

Bloody holes spattered up and down Ghost, small perforations in the front, big gaping wounds in the back. Chips of stone whizzed past Ocho as bullets missed and ricocheted, and then a mob of Eagle Guards fell upon Ghost.

Roaring and screaming. The ratcheting of automatic weapons. Blood mist in the air, a whirlwind of viscera and bones and bodies. Men seemed to disappear before Ocho's eyes, replaced by sprays of blood on the walls and columns.

In their rush to aid the Colonel, some of the Eagles had strayed into the half-man's reach. They simply came apart in the monster's grasp and then the monster had their weapons, and the rest of the Eagles were dying as well, gunned down with terrifying marksmanship.

Ocho dove for the ground and crawled behind a column, wishing he could find shelter. The half-man roared and fired, emptying clips. Men were screaming. A body tumbled down beside Ocho. He grabbed for the man's weapon as more Eagles boiled into the command center. They were ducking and dodging behind columns, snapping shots, but the half-man seemed to anticipate them. Every time a soldier showed himself, he took a bullet in the face.

Ocho belly-crawled behind a desk, hoping to make it to the door. He just had to get out...

He glimpsed the girl, still tied. Trying to lie flat as bullets whizzed around her. She was sobbing and trying to reach Ghost where he lay in a spreading pool of his own blood.

The half-man's weapon clicked empty.

Ocho wasn't sure if the other soldiers realized it, but the half-man was a sitting duck now. With a curse, Ocho took his rifle and leaned out, and then, with a prayer to the Fates, he slid his rifle across the floor, right to the monster.

The half-man caught it. Locked eyes with Ocho.

What am I doing?

But it was already done. When Ocho put the knife in the Colonel it was done. There was no going back now. Ocho crawled across to where the Colonel lay in a heap. He rolled the man over and started going through his pockets. The man flailed at Ocho, but Ocho shoved his hands away.

"Fight the good fight, soldier," Stern whispered.

"You got the key?" Ocho asked. "You got the key, Colonel?"

The Colonel looked at him. "You'll keep the fight going? You won't let the traitors ruin everything?" he gasped.

"UPF forever," Ocho said. "That's right. But you got to give me the key if we're going to fight. Gotta get that dog-face free."

The man's eyes narrowed. "You..."

But Ocho had found the key for himself by then. He pulled it from the man's breast pocket and hurled it toward the half-man as a blow like a fist hit him in the leg and spun him.

Ocho gasped at the numbness. He'd been shot. *Keep moving. Don't be an easy target.* He crawled toward Mahlia. He got out his knife, started sawing at her ropes. They gave under the razor edge, but when she got free, she went after him, beating at him with her stump, clawing at him with her last fingers.

"I didn't do it!" Ocho tried to fight her off. "It's not my fault!"

But she wasn't listening. Bullets whined and zipped around them. He threw himself flat, but Mahlia was stumbling to her feet. Ocho reached for her, but with a bullet in his leg, he couldn't prevent her from standing upright.

"Get down!"

Stone and marble and bullets ripped around her, a maelstrom of death, but she seemed unaware, uncaring. Like she wanted to die. She ran through the whirlwind, slid down beside Ghost.

Ocho pressed his hand to the bullet in his thigh, praying that it hadn't hit an artery. Fates, it hurt.

Suddenly, he felt something big rush past him, wind and movement. Ocho whipped around, but it was already gone. Before him, chains lay abandoned. Unlocked. The half-man was running free.

A roar reverberated through the crypt, a challenge that penetrated Ocho's bones and made him want to piss himself for fear. Gunfire chattered. Screams, high-pitched and terrified. More gunfire. The soldiers were trying to get a bead on the half-man. Ocho could barely keep track of the monster as it ducked between columns.

More gunfire. Six shots, fast and even. *Ch-ch-ch-ch-ch-ch.* Six electric lights shattered, plunging the place into gloom. The monster was taking out the lights now, too. Ocho thought he caught a glimpse of the half-man moving again. A shadow of death, there and gone. Someone was shouting orders, trying to get rallied, and then the man just started screaming and screaming. Another bestial roar numbed Ocho's ears. Fates, it was loud. Louder than war.

Mahlia wasn't paying attention to any of it. She was down on her knees beside Ghost, sobbing. Cradling her warboy to her.

"Mouse," she said. "Mouse."

The boy wasn't going to make it. Ocho didn't even have to look close to know it, but still she held him to her, his blood all over her arms and legs and body.

Ocho dragged himself over to them. He grabbed a dead Eagle's pant leg and slashed it with his knife. They had real uniforms, he thought inanely. He'd never had a real uniform. More gunfire echoed distantly, followed by the cries of soldiers begging for help.

"We got to get out of here," Ocho said. He cut another strip of cloth and bound up his bleeding leg. When she didn't listen to him, he tugged her shoulder.

"We got to get out, before they come back."

Mahlia whipped around, her face a mask of rage. "You did this! This is your fault!"

Ocho held up defensive hands. "He was my boy, too! We were brothers."

"He wasn't anything like you!"

Ocho started to stutter out an apology, but then a wave of his own anger engulfed him.

"None of us asked for this!" he shouted. "None of us! We were all just like him. Every maggot one of us." He dragged himself up against a marble column, set weight on his leg, wincing. "None of us were like this," he said again. "We aren't born like this. They make us this way."

Mahlia opened her mouth to retort, but Ghost coughed and she turned her attention to her warboy. Ghost's eyes were glazing, but he reached up to her. Pulled her toward him. Mahlia sobbed and cradled him close. It looked to Ocho like Ghost was trying to say something to her, whispering and coughing blood as he tried to talk.

Ocho turned away. What was he doing? He needed to get the hell out of here. Once the Eagles rallied, he was dead meat. He scooped up another abandoned rifle and started hunting for ammunition. He doubted the half-man—

A shadow fell over him.

Ocho looked up and gasped. The half-man loomed over him, his bestial face a mass of scars and battle lust. Blood drenched the monster's features. Ocho was suddenly aware of how many bodies littered the command center. How quiet everything had become.

The half-man had killed them all. Every last one of them. The ones the monster hadn't shot, he'd torn to pieces with his bare hands. Ocho had known the half-man was dangerous, but this was beyond anything he could have imagined.

The monster growled at Ocho and kept moving, dismissing him as unimportant, even though Ocho held a rifle.

What had he unleashed?

44

"Mouse," Mahlia whispered.

She cradled him in her arms. He seemed small. He'd always been small. But now, broken and torn, he was tiny. And pale. Much paler...

Blood loss, some part of her doctor's mind told her. He was losing all his blood. She kept running through procedures that might help, trying to find some solution to the pool of ruby that spread all around them, slick and sticky.

Direct pressure, surgery. Plasma. IVs that she didn't have. Painkillers. Raise the legs. Treat for shock. Airway, breathing, circulation. Stabilize. Operate.

All of it useless. She didn't have the tools. All of Doctor Mahfouz's teachings were useless.

Mouse reached up and touched her face. "How come I always got to do the rescuing around here?" he whispered.

Mahlia clutched him to her. "I'm so sorry." Tears ran down her cheeks. "I'm so, so sorry."

Mouse tried to talk. Coughed. "Can't believe you followed me."

"I had to."

"No." He shook his head, smiling tiredly. "That's how *I* do." He trailed his fingers through her tears, pushed at her chin, joking like he always had. "You're supposed to be the smart one." He coughed again, and blood stained his lips. He grunted in pain. "Should've listened to you, huh?"

A shell came down, shaking the building.

"I'm going to get you out," Mahlia said.

"If you knew what I done, you wouldn't say that."

"I don't care what you done. I'm getting you out of here." She tried to rise, but Mouse reached up and pulled her close, surprisingly strong. Holding on to her like a vise as he stared into her eyes.

"You got to get out," he whispered fiercely. "Get out and don't ever come back." His expression was fiercer than she'd ever seen. "You got to promise me not to die," he said, and then he smiled at her, and his breath went out, leaving Mahlia clutching an empty body.

Tool crouched down beside her. "It's time to leave. Long past time."

Mahlia didn't look up. She just held Mouse. "He's dead."

The half-man was silent for a moment. "I lost all of my pack as well. Remember him. Tell his story."

"That's not much."

"It's nothing. It's what we have."

The soldier sergeant, the one called Ocho, limped over. Mahlia could feel him looking down on her. "Get up, girl. You don't get up, you die."

"What do you care?" she said. "You're the one who was trying to kill me."

The soldier gave an exasperated sigh. "And now I'm the one that's trying to save your maggot ass."

The building rocked with another explosion. More followed. The ceiling rattled as shells crashed down in quick succession. Ocho and Tool looked up at the ceiling.

"Damn," Ocho said. "That's starting to sound serious."

"The Army of God will be preparing an assault," Tool said.

Ocho laughed at that, his expression grim as he scanned the command center. "They don't need to bother. It looks like you just about killed every single one of the command staff. They can roll in anytime and we won't know what hit us."

Tool growled agreement. "The UPF is headless. I left no commanding officers."

Another artillery round hammered into the building. Masonry fell from the ceiling.

"I got to get to my boys," Ocho said suddenly. "They're dead if they don't got someone to tell them what to do."

"Indeed," Tool rumbled. Mahlia was surprised to see the half-man hold out a huge hand to Ocho. "Thank you," he said.

Ocho looked at the half-man with an expression of shock on his face. For a second, Mahlia thought he was going to flinch away. But then he took the offered hand, his own smaller one disappearing in Tool's grip.

The sergeant looked down at Mouse, then at Mahlia again. "I'm sorry I couldn't save him," he said. "I tried. If I'd known what they were going to   " He broke off, took a ragged breath. "Anyway, I'm sorry." He turned and limped toward the door.

Mahlia watched the sergeant go. He was just a kid. They were all just kids. All of them waving guns and killing one another, while a bunch of men who claimed they were older and wiser pushed them around. Maggots like Lieutenant Sayle and Colonel Stern and General Sachs.

He was just some kid who'd been in the wrong place at the wrong time. A kid who turned out to be useful to men who didn't give a damn about him, except to make sure he did what he was told. Just like Mouse.

"Hey!" she called to him. "Soldier boy!"

Ocho turned. "Yeah?"

An idea was forming in her mind. A gamble. A big one. It wasn't the way she'd imagined it, but she thought it could work. She could make it work. She just needed to believe, and reach out to this soldier boy.

"You want to get out?" she asked. "Get out for good?"

She held her breath, praying that she wasn't just some civvy to him. That he didn't see her as a peacekeeper castoff or a traitor, any more than she saw him as a soldier. They were just two people, victims of something bigger than either of them. There weren't any sides, and there weren't any enemies.

She just needed to make him believe it, too.

"Out of here?" The sergeant smiled. "No way any of us is getting out. There's nowhere to go, and no one to take us. Blockades all around. AOG gunning for the triple hash." He touched his cheek. "There's no way out, not for any of us."

"Scavenge companies go in and out," Mahlia said.

"We ain't scavenge."

"What if I know where we could get some?" she said. "Rich stuff. Can you get us to the blood buyers? Can you get us and some scavenge to the docks?"

"That treasure room of yours?" Ocho hesitated, then said, "I can't leave my boys."

Mahlia almost gave up on the idea. The thought of all of Ocho's other troops scared the hell out of her. She swallowed. She was gambling, again. Gambling big.

"Can you lead them?" Mahlia asked. "Can you get them to follow you? To follow me? Can you give us protection?"

Tool looked at her with sudden surprise and respect as he figured out what she was planning. Another rumble of artillery rocked the building. Ocho looked up at the cracking ceiling, then at Mahlia.

"They'll follow me," he said. "If they're still there, they'll follow."

Mahlia's heart was beating faster. She was going to do it. For real. She was getting out. She hugged Mouse close, one last time, and let him go.

45

Chaos reigned in the palace. Artillery fire rained down. Soldiers milled in groups, unsure of what they were supposed to do.

A few Eagle Guards were still around, trying to organize, but it seemed that Tool had destroyed everyone who had witnessed what had happened in the command center. And now, under fire, people were scrambling, more concerned for their own skins than anyone else's.

Ocho led them into the rotunda, leaning against Mahlia and limping. His soldiers straightened and started to raise their weapons when they saw the half-man and the girl, but he waved them down.

"Where's the LT?" they all asked, staring.

"He's replaced," Ocho said.

"By who?" Stork asked.

"Me," Ocho said. Then he pointed at Mahlia and Tool. "And them. We're all together now."

There was a long silence. Ocho held Stork's gaze until the taller boy nodded acquiescence.

"Good."

Ocho started outlining orders to the platoon, organizing them all. He sent some to gather ordnance while he had someone strap his leg better, and then he had them all moving, a gathered knot of protection with Mahlia and Tool at their center.

Mahlia watched in awe as his platoon marched them right through the heart of the UPF. Soldiers ran hither and thither, preparing for a final battle that they couldn't win, but no one had time for an armed platoon that seemed to have orders. They made it outside, squinting in the bright sunlight. Down the length of the lake, Mahlia could see the mouth of the river and the sea. Her goal, beckoning.

Another artillery round came screaming down. The dome of the palace shattered, crumbling inward. Soldier boys screamed and scattered in all directions, but Ocho kept his command, ordering them all down the stairs for the water. Ahead, Mahlia saw blood buyers struggling to load scavenge into their zodiac rafts.

She pointed at them, and Ocho nodded and shouted more orders. Everyone changed course, preparing for a fight, but then Tool pushed into the lead.

It was like watching a hurricane. One moment he was

with her, the next he was among the blood buyers and their guards, hurling them aside. By the time Mahlia and the soldier boys reached the rafts, guards and blood buyers were thrashing in the water or running for their lives, all of them disarmed and harmless.

Mahlia and the soldiers piled into the zodiacs and fired them up. Tool leaped aboard. Mahlia's zodiac tipped threateningly under his weight, but then it was upright again and they were buzzing up the length of the lake, following Mahlia's directions, then cutting off into the canals.

All around, the city seethed with movement. People preparing for the Army of God's assault. Civvies running for cover, grabbing last belongings. Soldiers setting up defensive positions.

To Mahlia, it was so much like the last time the warlords came, when they'd swamped the place that she'd grown up in, that she couldn't help but feel terror at the approaching violence. She remembered troops storming from building to building, hunting every single person who had collaborated. Dragging people out onto boardwalks and executing them. Her mother trying to help her hide before the soldier boys burst in on them.

And now it was going to happen again. Another wave of violence as the UPF collapsed and new warlords rushed to fill the vacuum.

Ahead, her old apartment came into view. Mahlia pointed. Ocho nodded. "Yeah. I thought so."

The zodiacs slowed. Nearly two dozen soldier boys piled

out and dashed into the building. Mahlia pressed the hidden places in the wall, praying to the Fates...

It opened.

Before her, the warehouse lay waiting. Her mother's collection. Her father's hoarding. All of it still there. None of it looted yet. Stern hadn't had a chance to do anything with this news. Or maybe the lieutenant had never reported it. It was all here. Paintings and statuary and ancient books. The treasure trove of a dead nation.

"Round it up," Mahlia said. "Get as much as you can. Whatever fits."

They grabbed great armfuls of scavenge. Old muskets. Uniforms of blue and gray. Banners with circlets of stars on blue backgrounds. Yellowed parchments. Everything that they could find that was light and could be loaded into the zodiacs.

"Is this going to work?" Ocho asked as they heaved more pieces of art and history into the zodiacs where they bobbed beside the boardwalk. "You think we can really buy out?"

Tool answered for Mahlia. "With your soldiers to escort, and Mahlia to bargain with the blood buyers, it will. You will win free."

Mahlia looked over at Tool. Something in his tone worried her. "You will, too," she said. "We can all get out like this. There's plenty here to buy us all out."

"No." Tool shook his head. "They will not welcome my kind. I must go another way."

"But…" Mahlia hesitated. "What will happen to you? You can't stay here."

Tool almost smiled. "Let me be the judge of that. The Drowned Cities may not be a place for you, but to me…" He paused and sniffed the air. "This smells like home."

With a chill, Mahlia remembered what the Colonel had said when he had them trapped, about half-men not being able to live without a patron.

"You're not going to try to die?" she asked. "Like that other one? Like that other half-man? Keep circling back until you die?"

Tool's fangs showed in a feral smile, and he crouched beside her. When he brushed her cheek, it was surprisingly gentle.

"Do not fear," he rumbled. "I am no victim of war. I am its master." He glanced to the canal and the civilians. The soldiers rushing about like an ant's nest, kicked and frantic. His ears twitched, and his nostrils flared.

"The UPF will die, but its soldiers will need safe haven. They will hunger for a leader." Tool's low growl sounded of satisfaction. He looked at Mahlia again. "I have fought on seven continents, but never for territory of my own." He scanned the buildings. "Where you see terror, I see… sanctuary."

He straightened. "Go. The Army of God is only blocks away, and other warlords are stirring as well. It will be a long time before you can return to this place."

"What are you going to do?" Mahlia asked. "You're going to die."

Tool laughed. "I have never lost a war. I will not lose this one. These soldiers are wild and untrained, and they have never fought a true war. By the time I am finished with them, they will roar my name from the rooftops." He gave another growl of satisfaction.

Mahlia stared up at Tool. For the first time she thought she saw him true: not a mix of creatures, but a singular whole, built entirely for war. Entirely at home.

Gunfire echoed down the canals. A few shots, then more. A cacophony of weaponry that broke her thoughts and sent the warboys all scrambling into the zodiacs.

"Go!" Tool said. "Quickly! Before you lose your last opportunity! Go!"

"Come on!" Ocho said frantically. "Come on!"

When she hesitated still, Tool simply lifted her into the zodiac and set her amongst the troops. The soldier named Stork gunned their engine, and then they were speeding away from the half-man.

Mahlia looked back. Tool held up a hand in farewell, and then he turned and plunged into the canal, disappearing entirely. Mahlia stared after his disappeared form, wishing him well.

46

THE ZODIACS RIPPED down the canal, leaving frothing wake behind. Ahead, gunfire echoed.

"Here it comes," Ocho muttered.

"We going to make it?" Mahlia asked.

"It'll be close." The zodiac's engine whined higher as Stork ran the thing full out. Ocho pushed Mahlia down, covering her with his body. Bullets zipped and whined overhead. The UPF boys were all flopping down, lying low, returning fire. Shell casings rained down on Mahlia as guns chattered.

They shot across the leading edge of the AOG, running a gauntlet of bullets, firing all the while, and then they were past, and Ocho was shouting for his soldiers to report.

Mahlia straightened, trying to get her bearings. A soldier

boy with missing ears was frantically patching holes in the side of the zodiac, blocking the air loss. Mahlia leaned over to the kid. "How can I help?"

"Put your hand over this," the boy said, showing her a hole. "Cover this one, too. I got tape somewhere."

Mahlia awkwardly pressed her stump and her bandaged left hand over the tiny hissing holes while he rummaged through their treasures. He came up with a bag, stripped it open, and found tape.

"Last time we used this, I think it was on you," he said, grinning. Mahlia stared at him, trying to figure out if he was a threat, but the kid was like a puppy that couldn't control itself. He was practically bouncing up and down.

"I'm Van," he said as he slapped tape over the holes. Bullets started wailing overhead again, but Van didn't stop smiling. Just kept doing his job like it was the best thing in the world to be ripping down a canal with enemies closing in on them.

He was crazy, she decided.

But then, as she looked around at the other soldier boys, she realized they were all like Van. It was like they were alive with energy. Everything they did felt eager.

They were getting out. All of them. They were leaning into the wind, eyes brighter and more alive than anything she had ever seen. A whole pack of soldier boys, all pursuing a future that they thought they'd never be allowed to have.

Ahead, UPF sentries saw them coming. They lifted their rifles, but Ocho threw up UPF colors. The sentries lowered

431

their weapons and waved them on. Mahlia and the soldier boys shot past, three boats in a row.

Mahlia watched the checkpoint sentries, thinking how odd it was to simply whip past them like this. She wondered if any of them caught sight of her, and if they wondered what a castoff was doing, running with the UPF. And then they were past the final checkpoints, and they hit Potomac Harbor, and Mahlia stopped caring forever about what the UPF or any of the warlords thought.

Open water stretched before them, blue and wide, sunlight glittering on the waves. All across the harbor, clipper ships were readying their sails, preparing to flee. Some were already moving, their white sails billowing, filling with wind. She watched as one of ships rose on its hydrofoils and cut across the waters for the high seas.

It was beautiful, like a gull breaking into flight.

"Now what?" Ocho asked.

Mahlia scanned her choices. Pointed. "That one."

It was rich. Sleek and fast. A shining white hull and sails that were only now unfurling. A wealthy blood buyer, glutted on scavenge and now escaping as the violence once again overcame the city.

"You sure?" Ocho asked.

"They're just like the people my mom used to trade with."

Ocho gave the order, and their raft angled across the waves, chasing for Mahlia's chosen destination. She stared up at the gleaming ship as they approached, remembering

432

how she'd stood on the Potomac docks years before, begging and desperate for the peacekeeper ships to return.

You're not begging this time, she thought. *You're buying.*

"Is this going to work?" Ocho whispered as they closed on the clipper ship.

"Yeah, it'll work. Put up that old flag. The one with the stars in a circle, and the red and white stripes."

"That old burned thing?"

"Yeah. That'll get their attention. They'll want it, for sure."

Their zodiac hurtled across the waves, flying its ragged banner. Sure enough, the clipper ship's sails that had been unfurling halted, and started rolling themselves back up.

Mahlia could see people on deck, looking down on them with binoculars. Watching them. They'd want what she had to sell. Her heart beat faster. It was going to work. It was really going to work.

"Keep your guns down, boys," Ocho said. "Try to smile and look friendly."

Mahlia almost laughed at that. Ocho seemed to catch her humor, but his smile faded, almost as soon as it showed.

"You think they'll take us? Really?"

"They already are."

"No. I mean…" He touched his cheek and his brand. "They'll know what we did, right? They'll know what we are."

Mahlia looked at him, and once again, saw that other part of him. The part that was other than a soldier. Some part of whatever the sergeant had been, before the Drowned Cities had swallowed him up. The scared kid who'd been beaten and whipped and shoved around so long he'd almost lost every bit of his humanity. He was right there. A whole other person, trying to believe.

She started to answer, to try to tell him that everything would be okay. They could buy respect. They could go someplace where no one had even heard of the UPF or the Drowned Cities or the Army of God. Where none of it even existed. Beijing, maybe. Or Seascape Boston. Or farther even. They could disappear from everything that they'd been.

Somewhere they'd find a place, she wanted to say.

But then she looked down at her own hands, her missing right and the bandage on her left, and she wondered the same thing herself. What good was anyone going to find in a doctor girl who had only four fingers?

Finally she said, "One step at a time, soldier boy. We'll take it one step at a time, and we'll figure it out."

They swept up beside the clipper ship and it loomed over them. Someone threw a rope ladder down, and then soldier boys were scrambling up the ladder and climbing aboard. They went up one by one, and then the ladder was in front of Mahlia.

She took a deep breath, then reached up and hooked her arms through the rungs. The soldier boys helped her, shoving her higher, and then she was lifting free of the zodiac, climbing.

434

ACKNOWLEDGMENTS

MICHELLE NIJHUIS FOR TELLING me about the coyote-wolf hybrids that became the basis for coywolv. Ruhan Zhao for some desperately needed language expertise when my rusty Chinese skills failed me. Rob Ziegler for talking me off the ledge and keeping me from throwing the book away, yet again. All the folks at Blue Heaven who read this book, when it wasn't this book at all. My editors: Jennifer Hunt, who supported me and was willing to wait so that I could write the best book I could; and Andrea Spooner, for guiding me through the final miles to make it even better. My wife for having faith when it all took longer than it should have, and Arjun, because he makes this matter. Any errors or omissions are mine alone.